Death's
White Horses

A Jeff Trask Crime Drama

MARC RAINER

ISBN: 1495322335
ISBN 13: 9781495322334

Library of Congress Control Number: 2014901739
CreateSpace Independent Publishing Platform
North Charleston, South Carolina

Author's Preface

I have long maintained that the use of a term such as "police action" to describe a war is ill-conceived, and that the use of the term "war" to describe law enforcement operations is similarly misleading. After 28 years in the military and 30 years as a prosecutor, I have seen firsthand the confusion that such carelessly crafted labels cause with respect to both warfare and criminal justice.

We do not seek to bring national enemies "to justice;" we seek to kill them or cause them to unconditionally surrender. Such is the true nature of war. We do not fight "wars" on drugs or on crime, because there is no hope of ever winning such a conflict. These "wars" are usually fictions created by politicians for re-election purposes. Crime is an unfortunate certainty of the human condition, since there will always be a percentage of the population willing to engage in criminal activity. We have never won—nor will we ever win—a "war on burglary" or a "war on theft," for example. We continue to react to such crimes because we are a civilized people, but we know these problems will always be with us. To think we will win a "war on drugs" is therefore naive, but it does not necessarily follow that we should, as a nation, give up that fight. The costs of surrender would be astronomical, even when compared to the cost of the "war."

There is, however, an exception to these distinctions. When a nation's armed forces are actually outnumbered by its criminal elements and armed thugs, and when it is actually fighting for its national survival, then a police action and a war in the traditional sense can merge and become one. Such was the case in Colombia when the nation battled the Medellín and Cali cartels. Fortunately, the law-abiding forces and citizenry ultimately rose up in that country to conquer their national demons.

In today's Mexico, an even more serious conflict is underway. With a body count on the North American mainland second only to the United States' Civil War, the very viability of Mexico as a nation—and the corresponding well-being of America's border states—is being threatened by an actual war with criminals.

I have attempted to make this a contemporary, yet historical novel, incorporating many actual events into the narrative. Many of the scenes set in Mexico and fictionally portrayed in this novel are based in part upon actual events. Even the Texas Highway Patrol's gunboats described in the book are very real. Any reader who doubts the scope of the violence referenced in this novel is invited to plug the word "Zetas"—or the phrases "San Fernando Massacre" or "Cardereyta Jiménez"—into his or her favorite search engine, and become educated. The words taken from the signs posted by the cartels claiming credit for their gory handiwork are quoted. If anything, the violence described in this book is purposefully understated.

Some of the villains in the novel, such as Chapo Guzmán of the Sinaloa or Federation Cartel, and Heriberto Lazcano of the Zetas, are—or were—all too real. Others, such as Ramón and Vicente Dominguez, are fictional composites but are based upon real figures. Our heroes, Aguilar and Trask, are also fictional composites of good men I have known and studied. As always, I salute those on both sides of the border who are fighting the good fight. This book is dedicated to those heroes who continue to perform their duties with integrity, and to those who have already fallen; in short, to all those who protect and serve, regardless of the uniforms they wear.

Prologue

The jury would be out for a while deliberating. Trask elbowed his way through the crowded hallway, trying to reach the sanctuary of the office space reserved for trial preparation by the United States Attorney. The courthouse was packed with interested spectators, attorneys, and security personnel, and there was the usual crush of reporters clamoring for a statement.

"You folks know that you're supposed to contact our public affairs officer," he said, shoving at least three microphones out of his face with a single sweep of his hand.

"C'mon, Jeff, you know that if the jury comes back with the death penalty, it will be the first capital sentence in this town in decades. Give me a quote."

Trask stopped and looked at the reporter from *The Post*. He thought about saying something, but thought better of it. *I should just shove on past, get to the prep tank.* He looked at the man, half-smiled, and shook his head.

"You just asked those people to kill a man, Trask. You can't actually believe that's something civilized people should do. You can't believe that's justice."

Trask froze in his tracks, and turned to face the reporter.

"Now you're questioning my ethics and my own motives and beliefs, Rafferty, so I'll answer you. That defendant in there got his due process of law, more than he was ever actually entitled to. Don't you *dare* imply that I asked for the death penalty just to put some kind of notch on my gun. I don't need one. Capital punishment should always be the last resort, used only when we are certain as a society that it's appropriate. I'd *never* ask for it if I didn't think it was justified."

"So you're *that* sure? You're willing to let your own judgment play judge, jury and executioner?"

Trask stared hard, burning fires into the reporter's eyes with his own. "Rafferty, I couldn't say this to the jury. It would have been *the truth*, but *not allowed* under the law. There are times when the law *is* an ass, and some of those times the rules still have to be followed. But you're not a juror, and we're not in that room anymore, so make no mistake about it. If the jury comes back with a death verdict, and after all the appeals run out," he lowered his voice to a measured growl, "once they strap that monster to the gurney in a death chamber, if they ask me to push the plungers, I'll jump at the chance, and never think twice about it afterward. He actually deserves a lot worse. I'm only sorry that we're too civilized to give it to him."

Chapter One

Cuernavaca, Morelos, Mexico
December 16, 2009

Captain Luis Aguilar looked down at the bullet-riddled body lying on the floor of the luxury apartment. *Not so high and mighty now, are you?* Aguilar thought. The Captain saw a sergeant approaching him.

"What's the count, Gonzalez?"

"Five dead, counting their *jefe* there, *Capitán.* We got four of them. One shot himself as we were coming in the balcony door. We found about $40,000 in US cash, several thousand in Canadian money, and five assault rifles. Not quite as big a haul as in Ahuatepec. Except for Arturo there, of course."

"Exactly." Aguilar nodded in agreement. *Five days ago we just missed him. Another luxury home here in the "Beverly Hills of Mexico." Another party thrown by this scumbag, with the finest food and drink, twenty whores, and everything else dirty money could buy for entertainment. Three cartel gunmen dead, eleven arrested, but no Arturo. Two-hundred and eighty thousand in US currency, sixteen assault rifles, but no Arturo. Now that has changed. This operation is a complete success, at least for the moment. Arturo Beltrán-Leyva is dead, his cartel on the run.*

"How about our men? Casualties?" Aguilar asked.

"Just a couple wounded on my squad, *Capitán.* When we rappelled from the choppers, they started throwing fragmentation grenades at us—about twenty or so."

Another NCO walked in from the front of the room, his helmet in hand.

"I have one dead, sir."

"Who was it?"

"Angulo, sir."

"Thank you. I'll notify his family." *My most hated duty. My most necessary duty; one I owe to all of my fallen heroes.* "Where is he?"

"Just outside the door, *Capitán.* He was on point, and they were waiting for us."

Aguilar stepped into the hallway, bending down next to the body. Angulo's hand still held his weapon. A crimson hole in his neck told the story of his final moment. Aguilar held the young man's hand for a moment, still warm to the touch. He looked up at the sergeant.

"Guard him well until we can honor his life."

———

Mexico City, Distrito Federal, Mexico
December 21, 2009

The hearse carrying the body of fallen marine Melquisedet Angulo Córdova rolled past, flanked by a dozen hatless marines in uniform.

Brave young men. Aguilar shook his head proudly before snapping to attention and saluting the procession. *They refuse to hide their heads or faces as a tribute to their fallen friend. I am more proud of them than I have ever been, but I wonder if this is wise. The cartel spies are everywhere, taking photos, taking names.*

The funeral proceeded with full military honors. After the casket had been lowered, Aguilar ordered his driver to return him to the hotel, his temporary quarters for the now completed mission. He did not eat well. The image of the young marine's casket stuck in his mind. He showered and tried to sleep, finally drifting off well after midnight.

He had only been asleep for an hour when the phone rang.

"Yes?"

"I am sorry to disturb you, *Capitán,* but we have very bad news and I knew you would want to be advised," the corporal said.

"What is it?"

"The cartel has retaliated. Angulo's home in Tabasco was hit. His mother and three others are dead."

Aguilar's face froze in anger. *The cowards hit the helpless. My young hero's family is allowed to mourn him for less than a day before being murdered themselves.* Aguilar was awake now.

"Who found them?"

"Some of our men had gone to pay their respects to the family, sir."

"Any information from the scene?"

"Just a 'Z' painted in the victims' blood on a wall."

"Thank you."

Aguilar returned the phone to its cradle. *The Zetas. Intelligence had reported that they were aligning themselves with Beltrán-Leyva. We have replaced one enemy with a stronger one.*

———

Washington, D.C.
January 20, 2010, 11:49 a.m.

He leaned over and kissed her on the forehead, the usual signal that he was leaving her again. Their "early lunch" was over.

Another vote on the hill, or something else of critical importance. She pretended to be asleep, not wanting to say what she was thinking. There was no point in it at the moment, and she actually wanted him to hurry and go, if he was going.

She opened her eyes just a slit. *There it is,* she thought, seeing the usual flick of the gray hair about his temples as he checked himself in the hallway mirror before opening the door.

She counted to a hundred. *He's in the parking garage by now, ducking under his hat so that his face won't be seen on the security cameras. God forbid he should ever have to acknowledge even knowing me outside the dinner parties. I wonder how he'd act if we ever ended up at the same table again.*

She tossed the sheets aside and slid across the bed. She walked across the white marble tiles to the same mirror where he'd checked his hair. She stood in front of it, naked. Her body was good, young and firm. *Not bad. Good enough to*

3

keep him coming back to me. My hair's a wreck, though. The hell with it; I'll fool with it when I wake up again.

She opened her purse and took out the small nylon bag. The pill bottle with the powder came first, then the spoon, the lighter, and the syringe. *It was so good last time, I'll add just a little more.* She heated the powder in the spoon and drew the hot liquid back into the needle, smiling in anticipation as she did so. The needle went in between her toes.

She lay back as the first warm waves washed through her veins, moaning in pleasure. She giggled. *I think I made that same sound about an hour ago.* She walked to a window and stood there still naked, looking out at the river, seeing nothing, feeling nothing but the warmth in her blood. She smiled and took in a deep breath, then returned to her bed and drifted off to sleep—a very deep slumber this time—so deep that she never felt her breathing becoming shallower by the minute, or her lips turning blue from the lack of oxygen.

————

9:49 p.m.

He was surprised when she didn't meet him at the door to the apartment. He was already irritated. The votes on the Hill hadn't gone his way, and now she was playing games on top of everything else he'd been through. He saw that the bedroom door was ajar, and headed for it.

"Janie, where the hell are you? I left a message on your cell—"

He stopped frozen in the doorway. She was lying on the bed, motionless. He saw the syringe on the nightstand.

"Oh, Jesus, no. *NO!*"

He checked her neck for a pulse. There was none, and she felt cold. He stood up and waited for a moment, staring at her, trying to will her diaphragm to move, waiting in vain for evidence of a breath taken in or exhaled.

Think, don't panic.

He grabbed the syringe and threw it into the trash can under the sink in the kitchen. It took him nearly an hour to wipe down the place, trying to remove every fingerprint he might have left there in the course of more than a month of trysts. It was almost midnight when he started to leave, but he stopped near the door.

The phone!

He found the purse lying on the floor on the far side of the bed. The cell phone was inside it. He breathed a sigh of relief and stuck it into the side pocket of his jacket as he headed for the door. When the elevator opened into the parking garage, he grabbed his hat and pulled it low over his forehead as he walked to his car.

Instead of heading toward Georgetown and his own condo, he drove west, toward Arlington. As he crossed the bridge he pressed the button and lowered the passenger side window. The cell phone sailed over the guard-rail, falling into the dark waters of the Potomac.

———

Washington, D.C.
The Dome Racquet Club
January 22, 2010

Joseph Adipietro put his feet up on his desk and thumbed through the morning edition of *The Washington Post*. As he reached the obituaries he scowled and his feet fell off the corner of his desk with a thud. He stood and pulled a step stool to a corner, directly under the small surveillance camera that was always trained on the center of the office. He pulled the DVD from the back of the camera and replaced it with another, then took the disc he had just removed and put it in his briefcase.

Chapter Two

Washington, D.C.
January 23, 2010

Jeffrey Ethan Trask glanced at his name on the plastic strips resting in the brackets on the wall outside his office. Below his name were the words, *Senior Litigation Counsel.* He gave a slight shake of his head as he unlocked the door.

There were dozens of other prosecutors working in the Office of the United States Attorney for the District of Columbia who were senior in age or years of service to Trask. No one, however, was senior in terms of trial experience. After he'd graduated from the Air Force Academy, the brass had sent him to law school and assigned him to the JAG Corps. He had tried more than two hundred criminal cases in his years as a traveling circuit prosecutor for the Air Force. Trask had made the leap to the Justice Department after serving his commitment time, and soon made a name for himself in the District. In his last two major cases, he had worked with a team of federal and local investigators to bring down a major Jamaican cocaine ring and had also dismantled a very violent chapter of the MS-13, a notorious Salvadoran street gang. The United States Attorney, Ross Eastman, had accordingly rewarded him with a promotion to the office's position of lead trial attorney.

The promotion had come with a couple of other benefits of some considerable value to Trask. The first was a prized parking space in the basement of the building, a major perk since monthly parking for those who drove to work cost well over a hundred dollars.

The second was the support of Eastman in Trask's application—now approved—to carry a firearm to and from the building for self-defense. The

United States Marshals Service had initially balked at the request, but after Trask's former supervisor, Robert Lassiter, had been gunned down in the course of the Jamaican case, and after Trask and his wife had been attacked in their own home by the Salvadorans, the red tape had come down. Trask had to carry the same service weapon used by the deputy marshals, a standard-size Glock, but he was also allowed to wear a back-up. His choice was a Sig Sauer P239 compact 9mm, which he concealed in a leg holster. He was not allowed to carry the guns into his office, however. Both weapons had, according to regulation, been secured in a lock box in the lobby, along with the weapons stored there by all the cops and agents visiting the building.

The red light was flashing on Trask's phone as he entered his office. It always was. He had another voicemail.

"Mr. Trask, this is Julia Forrest."

Trask immediately turned back toward the door to the hall, recognizing the name of the United States Attorney's personal secretary. He paused at the door to make sure he knew the reason for the rest of the voicemail.

"Mr. Eastman would like to see you as soon as you get in this morning."

He was out the door before the beep signaled the ending of the message. Eastman was more of a career bureaucrat than a prosecutor. His political connections had landed him the lead job in the office, but he was a manager with integrity, and he was the boss.

As Trask reached the outer lobby to Eastman's office, he noticed a young man in a suit waiting in a seat against the wall, busily fiddling with an electronic tablet and a smart phone at the same time. Trask hurried by, figuring that Eastman was probably entertaining interviews for a job opening somewhere in the building. There were several hundred Assistant United States Attorneys in the DC office, and turnover was high.

Julia Forrest smiled. "They're waiting for you. Go right in."

They, he thought. *I wonder what little piece of paradise has been inflicted upon us now, and who's bringing it to us. I only get the major problems, or the sensitive ones.*

When he cleared the doorway to the large corner office, he saw that Eastman was there, as well as a shorter, plump figure in a five-hundred-dollar suit. The visitor stepped quickly toward Trask, smiling broadly.

"Jeff, how the hell are you?" asked Senator Sherwin Graves as he grabbed Trask's hand, then hugged him.

8

"Not too bad, Digger," Trask said, smiling. "How's Georgia? Or have you seen your state in a while?" Trask looked up to see Ross Eastman shaking his head.

"I should never be surprised with you, Jeff. How do you know—?"

"Before I entered politics," Graves answered for Trask, "I was Jeff's assistant trial counsel—that's JAG for prosecutor—when we tried a bunch of dope dealers in some courts-martial at one of the Air Force bases in South Carolina. I learned a lot of law from this guy."

"What brings you down off the Hill today, Senator?" Trask asked.

"The senator has asked *me*," Eastman said, reminding them that he was still present and relevant, "to appoint either my best prosecutor—or you, since he has a high opinion of your abilities—to work an important and sensitive case. I told the senator that since I thought those two attorneys were one and the same, you were perfect for the assignment. Have a seat, please."

They sat around a coffee table on the side of the office, away from Eastman's desk. The U.S. Attorney's seat of power was not appropriate for use when a political figure outranking him was in the room.

"Did you see the papers Friday morning, Jeff?" Graves asked. He was assuming control of the meeting.

"Sure. Anything in particular?"

"Yes," the senator said. "The obituaries."

"I don't usually read those," Trask said. "They remind me of my own pending mortality."

"Had you read them, they would have informed you of the mortality of one Jane Britt Heidelberg, the daughter of one Randall Hugh Heidelberg," Graves said.

The most powerful man in the Senate, Trask reminded himself. *And a Texas oil baron.*

"What was the cause of death, and where did it happen?" Trask asked.

Graves smiled, looking at Eastman while nodding in Trask's direction. "Same Jeff I remember and worked for. He's already on the case." The senator turned back toward Trask, a more serious look on his face. "She was found lying on her bed in the Watergate. The cause of death *may have been* opiate toxicity."

Trask leaned back and looked pointedly at Graves. "'MAY *HAVE BEEN*' something as specific as a medical examiner's code for a heroin overdose? Come on, Digger. If you want me to play in this sandbox, you play by my rules, which happen to coincide with the federal rules of evidence and criminal procedure. Don't bullshit me. How do you politicos say it—what do you know and when did you know it?"

"Fair enough." Graves stood and walked toward the window, then turned back and sat on the corner of Eastman's desk.

Space and power games, Trask thought. *Now HE's assuming the position of authority and speaking from a higher point. What's he up to, and what am I into?*

"The family paid for a private autopsy, hoping to keep this quiet for now," Graves said, "And—"

"And that's a problem," Trask interrupted. "That's not the way suspicious deaths are supposed to be handled in the District. We have a *real* medical examiner in this town, and having a corpse whisked away to be handled off the books is not only unusual, it's not legal. There's a protocol to be followed."

Graves was direct for once. "Is that a problem for you, Jeff?"

"You're damned right it is."

"Now, Jeff—" Eastman began.

"Sorry, Ross." Trask was shaking his head. "I love this job, but only if it's played straight. If this is my case, we're having the autopsy and toxicology done according to code." Trask looked at Eastman, his thoughts carving the expression on his face. *I owe you, boss, but we both get murdered in the press if we take shortcuts on this one and it goes bad.*

"That means a re-examination of the girl's body!" Graves protested.

"That's exactly what it means," Trask shot back. "Has she been buried yet?"

"No, but the funeral's Wednesday, just two days away, and—"

"And I know a very good assistant ME in the District office who can review the family's hand-picked pathologist's work, and the lab's toxicology results. If she can assure me that everything's kosher, she might not have to cut the kid open again. If you want me on this case, Digger, then we don't cut corners. Right now, I don't even know why you're here. If this is a run-of-the-mill overdose death, there's not normally a prosecution."

"It's Hugh Heidelberg's daughter, Jeff. Nothing 'run-of-the-mill' about it. What about the law—which I helped sponsor a few years back—that provides enhanced penalties for the distribution of drugs that cause death for the user?"

"You want me to find her pusher, fine. Then you tell your buddy Hugh Heidelberg that he'll get the best investigation I can give him, as long as he lets me do my job without interference and everyone involved plays by the rules, including Senator Heidelberg himself. A case like this is tough enough without having three bosses looking over your shoulder." Trask nodded toward Eastman. "One's all I can handle, and that's with one I trust." He gave Graves a hard glare. "Should I also assume that detectives were not called to her residence when the body was found?"

Graves' expression answered the question.

"Wonderful." Trask shook his head. "So instead of trained personnel processing what *may* have been a crime scene, we have—let me guess—some private investigator whose first instruction was to keep things as quiet as possible, and who *may* have had a secondary mission of figuring out who did what?"

Graves nodded.

"I'll need his name. Or hers. Whatever it is. Then we'll try and see what we can do with this little sow's ear of a case that you've dropped in our laps."

Graves nodded again. "Okay. We'll do it your way. I've seen you work in person. I told Hugh that if anyone could get to the bottom of this, you could. I'm sure you understand that, as a father, he's crushed. Janie was all he had left after his wife died of cancer last year. What's the name of that medical examiner?"

Trask shook his head. "No. This is a big favor I'm asking her to pull," Trask said. "I'll call her first. If she agrees to take this on, then I'll have *her* call the family's doc. Just get me *his* name."

"Okay." The smile returned to the Senator's face. "Hey, it was great to see you again."

Trask shook the extended hand, but did not return the smile. "You too, Digger."

Graves nodded to Eastman and walked out, collecting the young man in the lobby as he left.

Staffer, Trask thought. *Might have known.*

"I thought you and the senator were friends!" Eastman gasped.

"We are," Trask replied. "For now."

Five minutes later he was back in his own office, staring out the window at the National Law Enforcement Officers Memorial in Judiciary Square, a tribute to those killed in the line of duty. *I know people whose names are carved into that stone. I know others who almost had their names added there, my wife's and mine included.*

The Rolling Stones' "Sympathy for the Devil" started playing in his head. The songs were always there, filling the gaps in his thoughts, quieting the madness. *Every case has its own script, like a movie playing out on a really huge stage. The ultimate reality show, and each episode has its own soundtrack.*

He looked down at his left hand, which was shaking involuntarily. He tried to stop the trembling by grabbing it with his other hand, but the shaking resumed with every release. His mind drifted to another Stones tune. *Here comes your "Nineteenth Nervous Breakdown." Wonderful. I don't like the way this one's starting.*

Chapter Three

Reynosa, Tamaulipas, Mexico
February 24, 2010

"Another ghost town," Captain Aguilar muttered to himself. *Deserted streets, dead bodies lining the streets, lying behind cover that was insufficient to protect them from enemy bullets. I hope most of the dead were deserving of their fates.* He saw the lieutenant approaching him with a notebook, and returned the salute.

"The survivors we could find say it was a firefight between the Zetas and what is left of the Gulf Cartel, *Capitán*."

Aguilar mentally recounted the intelligence reports. *The Gulf bosses hired the deserters, Los Zetas—our former special forces operators—as muscle for their fight with the Sinaloa Cartel. A few disagreements, and suddenly the muscle is the monster the Gulf could not control. Now Heriberto Lazcano and his Zetas run the drug routes the Gulf used to control, and the Gulf bosses are asking their rivals in the Sinaloa Cartel for asylum. The old bosses now work for their old enemies, the new cartels are more dangerous than the old ones, and even more civilians are caught in the crossfire.*

"Take any wounded you find to the hospital," Aguilar said. "Guard any that you suspect of being involved in the shooting, and we'll transfer them to the jails when they're fit to travel."

Torres saluted and headed off.

"You are next on my list, Lazcano," Aguilar said aloud, but to himself. He stood alone in the center of the street. The odors of stale gunpowder and blood mixed with the dust in the breeze.

13

Hart Senate Office Building
Washington, D.C.
February 25, 2010, 10:35 a.m.

"It's been over a month. I had hoped you'd have some news for me by now."

Senator Heidelberg leaned back in the huge leather chair behind the huge mahogany desk. The old man was tall and lanky, his gray hair thinning on top but still thick and swept back along the sides. The blue-gray eyes sweeping the room were still sharp and alert. Trask sat to the right of Ross Eastman in one of three chairs facing the desk. He thought Heidelberg looked like an eagle.

"We were hoping to have something for you, Senator," Eastman said. "I assure you that we have our best people working every aspect of the case. Jeff here is my best prosecutor, and I let him pick his investigation team on this one. That's why Mr. Doroz is here."

"Agent Doroz is the chief of the FBI's drug and gang unit in the District," Trask explained, nodding toward the short, stocky figure seated to his right. "We've worked some major cases together, including the Demetrius Reid drug conspiracy, and the Salvadoran gang wars involving the MS-13 and the rogue hit squads that were shooting up the streets a couple of years ago. In my opinion, he's the best in the business."

"And I can tell you, Senator, that I consider Mr. Trask to be the best in his office, and as good an investigator as he is a prosecutor," Doroz said.

"I already know all that, and I appreciate that this little mutual admiration society has functioned well in the past," Heidelberg said, slowly measuring his words. "I'm no newcomer to this town, gentlemen, and I asked around a good bit about all of you. I know that Senator Graves—whom I trust completely—shares that high opinion of you, Mr. Trask. So why don't you tell me why you aces and experts have the square root of nothing to tell me about my daughter's death?"

"We have to have leads to follow, Senator." Trask met the old man's hard glare with a firm one of his own. "The only prints your PI found in her apartment were your daughter's. The only usable ones, anyway. Again—according to *your investigator*—there were a couple of partial prints that belonged to a male, but they were, as I was saying, partial prints. Not enough to identify anyone.

Even if they were traceable, they might have belonged to a friend who was in the apartment for an innocent reason."

Heidelberg said nothing, but raised an eyebrow. Trask took the cue to continue.

"There was a little of the heroin remaining in a pill bottle by her bed. It's a type called 'China White.' Very pure, potent, and not the usual variety we've seen in town before now. We're used to seeing dark goo called 'black-tar' and a brown powder we call 'Mexican Brown.' Both the tar and brown come from Mexico. The white stuff usually comes in from Afghanistan or some other part of Asia.

"The heroin seems to have been self-administered. There was a print on the pill bottle, and a syringe with a print in the trash. Both the prints were your daughter's. The injection site seems to be one she picked as well."

"I don't dispute that." Heidelberg was leaning forward over the desk now. "I realize that Janie overdosed. I've come to terms with that. I want to know where she *got* this poison, Mr. Trask. Who gave it to her?"

"I was hoping you might help us with that, Senator," Trask said, still squarely matching Heidelberg's piercing gaze. "Was she seeing—dating—anyone you were aware of? Or was your PI able to determine that?"

"You've made your point, Trask. I should have let the authorities handle it from the start." The old man leaned back, shifting his eyes toward the window. "Yes, she was dating someone, but she wouldn't share his name with me. She said she'd tell me when she thought I was ready." The eyes turned back to Trask. "I wasn't having her followed. She was an adult, with her own life. I tried to let her live it."

Trask nodded. He remained silent, wanting to let the senator continue. Maybe a lead would float out of the old man's reflections.

"I have her cell phone," Heidelberg said. "She left it in her car in the Watergate parking garage. Could that help?"

"It certainly could," Trask said. "Do we have your permission to download her contacts and stored information?"

"Of course. She would raise holy hell about it if she were still alive." The senator's gaze softened and tears appeared in the old man's eyes. "But she's not."

Heidelberg reached into a drawer on the right side of the desk. He handed the phone to Trask, who then passed it to Doroz.

"You'll keep me informed?" the senator asked.

"I'm required to do so by statute," Trask said. "I believe you co-sponsored the bill. The Victim-Witness Protection Act of 1982."

A slight smile appeared on the senator's face. "I guess I did. Never thought it would apply to me."

———

1:42 p.m.

Adipietro looked at the caller ID window, then picked up the handset of the phone on his desk. "I thought you weren't going to call for a while."

"How can you be so calm, you son of a bitch? It was *your* shit that killed her."

"It was Janie being careless that killed her, Ace. Or maybe *you* didn't warn her about measuring the dose like I told her. Anyhow, *you* gave her the shit."

"What the hell are you talking about? It was *your* stuff!"

"Yeah, that you paid for and gave to Janie. That's my story if anyone comes asking, Ace, and you know I can prove it. I suggest you do your best to make sure that doesn't happen. Anybody asking you questions yet?"

There was an angry pause at the other end. "No."

"Then my other suggestion is that you *man up* to your own role in this thing and *calm the fuck down*. Don't call me again." He slammed the set down in its cradle. *White bread, upper crust pussies. That's the last time I sell to any of 'em.*

Chapter Four

Washington, D.C.
555 4ᵗʰ Street, N.W.
February 25, 2010, 5:29 p.m.

Trask dialed his wife's desk telephone from his own. A former field agent for the Air Force Office of Special Investigations, Lynn was now happily "double dipping," collecting a military retirement check while manning an analyst's desk on the gang squad of the Washington field office of the FBI. Supervisory Special Agent Barry Doroz was her boss.

"Lynn Trask," she answered.

"Her dutiful servant," he said.

"What did you do with my husband, then?" she laughed.

"I'm sending him home for the day. It's five-thirty, and Willie's grand opening is tonight. Command appearance."

"I remember. I have to stop for dog food. I'll meet you there. How'd your meeting with the senator go?"

"Edgy. Didn't Bear fill you in? He should have a cell phone for you to analyze."

"He hasn't been back since your meeting; said he had to run some errands."

"The senator had his daughter's phone. He said she'd left it in her car. Know any female twenty-somethings who function for five minutes without missing their cells?"

"Can't name any. I'll see you at Willie's."

"Be careful."

17

Trask headed for the lobby and his gun locker. He unlocked it with his right hand only, keeping his left in a pants pocket. It was shaking again.

He left the District heading southeast on the Indian Head Highway, cut north on some back roads, and merged onto Maryland 5 after most of the traffic had already exited into other townships. He would normally have turned into the St. Charles subdivision in Waldorf toward home, but he kept heading southeast until he turned into a crowded parking lot under a bright neon sign that read "The Beverly." He got out of the Jeep and examined his left hand.

Steady for now. Good.

He felt like a regular from *Cheers* when he walked in, as a chorus call of "Jeff!" rang out from customers sitting around the square bar. The place was packed. Once his eyes adjusted to the light he recognized most of the patrons as DC cops, federal agents, and their significant others. The smells of fresh French fries and popcorn mixed with the scent of beer.

The layout reminded him that the place had been a chain restaurant before the economy had forced its previous owner into bankruptcy. The bar to the left had probably not required much in the way of remodeling. On the right-hand side, dining booths and tables had been removed to make room for a pool table, a small stage, and a reasonably sized dance floor. Trask saw a replica Wurlitzer jukebox in the corner. *It's playing CDs instead of 45s.* He recognized the oldie it was blaring. *"Kicks." Paul Revere and the Raiders. Sixties. Willie always said he wanted to run a juke joint when he retired. Guess he was serious.*

"What'll it be, counselor?"

Trask looked and found the source of the familiar voice. Willie Sivella, newly-retired from a post as a commander in the Washington, D.C., Metropolitan Police, and most recently the chief of the Violent Crimes Division, was tending his own bar. The white shock of receding hair was a bit longer than when he had been in uniform, and a goatee was about halfway in on the former commander's chin.

"Your best clean lager on tap, barkeep," Trask laughed. "The place looks good, Willie."

Trask sat down beside a black man in a business suit. "Whaddaya think, Dix?" he asked, as Sivella slid a frosted mug across the bar.

Detective Dixon Carter shook his head. It was large, shining, and shaved. He was a massive man, almost as wide and thick as he was tall. A native of the

District, he was in his mid-forties in age, and in his mid-twenties in experience investigating felonious conduct on the streets of the capital city.

"I think," Carter said, "that this was the job one Willie Sivella was born to fill all along. He's certainly more cut out for this than he was police work."

"I still have connections on the force, Detective," Sivella cracked. "I make the call and you'll be back in a squad car in Anacostia tomorrow."

"We were out there today." The voice came from the other side of Carter.

Trask leaned back around the big man and saw a tall, blond, blue-eyed figure dressed in a sports coat and slacks. He shook hands with the man, still leaning back on the stool behind Carter.

"How are you, Tim?"

"Still protecting the legendary senior detective in the department from his worst instincts," Detective Timothy Wisniewski said. "My partner tends to forget both his age and girth from time to time. He still thinks he's playing football for the turtles."

"*Terrapins*, damn it." Carter shook his head. "Maryland *Terrapins*. See what you saddled me with, Willie?"

Sivella laughed from behind the bar. "You needed a keeper, Dix, and he was the only one who could handle your sorry hide."

"I see who's handling yours now, Willie." Trask looked behind Sivella to see a petite blonde sneaking up on the bartender. She threw her arms around Sivella's waist and kissed him on the cheek. Kathy Davis, an assistant medical examiner in the District, had shared Sivella's roof and bed for a number of years. Trask guessed that she probably had both a personal and financial interest in the new establishment.

"Thanks for the favor on the senator's daughter, Kathy," Trask said.

"No problem. The private doc knew his stuff. The family hired a good one. We re-did the toxicology just to make sure, but it was a heroin overdose, plain and simple."

"Just the same, I appreciate it. I know it was a little outside your comfort zone."

"Most of your cases are, Jeff." Davis winked at him, earning a playful swat from a nearby bar towel.

"No disrespect toward our favorite prosecutor, young lady," Sivella quipped. "I think he got us all promoted once or twice."

"Teamwork, Willie. You know that." Trask waived a finger at him. "You guys do all the heavy lifting; I just talk about it in court."

"To teamwork, then," Sivella said, lifting his glass in a toast.

"Sir, do the Commonwealth of Maryland statutes allow bartenders to drink while serving others?" Wisniewski asked.

"Hell if I know, I haven't read 'em yet," Sivella said. "Shut up and drink."

Trask took a sip of his beer. It was good and cold, perfectly chilled. "I can see this place becoming the FOP East, Willie," he said, referring to the Fraternal Order of Police, the union of officers on the force in the District. "Why do you call it 'The Beverly'?"

"A thoughtful tribute to his late mother," Kathy Davis said approvingly.

Trask nodded her way, and raised his glass again. "To The Beverly."

"All law enforcement personnel are welcome to drive in to The Beverly at any time," Sivella beamed. "If they have too many, we'll find someone sober to drive 'em home. That's if we like 'em. If we don't, we'll drive 'em somewhere else. See if they can swim."

Trask laughed. A light from the opening door behind him made him turn on his stool.

"Happy Grand Opening!" Barry Doroz and Lynn Trask entered the bar together, each one carrying an end of an etched mirror that had to be five feet long. They walked through a swinging gate in the bar and hung the mirror on hooks that had been perfectly placed above the bottle shelves.

Sivella shot a knowing look at Kathy. "I wonder how those got there?" he mused, rubbing his chin in mock bewilderment.

"They knew where to go to get inside help," she said.

"Federal Bureau of Intoxication," Lynn said. "We're sneaky." She winked at Trask. "How do you like it, Willie?"

Sivella leaned back on the inside of the bar and read the lettering:

"*Willie's Bar at The Beverly — Serving Those Who Protect and Serve.*"

He bent his head for a moment and dabbed at his eyes with the bar rag. "It's perfect, guys. Thanks."

Chapter Five

La Campana, Cauca, Colombia
March 9, 2010, 1:34 p.m.

"Any problems at the borders?" Dominguez asked.

"Of course not, Ramón. Money talks, and we have more money than we can spend." Heriberto Lazcano Lazcano, "Z-3" or "El Verdugo" to his men, waved his hand to the side, dismissing the question. "How is the new crop?"

"Better than last year's. It should be an excellent harvest." Dominguez passed a pointed finger across the horizon. He could feel the cool damp air as he waved his hand through it. From the horizon, the high peaks of the Andes fell into steep hillsides covered with red, violet and pink flowers, in bloom as far as the eye could see. "The poppies love the climate here. We have about 20,000 acres under cultivation now in this area, more in Tolima state next door."

Lazcano nodded approvingly. "It is excellent work, Ramón. And your friends with the new processing methods have earned their pay as well. The Americans will pay top dollar for the white, whether it is from China or somewhere else. What they don't know is not our concern. They always like the white better than the black or the brown. That is their bias."

Both men laughed at the joke.

"It is a little more expensive to produce the white instead of the tar," Dominguez shrugged. "It should actually make little difference—the purity isn't really in question in either form. You're right, I think. The magic is in the packaging—all cosmetic."

A dark, stooped figure walked past them carrying a load of harvested flowers in a basket on her back.

"How much are we paying them?" Lazcano asked.

"The Guambianos? Almost nothing," Dominguez answered. "Certainly very little compared to our profits. The Indians here see nothing wrong with growing our crops, and the clouds from the mountains hide them from the government aircraft and their crop sprayers. The cocaine we buy is much more problematic. It is grown in lower altitudes, in big plots; it requires much more fertilizer and labor, and is easy to spot from the air. Our poppies are like weeds here. We spread a few around and they just take over."

"It has been a great venture, my friend," Lazcano said. "We are spreading it all over the United States, and our profits keep growing. The addicts don't turn down our rivals' products, because they are addicts. But they ask for our heroin first, and they pay us more. We have a best-seller."

"We will make even more soon," Dominguez said. "The white from Asia has been running about $115,000 per pound in the States. We've only been charging $36,000 per pound in order to get established and to steal the customers from our competition. Very soon, we'll be able to almost double our price, and the demand will remain high, with our prices still much lower than the Asians."

"You've done well, and at a critical time," Lazcano said. "The elections are coming up soon, and our friends in the opposition party have some financial requirements. If we can bring the PRI back to power and rid ourselves of that bastard Calderón and his damned marines, our lives will be much easier, and we will be free to enjoy some of the profits of your crops." Lazcano looked at his watch. "It's getting late, Ramón. We are miles from a paved road, and I'm due back in Nuevo Laredo tomorrow."

"I'll see you there on Friday," Dominguez said. "I have some payments to make, and another farm or two to buy."

Dominguez waved toward two jeeps parked up the trail. The vehicles' drivers immediately hopped into their vehicles.

"Friday then," Lazcano said. He zipped up his jacket. "It is cold here. It will be nice to get back home. We'll see some baseball when you get back."

"He should be there in about five."

"Great. Same price, bud?" Adipietro unlocked the bottom drawer of his desk and removed the stacks of bills.

"Yeah, for now. They tell me it might be going up, though."

"Figures. It's good shit, and my junkies love the white. Been back to the neighborhood lately, or are you just staying in Texas?"

"Nah. Too much going on down here. You?"

"Last week. Times Square, baby. I miss the buzz."

"Yeah. Me too, sometimes."

A short beep of a truck horn caught Adipietro's attention. "He's here. I'll call ya back if there's any problems."

"Yeah. Do that."

Adipietro hung up and opened the door in the rear of the building. A ton-and-a-half truck with Texas plates was parked in the rear lot, and a short man was standing at the door with a duffle bag. He handed Adipietro the bag, and Adipietro handed him another.

"Six, right?" Adipietro asked.

"Yep. See you next trip, Joe. I gotta get going."

"Sure. Tell 'em up the coast that I said hello."

The little man nodded and walked back toward the truck.

Adipietro walked to his office with the bag. He picked up the phone and made a call. He waited for the answering machine to beep and said, "See me at the spot at seven."

Chapter Six

Captain Luis Aguilar sat at the small dining table in his quarters at the Tampico Naval Air Station, reading the morning paper. He was shaking his head in disbelief.

"What is it, Luis?"

"Cartel gunmen in Chihuahua killed three Americans from the US consulate in drive-by shootings yesterday. Probably Federation Cartel. Chapo Guzmán's thugs. Two kids were hit, too. The bastards have no fear, and no sense of shame."

"That's horrible." Aguilar's wife Linda placed her hand on his shoulder and looked at the paper. "I see that both our presidents have condemned the attack," she said sarcastically.

"At least President Calderón gave us that fifty-percent pay raise couple of years ago," Aguilar said, patting her hand softly. "I think he really wants to win this fight."

Aguilar pulled his wife to him and kissed her. He had met her on a joint training exercise with the Americans in San Diego four years earlier. She had been an ensign on a U.S. Navy ship used by his marines to stage an amphibious landing. Their relationship had quickly gone beyond the professional to very personal when they had discovered they had grown up just a few miles of each other, on opposite sides of the Rio Grande. Linda Avila was from southern Texas, just south and east of Laredo, and Aguilar had grown up in the Mexican border town of Nuevo Laredo.

They found that they shared a love of the river, boats, fishing and diving, and each other. They had married as soon as her completion of her ROTC commitment allowed for her to be discharged.

"What do I smell?" he asked her. "Are you cooking this early? It's not even seven-thirty yet."

"Nothing much. Just some enchiladas for Sergeant Vaca's family. His wife has a fever, and his little ones need to eat. I need to get going. I was trying to get these over there before Vaca left for work."

"I love you." He kissed her again, and watched as she returned to her cooking.

She had been shocked by their domestic conditions at first, even though he had tried to prepare her for them. She had expected the same officer's salary, the commissary and medical benefits that she had enjoyed in the American navy. Instead, they had to manage on the equivalent of less than twelve-hundred dollars per month, even after the raise, and their on-base housing might have been condemned in some American cities.

She had made the best of it after the shock had worn off. The holes in the walls where the roaches lived had been patched with plaster while he went off to fight the cartels, and she had fashioned some respectable curtains for the windows out of bolts of cloth she had bought at a flea market.

As rough as their own situation was, Aguilar felt even worse for his men and their families. Most were from the poorest parts of the country, and had to make do on less than half his salary. Many were from Catholic backgrounds and had large families. They had little or no medical care, lived in squalor, and still went out every day to risk their lives for the Republic.

"That smells delicious. I know they will be appreciated." *She deserves all the encouragement I can give her. She has sacrificed a career for me, for us.* "Vaca's a good man, and you are an angel to help them."

She wiped her hands on an apron and came to the table to sit beside him. "They worship you, Luis, because you lead them by example and don't abuse them like so many of the other commanders. The least I can do is to help them on the home front."

He nodded. "I do my best." *We are outnumbered, outgunned, underpaid, and are still asked to fill the void that the corrupt police and politicians have left for us. But I love my country—our country—and cannot just stand by and do nothing.*

"I know," she said. "Did you see the billboard outside the gate when you came in last night?"

"Yes. Another damned Zeta recruiting poster. They taunt my marines where they live in these slums and promise them better pay and new cars if they will desert their country and join them." He shook his head again. "We've had over a hundred-thousand desertions since the Zetas created their cartel. The better pay we get now helps a little. Before the raise our NCOs were only making three hundred of your dollars a month—less than the corrupt policemen we've had to replace."

She saw he was looking at the editorial page. "How are the polls?"

"It doesn't look good for the next election. The country is tired of the killing. They think that if the Institutional Revolutionary Party—the PRI—returns to power, there will be fewer deaths. Maybe they're right. The cartels will just kill each other and any innocents in the crossfire, while the government looks the other way. The PRI has always had a soft spot for cartel campaign contributions."

"Will that put you in more danger?"

"We'll see. I will do my duty, but if the government does not support us, we—you and I—will have some decisions to make. I will not put you in harm's way."

"I am here with you. You are always in harm's way." She was wrapping up the enchiladas.

"Be very careful outside the base, my love. *Los Zetas* will not hesitate to hurt you if they know you are married to a marine."

"I will," she said, kissing him. "Don't worry."

———

8 Amwich Court
Waldorf, Maryland
7:42 a.m.

Trask stirred two teaspoons of sugar into Lynn's coffee—a light blend—while he waited for the Keurig to finish brewing his own cup, a dark roast. He felt a massive, furry head slide between his legs. He didn't have to look down. It had become a daily ritual.

"Morning, Boo," he said, scratching the big dog's head as he pulled his own cup from the machine and dumped in two packs of an artificial sweetener. He carried both cups to the table and looked at the morning edition of *The Washington Post* while he waited for Lynn to come out of the shower. *More trouble in Mexico. Our embassy folks are getting shot now. What a mess.*

The big dog was joined now by a smaller one. Trask now had one on each side of his chair.

"Hello, Nikki," he said, rubbing her head with his left hand while he continued to pet Boo with his right.

"What a nice family portrait." Lynn stood in the doorway, wearing a robe.

"I fed 'em already."

"Anything in the paper?"

"More trouble on the border."

"At least it's not close."

"Yeah. Don't need any gunfire here at the moment. Bad enough to have Ross and two senators breathing down my neck on a case with no leads."

"You'll come up with something. You always do."

"I wish I shared your confidence." He thought about his left hand and grabbed it instinctively under the table. It was good for now. He hadn't mentioned it to her yet. "Maybe I'll resign and do something else."

"Right. Like what? We have a mortgage, you know."

"I know." He leaned back in the chair and closed his eyes, pretending to be deep in thought. "I've been considering becoming a writer."

"Go for it. You've certainly got some plot lines in your case history to work with. You could probably crank out some good thrillers, and we wouldn't have to live in red-alert status."

She's right. Two attacks on the old homestead in the last case, and a dead cop and prosecutor in the one before that. Maybe that's why I have the shakes. He wondered if he should tell her about his hand, but decided against it. *I don't need to worry her until I know exactly what it is.*

"I was thinking more of romance novels," he said.

Lynn almost dropped her coffee. Her last sip was running out of her nose.

"Damn you! Don't do that when I'm drinking something."

"No, really." He began to type on an imaginary typewriter on the table in front of him. "*The Trapper and the Trollop*," by Jeffrey Trask. I need a subtitle, like the ones you see on all those hot-blooded book covers. A rhetorical question."

He air-typed some more. "Could this purring minx steal him away from his furry minks?"

"Oh my god!" she howled.

"Chapter One. Misty Gale was a steamy tramp as she descended the gangplank from the tramp steamer into the streets of Skagway—"

"Misty Gale? *Skagway?*"

"It's a real town in Alaska. I'm going for realism here, and there's no real town named 'Skankway.'"

"You're crazy."

"Probably. Let's see now." The air-typing resumed. "Misty had never met a man like—I need one of those soft porn names here—I got it. Misty had never met a man like Phil Sizemore."

"No, no, no, no, *NO!*"

"What, too low-brow?"

"I don't think you could sink any lower."

"Wanna bet?"

"I think you've already hit bottom, Mr. Author."

His fingers pounded the imaginary keys again. "'How was your inside passage?' Phil asked her. 'Pretty rough,' Misty replied, 'but then some nice seaman gave me some cranberry juice—'"

"OH MY GOD!" She turned and headed for the bedroom. "Stick to your day job, you crazy man!"

———

Tampico, Mexico
8:03 a.m.

Aguilar was almost out the door when the phone rang.

"Yes?"

"*LUIS!*" His wife's voice was a tortured scream.

"Linda—what's wrong?"

"It's the Vacas. *They're dead!* All of them, even the children. *They've been butchered*, Luis!"

Aguilar raced to his car, grabbing a radio as he lunged into the driver's seat. "Listen to me, Linda. *Get out of there. NOW!*"

Chapter Seven

El Huizachal Village
San Fernando, Tamaulipas, Mexico
August 24, 2010

Aguilar sat across the table from the young man. The boy, eighteen years old, was still in pain, but was holding up remarkably well after his ordeal. His head was heavily bandaged, and his speech was slow and somewhat slurred from the pain medications, but he was functioning.

The table was in what had once been the kitchen of a farmhouse. Aguilar could see through a window that his men were still swarming over the walls of a large building that had stood adjacent to the house. The roof was gone now, collapsed years before. From time to time, another body would emerge from behind one of the walls, carried out on a stretcher by two marines to a waiting truck.

"Just a few more minutes, Freddy," the Captain said. "You'll be on the way to a hospital very shortly, and we'll make sure your room is well-guarded. If you can, I'd like to make sure I have understood your story accurately."

The boy nodded. "I understand. I think I'll be alright for a little while."

Aguilar wondered if it was the drugs or the events of the day that made his witness speak in a dull monotone. "You were on the way to the US. You made your way here from Hidalgo, and you boarded the bus which was supposed to take you up to Nuevo Laredo." Aguilar looked up from his notes with raised eyebrows.

The boy nodded.

"Good." Aguilar wrote a checkmark by the paragraph on his notes. "On the 22nd, the bus that you and the others were riding in was suddenly surrounded by three trucks. There were eight men, all armed, who forced you and the others into their trucks, and they brought you all to this house."

Another nod.

"You remained here overnight, and were afraid to run because the men said they were all *Los Zetas*, and they seemed to be trying to recruit you as soldiers, or to force you or your families to pay a ransom. Nobody in your party agreed to join them, because everyone was trying to get to Texas to find work or relatives. No one had any money to pay them. When you all refused to join them, the Zetas took everyone to the old warehouse."

Freddy nodded again. Aguilar could see tears welling in the boy's eyes.

"Inside the warehouse, you were blindfolded and forced to stand facing the walls. How long were you standing like that?"

"I'm not sure," the boy said. He was sobbing now. "Maybe twenty minutes or so."

"This is important." Aguilar looked at his notes. "Tell me again what happened in the warehouse.

The boy seemed to go into a trance for a moment, then shook his head and started speaking.

"They started shooting. I could hear them coming down the line toward me. At first I flinched with each shot, but then I just listened . . . and *smelled*. I could hear and smell each gunshot. I heard the bodies falling and a few screams. Every time I heard a body fall, every time I heard a shot fired, I could tell they were getting closer to me. Then I could smell the gunpowder as the gun was fired at the man next to me. I heard and felt him fall to the floor. I smelled the gun, and knew it was being pointed at my head."

The sobs grew deeper, and the boy took another moment to recover.

"I must have turned my head just as the gun was fired, and the bullet just grazed me. I played dead until I heard the men leave in their trucks. I waited until nightfall. I ran toward some lights and knocked on some doors in the village, but no one would help me. They were afraid to open their doors."

The boy was crying again, catching fitful breaths between the gasping whimpers.

"You walked all night until you saw some of my men at a checkpoint," Aguilar continued for him, "and told them what had happened. You brought us back here, and showed us the warehouse."

Freddy nodded, sobbing pitifully. Aguilar reached across the table and put his hand on the boy's shoulder.

"My next question is also very important, and it is the last one I have for you today, Freddy."

The boy tried to stop crying, and looked up. He nodded once more.

"Did you hear any of these guys call each other by name, or by a number, or by any other title?"

"A couple," Freddy said. "One called the guy who seemed to be in charge 'Number Three.' I thought that was strange because he seemed to be running the show. He called another one 'Rider,' and another name I heard was 'Rat.' They called one guy 'Rat' behind his back, after he had gone outside. I also heard someone call one guy *El Wache*."

"Thank you, Freddy. You've been very helpful," Aguilar said. He turned to a sergeant standing by the door. "Take him to the medical facility in San Fernando. Guard him well."

The sergeant saluted and helped the boy stand before walking him slowly to a waiting ambulance.

Aguilar walked toward the warehouse. A lieutenant met him halfway.

"How many, Torres?" he asked.

"Seventy dead, *Capitán*. All shot in the back of the head. Two more alive for now, but not in very good shape. Two more missing, according to the survivors. Did the boy have any idea who did this?"

"*Los Zetas*," Aguilar replied. "Lazcano's crew. The kid mentioned *El Wache*. That's Édgar Huerta Montiel, one of Lazcano's top lieutenants. The Zetas all use little titles. *El Wache*, *El Toto*, The Rat, The Rider. Lazcano has taken to calling himself '*El Lazca*.' He probably took the two missing victims to his ranch to feed his damned tigers. That psycho thinks he's Pablo Escobar."

The lieutenant walked with Aguilar toward a waiting armored car. "Have you heard from your wife, *Capitán*?"

Aguilar nodded. "Yes, she is safe with her parents in San Antonio. I miss her, but after what happened to poor Vaca and his family—"

"You don't owe us an explanation, *Capitán*. If we could send our families to safety, we would all do so. You are still here with us, sir. We know you could have resigned and gone with her."

The lieutenant stepped back and saluted him.

———

Laredo, Texas
September 20, 2010, 9:19 p.m.

The stockbroker had retired early, before he was fifty. His success on the floor of the exchange had provided him a very comfortable living, more than he needed, and the extra cash had enabled him to buy the ranch north of town.

He watched in the moonlight as the ton-and-a-half headed up the gravel drive toward the gate. *The gate, the highway, the capital, the Big Apple*, the broker thought. He scanned the edges of his property. Nothing moving, no lights except for the truck. *Good. I'll see him in a week.*

He looked around the ranch again, the flats of south Texas. This was his mother's country, where the dark-haired Mexican girl had met his father, the Italian from Bensonhurst. His father had enlisted in the Air Force while 'Nam was in full swing, hoping to avoid the rice paddies. The old man had been assigned to Laredo Air Force Base as an aircraft mechanic, and had met his mother on one of his frequent adventures across the border. The broker had been born on the old air base before it closed in 1973, part of the force reduction as the war had drawn down. The old base's runways now served as the Laredo International Airport.

His father's skills with planes had landed the old man a job back in New York at JFK, and enough union money and benefits to get his son a decent education. He had degrees from NYU and Columbia, a BA and an MBA, and had eventually punched his ticket to the floor of the exchange.

He had been good in the city, and had wheeled and dealed his way through hundreds of thousands of dollars and dozens of pretty and willing young ladies. While young himself, he had been unwilling to give up the fast life for any commitments. As time passed, he found himself left more and more alone with his money and his receding hairline, and New York began to sour for him. He had always enjoyed his trips back to Texas with his mother. The visits with her family in Nuevo Laredo had always seemed honest and relaxed compared to his life in New York, so he emptied his bank account and headed south, arriving in Laredo in mid-2009.

He brought some of the city with him. He still knew how to cut the corners on a deal, how to get and use the inside knowledge he wasn't supposed to have.

He also brought to Texas a substantial appetite for cocaine.

It had worried him a little before the move. He told himself, in alternating moments of good and bad intention, that he'd just kick his expensive vice "cold turkey" and get healthy; the next minute he'd figure it would be easy to find a new plug. Hell, he was minutes away from Mexico, where you could score anything if you waited five minutes.

It had actually taken him about ten minutes in a Laredo bar and a knowing glance at a Mexican who looked like a rodent to line up not only a new source of supply, but a new career.

It had started easily enough. An ounce of coke here or there, some innocent chatter with the Mexican with the narrow jawline and protruding front teeth. They spoke in Spanish, his mother's native tongue. He told his new coke dealer about his friends in the city, that he could afford the ounces he was buying on a regular basis because he'd put up some money from his former life. He had some land north of town, he kept quiet, and never sold the stuff to anyone else. No need to worry. He was a safe customer.

He awoke one night to find someone prodding his foot with an assault rifle. The lamp on his nightstand had been switched on, and he had seen the formerly friendly face from the bar smiling—no, leering—at him, from the foot of his bed. There were others in the room. They called one *El Verdugo*—The Executioner. That had gotten his attention.

His visitors offered him a simple business proposition. He would help them by using his ranch and his contacts in New York to set up a new route for their products. He would hire and direct the transportation for these products to New York and other destinations en route as directed. He would be responsible for developing some marketing contacts and customers on the East Coast. His visitors told him they were sure that he already had some such contacts, given his love for the white powder. In return, he would be compensated handsomely. They were sure he would accept their offer, they said, because—if he refused— they would kill him. Slowly.

He had accepted their proposal.

Hiring the truck driver had been his biggest challenge, but he had been up to the task. He had, after all, been a professional gamer, playing the edges of the market very well for all those years, and he had learned to recognize the others who lived on those edges. There was always just something about them. The way they sat on a bar stool, smoked a cigarette, watched a room. It was something he couldn't define, but it was something he *knew*.

You could never trust the loud ones. They were trying to be noticed; it was why they were loud. The quiet ones came in two varieties. There were the ones who were a danger to everyone else—the seething, bitter ones who would remain quiet until they exploded in anger. He had learned to mark those men after very brief conversations. Once marked, they were left to their demons. The quiet, careful ones who had learned to live in the shadows were the ones he had always hired for anything not completely kosher. As long as they were paid, they stayed quiet. They would share information about their companies, their friends, their bosses. Stocks rose and fell on such tips, and those who knew how to ride those waves prospered.

He first saw the little man in the same bar where he had first met The Rat. Their conversation at the bar had not lasted long, and would not have meant anything to anyone who had not shared their view of the world and their view of what they believed to be business. The chat had concluded with a brief, yet informative, exchange.

"Been on the road?" he had asked the man.

"Quite a bit."

"CDL?"

"Yeah."

"Interested in hauling some small loads off the books? No scales?"

"How's the money?"

"Good. Real good."

"Sure. What the hell."

A business card had been passed. It had been enough.

Chapter Eight

555 4th Street, N.W.
Washington, D.C.
November 10, 2010, 8:30 a.m.

That damned light's on again. Trask punched the message button on the phone hard enough to rock the handset in its cradle.

"Jeff, this is Julia. Mr. Eastman would like you to come up when you get a chance, please."

Eastman was alone this time. He motioned for Trask to shut the door behind him.

"Jeff, you know the question before I ask it. I got another call from Heidelberg this morning, and—"

"And what exactly does he want me to do, Ross? Pull some evidence out of my backside after his private hires tromped all over our crime scene?"

"I know, I know. You just have to understand the pressure he's putting on this office, and—"

"I understand the pressure he's putting on *you.* I don't understand the pressure *you're* putting on *me.*"

"You don't?"

Trask took a deep breath, trying to measure his words. *Back off. This guy's backed every play you've made. It's not his fault. He supported Lassiter's decision to promote you out of cycle, kept the departmental know-it-alls calm when the Salvadorans were shooting up the town, and gave you a chance to solve the mess. Take it easy.*

"I'm sorry, Ross. You've been the best boss I could imagine, with all we've been through. I'm not blowing smoke up your skirt. You've kept the political hounds at bay in all my past cases, enough to let me focus on the real job at hand; enough to let me always do the right thing. It's just that—for whatever reason— I keep getting the feeling that the squeeze you're getting from Heidelberg may be more serious than what you've deflected in the past. Am I wrong?"

It was Eastman's turn to pause.

"Maybe not. I was told this morning that the senator is losing faith in my ability to handle this job. He's the most powerful figure on the Hill, Jeff. He could pull a lot of strings if he wanted to. He's very close to the president and the attorney general. I could be out the door tomorrow if he made the call."

Trask nodded. "Obviously, I hope to heaven that doesn't happen, and would feel horrible if it did, but I know that you don't expect me to create evidence, or to charge someone who may not deserve it just to satisfy some political or PR concern. I won't do that."

"I'm not asking you to. I am asking you to think the investigation through again, and to consider some avenues you haven't pursued yet."

"Sure. Got anything in mind?"

"Don't get defensive. Knock it around again with your task force, please. Anything to let me tell Heidelberg's office you're working on some new angle."

Trask nodded again. "Will do. There's something you can do for me, though."

"What's that?"

"In your most deferential, political, and diplomatic fashion, please inform Hugh Heidelberg that my oath of office—like his—is to the Constitution, and that our canons of ethics require us to do the right thing. This isn't Rome, and we don't swear allegiance to some consul or tribune."

"I'll work on that. Maybe. Cool off and go see your team."

Trask headed back to his own office and dialed a number from memory. He never forgot the important ones. He could still remember the two his mother had told him to memorize as a child in case of emergency. One at home, the other of some family friends. *The Munns. 583-1328.*

"What's up, Jeff?" Barry Doroz asked.

"Squad meeting in your conference room in about fifteen?"

"Sure. We can do that. What case?"

"The Heidelberg girl."

Doroz sighed audibly. Trask could visualize him rolling his eyes at the ceiling.

"We need to look at some new directions, Bear."

"You have some in mind?"

"See you in fifteen." Trask returned the handset to its cradle, and rolled his own eyes upward. *No, I don't have anything in mind at the moment.* He stood and headed for the hallway, pausing at the door when he saw his overcoat hanging on a wall hook. He left it. *It's not that cold today, and I'm not going far.*

He paused again when the elevator opened on the lobby floor. *Guns? Naah. Not just to cross the street. Too much of a hassle.* He took a right outside the front of the building, heading north. He stopped at the curb even though there was no traffic, and stared at the corner across the street.

It was just a few months ago. That mutilated gangbanger's body dumped right there in the middle of the night. In front of an FBI office, for Christ's sake. Salvadoran gang warfare in our capital city. Maybe I should go back for the weapons. He shook his head as if to banish the memory. *Your antennae are working overtime today.* He looked left and right—not just for traffic, but for anything out of the ordinary—a face, a parked car, someone waiting just a bit too long in one spot. He felt his left hand start to quiver again. He shoved it into his pants pocket and crossed the street.

The Gang Squad conference room of the Washington Field Office of the Federal Bureau of Investigation was full of familiar faces as Trask walked in. Detectives Dixon Carter and Tim Wisniewski, federally deputized officers of the Metropolitan Police serving as FBI task force officers or "TFOs," had joined Doroz and Lynn at the large table in the center of the room. They had left the chair at the head of the table for him. He bypassed it and sat in a vacant seat beside Lynn, across from Carter.

"So what's the new plan?" Barry Doroz asked. "I think we've about beat this dead horse into dog food. No clues, no evidence. Lynn dumped the phone you got from the senator, and we ran down every contact in the thing. Nothing but air-tight alibis and straight shooters. Dead ends."

"I can't disagree with that," Trask replied.

"Why are we here then, Jeff?" Dixon Carter's deep baritone took Trask back to a night a couple of years earlier, when he'd first heard that voice. *Night papering in Superior Court. Dix and Juan Ramirez, rest his soul, bringing in a dope dealer. Another cop had been in line in front of them.* A disco tune started playing in his head. *"I Love the Nightlife." Alicia Bridges, a former hooker turned diva.* He smiled and looked back at Carter.

"Hammer," Trask said.

Carter looked puzzled for only a second, then the light went on, and he nodded. "Just might work. Can't hurt."

"Screwdriver," Lynn said. "What the hell are you two talking about? Some secret guy tool code thing?"

"Hammer is the nickname for Detective Gordon Hamilton, our resident expert in the District's vice trade," Carter explained. "Your husband met him the same night he met me. He knows every hooker in DC, their habits, pimps—"

"And addictions. I get it." Doroz was nodding in agreement. "That includes heroin."

"Exactly," Trask said. "Our dead junkie can't tell us anything, and neither could her very expensive apartment, so let's find some live junkies and see if we might stumble across a mutual supply line."

"L-O-O-O-N-G shot, don't you think?" Wisniewski was skeptical. "Senator's daughters and streetwalkers don't normally hang together."

"It certainly is a long shot, Tim," Trask admitted. "But worst-case scenario, we might make some good heroin busts, and if we get lucky, we throw the cuffs on someone who sings. For all we know, little miss senator's princess could have been hitting the hood to get her fixes, and one of the working girls could have been making some money on the side, ordering double doses and selling one at twice the going rate. If Janie Heidelberg was new to the game, she wouldn't have known the difference, and God knows she could pay *whatever* the asking price was."

"Long shots are our specialty," Doroz said. "Dix, make some calls in your department and see if Detective Hamilton wouldn't mind being deputized for a month or two."

"I'll make the calls," Carter said, "but what happens if he says no? Hammer likes his gig, for some strange reason. He's done it for years, and he might not want to give it up."

"Tell him it should be temporary, Dix," Trask responded. "In the event that your legendary powers of persuasion fail us, I'll make some calls to Senator Heidelberg, and he'll make some calls—"

"And I've got the picture," Carter nodded. "Hammer will be here tomorrow."

———

Tampico Naval Air Station
Tamaulipas, Mexico
7:15 p.m.

"It's been a hell of a week, my love," Aguilar said, shifting the phone to his left hand as he warmed his dinner in the microwave. "We got Cárdenas Guillen in Matamoros. He was one of the heads of the Gulf Cartel. It was a battle. Fifty of his gunmen joined him in the morgue."

"Oh my God!" Linda's voice was shaking. "Are you alright, Luis? Were you hit?"

"Just a scratch, nothing more." Aguilar looked down at the bandage on his right forearm. "The day before the fight, we found eight beheaded corpses in *Ciudad Mante*. That was probably Cárdenas Guillen's handiwork. There was a poster nearby claiming credit for the Gulf Cartel and saying the same would happen to anyone supporting *Los Zetas*. The old Gulf bosses keep trying to reclaim what the *Zetas* took from them. They don't have the men to do the job, and keep losing ground. At any rate, those Gulf bastards in Matamoros won't be swinging their machetes anymore."

"I worry about you so much, Luis." Her voice was cracking, and she took a moment to steady herself. "Is this the end of the *Gulf* Cartel, anyway?"

Aguilar paused. He couldn't lie to her. "Not yet. They executed one of the mayors in a town near the border yesterday for supporting *Los Zetas*. We expect retaliations from Lazcano's traitors now. They'll kill any Gulf survivors that we missed, and then *we'll* track the *Zetas*."

"How long, Luis? How long until they kill you, too? Am I going to read a letter from one of your men saying *you've* been decapitated? Are they going to leave me anything to bury, if I can even find your body? Come across the border and *live with me*. You've done enough—all you can—and the killing just keeps getting worse. *Please*, Luis."

"We've been through this, Linda. After the elections we'll weigh the options. Until then, I promise I'll be as careful as I can, but I cannot desert my marines. You be careful, too. Good night. I love you."

He waited for her reply, but heard only a dial tone.

Chapter Nine

Waldorf, Maryland
November 12, 2010, 3:15 p.m.

Trask took 301 North out of Waldorf toward Brandywine until he reached Surratt's Road. He'd left work early, gone home and changed into his shooting clothes. It was Friday, the day he'd picked to meet the periodic requirement to qualify. If he wanted to keep carrying the weapon, he had to prove he could use it correctly. He made the first left onto Dangerfield Road. At a stop sign he took another right, and another turn took him to the main gate of the Cheltenham Federal Law Enforcement Training Center, FLETC or "fletcee" for short. The US Marshals' firing range was in the back.

He pulled his range satchel from the passenger floor board with his right hand, then froze. His left hand was shaking again. The Cars' "Shake it Up" started playing in his head. *Not funny. Knock it off.* He waited to see if the tremors were going to pass, then shook his head. *No such luck.* He grabbed the bag again and headed into the facility. *Glad I loaded the magazines before I left. That would be a show with the shakes—rounds falling all over the place as I try to squeeze them into the clips.*

He recognized the deputy on duty. *Shane Lightsey. Good man. Agreeable sort. Maybe I can pull this off.*

"Afternoon, Shane."

"Jeff. That time again?"

"Yeah. Mind if I try something a little different today?"

"What did you have in mind?"

"Some tactical barrier, one hand stuff. I haven't tried that yet. Everything up to now has been Weaver stance, two hands."

"Sure, long as you hit the silhouette. Go for it."

Trask grabbed one of the paper targets—an outline of some thuggy-looking character. He hung the target, and started firing with his right hand from the various prescribed distances. He hid his left behind him, securing it by gripping it tightly with his thumb behind the belt. Twenty minutes later he returned the target to Lightsey, who raised his eyebrows at the holes scattered all over the target.

"Not your usual tight pattern, Jeff, but you didn't miss him. You're qualified again."

"You guys are all obsessed with heart shots," Trask said. "I wanted to work on all the organs today."

Lightsey laughed. "I think you got 'em all. Yep. Both lungs, gut, liver, spleen, kidneys. Good shooting, I guess. Want to try the left hand today?"

"Not today, got an appointment. Maybe next time."

"See you then."

Trask checked his watch when he was back in the Jeep. *Just after four. Maybe I can get in before the rush.* He headed back toward Waldorf.

The sign at The Beverly still said 'Closed,' but he saw Willie's Honda parked in the back. He knocked, and the door to the bar opened.

"Sign says open at five, sir," Sivella said, straight-faced.

"Sorry, guess I'll come back later." Trask did his own best deadpan.

Sivella grinned. "Always open for you. Get your ass in here."

Trask sat at the bar while Willie poured him a beer in a frosted mug.

"It was a Michelob Ultra, right?"

"You'll do well here, Willie. Spot on, and I only had a couple when I was here last."

"Part of the new gig. Faces, license plates, names, times—I used to file those away pretty well. Now it's customers and drinks. Not that hard."

Trask held the mug up in a mock toast. Sivella winked back at him.

"What's wrong, Jeff?"

Trask sighed. "You're still on the job, Willie."

"Memory work is one skill that translates to this job from the old one. Amateur shrink is another one, and you know as well as I do that none of us in this business ever want to have to see a real one. The paper trail gets messy for clearances."

"Exactly," Trask said. He held up his left hand above the bar. It was still shaking.

"Um-hmmm." Sivella nodded. "I'm not surprised."

"You're not? Explain that, please."

"Just lie back on that couch, young man, and let Dr. Willie go through this with you. It's not my first contact with this type of case. You're lucky you're right-handed."

"Yeah, I know. I had to shoot today. Just used the right. I told the deputy at Fletcee I wanted to fire tactical."

"How'd that go?"

"I got by," Trask said. "Still licensed to carry."

"All you guys should be," Sivella said. "I think about Bob Lassiter every day. If he'd been armed, it wouldn't have made any difference, of course. Sniper shot. But I think it makes you more aware of your surroundings in general when you're armed, wouldn't you agree?"

"I do, and I am."

"Thought so. Let's get back to your hand there. When did that start?"

"The day Eastman handed the Heidelberg mess to me."

Sivella nodded. "Figures."

"Damn it, Willie, why is that?"

"This session is free, Jeff—and so is that beer, by the way. Think of it as 'very happy hour.' So don't interrupt the therapist. You'll live, I promise."

Trask sighed and rested his arms on the bar.

"Bob Lassiter's gone, and his deputy—was it Bill Patrick? Retired now?"

"Yeah."

"So you're the big dog now. You're your own boss, except for the politibrat?"

Trask smiled. *That's what Lassiter and Patrick used to call all the US Attorneys.* "Ross Eastman, Willie. You know that."

"I know. And I know he's just a figurehead, and leaves things up to you case-wise, right?"

"I'm not so sure this time."

"Again, it figures. Pressure from big-shot senator to Eastman to you, and you've got no buffer or Buddha like Patrick or Lassiter to screen the shit flowing downhill."

"True, but—"

"But you think you're used to that, and you might be, under more normal conditions." Sivella took the mug sitting in front of Trask. "Let me top that off for you."

"I'm used to pressure, Willie, even the political nonsense."

"You've still always had a shit screen protecting your head, Jeff. Eastman had done that himself a couple of times, as I recall."

"He has."

"How about now?"

"Not so much."

"My point exactly," Sivella said. He reached across the bar and gave Trask a fatherly pat on the shoulder. "What position did you play in baseball?"

"Catcher."

"Football?"

"I was small, started late. Some linebacker later. Mostly safety."

"Other sports?"

"Water polo at the Academy. Intramurals. Goalie."

"See the pattern?"

"Not really."

"Come on, Jeff. You're smarter than this. I'll spell it out for you. You're used to having everything in front of you, being the last line of defense. You play the same role in your job—the last guy between society and the perps in court. I used to tell the guys on your cases that they better have everything fleshed out because if they didn't, you'd embarrass them and do it yourself. You're not comfortable when there are variables you can't see, questions you can't answer, and now the pressure is coming from a higher plane that you sure as hell can't control. You're one of the best prosecutors I've ever seen—maybe the best—but you're not going to be any match for Hugh freakin' Heidelberg if you try to tangle with him on his turf."

"What do you suggest?"

"Get him off his playing field and onto yours."

"As a victim's father? He's not even a witness to anything that I know of."

"Not yet. There's a connection somewhere. You'll find it. Just stay in *your* game. Don't play his." Sivella paused for a moment. "You were a catcher. What would you tell your pitcher if he was overthrowing and trying to win a game all by himself?"

Trask smiled. "You know the speech: 'You have seven guys behind you who'll be glad to help if you let them; pitch to contact and let 'em play some defense.'"

"Exactly. You have a team of some damn fine ferrets who're trying to help you figure things out here. Doroz, Carter, Wisniewski, that wife of yours. Stop trying to win the game by yourself. Now finish your beer and get out of here. My paying customers will be coming in soon."

———

Washington, D.C.
9:38 p.m.

Detective Gordon Hamilton slowed his car as he approached the intersection of K Street and 11 Street NW. "The track," as it had always been known to him while working Vice, had migrated a bit from time to time, as the pimps and prostitutes flowed like water toward the points of least resistance through the District. Thomas Circle was usually ripe for an arrest or two. A block to the southeast, the 1100 block of 13th Street had been easy pickings for a while, at least until the Washington Bureau of the Associated Press had gotten the department brass to declare the block a "prostitution-free zone," and had turned up the heat so that the ace investigative reporters from the AP weren't subjected to risqué sights and sounds that were somehow just too much for them.

K Street, unlike the other areas, never seemed to change. When he first hit the force, Hamilton heard old-timers talking about the hookers on K Street in the late seventies. "Two on every meter, knocking each other out of the way anytime a potential 'date' rolled down his car window." He was glad some things were constant, and he was even happier when he spotted her in her usual spot, a little south of the corner, away from the other girls in their ridiculously short skirts barely flashing a hemline out from under their winter coats.

He had arrested her five or six times over the years. She'd been able to provide information for money on several other occasions. She kept her ear to the ground, and knew which pimp was getting too violent, which girls might be spreading AIDS. She was also a seasoned pro, and knew that the separation from the crowd on the corner gave her the best shot at a first approach to a slowing car. He pulled to the curb, and hit the button to drop the passenger side window. He leaned to his left, into the driver's door and away from the curb, knowing that she'd have to stick her head into the vehicle before she could recognize him.

"Hey baby, you need—aw shit, Hammer." Her come-on smile turned to a distressed frown immediately. "Why you got to sneak up on a girl like this?"

"Get in, Bootsy. I'm not arresting you tonight. Just need some info, and I'll pay your going rate. We'll just drive, and I'll bring you back in a bit." He held up three twenties. He knew it was probably more than her usual fee, but flattered her with the offer. She climbed in and shut the door.

"You know I'm worth more than this," she said, stuffing the cash into her bra.

"I'm sure you are, baby, but that's what the G gave me to spend tonight."

"The G? You mean the city?"

"No, I mean the big G—the federal government. I'm working with them for a while."

"What do the feds care about workin' girls?"

"Believe it or not, some of us in law enforcement care about all our citizens, so buckle your seat belt. I was lookin' for you to find out if any of the other girls are having any new problems." He pulled away from the curb, back into the flow of traffic.

She scowled as she buckled the belt. "Hammer, you been workin' Vice for as long as I been on the track. You know our problems. Mean johns, bad pimps, cops like you bustin' us twice a month, and dates who don't pay. Ain't *nuthin'* new in the oldest profession."

"I'm not exactly askin' about your work, Boots. Anybody gettin' any bad dope? Girls gettin' sick?"

"Gettin' sick, no. Droppin' dead, a few. The ones doin' smack, anyway. There's some new white shit out lately. *Strong* shit. Some of the new girls hittin' it for the first time hit it too hard, and they don't wake up. Even a couple of the older girls done gone to the morgue. Guess they took their regular dose, and it wasn't really regular."

"Any idea who's been pushin' it out?"

"No. You know me, Hammer. I'm a weed girl. I only hit the crack pipe once or twice, and I didn't like it much. I like my herb. Hate needles. Smack scares me."

"It should, Bootsy."

"Yeah. And it does. I'll keep my eyes on it, though. Call ya at the same number if I hear anything? Same money as this time?"

"Same number, and the same money. I told you. It's the G." He made another right turn and pulled to the curb at the same spot where he'd picked her up. "Short enough date?"

She giggled. "Yeah, anytime you want it for real, you know where to find me, baby."

He held up his left hand and pointed to his wedding ring. "Thanks anyway, Boots. Be careful, now."

She got out and walked back to her spot. She waved as he pulled away. He made the light at the intersection, and noticed in the mirror that another car had pulled to the curb behind him. Bootsy was getting in the car. He shook his head while dialing the phone.

"Dix? We need to pay the ME a visit."

Chapter Ten

Laredo, Texas
November 13, 2010, 11:56 p.m.

The broker saw the truck's lights coming down the road to his ranch house. It was followed, as usual, by a red Bronco.

The Rat trusts no one. He has to be hands-on about everything. The broker stepped out onto the porch of the house, and watched as the driver of the truck and another man jumped down from the cab and began unloading the bags of feed into the barn, to his left along the side of the house. A hog pen was just behind the barn down the road that separated it from the house, and the three big sows in the pen started snorting, already smelling the feed. The Bronco, as usual, pulled up in front of the house.

"Hello, my friend!" Ramón Dominguez appeared from the front of the Bronco. He walked to the porch, grinned and held his arms in a wide embrace as if approaching a long-lost brother.

"Ramón." The broker extended his hand, forcing a smile of his own. "How many this trip?"

"Ten pounds for your friend in your capital, and ten more for his friends in New York. The same as the last trip, as you requested. They are hidden in the usual location." Dominguez looked toward the barn, and saw that his men had finished unloading the bags of feed, the mask cargo for the trip across the border. He grinned again. "Between our special friend in your border patrol, and our special mix of feed, there was no problem in making the crossing at the

51

checkpoints. Our friend waved us on through. Even if another guard had tried to detect something with his dog, all the dog could have smelled was the feed. There's enough smelly stuff in those bags to gag a skunk. I hope your hogs like their dinner."

"I hate those damned pigs, Ramón. They smell like shit, and just make more shit to make more stench. Can't we find another way to do this?"

Dominguez laughed, but shook his head. He slapped the broker on the arm. "It is the approved solution for now, my friend. We will consider something else if you can find another method as cheap and effective."

Cheap and effective for you. A stinking pain in the ass for me. The broker nodded. "I'll think about that. My man will leave tomorrow." He reached inside the doorway and pulled out a small duffle bag. "Here's the money from the last run. I deducted the expenses plus two-thousand a pound, as we agreed. I'll see you in about ten days."

Dominguez grabbed the bag and grinned again. "Make sure you do." He waved toward the men by the barn. They trotted over and got into the back seat of the Bronco. Dominguez started to get into the driver's seat, then stepped out again. He tossed the broker a set of keys. "You might need these," he said, laughing, "for the truck."

The broker nodded, and gave a half-hearted wave as the Bronco headed up the road toward the gate. *What an asshole.*

He took the cell phone out of the clip on his belt and pressed a contact icon.

"The truck ready?" the little man asked.

"Yeah. They just left. You'll need to stop at the warehouse and pick up a cover load on the way out—some more of those cheap leather coats or something. Just put some boxes on the truck and tie 'em down."

"On my way."

———

Waldorf, Maryland
November 15, 2010

Trask beat her home, so it was his job to feed the dogs. He opened a can of the expensive, healthy stuff Lynn always bought, mixed it with some just as expensive dry food that was supposed to be just as healthy, and measured the portions into two bowls.

Even if Nikki was half the size of Boo, she was always fed first since she was older and the alpha female of the pair. Trask put the smaller bowl into the stand in front of the smaller dog, gave her a pat on the head, then did the same with the large bowl and Boo. Once the dogs were eating, he crossed the den to the couch and turned on the television, flicking the remote buttons until he recognized the channel indicator for C-Span.

Good. I need to watch Heidelberg at work. Don't know why, just know that I do. Credence Clearwater Revival's "Fortunate Son" started playing in his head. *Not-so-fortunate daughter, in this case, Fogerty.*

The Senate Foreign Relations Committee was having another hearing on how much funding was appropriate for the war in Afghanistan. Trask mentally checked off the names of the majority members as he recognized the faces. *Heidelberg of Texas, Chairman, Craig Funderburk of Colorado, Digger Graves of Georgia, Heidelberg's gofer and lapdog. I wonder when Digger last had an original thought of his own? John Clark Arthur of Oklahoma, Robert Tatum of Maryland, William Pope of Pennsylvania, Tom McWhorter of Alabama. Their opposition, Robert Anderson, the ranking minority member from Illinois, Scott Holland from Tennessee, Susan Sims Brockman from Maine, Chancellor Kirkland from Nebraska, Michael Baker Weilepp from North Carolina.*

Trask watched as the hearings continued, with a couple of witnesses from the Pentagon fidgeting nervously as they waited for the senators to ask their "questions." *Questions, hell. All I've heard is the usual round of sound-bite speeches tailored for the party bases back home. They don't really care about any answer, just their own face times before the cameras. Transparency may be a good idea in theory, but I bet they'd get more work done if they thought nobody was watching.*

He heard the door close, and Lynn walked in, carrying some take-out fried chicken.

"Will this work for dinner? I just don't feel like cooking tonight." She turned toward the TV. "C-SPAN? What's the plot?"

"I'm not sure. Thought I might see something, anything that might poke me in the head about Heidelberg's daughter."

"In a Senate hearing?"

"I know, another real long shot."

"And what have you discovered, watching the wheels of government grind something else into mush?"

"Absolutely nothing. They all hate their counterparts on the other side, or pretend to, and all love to hear themselves talk."

She paused and watched for a moment as Heidelberg and Anderson discussed some opaque point of senate procedure. "Those two are at least civil today."

"Yep. They seem to be the adults in the room for now. Should be, they've both been in the Senate since the earth cooled."

"Come eat this chicken before *it* gets cold. You can return to this thrilling serial after dinner."

"I've seen enough already. Nothing, to be exact."

Trask pushed the off button on the remote. *Fade to black. Just like a junkie on her last trip.*

Chapter Eleven

Washington, D.C.
November 16, 2010, 9:38 a.m.

Assistant Medical Examiner Kathy Davis pointed to the arms on the corpse. "Tracks. The toxicology report won't be back for another couple of days, but I know what my cause of death will be before I see it. I already wrote the report, and I know I won't have to change it. Opiate toxicity. Very probably a heroin overdose." She looked up at the others surrounding the table. "She's the fifth this month. I'm sorry I didn't think to call you, but I didn't see any connection between these hooker ODs and the senator's daughter."

"That's okay, Kathy," Trask said. "There may not be a connection. We're kind of grasping at straws here, and hoping."

"There's some really strong new junk on the street," Detective Gordon Hamilton looked at the body, shaking his head. "The junkies aren't used to anything this pure, and they're dropping all over the metro. This girl was new to town. I hadn't met her yet."

"Any personal effects sent over from the hospital, Kathy?" Tim Wisniewski examined the scars on the girl's arm as he asked the question.

"Just some cash—about forty bucks—probably her cut from the last two tricks of the evening." Davis retrieved a plastic bag from a nearby counter and handed it to Wisniewski. "Oh, and a cell phone. It's in here with the money."

Trask circled the body on the autopsy table. *Just another dead junkie-hooker, except to her parents, or a sibling, or—God forbid—a child. We'll be lucky to ever get a real ID on her. The body's just a shell now. Just evidence. Nobody's home anymore. Stay detached. Time to analyze now. We can ask a jury to sympathize later.*

Trask gathered himself. "If we can identify the source of this poison—one pusher or a conspiracy group—we'll take it on the federal side. A conviction for distribution with death resulting from use of the stuff is a mandatory twenty years. If anyone in the chain of distribution down to the victims has a prior conviction on a drug felony, he gets mandatory life." He looked up at Dixon Carter. "Any of the other victims have cell phones on them, Dix?"

"One. Found in her hotel room. I stopped by the computer lab and picked up the file. The other three dropped while they were out on the streets soliciting. A free cell phone doesn't stay with a dead owner very long on the track."

Trask nodded. *It's almost always 'the track.' 11th Street, K Street and New York Avenue. If you're out for a 'date,' there's never a wait on the track.*

"Let's have the computer guys crack *all* the phones open that we *do* have and dump the call history," he said. "Then get the files to Lynn and have her start looking at them. See if we can ID some common calls, in or out, someone other than the johns. Maybe a pimp's pushing the stuff to his stable, maybe the dope is outside the pimp's control."

"Probably the latter," Hamilton said. "No pimp is going to want to see half his girls dropping dead. Bad for cash flow."

"We'll put out some feelers to the guys in Maryland and Virginia, too," Wisniewski added. "Maybe they've picked up some phones we can throw on the pile."

"The more the better," Trask agreed. "Lynn's good with the phone programs. If there's anything in common, she'll see it."

Trask left the morgue, walked out into the sunlight, and climbed into the driver's seat of the Jeep for the drive back to his office. The lyrics hit his mind almost involuntarily.

Laid Back. Danish techno group. Early '80s. "If you want to ride, don't ride the white horse." Even the hookers usually know not to mess with heroin. Most of them are crack addicts. Coke can kill, but not as frequently as the 'horse.' "If you want to ride, then ride the white pony." Yeah, right. Coke starts safer, but then they have to have more and more to get high, and finally even more just to get back to normal. They turn to heroin because it eases the crashes between the highs. Some even end up 'speedballing' both drugs in the same syringe.

He pulled the Jeep into the underground parking garage, parked and started the short walk across the street to the FBI field office. *The coke and crack users are used to doing half-grams, big fat lines. High-potency heroin is properly done in 'points,' or tenths of a gram. A new user can easily overdose on what looks like a fraction of her usual coke or crack hit.*

Trask walked to the entries of one of the cubicles in the squad room and kissed Lynn on the back of the neck. She turned and smiled.

"Hi, babe!" She smiled up at him from her chair. "What's up?"

"Back from a cheery visit to the local morgue." Trask looked toward the squad supervisor's office. The door was shut, a sure sign that Supervisory Special Agent Barry Doroz was out.

"When does the Bear return to his lair?"

"Monday," Lynn said. "He's down in Texas at some kind of conference. Cartel stuff, I think."

"Who's in charge 'til he gets back?"

"Officially or actually?" she asked.

Trask didn't have time to sort that out.

"I'm the operational supervisor." The deep baritone of Dixon Carter boomed across the room as he and Wisniewski entered.

Trask smiled. *Bear couldn't officially leave one of the TFOs in charge. They weren't full-fledged FBI agents. That hadn't stopped Doroz from telling the squad that Dixon Carter was actually running things, even if some baby fed had to sign off on something to make the paperwork pass muster.*

"In that case, Dix, I have to ask you to approve the assignment I have for your squad analyst here. Running the phone analysis on our dead addicts."

"So be it." Carter waved his hand in the air, sprinkling imaginary holy water on an imaginary edict. "I'm surprised you need my approval for that, Jeff. Didn't she promise to love and obey and all that?"

"They seemed to have left that out of our vows," Lynn said. "At least I can't recall hearing that part. What about you, babe?" She turned to Trask. "You remember everything. Was that in there?"

"I don't remember anything about that day. I think I'd been drugged. The whole thing could be annulled anytime now."

"See?" Lynn turned back to Carter. "No witnesses, no vows."

"Here's your first stack," Carter said, dumping two inches of paper on her desk. "The phone dump on one overdose victim from the geeks in the computer lab. More to follow. Look for patterns in this one, then we'll see if anything similar pops up on the other vics' phones. We're looking for their dealer, not their pimps."

"Yes, boss," she said. She looked at Trask. "I didn't mean you."

"I know," he said. "The thought never entered my mind."

———

Ciudad Victoria
Tamaulipas, Mexico
November 22, 2010, 11:48 p.m.

The old man held the photo of his wife as he spoke to her. She had been dead for more than a decade, but he made it a practice to kiss her before retiring every night. Tonight, however, he knew there would be no sleep for him; at least there would probably be no sleep from which he would ever awake. He looked at the clock over the mantle, and saw that it would be soon chiming midnight.

"They will be coming soon, *mi corazón*. I will be joining you tonight, God willing. I hope you understand. They wanted me to give them our home, the *hacienda* we worked so hard to build, where we raised our children. I have not told the kids. Manuelito would surely want to stand with me, but he has a family of his own now, and I cannot let him make such a sacrifice. I will defend our land against these scum like the man you knew me to be. I will try to make you proud of me. With any luck, I can take a few of them with me. I love you."

He kissed the photograph and returned it to the mantle, positioning it so that she had a good view of the room. He turned out the last lamp, grabbed his rifle and waited.

The first bullets crashed through the windows just as the clock began to chime. A burst of automatic weapon fire interrupted the bells by smashing the old clock, making the midnight hour the last one that it would ever mark. The old man knelt behind an oak table he had positioned against the window for cover. He cradled the rifle as he had so many times before when shooting the coyotes on his ranch. He could make out some of the human varmints approaching the house in the moonlight. He took aim and fired, and smiled as the shadows began falling.

There are too many of them, my love. I am coming to be with you soon.

He felt a bullet slam into the top of his left shoulder. His left arm could no longer support the weight of the rifle. He dropped lower, resting the barrel on the window ledge. He saw another silhouette and fired again.

Chapter Twelve

Washington, D.C.
November 24, 2010, 2:38 p.m.

Officer Thomas Thaggard McInnis of the Washington, DC, Metropolitan Police Department looked around as his partner pulled the marked cruiser to the curb at the convenience store.

"Need anything, Sam?" his partner asked.

"Nah, I'm good for now," he said. "On second thought, maybe just a Diet Coke. Bottle."

He reached for his wallet, but she slapped his hand away from it.

"I gotcha."

"Okay, thanks."

While she went inside, he rotated the side view mirror and looked at his right eye. It was still black from the tussle he'd had with a perp the night before. *Sam,* he thought, shaking his head and smiling to himself as he looked in the mirror. Growing up, his first two initials had earned him the nickname "T-square" from friends in school. In the police academy, however, his flaming red hair, matching moustache, and Irish temper had combined to tag him "Yosemite Sam," after the cartoon character of the same name. He'd tried to fight off the moniker at first, but had eventually given up. The name had stuck, and he'd answered to "Sam" for over twenty years now.

"You're still beautiful. Quit preening." She was back in the car now, handing him the soda.

"Just checking the eye," he said. "I must be slowing down. That dude from the traffic stop last night really got in a good shot before you tased him."

"He was an asshole, and deserved every volt."

Officer Miranda Rhodes winked at him. Sam chuckled. His partnership with the rookie cop was running smoothly now. They knew each other's moves, the strengths that could be counted on, the weaknesses to protect. It hadn't started as smoothly. Sam's previous partner, a guy named Stewart, had quit the force to go into flipping houses. When his replacement turned up in the personage of Officer Rhodes, Sam had gone through every instant adverse reaction that could have been expected of a veteran cop used to working with other veteran cops. Other *male* veteran cops.

Randi, as she was known to her friends, was certainly not a male. A very pretty brunette of five-seven, she could only be thought of as a cop when in uniform. Out of uniform, she could have been a model, and Sam had caught himself lately thinking of her in some very out-of-uniform scenarios.

Gotta keep this professional, Sam told himself, shaking his head slightly. Randi had dispelled his initial misgivings in almost no time. She was a very capable cop, and her recent taser shot had not been the only time in the past year when she'd proven herself to be more than up to the job.

He valued their partnership now, really liked her, wanted to keep everything good. *Hell, I'm fifteen years older than she is anyway,* he thought. *Old enough to be her daddy in some parts of the country. Don't know if I could survive her turning me down, anyway. We wouldn't be just partners anymore. We'd be the hot young cop and the old fool who was stupid enough to make a play for her. I've stayed single this long. Might as well just maintain status quo. Don't mess up a good thing.* He readjusted the mirror. *Wonder if she's dating anybody at the moment. She never talks about it.*

"You giving me the silent treatment?"

Her question brought him back to reality.

"No, sorry, I was just thinking about—"

Before he had to come up with a white lie to finish his answer, he was getting out of the cruiser.

"Sir!" he called after the small man who was walking away from the convenience store's front door.

"Yeah, somethin' wrong?" the man asked, turning to face him.

"Not unless you don't need this anymore," Sam said, picking up an object from the sidewalk. "You dropped your cell phone."

"Oh, thanks a lot," the little guy said nervously.

"Good number, too," Sam said, looking at the digits displayed on the phone's screen.

"Yeah, thanks again. I appreciate it," the man said, almost snatching the phone away.

"No problem. Have a good day," Sam said.

The smaller man spun around, almost bumping into Officer Miranda Rhodes who had assumed a support position toward the rear of the cruiser.

Always where she should be, Sam thought. *Good girl. Good cop.*

"Good number?" she asked when they both got back inside the cruiser.

"Last four anyway. 1969."

"Pervert."

"Oh hell, Randi. It's the year I was born." Sam pulled out a small notebook and wrote down the entire phone number.

"You think he's wrong, Sam?"

"He was acting pretty squirrelly. Hmm," he said, looking at the number. "He got into that ton-and-a-half. Texas plates. The phone number had a south Texas area code, too. Why don't we follow him for a while?"

"Sure," she said. "Quiet day so far."

"Stay back and play him," he said. "Not too close."

"Yes *sir,*" she said, a little edge to her voice.

"Keep it even. I would have said the same thing to Stew. Just thinking out loud, doing the mental checklists. Reminders never hurt, and are never personal."

"Sorry," she replied. "I'm on him."

They followed the truck until it pulled into the back of a tennis club just south of Capitol Hill.

"The Dome Racquet Club," Sam said as he made more notations in the notebook. "Our truck driver from Texas doesn't look like the athletic type to me, and I can't think of a reason that a DC racquet club would be ordering supplies from down there."

"Any ideas?" she asked.

"Only that it was a shame he was driving so carefully. Any violations and we'd have pulled him over and called a dope dog. The bed on that truck looked awful thick to me—may have had a false bottom underneath all those boxes. Oh well, file for future reference."

He pulled out a zippered binder and stuck the page from the notepad into a pocket of the folio. "Let's get back to it."

She nodded and made two lefts, heading back toward Georgetown.

———

Waldorf, Maryland
11:35 p.m.

Lynn Trask paused for a moment as she approached the doorway to the den. She stood in the shadow, watching her husband. He was watching television, his eyes fixed to his left. He had his right hand on Boo's head, gently petting the big dog. His left hand was resting on his lap, only it wasn't resting.

Is he drumming again? Keeping time to another one of those songs in his head? No, there's no rhythm to that movement. It's involuntary. It's just quivering.

He noticed her and his left hand slipped out of his lap, behind his left leg. She smiled. "I'm going to bed, Jeff."

"Be there shortly."

She headed toward the bedroom. *He'll tell me when he's ready.*

Chapter Thirteen

Ramón Dominguez ushered Heriberto Lazcano from the main house to what had been a barn in the hacienda's more legitimate days. The barn had been stripped of any stalls, feed, and livestock, and was now buzzing with both Mexican and Thai workers who were rolling fifty-five gallon drums—some empty, others full of chemicals—into their designated places.

"The hacienda came at a higher price than we expected," Dominguez explained. "We lost four men before we were able to kill the old man. In the long run, it will be well worth our trouble."

"It is a good location," Lazcano agreed. "We control the whole process now, from the cultivation in Colombia through the processing here to the distribution in the North. Speaking of that, how is your American connection working out?"

"Very well, for now at least. I am having both our broker friend and his driver monitored. So far, no problems."

"Good." Lazcano pointed to a group of the Thai workers in one corner of the barn. "What exactly are your Asians up to?"

"That is where the actual refining lab will be located. The Thais are experts at refining the heroin." Dominguez pointed to the other end of the barn. "The raw product comes in there. We receive the gum here in our trucks from Colombia. Our soldiers and money protect the routes. We first have to convert the opium gum into morphine by boiling it in some of the barrels, filtering it with burlap, and then we press the morphine into bricks. We convert the bricks into heroin by using acetic anhydride and some other chemicals—sodium carbonate, ammonium chloride, some charcoal. The heroin our experts from the East produce is more than 90% pure, but we dilute it with some white additives. It cuts the purity a bit, but looks the same, and the final product still looks and kicks better than most of the tar our competition makes. In addition, by cutting it a little, our profits are better."

Lazcano nodded approvingly. "The location is superb. We have clear fields of fire on all sides. If Guzmán's bastards or those damned marines try to attack us, we can cut them down easily; there's nowhere for them to hide, no cover. Well-selected. Well-protected."

"That's why the old man was such a problem for us," Dominguez agreed. He barked an order in the direction of the Thai workmen, which was translated by a Zeta standing near them. The workers began moving the barrels further away from the wooden walls of the barn.

"We don't want the heat too close to the dry wood of these old walls." Dominguez shook his head. "It would burn the building down on top of us. I have some asbestos coming to make sure that doesn't happen."

Lazcano pointed to one of the Asians. "One of your hired hands seems grumpy."

Dominguez turned and saw that one of the Thai men was saying something to the others in his own tongue, apparently complaining about having to move the barrels. Dominguez started to say something, but Lazcano was already in motion, shouting at the Zeta translator.

"Yes, Rios, that one. Bring him here. Now."

The translator ushered the offender toward Lazcano at gunpoint, and forced the man to his knees.

"Now tell them what I'm saying," Lazcano commanded. "Word for word."

The translator ordered the workers to stop and listen. Most, seeing one of their own at Lazcano's feet, had already done so.

"We ask only a few simple things of you," Lazcano began. "One, work hard. Two, keep your mouths shut when you go home at night. Three, do what you are told, and do not question orders. Do these things and you are paid well. Is that not true?"

The translator spoke, and the men—including the one on his knees before Lazcano—nodded.

Lazcano pulled a pistol from the holster at his side and pointed it at the man's head. "You say you understand now?"

The man nodded and bowed. Lazcano fired into the back of the man's head. The body slumped at his feet.

Lazcano faced the Asians, pointing to the dead man with his pistol. "He said he understood, but we have said these things to you before, so either he lied, or he refused to obey. This is a good lesson, because all of you understand even better now, no?"

The terrified workers all nodded their heads in agreement.

"Excellent! Because each of you now gets a raise! A share of this fool's salary. Now back to your assignments." Lazcano turned back to Dominguez. "Excellent work as usual, Ramón. And the facility in Nuevo Laredo?"

"We are removing the small lab there, and bringing the whole refining operation here. The hacienda in Nuevo Laredo will be used for storing and shipping, and will continue to serve as our main armory."

"It is exactly as we had discussed. More money means more soldiers for us, more bullets, and fewer marines and enemies. Soon I hope that we have a new government. It might leave us to solve our own problems, and we can just deal directly with Guzmán and his Federation cowards. We still have a year to go before the elections, however. More skirmishes with the marines."

"We will be ready for them. We even have some anti-aircraft weapons on site here if they try to come in by helicopter."

Lazcano laughed, and patted Dominguez on the back. "You leave no stone unturned, my friend." He motioned to another one of his entourage and headed for the door to the barn. As the man neared, Lazcano pointed back to the body on the floor. "I don't want that cat food to go to waste. Make sure it gets on one of the trucks."

———

Washington, D.C.
4:05 p.m.
11:20 p.m.

Joseph Adipietro left the gym bag inside the locker on the end of the row, re-locking it as he greeted the customers entering the locker room after their game.

"How's the backhand, Monty?" he asked the taller of the two.

"Much better, Joe. The change in the grip made all the difference. Thanks for the tip."

"No problem. Keep practicing. Muscle memory's the key."

The man nodded. "Will do."

Adipietro headed for his office. He locked the door behind him before making the call. He picked up the desk phone and dialed. When the voice answered, Adipietro was brief. "One in your locker. Usual time." He didn't wait for a response.

He got up from the desk and headed for the courts. There were three couples still playing.

"Wrap it up folks, as soon as you can please. It's getting dark and cold out here. If you want showers inside, remember we close at five."

His members were out on time. Before Adipietro locked the front door to the club, he saw a van pull into the space by his own car in front of the building. A sign on the van read "Metro Maintenance Services." A stocky black man in a janitorial uniform smiled as he passed Adipietro on the way inside. A nametag on the man's jacket read "Roscoe."

"One in the bag," Adipietro said. "How long?"

"About three days, between the track and PG County," Roscoe said. "Lots of hungry people out there."

"Good. Our suppliers are hungry, too. For their money."

"No sweat. I'll have it Friday night."

"Good. Make sure you hit the corners in the guys' showers tonight. Thought I saw a little mold starting to form."

"No sweat. Got my bleach."

"Friday, then."

———

11:20 p.m.

Detective Gordon Hamilton pulled to the curb. The woman climbed into the car and handed him the phone. He pulled back into traffic, making the block.

"Hiya, Bootsy," he said. "Here's your money. Sixty for your time, a hundred for your info, and another hundred to replace what you paid for the cell. We good?"

"We're v-e-e-r-r-y, good, baby." The hooker flashed a wide smile as she tucked the money into her bra. A small diamond gleamed from the center of one of her front teeth.

"Good. Tell me how you know this came from an OD?"

"Her street name was Misty. I never got close enough with her to find out her birth name or nuthin'. One of my girlfriends had done some double dates with her—you know—two girls on one guy? Anyway, my girlfriend said that after one trick, she pulled a needle after the trick left, and shot up right there in the hotel room. China White. Girlfriend had the room for the night, and told Misty to clear out 'fore she came back with another customer. She comes back a little later with another trick, and Misty's dead on the bed."

"What's the girlfriend's name, Bootsy?"

She gave him a look. "I ain't goin' there, Hammer. Like I said, she's a friend. Anyway, girlfriend was pissed 'cause her trick ran off. She kept the phone since she lost money. Know what I'm sayin'? Like I told you, Hammer, I had to pay her a hundred to get it. I told her my phone died and I lost the charger so I needed another one."

Hamilton nodded. "Thanks for the help. You wouldn't know who the trick was that ordered the double date, would you?"

"Naw. I can try and hint around it. Maybe girlfriend wants to do another one with him sometime. I don't usually do those. I just sticks to my safe old boring regulars. I'll keep my ear to the street for you, though."

"Same number and same money if you hear any more." He pulled to the curb and let her out. He looked ahead to the corner of the intersection where most of the girls were working. A commercial van had pulled in at the curb. Hamilton made a mental note. *Metro Maintenance Services.*

Chapter Fourteen

FBI Field Office
Washington, D.C.
December 1, 2010, 10:15 a.m.

"I need a reference for this one," Lynn said, holding the phone up that Hamilton had just handed her. "Want me to just mark it 'Jane Doe number four,' or did you get a real ID on this one?"

"Kathy said they logged her in as a Jane Doe at the morgue," Trask replied. "Did you get a name for her, Hammer?"

"Just a first name. Misty."

Lynn shot Trask a look before he could react. "If he says her last name was 'Gale,' I'm going to start throwing stuff at both of you."

"She throws stuff?" Wisniewski asked, rolling his chair backward and out of his cubicle.

"Yeah. Accurately." Trask shrugged. "Fortunately, most of what she throws is soft. Pillows, boxes of tissue."

"Who's Misty Gale?" Carter asked.

"I have no idea," Trask said. "Lynn must be having some jealousy dreams again."

"I really am going to start throwing stuff," Lynn warned, grabbing a stapler.

"I just know her street name was Misty, so call her Misty Doe," Hamilton said. "You day cops are crazy. Keep your shit on your desk, Lynn. I'm going home to get some sleep."

"I'll see if Misty here was making common calls with our other Doe-girls, then," Lynn said, still staring suspiciously at Trask and waving the phone like it was a boomerang.

He raised his hands in denial. "I swear. No collusion."

Lynn was still holding the phone in the air when it was snatched from her hand by Barry Doroz, who appeared from behind the wall of the cubicle. Doroz put it in his jacket pocket.

"I'll take this to our computer geeks to do an official, forensic download, and bring it back to you for your analysis," Doroz said. "That way, we don't lose any data when you throw it at your husband."

"That's okay," she said, picking up the stapler again. "I have other ammo."

"So how was the conference in Texas?" Trask asked, changing the subject.

"Informative, and scary," Doroz said. "If we can get all you pirates in the conference room, I've got some notes to share."

They all followed him into the room used by the squad for conferences, lunches, planning, and any other function requiring space outside the cubicle-filled bullpen. Trask grabbed a soda from the fridge in the corner, and tossed another to Wisniewski before sitting down.

"This may actually have been the rare, productive G-fest. It certainly wasn't one of those GSA boondoggles," Doroz began. "We had people there from the El Paso Intelligence Center, DEA, ATF—"

A round of boos interrupted him.

"Yeah, I know. We're all furious about Fast and Furious," Doroz continued, "especially since a lot of those guns ended up in the hands of the Federation Cartel. Like all of our agencies, ATF has their rank-climbers who wish to work in headquarters, and they have worker bees, mostly good guys. I didn't see any F&F planners there.

"Anyway, the cartel wars in Mexico are something I hope we never see on our side of the border. The main conflict now is between Chapo Guzmán's Federation Cartel—we used to call them the Sinaloa Cartel—and with the Zetas, a bunch of former military special ops troops who went bad and took over the old Gulf Cartel from the inside."

"I thought we were done with paramilitary bad guys," Carter said. "Those Salvadoran hit squads we ran into on the MS-13 case were bad enough."

"The Zetas are worse, Dix," Doroz said. "It's like some of our Seals and Green Berets crossed the line and started working for drug lords. In this case, the Zetas now *are* the drug lords. In fact, they were trained by some of our own special operators—Seals, Rangers—and by the Israelis, too. They kill for show, to control the population in their areas, and the latest intelligence is that they're starting to grow their own heroin poppies in Colombia and process the gum into China White."

"Any indication that they're the source of what we're starting to see here?" Trask asked.

"Not specifically, Jeff, but some of their dope has already showed up in Chicago and Atlanta."

"How's it getting in?" Wisniewski asked.

"Through that joke of a border," Carter snorted. "Same as always."

"To be determined," Doroz said. "But there've been arrests of confirmed Zetas in several cities north of the border. Some tied to the dope, others to homicides."

"It's a *possible* source, anyway," Trask said. "Maybe even probable. I haven't seen anything in the other intelligence reports about an increase in the traditional China White routes—you know, the Nigerian balloon swallowers gulping down condoms full of the stuff and then flying in from Europe."

"Disgusting." Lynn shook her head.

"Especially when the balloons rupture in their guts," Doroz added. "Then they come off the planes in body bags. You're right, Jeff. This could be our source."

"We're just seven stages separated from any proof of it for now," Trask said. "One step at a time. Connect the dots from the bottom up. Let's keep our eyes and ears open for any linkage, at any level." He looked at Lynn. "Starting with the dots in those phones."

"Working," she replied. "Maybe Misty Doe's phone has some tales to tell. No telling what's on *that* phone."

"We'll get the info dump this afternoon," Doroz said. "Lynn can do her magic; maybe then we'll have something to follow-up with."

5:30 p.m.

The Metro Maintenance truck pulled into a parking slot in front of The Dome Racquet Club, and Roscoe Briggs hopped down from the driver's seat. He opened one of the side panels on the vehicle, removing a toolbox and a small duffle bag. He unlocked the front door, and headed for the locker room. Reaching the last locker on the end, he located another key on his ring and opened the locker, leaving the gym bag inside it. He sat down on one of the benches and opened the tool box. The smell of Kentucky Fried Chicken filled the room as he pulled the box containing his dinner from the top tray.

Gotta wait a few minutes to make it look like a service call. Might as well make use of the time, he thought.

———

Tampico Naval Air Station
Tamaulipas, Mexico
11:23 p.m.

"Will you at least be here for Christmas, Luis?" she asked. "I had to spend Thanksgiving without you, and I'm not spending another holiday alone. If you won't let me come down there, you're coming up here."

"I will be there, my love," Aguilar said. "I already have the leave request approved. We will have two weeks together. Lieutenant Torres has agreed to take my company for that time, and he's becoming a fine officer."

"He has a good commander as a teacher."

"I hope so. How are your folks?"

"Good, Luis. Daddy's diabetes is back, so he's having to watch his diet; otherwise everyone is fine. How are you?"

"Too tough and sneaky for the Zetas, so don't worry."

"You know that's impossible—on both fronts."

"I'll be careful. Please do the same. I'll call again soon. And I *will* be in San Antonio for Christmas."

Chapter Fifteen

South of Nuevo Laredo
Tamaulipas, Mexico
December 17, 2010, 10:13 a.m.

Heriberto Lazcano and Ramón Dominguez sat down beside the blindfolded and terrified man, who was shaking in his chair. Lazcano sat on the man's left, while Dominguez flanked him on the right. Lazcano nodded, and Dominguez reached up and untied the man's blindfold.

"We will wait for your eyes to get adjusted to the light, warden," Lazcano said. He waited for a moment until it was clear that the man's ability to focus had been restored. "Better now? Excellent." Lazcano saw that the warden was taking in the scene around him.

Lazcano's ranch was ornately decorated with the usual trappings accumulated by one of low birth with too much money to spend. No expense had been spared in the course of ensuring that things appeared expensive. The chairs the men sat on were upholstered in a gaudy, gold-trimmed, red crushed velvet. The cart in front of them was a pure silver serving piece. On it was a bottle of Lazcano's best champagne, three golden goblets, and three large stacks of American currency.

Just in front of their chairs, the ground opened into a square pit, approximately twenty feet deep. A metal railing surrounded the pit, with the exception of a gap, about five feet wide, directly in front of the chairs occupied by the three men. Each had an unobstructed view of the bottom of the pit, and of two metal doors on opposite walls of the hole.

"I must apologize for the manner in which you were brought here, warden," Lazcano said, "but you had refused our invitation to come voluntarily. I assure you that—assuming we can come to some reasonable accommodation today— your wife and children will not be harmed in any way. What I am proposing will, I hope, be a clear choice for you. I do not choose to rule by force unnecessarily; I always try to present an option—an opportunity—to avoid the use of force."

Lazcano waived his hand and a Zeta standing across the open expanse of the pit pushed a button on a control panel. One of the doors in the pit opened, and a man was shoved into the center of the pit, falling on his side in the middle of the floor.

"Carlos!" the warden exclaimed involuntarily.

"Yes, I do believe you know this man. You do, don't you?" Lazcano asked, smiling at Dominguez.

"He is my deputy," the warden said, looking first at Lazcano, then at Dominguez, his eyes imploring them not to harm his co-worker. "He is a good man, with a family—"

"I am sorry, my friend, but you are wrong on both counts," Lazcano interrupted, shaking his head in disagreement. "He is not a good man; he is a foolish man, and he no longer has any family. He stupidly refused the same offer I am about to propose to you."

Lazcano nodded again to the man at the control panel, and the same door which had opened previously opened again, and gloved hands rolled three human heads—one of a woman, and two of young children—onto the floor next to the man in the pit. The man collapsed to his knees. A pitiful cry of agony wailed from his throat. The warden stood, staring at the floor of the pit in horror.

Lazcano grabbed the back of the warden's belt and pulled him violently back into the chair. "Careful, my friend, you don't want to join him down there, and you might fall." He nodded again, and the man at the control panel pushed another button.

The warden looked as the other door to the pit opened, a metal plate rising slowly from the floor. As soon as the plate had risen about three feet, a black and yellow shape streaked across the bottom of the pit. A huge tiger was upon the deputy warden in an instant, giving him time for only a brief, terrified shriek. The big cat's jaws clamped upon his throat, and three hundred foot-pounds of pressure simultaneously severed the arteries to the man's brain and broke his neck. When the body ceased its involuntary spasms, the tiger began feeding.

"I call him Felix—Felix the cat—probably a poor joke, but a fitting name, don't you think?" Lazcano asked.

The warden said nothing, vomiting instead.

"Pour the man some champagne, Ramón," Lazcano instructed Dominguez. "He'll need to get that taste out of his mouth."

Dominguez handed the goblet to the warden, who took a timid sip with shaking hands.

"I assure you that the champagne is free of any harmful additives," Lazcano said, pouring himself a drink. "In fact, Ramón and I will toast you from the same bottle."

Dominguez took the cue, filling his own goblet, then raising it as Lazcano did the same. They each took a drink.

"Now, let's get down to business," Lazcano said.

"What do you want from me?" the warden asked, his voice quivering. He looked down into the pit, where the tiger was gnawing on one of the severed heads.

"A simple—and as I said earlier—clear choice," Lazcano replied. "You can refuse us, and try and tame poor Felix down there, who is not fed on a regular schedule, or you can open the doors to your prison tomorrow. We have many friends inside your facility, and they tell us they do not care for it much. They simply wish to rejoin our ranks, and with the doors unlocked, they can return to us without the need for harming any more of your staff. In addition, the money before you is yours to take for your trouble. I know we have somewhat inconvenienced you today. So," he paused, "what will it be? The money or the tiger?"

"I will do what you ask," the warden said, hanging his head.

"A very wise decision," Lazcano said, patting the warden on the shoulder, "and one that tells me we will be able to do more business together in the future." He nodded toward Dominguez. "Ramón, please see that our new friend arrives home safely. His family is waiting for him."

————

Tampico Naval Air Station
Tamaulipas, Mexico
December 19, 2010, 10:27 a.m.

"What is it, Torres?" Captain Luis Aguilar looked up from his desk when he saw the lieutenant standing in the doorway. "You look confused."

"Pardon the interruption, *Capitán*. I just got a call from one of our men outside Nuevo Laredo. There's apparently been a mass escape of sorts from the federal prison there."

"What do you mean 'of sorts'? Is it an escape or not?"

"According to the report, a hundred and fifty-one Zetas escaped yesterday. They appear to have just walked out the front door. Someone left it unlocked."

"They left it unlocked just for the Zetas? How many of them were on our high-priority list, or do we know that yet?"

"We know, *Capitán*. One of our detachments is at the prison now. The warden just resigned and left the area. We are looking for him now. The deputy warden has disappeared, along with his family. The remaining guards have performed a head count, under our supervision. Fifty-eight of the escapees were high profile."

"Thank you, Torres. Keep me informed."

"*Sí, Capitán.*"

The lieutenant shut the door behind him. Aguilar buried his hands in his face for a moment. *Beautiful. Those we succeed in arresting merely wait in their cells to be released—not by the courts—by their cartel bosses. Our judicial system is completely broken now. My poor Mexico.*

————

FBI Field Office
Washington, D.C.
December 20, 2010, 11:15 a.m.

Lynn Trask spread the pages of the cell phone records across the squad conference table and began pointing out highlighted lines on the pages.

"See, we have fairly regular calls to the same number from four of the dead hookers' phones." She looked up at her husband. "Your favorite 'Misty' called this number a lot. There are a few common numbers between some of the phones, maybe regular customers or something else like clothing stores, but this is the most frequently called common number with links to all the overdose deaths."

"So who is our mystery caller?" Trask asked her.

"The subscriber for this phone is Metro Maintenance Services, which appears to be a one-man janitorial firm run by a guy named Roscoe Briggs."

"Does our man Roscoe have any history?" Dixon Carter asked, picking up the phone records and examining the highlighted calls.

"None that I could find," Lynn replied. "Nothing serious anyway. His company truck has a bad habit of attracting parking tickets."

"We have dates and times on those citations?" Doroz asked. "Anything that lines up with our overdose locations or crime scenes?"

"Damn." Lynn rolled her eyes. "I thought I'd anticipated all these questions in advance, Bear. Hadn't got to that one yet. I've just been working from the phone data so far."

"Tim—" Doroz started to assign the lead, but was cut off.

"I'm on it, Bear," Wisniewski said. "I'll pick all the citations up from traffic and see if there's any linkage." He grabbed a jacket and headed for the door.

"What did you say the name of that company was, Lynn?" Gordon Hamilton looked like he was coming out of a mental fog. "Sorry, these morning squad meetings after my night shifts are screwing up my body clock."

"Metro Maintenance Services."

Hamilton nodded. "I'm sure I saw that truck out on the track on one of the meetings I had with Bootsy. It looked like some of the working girls knew him from more than just clean-up or handyman work."

"Dix, you and Tim need to pay this guy a visit," Doroz said. "I'd go with you, but let's make this look like some routine police inquiries first. No Bureau presence on the initial contact. Get a story from him. If it doesn't line up, we'll start watching him. Hammer, keep your eyes out for him on your nightly rounds, if you can keep 'em open. Go home and get some sleep."

"Can I make a suggestion?" Trask asked.

"Of course," Doroz said. "Didn't mean to cut you out of the discussion."

"You didn't, Bear. I just think it might be a good idea to see what kind of account sheets Mr. Briggs keeps. If he's cooperative, tell him we might like to look at his customer records—to help identify some of our Jane Does—something like that. We might want to see if he's servicing anyone besides hookers." Trask felt himself doing a double-take. "That didn't exactly come out right, did it?"

"I got the idea," chuckled Carter. "We'll see who does his taxes, too, in case we want to throw a subpoena at them."

"Good," Trask nodded. "And speaking of subpoenas, let me know which phone company provides service for Metro Maintenance. We'll hit them with a Grand Jury subpoena for Briggs' phone records, and see who he might be calling besides dead hookers. I'll put a 'do not disclose' letter in with the subpoena so that his phone company won't tip him off. Keep me posted, please. I have gods on Olympus who require frequent input."

Chapter Sixteen

Nuevo Laredo
Tamaulipas, Mexico
December 24, 2010, 5:00 a.m.

Captain Luis Aguilar mentally patted himself on the back. *Just as I suspected. Even thugs have to sleep sometime.* The streets of Nuevo Laredo, the headquarters city of *Los Zetas*, were deserted. Aguilar steered his car, a 2003 Toyota Corolla packed to the roof with boxes and clothing, through roads almost completely barren of traffic. *The cartel sleeps, and the good people hide from them.* He reached the border gates, showed his military ID on the Mexican side, and was waved through to the American side. There, his status as the spouse of an American citizen got him another nod of approval after a drug dog declined to alert on his car, much to the surprise of its handler, who was sure that the fully loaded vehicle must have been hiding contraband of some variety.

Once inside Texas, he headed southeast, reaching the community of Zapata just as the sun was coming up over the Rio Grande. He was glad Linda had changed their holiday location from her parents' home in San Antonio to the house on Falcon Lake. They would have some much needed privacy for a day or two before heading north for a late Christmas with her family. He had asked for two weeks of leave, but had been granted ten days to spend with her, the first vacation time he'd taken in more than a year.

He reached the lake house, parked the car and headed inside, finding the front door unlocked. He went into the bedroom and saw her through an open set of sliding doors. She was on the deck overlooking the water, watching the sunrise and tending to some blue flowers in a planter on the rail. She felt his footsteps on the planks behind her and turned, kissing him hard, pouring her relief and desperation into him.

"I saw the blue curls," he said, pointing to the flowers. "My favorites. Where did you find them?"

"On the side of the road driving down from San Antonio. My favorites, too."

"You left the door unlocked," he admonished her gently. "Not wise."

"As if driving through that hell-hole Nuevo Laredo alone was a good idea," she shot back. She put his face in her hand and kissed him again. "I was worried sick about you. You should have taken a safer route, or flown into San Antonio."

"If I had flown, there wouldn't have been room for all the things you wanted me to bring from the house."

"If you'd let me stay with you in the house, that wouldn't have been necessary."

"We settled that some time ago. You're safer here in the States, and it was cheaper for me to drive your things up than to ship them, or for you to buy everything new. Anyway, I'm safe, I'm here, and I have missed you terribly."

She kissed him again. He wrapped his right arm around her shoulder, and swept her legs up with his left. He carried her into the bedroom, where they raced to see who could undress the fastest.

An hour later, he held her, looking over her shoulder as they both looked at the water through the glass doorway.

"It looks so peaceful now," she said. "It's hard to believe that three months ago, that poor woman watched her husband getting shot off his jet ski."

"More evil from Lazcano's Zetas," he said. "And after killing your tourist, they murdered the lead investigator trying to solve the case, and sent his head to us in a box. His name was Rolando Flores. I had met him once or twice at some conferences. We were still trying to work with our local law enforcement agencies, before they were all compromised or wiped out. He was a good man; fearless."

"How did it come to this, Luis?" she asked, shaking her head.

"Your country's *demand for* illegal things, and my country's supply of men willing *to do* evil things. It's one of those perfect storms you talk about, and we seem to be in the middle of it." He kissed her bare shoulder. "That lake out there was formed when our countries could actually work together."

"1953. Daddy told me the story when he first bought this place. It's supposed to be a neutral, international playground, supplying some electricity for both sides of the border. Now it has pirates. Your Zetas are robbing fishermen, terrifying everyone. All the boats hug the American side now. They're afraid to go too far out. Daddy used to take the boat all the way to the point on the other side to fish." She looked down from the deck toward the boat dock where an old but well-maintained wooden bass boat was tied up. "Now he won't go out of sight of the house."

"I used to fish that point from the bank on the other side," he said. "Cane poles, of course." He patted her shoulders. "We're working on it. Give us time. We're making progress."

She rolled over and kissed him again. "I know you are. I just don't want you to be a casualty of all this, before we can live together normally, before we can start a family—*be* a family."

"If that ever happens, you can give me a Viking funeral."

"*WHAT?!* Don't even joke about that!" She sat up, the sheet falling off her shoulders. "Why Vikings, anyway? What brought that up?"

"I am a marine. In many ways, the Vikings were the original marines, the first to do amphibious assaults."

"I see."

"Nothing fancy, really. A small longboat will do. You'll just have to find an archer who's good enough to light the boat with a flaming arrow once it has been pushed away from the shore."

"Oh good grief!" She fell back onto the bed and started to giggle. "Luis, you are certifiably nuts sometimes."

"You could do it here. At the beach house, on the lake. Surely there's a good longboat builder around here somewhere."

"In south Texas?"

"Perhaps the bass boat, then."

"Enough of this, Luis." She wasn't giggling anymore.

"I have a man inside the Zetas now," he said, running his hand down her cheek. "He usually keeps me a step ahead of them. I trust him completely, and his information is always accurate. It won't be long before we capture or kill Lazcano. The snake can only grow so many heads if we keep chopping them off. In the meantime, I'll be careful."

"Just promise me that if you see things going the wrong way, you'll get out in time."

He looked into her eyes and kissed her again. "I love my country and the men who fight with me, but if I ever see that all is lost, or that I cannot do my job anymore, you have my word. I feel like I live in two worlds sometimes. I love them both, you know. You and your country, my own as well."

"I love them both, too, and I love you. Now you can love me again." She threw a leg over him, and pushed up, her breasts brushing his face.

———

Waldorf, Maryland
December 24, 2010, 4:16 p.m.

Trask left the mall empty-handed. *What in the world am I supposed to get her this year? Some guidelines for shopping! No clothes, no jewelry, no candy, no perfume. Gift cards are so impersonal. She'd hate that, or maybe she wouldn't. Not much time left. Gotta pick up dog food, as usual. Might as well get that out of the way first. Maybe I'll think of something on the way. I shouldn't have waited this long. Too late to do anything online.*

He left the highway and drove to the shopping area in the center of the St. Charles subdivision, heading for a large pet store that carried the super-healthy, super-expensive stuff that Lynn demanded for Nikki and Boo. The parking lot was packed, the result of a pet adoption/foster care group that was taking advantage of the Christmas season to display some of the dogs and cats they'd saved from pounds in the area.

Good luck, little guys. Trask smiled as he passed several crates containing some medium-size dogs inside the front door of the store. *Impulse Christmas pets. Not usually a good idea, but these folks check out prospective new owners first. Hope they all get a home soon. I know ours have been worth the effort. Boo even saved Lynn's life chasing off one goon, and they make us both smile.*

He grabbed a cart and pushed it to the aisles in the back where the food was stocked. *Big bag of dry, and a case of the cans of wet stuff. Nikki's picky, doesn't like the chicken. Boo would eat anything I put in her bowl.* He sorted the cans into a gourmet dog feast. *Wild Boar and rice. Venison and sweet potato. Lamb and brown rice. Duck and potato. I'll probably have hamburger. What a world.*

He pushed the cart back toward the front of the store and the checkout lanes. There was another row of crates, this time containing smaller dogs. He stopped when he saw a dark brown little mutt, sitting stoically by herself in a pen at the end of the row. Her hindquarters had been shaved and were covered with scabs and some kind of medicinal cream. She looked up at him with what he thought had to be the cutest face he'd ever seen.

Trask caught the attention of a middle-aged woman wearing a T-shirt that identified her as one of the foster service volunteers.

"What's the story with this little pup?"

"That's Tasha," the woman said. "I've been fostering her. She's actually six years old, and a full-blooded miniature schnauzer. We rescued her from an owner who just left her outside and threw food in her bowl. She was so flea-infested we had to shave her down and treat her with steroids. Our vet said she wouldn't have lived much longer if we hadn't taken her."

"How do you do that?" Trask asked. "Take them, I mean."

The woman smiled. "We inform the owner that they can voluntarily surrender the animal, or we can inform the police. The one's that really don't care about the animals just hand them over. Some, like problem hoarders, force us to go the other way."

"Mind if I walk her around a little? My wife has made it impossible for me to shop for a Christmas gift, and she might be the answer."

"Do you have a vet you regularly use?" the woman asked. "The only way I can let you take her tonight is if your vet vouches for you."

Trask gave her the veterinarian's name and number, and put the little dog on a leash. She pranced alongside him quietly as he walked her around the store. *Lynn loves the two we have already, but always wanted a lap dog. This little girl is cute as hell, and would be gone already if her butt wasn't shaved down. Well-behaved and quiet, too, despite her past ordeals.* He led the little dog back to the front of the store.

"Your vet says you're good as gold," the woman said. "He says you and your wife are the ideal puppy parents. You can take her tonight if you want. There's just an adoption fee and some quick paperwork."

Trask bent down and petted the little dog's head. She instantly stood up on her shaved back legs and licked his face. He looked up at the woman. "Will you take a check?"

———

Zapata, Texas
11:18 p.m.

Aguilar was almost asleep when the cell on the nightstand rang. He rolled away from Linda, who was sleeping soundly, and picked up the phone.

"Yes, my friend. Is something wrong?"

"No, *Capitán*. I just needed to say Merry Christmas to someone."

"Merry Christmas to you, my friend. This must be a very lonely time for you."

"It is, but I'll be all right. Merry Christmas again, *Capitán*."

"And to you, *amigo*. Good night, and stay careful."

Chapter Seventeen

FBI Field Office
Washington, D.C.
December 28, 2010, 8:50 a.m.

Dixon Carter entered the squad room and saw Doroz and Trask leaning over Lynn's shoulder. Both were looking hard at her computer terminal.

"Major break-through?" Carter asked.

"Don't I wish," Trask replied. "No, just taking another look at Roscoe Briggs' phone history before you take a shot at him this morning. He's supposed to come in at 9:30, right?"

"That's the plan. Spot anything we didn't notice before?"

"Not that I can find," Lynn said. "Calls to the dead girls, calls to a racquet club on the south side of Capitol Hill. I ran the racquet club owner and his property records, and he seems to be the landlord for some of the dead hookers, so both ends of that connection could be legitimately work-related for our Mr. Briggs. Tenant calls owner over a leaky faucet, owner calls Briggs and tells him to fix it, Briggs calls tenant to set up an appointment. Just one thing, though, the owner—a guy named Adipietro—is originally from New York, and has a rap sheet. Extortion, assaults, some car thefts in his younger days. May be mobbed up—a real wise guy."

"Interesting," Carter said, raising his eyebrows. "Good to know. Jeff, do you think Bear's ATF buddy from Brooklyn would know this guy?"

"He would and did," Doroz said. "You don't think of *everything* first, Dix. We just hung up with Joe Picone. He said that our man Adipietro used to be part of the Gotti crew before the Teflon Don took his big fall years back. It's the years back that complicates things a little. All of Adipietro's priors are at least twenty years old."

"So he's either gone straight—"

"Or gotten smarter since he left the big town." Trask finished the sentence for Carter. "Anyway, we thought you might find the intel useful in your session this morning."

"I certainly might. Thanks," Carter said. "Did you two have a good Christmas?"

"No," Lynn said, wrapping her right arm around Trask and hugging him. "I had a *wonderful* Christmas. Got the best gift anyone has ever given me."

"Spill the beans, Jeff," Carter said. "I might find that information more valuable than your intel in the future, assuming I can ever find another lady friend to exchange gifts with."

"I'm sure you will, Dix." Trask shrugged and threw up his hands. "No clever master plan this year. I went in for dog food Christmas Eve and walked out with a dog."

"She's a little doll," Lynn said, holding up a picture she'd already framed. "A real cuddle puppy."

"She is a cute one," Carter agreed. "Is she actually a puppy?"

"A perma-puppy," Trask said. "Mini-schnauzer. A rescue service had her out at the pet store. She's actually six years old already."

"Does she get along with your other dogs?" Doroz asked.

"Already part of the pack," Lynn said. "Boo thinks she's *her* puppy, too."

"Looks like you hit a home run this year, Jeff," Carter said.

"Maybe, but now I'm screwed for Christmas shopping next year. Three's the city limit for dogs, and I'm not sure we could afford another one anyway. My guidance was no jewelry, no clothes, no perfume, and now I can't bring home any more pets."

Tim Wisniewski stuck his head in the squad room. "Dix, our interview's waiting downstairs."

"On my way," Carter said. "Put him in the room and have him wait for a minute or two. I want to watch him through the one-way before we start."

"He's already in there," Wisniewski said. "I've done this with you before, remember?"

"Mind if we watch?" Trask asked.

"Be my guests."

The interview room was just like the ones Trask had seen in countless cop movies and TV shows. A main room with a table and chairs served as the actual interrogation arena. An adjoining, dimly lit room provided spectators a view of the event through a one-way mirror. The subject could not see the witnesses, one of whom might be called upon from time to time to identify a perpetrator.

At least the movies got something right, Trask thought as he took one of the folding chairs next to Lynn. Doroz stood behind them.

Carter stood next to Doroz, eyeing Roscoe Briggs through the one-way. The janitor seemed completely at ease, checking something on his smart phone.

"Cool customer, at least for starters," Carter observed. "Let's see what he has to offer."

He left the observation area, and Trask and Lynn watched as Carter and Wisniewski joined Briggs in the other room. Carter was carrying a large envelope. The detectives introduced themselves and shook hands with Briggs before sitting across the table from him.

"You're not a suspect or anything at this point," Carter began. "But we believe you might be able to help us identify some recent overdose victims, and we'd like to see if you've come across any other information that could lead us to whoever it is that's been dealing to these girls."

"I'd be happy to try and help," Briggs said in a matter-of-fact tone. "You must be talkin' 'bout some of those poor hookers down off the track."

He's sure not trying to hide anything, Trask thought.

"We *are* talking about them; that's correct," Carter said. "What did you know about those girls?"

"Not much," Briggs replied. "A name or two, the ones they used on the street, anyway. They was rentin' apartments in a building 'bout a block east of the track. My boss owns the place, and I was the superintendent, so if any of 'em had a problem with the place I'd get called out to go fix it."

Trask looked at Lynn. She smiled, having anticipated the story perfectly.

"What are your work hours?" Wisniewski asked.

Good question, Tim, Trask thought. *Let's see if he wants to deny being on the track in the middle of the night—when Hammer saw his truck out there.*

"Whenever somethin' breaks." Briggs shrugged his shoulders. "I'm on call twenty-four-seven. Busted appliances and plumbin' don't keep regular hours, so neither do I."

"You work any other facilities besides that building?" Carter asked.

"Just my boss's Racquet Club, down off the Hill."

Trask looked at Lynn again. *He's not trying to hide that, either.*

"I thought you were self-employed," Wisniewski commented.

"I am—own my own company, but Joe—Joe Adipietro—I call him my boss 'cause he gives me enough business between his club and the apartments to keep me busy and paid. I still do my own taxes. He doesn't withhold for me or nothin' like that."

"We're not investigating a tax case, Mr. Briggs," Carter said reassuringly.

"Oh, okay, good." Briggs chuckled a little.

That looked natural enough, too, Trask told himself.

"Why do you say that's good?" Wisniewski asked.

Nice work, Tim. That would have gotten by me. Glad you're alert.

"Well," Briggs paused. "I get some benefits from the work that I don't exactly know how to declare. Know what I mean?"

"Not really," Carter said. "What do you mean?"

"Well," Briggs paused again. "Let's say it's early in the morning on a Saturday—you know, 2:30 a.m. or somethin' like that. One of the girls has a problem with her place, she ain't gonna call Joe at that hour. She calls me direct. Maybe I don't want to get outta bed at that hour if it ain't a real emergency, but them girls don't keep normal hours, either. They be up all night and sleepin' all day long sometimes. They want somethin' fixed at that hour of the night, some-times we agree on a little *surcharge.*"

"What kind of surcharge?" Wisniewski asked.

Oh, God, Tim, I thought you were the fast one in the room. Trask looked at Lynn, who was rolling her eyes upward. He looked back into the interview room. Carter was staring at his partner with his mouth open.

"They're hookers, my man," Briggs said. "*That* kind of surcharge. I'm a sin-gle dude, you know."

"Of course," Wisniewski said quickly. "Just making sure I understood."

"I didn't charge 'em extra or nothin' like that, know what I'm sayin'?" Briggs added.

"I understand." Wisniewski had his hand up and his head down.

"No, really, I wouldn't know how to declare them benefits—"

"We're not asking you about those," Carter said, shooting a disbelieving glance at Wisniewski. "Let me see if you know any of these girls," he said, reaching for the envelope on the table.

"I'll tell you 'bout 'em even without whatever's in there," Briggs said. "One's named Connie, one called herself Donna, one was Misty, and the other one—from my building anyway—said her name was Sherry. One day they was there, and then all of a sudden, I'd be havin' to clean out their rooms 'cause they were gone. Overdosed, like you said. Real shame. Couple of 'em was real nice to me. Them surcharges I was talkin' about, you know?" He was looking at Wisniewski now.

"Yes. I do know," Wisniewski said.

"Let me show you the pictures anyway," Carter said. "It might help us to notify their families if we can establish who they were."

He laid the photographs, each a facial shot from one of the dead women, in a row on the table.

"Donna, Connie, Sherry, Misty." Briggs went down the row naming each one in quick succession. "How'd I do? Did that help?"

"It might," Carter said, making some notes in a pocket tablet. "You didn't get any last names?"

"Never did," Briggs said, shaking his head.

"Did you ever see them taking any drugs? See any in their apartments?" Wisniewski asked.

"Naw, I ain't into any of that." Briggs was shaking his head again.

"Any of them ever *talk* about dope?" Carter asked.

Briggs paused. "Yeah, poor Misty there. She told me she was afraid she was gettin' hooked on somethin' and needed to kick it cold, get herself right, know what I'm sayin'?"

"She didn't say where she might be getting her fixes, maybe during one of those *surcharge* moments?" Carter asked.

"Nope."

Very matter of fact again, Trask told himself. *If he's not straight, he's very good at acting straight.*

"Thanks for coming in, Mr. Briggs." Carter announced the end of the session. He and Wisniewski shook the man's hand again, and showed him out.

Trask and Lynn waited long enough for Briggs to be led out, then went into the hallway. Carter and Wisniewski were coming back from the lobby.

"Dead end?" Wisniewski asked.

"Maybe—except for one thing that will *never* die," Lynn said. "*WHAT KIND OF SURCHARGE?*"

———

Roscoe Briggs pulled away from the parking lot. He cued the Bluetooth telephone connection on his headset.

"How'd it go?" Adipietro answered the call.

"Piece of cake. Just like we talked about."

"You being followed now?"

"Oh *Hell*, no. We cool. No worries."

"Good. See you tomorrow night."

"Somethin' in my locker?"

"There will be."

"Tomorrow night then, boss."

Chapter Eighteen

Tampico Naval Air Station
Tamaulipas, Mexico
January 4, 2011, 7:30 a.m.

"What did I miss, Torres?" Aguilar shuffled the papers on his desk, trying to prioritize ten days' worth of reports. Some required action; others were simply depressing. "I see there was a cartel takeover of Tierras Coloradas over in Durango. Anything requiring our immediate action?"

"No, sir. There was a pipeline explosion last month in Puebla. Some Zetas were over there trying to siphon off some oil."

"Anyone hurt? Besides the Zetas, I mean. I hope some of those traitors went up in their own flames."

"Twenty-eight dead, fifty-two injured, more than a hundred homes damaged or destroyed. I don't know how many of the dead were identified. I imagine the bodies were in pretty bad shape."

Aguilar nodded. "Have the national casualty figures for the year come in yet?"

Torres handed Aguilar a sheet of paper. "I knew you would want them, sir."

Aguilar looked at the report, scanning for the total at the bottom. "'Drug-related deaths for calendar year 2010: 15,273.' That's without knowing how many more are in mass graves scattered around the country, the ones the cartels don't want us to know about yet." He shook his head. "Lieutenant, you'd think we were at war, wouldn't you?"

"Yes, sir. Did you at least have a nice holiday, *Capitán?*"

"Wonderful, Torres. Thank you for covering for me. I needed the break. I hope you were able to celebrate a little yourself."

"Yes, sir. Glad to be of service."

"Your service has been exemplary, Lieutenant. I hope to see your name on the next promotion list. I have recommended it."

"Thank you, sir. There's one more thing. We are starting to hear rumors of kidnappings in Acapulco."

"That is troubling. If the cartels start shooting up the resorts, the tourists will stay home. Lots of consequences for our economy. So far, the resorts near the Yucatan have been off limits. Several of the cartel bosses have their own vacation homes there. I'm glad Acapulco's not in our district. Let me know if we hear about any trouble in our own resort areas."

"*Capitán.*"

———

FBI Field Office
Washington, D.C.
January 5, 2011, 10:15 a.m.

"What do you think about putting a surveillance camera of some sort on that racquet club?" Trask asked. "You know, Joe what's his name's place—the guy Briggs called his boss."

Doroz looked up from the papers on his desk. Trask was taken aback for a moment. The FBI supervisor did not appear to appreciate the suggestion.

"Shut it please, Jeff." Doroz motioned to the entry to his office.

"Sure." Trask reached back and gave the door a shove, just hard enough to make the latch close. "What's going on, Bear?"

"This thing with Heidelberg's daughter is tying up too much money, too many man-hours, and we're getting nothing out of it. Despite the juice the old man has on the Hill and across town, I'm taking some flack from the bosses here about playing at all in that sandbox. Technically, it shouldn't be an FBI matter unless we get some indication of a gang connection. After our missions changed following nine-eleven, we had to basically forfeit all the drug turf to DEA. Hell, you know that already. I just don't think I can justify spending the money for the video feed at the moment, much less detailing somebody to monitor the damned thing. On top of that, the consensus here is that our friend Roscoe Briggs didn't have anything to hide."

"That's a pretty detailed 'Hell, no,' Bear." Trask said. *What do I do now, Willie? My ace is starting to shake me off. He doesn't like the pitches I'm trying to call.* "I'm not convinced Briggs *was* being straight with us. Without something to throw back at him, we're just chalking it up as a dead end."

"It *is* a dead end for now, Jeff. *The whole investigation* may be a dead end. We have other cases to work, you know. Cases with more than one well-heeled victim. I don't care how connected she was or who her daddy is, or what that means for folks in your chain-of-command. There are other real people out there who deserve more than we've been able to give them because of this thing." Doroz shook his head. "I'm sorry, but for now it's a no-go. We're more than willing to ramp back up if we get something to follow. Right now we've got nothing."

Trask stood and opened the door. He started to say something, but thought better of it. He shook his head and left the office, shutting the door behind him. *I know he hates to have it shut. He can open the damned thing himself.*

———

Waldorf, Maryland
6:16 p.m.

Trask took a sip of the Michelob and waited for Sivella to complete his pleasantries with a couple seated a few feet away, down the bar.

"Somethin' wrong with the beer, Jeff?" Willie asked as he leaned over the counter. "Your face says it's sour."

"Nothing wrong with the beer. Barry Doroz is shutting down my investigation, Will. He thinks it's a dead end."

"Wow. Even with all the pressure from the senator's office?"

"That's the way it looks for now."

"Did Lynn give you the heads-up?"

"No, Doroz told me himself. At least he had the decency to tell me face-to-face. I don't even know if Lynn's aware of it yet. She hasn't said anything. She did say she'd be a little late getting home, so I stopped in here."

"Anything I can do?"

"Not unless you can put a surveillance cam on The Dome Racquet Club for a while. Got one under your counter there?"

"Not at the moment, but I know some folks who do. Let's say I get you your video feed on the hush-hush. Would anybody have to ever testify about it?"

Trask took another sip of the cold beer. It was the best thing that had happened to him all day. "No. I probably shouldn't say that, but I'll personally guarantee it. I'm not looking for actual proof of anything at this point. Just something to put the train back on the rails."

"Your word's good enough for me. Who's going to be reviewing the video?"

"If you can put it on a DVD, I will. I'll run it on my office computer. Bear and his squad won't even know I'm end-running 'em unless and until I have a real good hand to throw on the table. If he's right and we're in the back of a blind alley, it'll never come up."

"Good enough. I'll make some calls for you. This is the little tennis club a couple of blocks off the Hill, right?"

"Yeah."

"I'll call you when your movies are ready."

"Thanks. I owe you."

"No you don't. You never will."

Tampico Naval Air Station
Tamaulipas, Mexico
January 8, 2011, 7:45 p.m.

Aguilar sat in his office, staring at the television. The news reports from Acapulco were horrific. Twenty-eight bodies had been found. Fifteen—all young men— had been decapitated, their torsos and heads scattered around the outside of the Plaza Sendero shopping center. The phone rang on Aguilar's desk.

"Yes?"

"How unofficial of you, old friend. Just 'Yes.' Not '*Capitán* Aguilar' or even 'Company Commander.' You run a very informal unit there."

"Jorge, it's Saturday night, you maniac." Aguilar recognized the voice of Captain Jorge Lopez, the commander of a marine company on Mexico's Pacific coast. "I'd be at home if I could stand the silence. I'm the only one here at the moment. Linda's still up in the States where it's safe, so I came in and sent the weekend duty officer home to be with his family."

"Very big of you, Luis. Have you seen the news today?"

"Watching it now. That's in your sector, isn't it?"

"I'm afraid so. We found messages signed by Chapo Guzmán among the bodies. The old Sinaloa crew, or the 'Federation'—whoever they think they are for now—is taking control of the coast here; in the north, anyway. There's a cartel based in Michoacan calling themselves the Knights Templar. Rough bunch. Almost as bad as your Zetas. Guzmán hasn't tried to mess with them yet."

"The news broadcast was carefully ambiguous, as usual. Was it twenty-eight dead?"

"Yeah, they got that much right. Fifteen kids beheaded. Six more bodies in a taxi behind a grocery, four perforated to hell and back with bullet holes in a residential area, and three more scattered around the rest of town. Guzmán is trying to wipe out the remains of the old South Pacific cartel. The kids were probably nothing but low-level street dealers, if that. Half the time these bastards just kill because they want to, then make up the connections of their victims for the terror value."

"I know. We've seen the same thing here with the Zetas. Are you hearing anything of Lazcano's crew on your side of the war?"

"Nothing other than a rumor here or there. He has *your* coast, Luis. Guzmán has mine. I am getting reports of more clashes between them in the center of the country—your Zetas trying to move westward into Federation turf."

"They're running away from my marines," Aguilar quipped. "Don't I wish that was true." He paused. "It's good to hear your voice again, Jorge. Stay safe, and let's keep each other informed."

"You too, my friend. Give Linda our best when you speak with her again, and be careful."

Chapter Nineteen

Hart Senate Office Building
Washington, D.C.
January 20, 2011, 10:20 a.m.

"Do you know what the significance of today's date is, gentlemen?"

Trask nodded. He had anticipated the question, had even anticipated the meeting before he had gotten the call from Eastman. Now they were both in Heidelberg's office again. Senator Graves was also present, sitting to his mentor's right on the side of the huge mahogany desk.

"It's the anniversary of your daughter's death, Senator." Trask felt like a rabbit about to be shredded by the papa eagle, breakfast for the fledgling. *Why are YOU here, Digger? Come to participate in the flogging, or just observe?*

"That is correct, Mr. Trask. At least you have the courtesy to recognize that fact." Heidelberg was drumming a ball-point pen on his desk, peering over the top rim of his glasses. "I've received no updates that I consider to be of any real merit during this full year of your investigation, Mr. Eastman. Why is that? And where is the third member of your club, Agent Doroz?"

"Mr. Doroz is working other cases, Senator," Trask responded. *Stay behind me, Ross. I'll take the fire as long as I can. None of this is your fault.* "While we've given your daughter's case a top priority, we have other victims, other grieving families to deal with as well."

Heidelberg paused. Trask could see that the old man knew he was being challenged. *The next answer will be a mild retreat—something politic and deferential—before we get back to the grilling.*

"I'm sure that's true, Mr. Trask." Heidelberg said. "And how many updates have you been able to give *those* grieving families?"

Remember what Willie said—get him off his own playing field and onto yours. "Those are confidential matters which are restricted by privacy concerns, Senator," Trask said. *See if you can put him off-balance. Fudge a little.* "I can tell you, however, that I believe there may be some connections between those other cases and your daughter's, and that we've been pushing even harder on these other death investigations because of the fact that they may be related to Janie's death."

"Why is today the first time we're hearing of this, Jeff?" Graves asked.

The puppet has a voice box. "In part because of those privacy concerns that I mentioned," Trask replied, "and in part because we're not sure yet. The leads are promising, but they aren't fully developed yet, and it's not my job to be making promises I can't keep, especially on something as important as this. I'm sorry things haven't progressed as quickly as we all would have liked, but we can't manufacture evidence."

"What *can* you tell me about these possible connections?" Heidelberg asked. He was genuinely curious now, his voice less accusatory.

"I had told Jeff to exhaust every theory he had," Eastman said. "He's been beating his head against a wall reviewing the particulars of your daughter's case, so he came up with the idea of trying to identify some heroin suppliers first—through the other victims if necessary—then trace the drugs back down from the suppliers to your daughter, rather than from your daughter's death upward. It's been productive, even though there are still some significant gaps to be filled."

"That's correct." Trask took his cue. "China White heroin is pretty rare in these parts, and it's quite probable that if we can identify the source of the dope, we can develop some intelligence that will point to the party who provided it to Janie."

"You've made some progress in that regard?" Graves asked.

Is your nose just up Heidelberg's ass as usual, or are you really interested in this investigation, Digger? Trask gave the junior senator a brief glare, then returned his attention to Heidelberg. "Our best evidence so far is that the supply line for this stuff may go all the way to Mexico, to one of the cartels there. If we're able to get enough information to trace the flow into DC, we may be able to solve several overdose deaths, including your daughter's."

"Does the fact that the source is in Mexico present any special difficulties?" Heidelberg asked.

Good. He's completely off the attack for now. "Not at the moment, Senator." Trask paused for a brief instant. It was a device he'd used hundreds of times in front of juries, the seconds of silence serving to underline the importance of what was to come.

"Because we're dealing with international suspects, we may have our hands tied down the road, even if we're able to fully flesh everything out. We have, as you both are very much aware, an extradition treaty with Mexico, but I can tell you from personal experience that the Mexican authorities extradite for American prosecution only those whom *they wish* to extradite. I have one pending extradition case that's actually been approved by the Mexican government, but the guy's been in jail down there for three years and we haven't seen him up here *yet.* Sometimes I think it's a matter of political connections and money." Another brief pause. "The bigger problem for us may be the violence going on in that country."

"I don't follow—" Graves started to say.

"You wouldn't unless you'd been trying to deal with Mexican defendants for the last five years or so," Trask cut him off. *My field, my expertise now, boys. I'll tell you some things you both don't know.* "It's not like dealing with a home-grown criminal. If I get a dope dealer from Anacostia, his only concern when it comes time to sing or clam up is *time*—the time he's going to have to spend in a federal pen. Sure, some of them are worried about threats from others in their own circle, but if we can round all those others up, the threat goes away when we lock them down for years, and we trade our songbird some time for his tunes.

"It's not like that for Mexican nationals. If we pick up a low-level mule at Union Station carrying a load for his bosses down south, he's telling us nothing, and no offer of a reduction in prison time is going to change that. That's because if any hint reaches his bosses that he's cooperating with us, his mother, his wife, and his kids all get shot or beheaded. He's much more likely to just plead guilty and go do his mandatory sentence, even if it's twenty years or more."

"If that's the case, how do you follow the trail?" Heidelberg asked. "Whether you try to climb the ladder, or go down it, don't you need someone to talk?"

"Usually," Trask said. "Not always. If we're able to identify the means they're using to move the dope, sometimes we can put a net over everything with surveillance. That surveillance can be physical—cops with eyes on the prize following the bad guys around—or electronic as in a wiretap. At any rate, once we track the dope to an American suspect, the usual formula works. Time becomes currency, and we can barter. We're hoping we can find a local perpetrator who will be willing to provide the linkage to the supply funnel. That does bring up one other problem, Senator.

"Assuming we're able to identify the largest local pusher—the one mainly responsible for the overdoses, the one receiving the heroin from the smugglers and spreading it across town—that target may be the only one who can identify his worker bees, and he may be the only one who can point us to the party who gave the dope directly to your daughter. Would you want to give a break to the more culpable target to get to your daughter's direct supplier, even though that bigger target might be responsible for several other deaths?"

The question caught Heidelberg completely off guard. It called for an answer with both moral and political consequences, especially if that answer ever left the room, and the way Trask had phrased it left no doubt that it might. The old man took his time before answering.

"No. Of course not." Heidelberg stared hard at him.

"I hoped you would say that," Trask said. "Like I said, we have other victims and their families to consider, and to consult." *Good. We understand each other and where the lines are drawn for now.* "We'll continue working the other cases and supply lines, and I promise that if we make the connection to Janie, we'll let you know immediately."

"That will have to do then," Heidelberg said, standing to signal the end of the meeting. "Just understand me, gentlemen. My patience has reasonable limitations, and I do not want to see another one of these anniversaries without significant progress."

———

"I didn't realize you'd tracked the drugs to one of the cartels, Jeff," Eastman said as they left the building and headed for a Metro stop.

"We haven't." Trask kept walking, but had to look back when his answer froze his boss in his tracks. He walked back to where Eastman was standing. "My exact words were that we *may* have traced it to a cartel, and that such was our best evidence. Doroz got back from a conference in Texas and heard that one of the gangs down there had figured out how to make China White. I'm sorry, Ross, but we need more time, and that's all I had to feed Heidelberg."

"How do you plan on following up on that? Does Doroz have any ideas?"

"Actually, Doroz has closed the case for now on his end. I'm going to have to reach out to some other agencies if something doesn't break soon."

"Oh my God. I guess I should start looking for other employment after the first of the year."

"You have my word that I'll do everything I can to prevent that from becoming necessary."

"You already have, Jeff. I know that. It just might not be enough."

"The cops have a saying, 'I'd rather be lucky than good.'" Trask said. "I'm starting to hope I get lucky."

———

Waldorf, Maryland
10:45 p.m.

"I'm sorry about Bear cutting you off," Lynn said, patting his thigh.

They sat on the couch watching the news. The dogs weren't interested in the commentary. Tasha was happily sprawled across Lynn's lap. Nikki was asleep on the other end of the couch, and Boo was snoring at their feet.

"Not your fault," Trask replied. "Not Bear's either. The politics has all our priorities upside down. It always does. Bear's right to put it on the back-burner for now."

"What's your next move?"

"Keep my eyes and ears open and if nothing pops, get away from it. I've got to do my two weeks stint for the reserves sometime in the next couple of months. I think I'll schedule it and get out of town for a while. The Air Force circuit guys in San Antonio are having a conference in March. That'll give me some time to clear up some things on my docket. Would you be okay with the pups for a bit?"

"Sure. The pups, the shotgun, my .45 and the alarm. Since we don't know who the bad guys are this time it's a safe bet that they don't know who we are, either. I'll be fine."

"Good. Thanks." He looked at the dogs again. *Everything's good at Castle Trask for once. At least the home front's secure.* His left hand started shaking again. He tucked it under his leg.

———

Tampico Naval Air Station
Tamaulipas, Mexico
11:52 p.m.

Aguilar shut the front door and cranked the locks on both the deadbolts. He surveyed the silent house. He'd moved the lamps close to the walls so that there was no danger of his shadow being thrown on a window by walking between a light source and a curtain, even though he kept all the blinds and drapes closed.

It's like a tomb in here without Linda. Maybe I'll get a dog. No, they'd just poison or shoot it. If I do move to Texas, we'll get one, live a life for a change.

He checked to make sure that there was a round chambered in the pistol on the headboard, and put his loaded assault rifle on the floor beside the bed. He turned on the television, keeping the volume low enough to hear anything unusual outside the house. He stopped channel surfing at the most mundane program he could find. It still took over half an hour to bore him to sleep.

Chapter Twenty

"It's a ghost town now, *Capitán*." The lieutenant shook his head.

"I'm afraid you're right, Torres." Aguilar nodded sympathetically. They continued their patrol of the silent streets, riding in the front seats of an armored car. Torres was driving.

It had been almost a year to the day since several violent weeks of turf warfare between *Los Zetas* and their former employers in the Gulf Cartel had turned the northern border town into a combat zone. Any resident with transportation had fled the city. Others were hiding. Others were dead.

Aguilar looked about the streets of Lieutenant Torres' home town, knowing what the young man must be thinking. *He sees nasty pockmarks left on the walls of the store fronts and houses left by the impacts of thousands of bullets. He sees empty streets that were full of people when he grew up here. He hears silence in the markets where he remembers laughter and conversation.*

"We are making progress now." Aguilar patted the younger man on the shoulder. "We have them on the run, hiding. It will take time, but we will fill these streets again. People will return to their homes. And we will get Lazcano."

"I hope so, *Capitán*." The lieutenant paused. "I wish I could be sure."

"This is not for dissemination, understand?" Aguilar's tone shifted from sympathy to a stern warning, his voice to a whisper barely discernible over the drone of the vehicle's engine.

"Yes, sir." Torres took his eyes off the street to meet Aguilar's gaze. "I understand."

"We have a good man on the inside now. It's just a matter of time."

―――――

Columbia, Missouri
February 27, 2011, 8:23 p.m.

The ton-and-a-half pulled into the pumps outside the convenience store off Interstate 70 just east of town. Its driver, a small figure, hopped down from the cab and inserted the nozzle into the tank, then stood waiting impatiently for the dials to stop spinning. When they finally stopped, indicating that the truck was fully fueled, he looked into the plastic window for the receipt. He found two.

Somebody forgot to grab theirs.

He started to toss the extra receipt into the trash receptacle between the front and rear pumps, but caught himself before doing so.

That silly, paranoid bastard is making me keep receipts for doing dope runs, leaving a paper trail when we should be just scrapping everything. I take all the risks on the road, and he gets more money for it than I do. I've seen him add 'em up before he pays me for the expenses. He doesn't read 'em; he just adds 'em up and pays me. He wants receipts? I'll give him receipts.

He walked around the other pumps and found one more that had been left by another customer in a hurry. He mentally added the two slips of paper. *Another $74.50 in my pocket. As long as I don't get too greedy, he'll never double-check these.*

He entered the store, used the restroom, bought a couple of energy drinks, and climbed back into the cab. *I can stay awake to St. Louis. I'll stop there for the night.*

―――――

Tampico Naval Air Station
Tamaulipas, Mexico
February 28, 2011, 8:30 a.m.

"What's the bad news this morning, Torres?" Aguilar looked up from his second cup of coffee.

"Plenty, I'm afraid, *Capitán*. The Federation Cartel apparently has a new tactic. The cops in Mazatlán found seven bodies hanging from a bridge this morning. A big sign—one of those *narcomantas*—hanging with them said that the dead were all members of the South Pacific Cartel. Guzmán's finishing off another rival gang."

"Wonderful." Aguilar's comment was heavily laced with sarcasm. "Next we'll see the Zetas copying that little trick over here."

"We do have some good news," the lieutenant said. "Our guys in Saltillo captured '*El Toto*' yesterday."

"That is good news. The Americans will be pleased. When was their agent killed?"

"About ten days ago, sir. His name was Zapata. He was one of their Immigration and Customs Enforcement officials. He was ambushed on his way to Mexico City from Laredo. '*El Toto*' and some other Zetas shot him in San Luis Potosi. Another ICE agent was wounded. The Americans identified themselves as diplomats, but the Zetas—about fifteen of them—just said they didn't give a shit and started shooting. The Americans were unarmed."

"That's right. I remember now. So another one of Lazcano's boys bites the dust; at least until he can buy his way out of jail. How's the other American agent doing?"

"He is expected to recover."

"Good. What's our latest information on where the Zetas are focusing their efforts?"

"We had reports last night of sightings of a Zeta convoy in Valle Hermoso."

"A convoy, Torres? How many vehicles?"

"About fifty, *Capitán*. Most marked with the 'Z' on their doors."

"Get the men together, Torres, and line up the chopper transports. I'm not going to have those bastards invading our towns like an army of occupation. We still have a government for now. We leave tonight."

———

Trask looked up from what had been a heaping plate of beef stew over rice. The plate was now empty. Trask was not.

"You know you could make a good living selling that stuff."

Lynn leaned over from her chair at the table and kissed him. "I'm glad you liked it, but I am *not* getting into the restaurant business. I'd want to shoot some of the customers even more than some of your gang-bangers. Did you hear from your reserve coordinator?"

"Yep. I'll be in lovely downtown Randolph later this month. Air Force circuit prosecutor conference. They've penciled me in as a guest lecturer. I just have to make sure the uniforms still fit, and come up with something to yack about for an hour. The rest of the two weeks will be consulting with the active duty crew on trial tactics. You know, telling war stories to the kids while they sit at my feet."

"You have a lot to teach them, and you should take it seriously."

He leaned over and kissed her this time. "And *you* know that I actually do. I just find some of the legend to be just that—legend—and a bit overblown."

"I lived some of that legend with you, remember? I'm not sure any other JAG could have pulled off some of the results that you did. Just teach them well. We'll miss you, but I know it will be worth it for the difference you'll be making. Clone that trial head of yours into some of those young pups down there, and spread the word."

"It helped that I had some great teachers, and the best undercover narc in the Air Force as a witness."

"I'd had a lot of other prosecutors plead my cases down to almost nothing. They were afraid of going to trial. You never were."

Trask leaned back, rocking on the rear legs of the chair. "It's like Lassiter used to say, "Trials are just a silly constitutional prerequisite to sentencing.""

―――

Valle Hermoso, Tamaulipas, Mexico
March 1, 2011, 7:34 a.m.

"How's the pain, *Capitán?*"

"I'll live, Torres. It's just a shoulder, and my left one, thank God." Aguilar said, wincing as the medic kneeling beside him finished the field bandage. "What's our count?"

"You are our only casualty, sir. We found the bodies of eight Zetas once the firing stopped. They tried to retreat into the brush once we repelled the ambush of our vehicles. We also recovered five of their SUVs."

"Good. Some of the bastards will have to walk, or ride in each other's laps."

Aguilar's quip drew appreciative chuckles form the marines gathered around him.

"We got some weapons, too, *Capitán.* Twelve assault rifles, a grenade launcher, four grenades, and about two-thousand rounds of ammunition."

"Good work, Torres. I expect you'll be in charge of things again until I get back." Aguilar looked at his bandaged shoulder; the blood was seeping through to the surface. "It looks like this one might take a while to heal."

―――

Nuevo Laredo, Tamaulipas, Mexico
11:48 a.m.

"Bad news, I'm afraid." Dominguez returned his cell phone to his pocket.

"What now?" Lazcano asked, looking up from his lunch. "More trouble with our former friends from the Gulf, or is Guzmán pushing this way again?"

"Neither. The marines hit our convoy at Valle Hermoso. We lost eight more men."

"How many marines did they kill?"

"I don't know. At least one was hit, but he appears to have survived. That's the only good news."

Lazcano slammed his fork down with such violence that the plate jumped off his desk, rattling around for seconds before it came to rest again. "Why the hell is that *good* news?" he growled. "We try and train our recruits to fight, and the damned marines have one wounded to our eight dead. Explain to me why that is *good* news, Ramón."

"My apologies. I should have explained my remarks at the beginning. The wounded marine was their commander, Aguilar."

Lazcano sat back in his leather chair, thoughtful for a moment. "Give the man who wounded him an extra ten thousand dollars; that is, if our man's not one of the dead. Tell *all* the men that we'll pay fifty thousand for the man who brings me that bastard's head. He's caused us enough trouble. I want him dead."

"I understand."

"And, Ramón—"

"Yes?"

"I am tired of the Americans coming to Mexico City and demanding things. How many of our men were arrested for that incident with the American agents?"

"*El Toto* and seven others, I think."

"The Americans send their police to our capital city to make demands, and that weak bastard Calderón bows and obeys. Their ATF gives guns to Guzmán, and his men hunt us with the Americans' weapons. We need to send them a message. A clear message. Be looking for an opportunity to do that."

———

Hospital Naval de Tampico
Tamaulipas, Mexico
10:41 p.m.

Aguilar's eyes blinked open and he began to focus on his surroundings. He became aware of the sling around his shoulder, and noticed that he was lying back, inclined. His eyes followed an IV line from a bottle hanging on a rack down to a bandage on his left hand. *Hospital bed. I wonder how long I've been out.* He heard voices outside the room, and saw the door open a crack, then fully. He recognized the figure that entered the room.

"Hello, Torres. What time is it?"

"Almost eleven, Major."

"What, why did you call me——?"

"You had a visitor, sir. Admiral Campos came by before you woke up. He left you three presents. The first is a set of major's epaulets. The second is this."

Aguilar looked to the table by his bed where Torres was pointing. A military decoration was lying next to a bottle of medicine with his name on it.

"Congratulations, Major. You've been awarded the *Condecoración al Mérito Naval.*"

Aguilar nodded. *The Naval Medal of Military Merit.* The decoration meant little to him personally. He would announce it as a tribute to all the men in his unit. *I wonder if it's actually for merit, or for being shot.* "Any other news, Torres?"

"Yes, sir. The doctor said that your surgery went well, but you've been placed on non-combat status for six weeks."

"You'll have the unit for a while, it seems."

"Yes, sir." He smiled. "I've been promoted as well."

"That is excellent news, *Capitán* Torres." Aguilar started to stretch forward, extending his right hand, but a jolt of pain in his wounded shoulder stopped the movement.

Torres stepped forward and returned the handshake. "Rest easy, sir. Your third present from the admiral is that you're being rotated into the consulate in San Antonio as an attaché until you're fully healed. I assumed you'd be staying with your wife. She called. I told her your wound was not serious, and that you'd be seeing her soon. Don't worry. I'll take good care of the men until you get back."

"I know you will, *Capitán.*" Aguilar said. "Stay safe yourself."

"I will, Major."

A nurse entered the room and smiled at both of the men. She injected something into Aguilar's IV. He started to say something else, but the injection did its work, and his eyes were closed before he could form the words.

Chapter Twenty-One

San Antonio, Texas
March 7, 2011, 1:36 p.m.

Trask saluted the gate guard and drove toward the "Taj," as the locals called the base headquarters building due to its modest resemblance to the center of the Taj Mahal.

Randolph Air Force Base. Oops! Joint Base San Antonio, now. Trask mentally corrected himself. *Some general or DOD bureaucrat made another star or promotion charting all the savings these inter-service consolidations would provide. So now Kelly AFB, Brooks AFB, Lackland AFB, and Fort Sam Houston, the Army post, are all under one big umbrella. I'll give it five to ten years before another bigwig proves that it would be cheaper to split them up again, and then it'll be just like the good old days. Separate bases and forts. That guy will get promoted for saving millions, too. Our government at work.*

He found the check-in desk for the visiting officer's quarters or "VOQ," got his room key, and drove the rented Ford Edge to a parking spot in front of what once had been the living quarters for pilot trainees during World War II. *The West Point of the Air. Before blue suits, when the Air Force was the Army Air Corps. Aviation Cadets learning to fly, and others learning to be instructor pilots.*

He'd spent years traveling from base to base in his former life as an Air Force JAG circuit prosecutor, and the memories flooded back to him. *Get to one base, prepare for a week, try a General Court-Martial, then drive to the next one and start all over again. New base, new case. Great professional experience, miserable personal life. Three-hundred days a year on the road.* He'd learned to hate VOQ rooms, but those at Randolph had always been a pleasant cut above the rest. He looked up at the old two-story building with its open verandas, a white-washed stucco structure with a red tile roof, two wings extending forward from a long center section. *Nice architecture. Spanish Colonial Revival style, I think.*

He knew what the room would look like before he unlocked the door. *Good. This hasn't changed. Two-room suite. Sitting room with a couch and TV, bedroom and bath in the back. I can stand two-weeks here.*

He unpacked and checked his uniform in the mirror. The short-sleeve light blue shirt still fit. The epaulets bearing the silver oak leaves of a lieutenant colonel were properly buttoned on the shoulders. The "gig line"—a phrase he'd picked up at the Air Force Academy—was good, with the edge of the silver belt lined up with the row of buttons on the shirt. He checked the flight cap to make sure the rank insignia was mounted at the proper angle. *Good to go. Back in blue.* He walked back down to his car and headed across the base.

All of the Air Force's traveling prosecutors had convened in San Antonio for their annual training and status meeting. Trask walked into the back of the circuit's conference room just as the "CTCs" were breaking from their second session of the afternoon. One of the captains—the last name "Castle" displayed on his name tag—beamed when he saw Trask, and walked over to shake his hand. Trask recognized him as a former trial assistant from a court-martial he had tried three years earlier at one of the bases in Florida.

"How are you, Josh?" Trask asked. "It's been a while since I saw you at Tyndall. So you're a circuit prosecutor now?"

"Yes, sir. I'm just trying to follow in your footsteps. I'm really glad you could make it for this. I'm sure we'll all get a lot out of your presentation."

"Had to squeeze my active duty tour in *somewhere* on the schedule. Seemed like a good fit. When am I on?"

"Twenty minutes. Sixteen hundred. You're our final speaker today. They left it up to me to draft the schedule and I figured you could wake everybody up."

Trask laughed. "I'll do my best." He looked around the room at the conference attendees. There were about twenty-five majors and captains, the current trial elite of the Air Force prosecutors, and one uniform Trask didn't recognize. He walked over to the officer, a short, powerfully built man whose left arm was in a sling.

"Jeff Trask," he said offering a hand.

"Very glad to meet you, Colonel," the man said, bowing his head slightly. "I am Major Luis Aguilar of the Naval Infantry of Mexico—what you would call the marines."

"Welcome," Trask said. "Would you by any chance be attached to your consulate here?"

"Yes. I just arrived this week."

"Oh, I thought you might have spoken at another conference recently—one an FBI friend of mine recently attended."

"No, that would have been Major Castillo. I am replacing him for a while, at least until this heals." The major nodded at his left shoulder.

"How did that happen, if you don't mind me asking?"

"I was wounded in a firefight with some of our cartel gunmen. They are our biggest problem at the moment."

"From what I hear, they are *our* problem as well," Trask said. "Are you speaking at our conference?"

"I am," Aguilar nodded. "Tomorrow morning."

"I look forward to your presentation," Trask said. He saw that Captain Castle was giving him the nod from the front of the room. "It was good to meet you, Major. Looks like I'm up."

Trask walked to the front of the room and stood beside Captain Castle, who made the introduction.

"Our final speaker of the afternoon is Lieutenant Colonel Jeff Trask. I had the pleasure of trying some courts-martial with Colonel Trask at Tyndall Air Force Base. Colonel Trask is, in civilian life, the Senior Litigation Counsel for the Office of the United States Attorney for the District of Columbia in Washington. I could try to list all of his trial accomplishments for you, but we'd be here until after dinner. Let me just say that our profession is full of folks with super-egos. You'll probably run into one of those attorneys in the future who claims to be the gold standard of trial attorneys. I have. I told the last one who made that claim that I've *seen* the gold standard of trial lawyers, and that his name is Jeff Trask."

Castle stepped aside, offering the floor to Trask, who nodded while the applause died down.

"Thank you, Josh. A very kind introduction which I'm sure I'll completely fail to live up to." Most of the attendees chuckled politely. *Good. They're still awake.* Trask picked up a remote and a drop-down screen descended at the front of the room.

"My topic for today is joint trials and conspiracy cases. My hope is that the kings of JAG-dom will someday realize that the best and brightest of our JAG

Corps—those assembled here today—are completely capable of trying cases in which multiple defendants are tried and, of course, *convicted* together." There was more laughter.

"We do this every day in federal court, and many of those cases are prosecuted by attorneys who are far less capable than some of you in this room. I used to work for a gifted attorney in our office who had a saying: 'Governments never react very well, but they over-react superbly.'" More laughter. "When I checked into the VOQ today I almost broke a toe kicking a table leg that I thought was a bit out of place. Had I been a general officer, I might have made a remark about my toe to an aide, and I'm sure that by noon the next day, there would have been a published base regulation on proper furniture arrangement in all visiting officers' quarters." The laughter was a bit longer this time.

"Unfortunately, at some point in the distant past, someone screwed up a joint court-martial, it got reversed on appeal, and those in command naturally inferred that because one of their hand-picked superstars had been incapable of trying such a case correctly, *nobody* could handle the job, and joint trials essentially became forbidden in the Air Force as a matter of JAG policy. At some probably not-too-distant point in the future, some of you will hold positions of authority. I'm hoping that you'll remember my little talk today, and that we can begin saving hundreds of hours and thousands of dollars by doing what other federal courts in the nation do on an everyday basis. Let's get to the meat of this."

Trask stepped aside so that the screen was unobstructed. "As a practical matter, co-conspirators tend to bond together in fairly tight groups. As we say in today's slang, they tend to hang together." He pressed a button, and a photo of the Surratt conspiracy executions following the Lincoln assassination appeared on the screen, the conspirators' bodies dangling side by side from nooses. A chorus of groans erupted at his pun. "Just a little gallows humor," Trask said, and the groans grew louder.

"As you all know, most of the issues surrounding joint trials stem from a failure to understand the mandate of the Supreme Court in the 1968 case of *Bruton v. United States*, which forbids using the out-of-court statement or confession of a non-testifying co-defendant against his or her co-defendants at trial. That violates the rule against hearsay because the defendant who confessed and dirtied up his fellow defendants isn't on the stand and isn't subject to cross-examination. Does anyone here have a suggestion as to how we might deal with that complex issue?"

Captain Castle raised his hand from the front row.

"Yes, Josh?"

"Have the confessing defendant testify?"

"You're a legal scholar and a genius," Trask said. "That is *exactly* how simple the matter is. If you want to use the confession and your confessor is cooperating, have him plead guilty first and then testify at the trial of his co-defendants. If he's not cooperative and wants to recant his confession, then you *do* need to try him separately in order to use his confession against *him*—*if it is essential to your case*—so that the jury will hear the confession. If you don't need the confession because your other proof is overwhelming, don't use the confession and try him with the others. It's that simple. There are, of course, some cases in which it is possible to use *part* of a confession—by removing any reference in it to the other defendants—even if the confessing defendant refuses to testify. Let's talk about that for a while."

At the end of the hour, which seemed to fly by, Trask dismissed the group and waited to entertain any individual questions that might be pertinent.

"What if none of the conspirators want to cooperate, and you *need* one to cross the line?" Captain Castle asked. "I have a case pending trial here at Randolph where four guys—we think they're drug dealers—kidnapped another guy who's probably a member of their competition and threw him out of a car going seventy-five on the beltway. They're holding firm, not breaking ranks."

"Was the rival dealer killed?" Trask asked. He saw that Major Aguilar was standing a few feet away, listening intently. "No state secrets here, Major. Feel free to join in."

"He survived," Castle said. "He's not being fully cooperative either. After being nearly flayed on the highway, he managed to reach a home in an adjacent subdivision, and got the owner to call an ambulance. He identified the four airmen who did it, but claims he has no idea of why they sent him body surfing on the concrete."

Trask saw the puzzled look on Aguilar's face. "Our uniformed services are microcosms of our society, Major. We unfortunately have drug dealers in uniform from time to time, even some rapists and murderers. That's why the ladies and gentlemen in this room have their current assignments. You don't have similar problems in Mexico?"

"On a more limited scale," Aguilar replied. "When our men go bad, they join the cartels. When that happens, we don't court-martial them. We shoot them."

"Understandable," Trask responded. "Fortunately we haven't reached that point. Not yet anyway." He returned his attention to Castle. "Josh, are these four locked up?"

"Yes, sir. Pretrial detention was ordered for all of them."

"Are they detained here at Randolph?"

"Yes, sir."

"Let's take a ride then. Major, you're welcome to come if you like."

"Yes. I'd like that."

They got into a staff car that Captain Castle had reserved for the conference, and drove to the base detention facility.

"I just want to take a look, Josh," Trask said. "More often than not, the solution to something like this can't be found in a law book."

A security police sergeant at the desk stood up and ordered the room to attention when they entered.

"At ease," Trask said. *He's the only one in the room. I wonder who he was calling to attention.* "Just want to do a quick walk-through." He saw the sergeant's curious glance at Aguilar. "He's with us, sergeant. We just want to see the facility. We'll be out of your hair in five minutes."

"Yes, Colonel."

The sergeant grabbed a ring of keys and opened a metal door on the rear wall. Trask and the others entered a hall that had four large cells, two on each side of the hallway. Each cell contained four bunk beds, a stack of two bunks lining each cell wall. In the first cell on the left, Trask noticed four men in fatigue uniforms, each lying on one of the bunks. The detainees jumped down and stood at attention when they saw the officers in the hallway.

They're getting good advice from their defense counsel, Trask thought. *Behave like good little airmen prior to trial. Act like military men, not pushers in uniform. Even the confinement NCO might end up testifying for you as a character witness if you can pull the wool over his eyes for a few weeks.* Trask and the others returned to the front area and waited for the sergeant to lock the door to the cell hallway.

"Josh, has your investigation indicated which one of those guys is your least culpable defendant?"

"Yes, sir. Airman Moore, the driver. The victim said Moore looked surprised when the others were trying to push him out of the vehicle. He may not have known it was going to happen."

"Good," Trask said. "Sergeant, could you do us a favor and take Airman Moore out of his current cell and move him to one down the hall? And one more thing. For dinner tonight, make Moore's portions just slightly larger—just enough to be noticeable. He showers alone, too. Any problem with those requests?"

"Not at all, Colonel. I can handle that."

"Great. Thank you."

They returned to the staff car and headed back to the conference room.

"Any questions, Major?" Trask asked.

"*Divide et impera?*" Aguilar asked. "Divide et impera"

"Precisely." Trask saw the puzzled look on Castle's face. "The good major quotes Julius Caesar in Caesar's native tongue, Josh. Latin for 'Divide and Conquer.' Your three *most* culpable dopers will now think Airman Moore has crossed the line to become one of your witnesses. He's in a cell by himself, getting more grub and private bath time. Even though he's actually done nothing to cross his buddies yet, they are—at this very minute unless I'm way off base—calling him every name in the book and threatening him with every evil under the sun. His protests to the contrary will not be believed. He will sit on his bunk tonight and come to the conclusion that—since they already believe he's a rat—he might as well become one and get something out of it. He will also need and ask for your protection against them, and you will assure him you'll do everything you can, in return for his truthful testimony."

"Got it," Castle said, shaking his head. "I should have thought of that myself."

"You will, in time. It takes times to learn the tricks of the trade in any job. Oh, and your semi-cooperative victim—"

"Yes, sir?"

"Order him to report at 0730 every morning to your office. If, at the end of the fourth day he still sticks to this story about having no idea why it happened to him, tell him that you're going to have to release those four clowns and dismiss their charges because you have nothing to explain their motives for trying to kill him, and it just looks like an accident. I know that's not true, but we're still allowed to use ruses in this business. We'll see who he's most afraid of—you or the guys that already tried to off him once."

Castle smiled. "I don't think it will take four days. He'll have to come clean about his own dealings and the others' motives or they'll be out looking to finish what they started. Got it."

"Good." Trask turned toward Aguilar. "What are you speaking on tomorrow, Major?"

"Something closely related to your topic of this afternoon, Colonel. Just a different solution."

Chapter Twenty-Two

San Antonio, Texas
March 8, 2011, 7:21 p.m.

"That was Torres." Aguilar explained to his wife, laying his cell phone on the table. "Sorry to interrupt our dinner, Colonel. One of my officers. My company has been ordered to move to Abasolo in Tamaulipas state. There've been several deaths as the result of an ongoing feud between two of the cartels. The Zetas and Guzmán's Sinaloans have been shooting the town up again."

"No need to apologize for one's duty, Major," Trask said. "The food is wonderful, and I always enjoy the Riverwalk." He looked around at the tables all lit with candles, and smelled the aroma of an order of fajitas being delivered to a nearby party. A barge full of waving tourists floated by on the river. Trask cut another bite of his enchilada with his fork, and was about to raise it when a trumpet blared behind him. He dropped the fork onto his plate, managing to catch it on the bounce to prevent it from falling off the table.

"Damn." Aguilar stood and walked over to the Mariachi band. Trask heard him say something in Spanish, after which the band members scowled and scurried away.

"Thanks," Trask said. "A bit too loud and close, I'm afraid. How did you get them to leave?"

"I must apologize for that, Colonel. I love my country, but not *all* of her exports. I have never been a fan of Mariachi music myself. The band leader wanted to know if I had a request, so I asked him if he knew the 'Ballad of Davy Crockett.' Apparently his band did not know the song."

"Or appreciate your request," Trask said, laughing.

"I thought it was appropriate," Aguilar replied. "After all, we're just a couple of blocks from the Alamo, and just under the street named for Crockett himself. At any rate, it's simply rude to sneak up on a dinner party like that."

"What kind of music *do* you enjoy?" Trask asked.

"He likes the newer classical composers," Linda Aguilar said. "Especially Aaron Copeland."

"Really?" Trask asked. "One of my favorites as well. 'Rodeo,' 'Billy the Kid,' 'Appalachian Spring.' By the way, Major, you don't have to call me 'Colonel' the rest of the evening. Please call me 'Jeff.' I'm just a reservist now anyway, and all the formality makes me almost as uncomfortable as that trumpet in my ear. Even if you don't, I'm going to start using *your* first name, my friend, so we might as well be even."

"Very well, Jeff," Aguilar said, smiling and lifting his glass.

"Thank you, Luis. By the way, I found your presentation today to be fascinating, and troubling. I had no idea things were that bad in Mexico. I'd like to know more about your cartel problems."

"Good." Aguilar was not smiling anymore. "My country is falling apart, Jeff. My wife is an American. I attended university in California. I have many friends on your side of the Rio Grande, and I do not wish to see your country suffer as mine has. You need to be very much aware of the threats our enemies—and they are *our* enemies—pose. That is one reason we invited you to dinner tonight. I was impressed with your talk as well, and with the way you handled Captain Castle's problem."

"Josh is a sharp man. He'll pick it up in time. He just needed to get his head out of the law books for a minute or two."

Aguilar nodded. "He reminds me a lot of Torres, the Captain who called a moment ago." He adjusted his left arm in the sling.

"Healing up as expected, I hope?" Trask asked.

"Yes, I've been lucky."

"Lucky enough to have been wounded twice in the last year, you mean," Linda snorted.

"I was very disturbed to hear that you believe your law enforcement agencies have essentially collapsed, Luis," Trask said, trying to deflect what was obviously a subject of tension between Aguilar and the major's wife. "How do you hope to restore any rule of law with your police and courts so compromised?"

"I'm afraid we are beyond that in Mexico for now." Aguilar tossed back the last bit of Tequila in his glass. "You see, I do enjoy *some* of my country's products." He looked at Trask for what seemed to be a full minute before speaking again.

"You are both a military man and a man of the law, Jeff. The corruption of my country's legal and law enforcement communities has forced me to assume one of those roles as well as my normal military mission. My marines are now the closest thing to a police force that our people know—the only police they can trust, anyway. For a time, we tried to work with our police, but any intelligence we shared with them went straight to the cartels. We've had to assume that all the local police forces have been compromised by the money that Guzmán's Federation Cartel and Lazcano's Zetas have been offering. Those that refuse the money die."

"In your talk today, you seemed to be emphasizing more of a military solution than a legal one," Trask said.

"That is *exactly* my point when I say we are beyond any rule of law for now. Let me ask you, Jeff. What did you think at the moment that you heard your President Bush, after the planes struck the World Trade Center, talk about bringing your enemies 'to justice?'"

Trask nodded. "I see your point. I admired his resolve, but not his choice of words. War is not a law enforcement initiative, and combat isn't a 'police action.' Our politicians seem to have lost the distinction ever since World War II."

Aguilar smiled. "I knew that you would realize the difference. We in Mexico are in the combat phase now. Our legal system was not up to the task, and so we are at war within our own borders. Only when we reach a military victory can we have real trials again, with real consequences. One must have stability and control before laws can have any meaning."

"Here's to Mexico's victory, then," Trask lifted his glass. "I hope it comes soon, for the sake of both our countries. I'd still like to pick your brain some more about the cartels, since they do seem to be a common enemy for both of us."

"You're here for two weeks?" Linda asked Trask.

"Yes, the duration of the conference. I have that active duty commitment every year so that they'll pay me some kind of retirement when I turn sixty."

"What are your plans for the weekend?" she asked him.

"The usual San Antonio sights. The Alamo—"

"Nonsense. We have a house in Zapata on Falcon Lake." She looked at her husband.

"Linda is way ahead of me as usual," Aguilar said. "There is plenty of room. We'd love for you to join us."

"If I'm not imposing."

"Not at all. We'll pick you up after the conference session on Friday."

———

Laredo, Texas
March 11, 2011, 2:14 p.m.

"I am concerned about something, my friend." Dominguez' looked down at the duffel bag, then stared hard at the broker.

They stood on the front porch of the ranch house. The Bronco was pulled in front of the house with its engine running.

"What's that, Ramón? It's all there—less my cut and the expenses. Same as always."

"It's the expenses, *amigo*. Surely you have noticed that they've been going up."

"Gas has been going up, Ramón. I make my driver turn in his expense receipts so he won't gouge us. I add them up and that's the figure I give to you. I just finished them before you got here."

"Do you still have them?"

"No, I shred them as soon as I'm done with the totals. Don't want to leave a paper trail in case anyone comes looking."

"The expenses are up more than the gas prices, *amigo*."

"I told him to take different routes going north and east. Sometimes he drives more miles. Maybe something's going on with the truck."

"Maybe. We'll check it out. Save the receipts for me next time, okay?"

"Sure, Ramón. No problem."

———

Zapata, Texas
4:43 p.m.

Trask and Aguilar sat on the deck of the house and looked out over Falcon Lake.

"Zapata, Texas." Trask took a sip of the cold Dos Equis. "Named for your General Emiliano?"

"Actually, no," Aguilar replied. "Another revolutionary hero, but less well known. The place is named for Colonel José Antonio de Zapata, a cavalry commander in the Republic of the Rio Grande. When Santa Anna seized central power in the 1830s, your Texicans at the Alamo weren't the only ones who tried to secede from Mexico. There were also secession efforts in Zacatecas and the Yucatán, and here along the river. Colonel Zapata was unfortunate enough to suffer the same fate as your Colonels Crockett and Travis. He was defeated by Santa Anna's forces. He actually survived the battle, but was executed afterward."

Trask raised his bottle. "To those who oppose tyrants."

Aguilar tapped Trask's bottle with his own. "To patriots."

"Tell me more about your Zetas, Luis." Trask leaned forward across the table.

"Former military special forces deserters who have left their country for the lure of drug money. Originally trained by your own Green Berets and others, including some Israeli specialists. Ruthless. Their current leader is a thug named Lazcano. They specialize in rule by terror, and will kill anyone who opposes them. Sometimes they kill just to kill."

"And your civil authorities are powerless to do anything about them?"

"The cartels have more guns than all of our police forces combined, and also outnumber those in the military ranks. As I said on the Riverwalk, we are at war."

Trask nodded. "Any idea on which cartel is moving heroin into the US at the moment?"

"All of them. Along with cocaine, meth, marijuana, ecstasy, you name it."

"How about China White heroin?"

Aguilar put his beer down and studied Trask's face. "The Zetas. *They* are your targets, but understand this. To me, they are not criminal defendants anymore; they are the enemy. When we see them, they shoot at us. We shoot *them*, unless they surrender. In that case we lock them up, they escape, and they shoot at us again." Aguilar turned his gaze out toward the lake. "Let me ask you something, Jeff. Assuming that my *military* solution for these bastards fails, what do you think your system—the American courts—can accomplish?"

"Only what is constitutionally allowed in the States. Prosecution and incarceration. In the case of murder, sometimes the death penalty, but our extradition agreements with your country are a problem there. Mexico won't allow us to execute Mexican citizens, so your government refuses to extradite them if they're facing a death penalty in our courts."

"You could try Lazcano in your courts?"

"If the proof is there to tie him to our heroin trade in DC, yes. But the extradition process is very iffy, and you'd have to have him in custody first. And as I said, Mexico would not hand him over if we planned to execute him, but that wouldn't be an issue right now. I *do* have a lot of people dying from using white heroin at the moment, Luis. I *don't* have proof of where it's coming from yet, and even if I did, drug distribution alone is not a capital crime in the US."

"Then we will execute him here. No trial required. He is—as you call *your* terrorists—an 'enemy combatant.'" Aguilar paused for a moment. "I seem to recall that your courts *have* executed some Mexican citizens in the past."

"That *has* happened in some cases, but it involved defendants who were already in the US when they committed their crimes, and who were captured on this side of the border. No extradition was required."

"I see." Aguilar shifted his gaze from the lake back to Trask. "My intelligence concerning the Zetas is quite good at the moment, Jeff. I want to help you because helping you hurts the Zetas; if you stop their business, it robs them of their cash flow. But understand this. My first goal is to kill them. No trials, no courts, no prisons from which they can escape. I will try and get you whatever information you need to do your job on this side of the river, but for my nation's security, I will hold close any information that helps me track down and kill Mexico's enemies."

Trask nodded. "I understand. I'll take whatever help you can give me, Luis. I only wish I could give you as much assistance in return." Trask passed a business card across the table. "My cell number's on the back."

"You *can* do one thing for me," Aguilar said, putting the card in his shirt pocket. "Even if your investigation gives you enough to indict the Zetas, promise that you'll give me first crack at them before you try and extradite them. My solution is more final, and more appropriate."

"I promise I'll call you first, Luis. That's the best I can do. I won't have the final decision on anything else. My superiors will."

Aguilar nodded. "That is acceptable." A door behind them slid open.

"Dinner's ready," Linda said. "Let's eat."

An hour later, Trask followed his hosts down to their boat dock. They pulled life vests on, and Trask sat in the back as Luis took the little boat out around a point and into the main channel of Falcon Lake.

"Any risk being out this close to dark?" Trask asked his hosts.

"At the time David Hartley was shot off his jet ski, the answer would certainly have been yes," Linda shouted over the noise of the outboard motor. She smiled and pointed to another, larger boat approaching them from the center of the channel. "Now, not so much, as long as we're in US water and those are around."

As the bigger boat drew closer, it cut its engines and Trask could read the words "Texas Department of Public Safety" and "Texas Highway Patrol" painted on the side. *Some highway,* he thought.

The big craft pulled near and a tall figure wearing a badge tossed a rope to Luis, who tied the bass boat alongside. Aguilar motioned Trask to follow him as he climbed the ladder up the stern and into the patrol craft. Linda followed Trask. There were three uniformed men on board, and Linda gave the tallest one a warm embrace as she climbed into the big boat. Luis laughed as he saw the confusion on Trask's face.

"Jeff Trask, meet my brother-in-law, Sergeant Jimmy Avila. He's a member of either the Texas Highway Patrol or the Texas Navy, depending on how many beers he's had before you ask him."

Trask shook hands with Avila, a broad-shouldered tank of a man with a dark moustache.

"This is some kind of canoe you have here," Trask said, surveying the boat.

"Let me give you a tour," Avila said.

Trask followed him forward to one side of the boat, where two light machine guns were mounted between armored cover plates.

"They fire 7.62x51 mm NATO rounds," Avila said. "We have five on the boat. A dual mount on each side, and another one up front. We have a couple of .50 cal sniper rifles on board, some hand held submachine guns, and grenade launchers. We've also got the latest in night vision technology. She's 34 feet long, and powered by three, 300-horse outboards on the stern."

"And this is a *Highway Patrol* asset?" Trask asked.

"Yep. The governor decided that the feds weren't living up to their obligations to protect our folks down here, so the state bought six of these beauties at over a half-million bucks per boat. When I heard that we—The Patrol—were getting 'em, and that I had a chance to get back on the lake where I grew up every summer, I kidnapped, bribed and may even have shot a couple of guys to get to the head of the line."

"Jimmy knows both sides of the lake better than anyone I know, with the possible exception of Luis," Linda said. She smiled at her brother. "I should have told you that Jeff was 'a fed' before you went off on your rant. He's an AUSA up in DC."

"He's on *my* boat, now," Avila said. "Texas turf in Texas waters. Luis, if you'll untie and hang tight for a minute, I'll show our fed what a Texas boat can do."

Aguilar jumped back into the bass boat and cast off from the bigger craft.

"Better sit down and hold on, Jeff." Linda waited for Trask to grab a rail, and she smiled at her brother, who had moved to the controls.

The gunboat lurched forward as the outboards growled, the bow of the vessel lifting above the water as the craft raced across the lake. Avila motioned Trask forward. He made his way slowly up the boat, grabbing rails and chair backs to maintain his balance, and stood beside Avila, who shoved the throttles even farther forward. The engine growl became a steady, humming roar.

"She's the fastest thing and the best armed boat on the lake. We can be anywhere in our patrol area in a few minutes, and when we get there, the bad guys better be gone. If they're not, they're either swimming or floating."

Trask nodded. "Very impressive. Glad you folks are out here now. I hear there are some very bad actors on that other shore over there."

"The Zetas? Yeah, they're real assholes. I keep hoping they'll come out to dance. So far they've declined our invitations. As fast as we are, they run back into their waters at the first sight of us. We grab a lot of their dope out here, beating their boats to the stuff they drop into the water from their planes. They drop bundles of coke, weed, and meth into the water and try to get it across in the middle of the night. We call 'em splashdowns. We keep waiting, but they don't seem to want to fight us for their merchandise."

Avila turned the boat back toward where they'd left Aguilar. Minutes later, Trask and Linda were climbing back into the bass boat.

"Thanks for the ride," Trask called up to the sergeant.

Avila waved and hit the gunboat's throttles again, pulling away and back out toward the center of the lake.

"Helluva boat," Trask remarked.

"Yes," Aguilar said, "but lousy for fishing. Too loud, and he can't get close enough to the banks to use worm lures."

Chapter Twenty-Three

"So how was the conference?" Sivella rested his elbows on the inside of the bar after pushing the beer toward Trask.

"Interesting. A vacation of sorts until the first weekend, anyway. I bumped into a major in the Mexican marines who has an inside track on the cartel that is probably supplying our heroin. Brutal bunch. I *was* able to help one of our blue-suiters solve a much smaller conspiracy case while I was there. Not a bad trip overall. How've you been?"

"Every day's a vacation for a retired cop. Even one tending bar. At least it *would* be if that retired cop didn't have to keep playing spook to help out his friendly federal prosecutor." Sivella reached under the bar and tool out a manila envelope. "Your DVDs of the racquet club are in there. Hope they help. How's the hand?"

Trask reflexively raised his left hand. It was steady. "Making a liar out of me. No problem while I was in Texas. I even had some of the docs at the Air Force hospital run some neurological tests. They couldn't find a thing."

Sivella shrugged. "No news is good news, right?"

"I suppose."

"Lynn and the dogs make out all right while you were gone?"

"Yep. Not a ripple on the moat."

"Great. Did your new friend from Mexico give you enough to reopen channels with the Bureau?"

"Not yet. He did say he'd have his intel guy look into some stuff. Can't hurt."

"Never does, unless you run into one of those one-way-street information streams like you had with DEA on the Jamaicans. They actually stole your case files and refused to share anything with you, didn't they?"

"Yeah. I had to have the marshals seize my own case files with a subpoena after DEA broke into our office and ran off with them. Two of their field office bosses ended up getting fired over it."

"Unbelievable."

"I wish I never had to believe it. The DEA office here still hasn't made peace with me, even though they were the ones in the wrong, and now I've got FBI—or what's left of it after nine-eleven—shunning my investigation, and my best lead so far is in another country. What would you do in my shoes, Willie?"

Sivella shoved the mug at him. "Have another beer."

———

Washington, D.C.
March 22, 2011, 10:45 a.m.

Trask fast-forwarded through the recorded video on the discs playing on his desktop computer. The angle of the camera on the racquet club left a lot to be desired. It was a narrow-width view of the front of the club, with the left side of the scenes clipped so that only a fraction of the driveway to the rear of the building was shown. *Oh well, beggars can't be choosers. Whoever Willie's friend is can't have much field experience. Nobody just watches the front door. I've watched three weeks of running video. The Metro Maintenance truck comes and goes at what look like regularly scheduled intervals. Nothing suspicious there unless our man Roscoe is more than he seems to be.*

Trask froze the frame on something he thought he'd seen before. What appeared to be a light colored truck turned through just enough of the scene so that he could make out the vehicle before it disappeared behind the building. He checked his notes, pulled out the disc he was watching, and replaced it with one he'd already reviewed. *There it is. Ten days before. Could be the same truck. Can't see the plates. Same size, same color.* He noted the arrival and departure time, then put the other disc back into the computer.

He advanced the frames at regular speed this time, then froze the frame. The truck had left the driveway and turned *in front* of the club this time. *Gotcha. Maybe.* The angle still didn't permit a view of the truck's plates. *Damn. Oh well. Light-colored cab. Ton-and-a-half from the looks of it. I thought it was too big to be a pickup.*

The phone on his desk rang. He looked at the caller ID window before picking up the handset.

"What's up, Bear?"

"Doing anything for lunch?"

"No plans at the moment."

"Why don't you head this way about twelve. I don't like where we left things. I'm buying. We're all going to the FOP."

"Twelve then. I'll meet you there."

He hung up the desk phone, but felt the cellular phone vibrating in the holster on his belt. The number shown in the caller ID box identified the new caller as a subscriber in Mexico.

"Luis?"

"Yes, Jeff, how are you?"

"Been better, been worse. How's the shoulder?"

"About eighty-five percent now; improving. I have some news regarding the American distributors moving your heroin. They're based in Laredo, and are probably supplying your capital city and some others on your eastern seaboard. My man with the Zetas tells me you should be looking for a truck with Texas plates—"

"A ton-and-a-half with a light-colored cab?"

"Exactly. I see you've made some progress on your end as well. Excellent."

"I'm looking at a still shot of it right now on my computer. Part of a surveillance camera feed. Got any names for me to go with the truck?"

"Not yet. I'll work on that. On your side, at least."

"Yeah, I remember our deal. No indictments or extraditions of your Zetas until you've had your chance at them."

"Thank you, my friend. I'll call again when I have more."

———

12:02 p.m.

The DC Chapter of the Fraternal Order of Police was located at 711 4ᵗʰ Street, N.W., about a block north of the FBI field office, so it was a short walk for Trask. Once inside the entrance to the dining room, he was hailed by Doroz, who waved him over to a large table. Lynn was there, along with Dixon Carter, Tim Wisniewski, and two uniformed DC cops in uniform, a male with flaming red hair and a moustache, and a very attractive female officer. Trask stood behind the seat Lynn had saved for him.

"We have a couple of party crashers, Jeff," Dixon Carter said. "This is Tom McInnis. I was his training officer a few hundred years ago."

"Call me Sam," McInnis said as Trask shook his hand.

"Sam," Trask nodded. "No explanation required. The resemblance is uncanny."

"I guess so. Everybody says that," McInnis shrugged. "This is my partner, Randi Rhodes."

"Pleased to meet you, sir," she said, extending her hand to Trask.

"Oh for God's sake, don't 'sir' him," Lynn snorted. "His head is big enough as it is."

"Alright, Mr. Trask, then," Rhodes said, smiling. "So Detective Carter, I have you to blame for training *my* training officer?"

"I'm afraid so. Not too tough on you is he?"

"I'll survive him," Rhodes said. "So what kind of team are you guys on now?"

"We've been adopted and deputized by the man, the myth, and the legend, Barry Doroz, whom you've just met, as members of an FBI squad. We basically protect the city and other parts of the republic as directed by Supervisory Special Agent Doroz."

"More accurately put, Randi, Detectives Carter and Wisniewski have proved themselves to be very valuable in the past working against some very dangerous criminal drug-trafficking organizations," Doroz explained, "so I arranged with your department to have them permanently—I mean temporarily—assigned to my squad at the Bureau. Jeff here is our favorite prosecutor. Not only because he's damned good at it, but because we have his wife Lynn here as part of the package deal. She's a former Air Force OSI agent, and our squad analyst."

Trask noted the compliment. *More apologies from the Bear. Good to see the bridge isn't burned.* He looked down the table at Wisniewski. Sitting directly across from Officer Rhodes, he was strangely quiet, and Trask saw that Tim was trying very hard not to stare at her. He focused on McInnis for a second, and saw that Rhodes' partner had also noticed the attention being paid to her by Wisniewski. *Is that jealousy I'm seeing, or just a protective brother in blue?* His left hand started to tap a rhythm on his thigh, enough to grab Lynn's attention. Her right hand closed softly on his left.

"So, Lynn, you actually do the brain work for these guys?" Randi asked.

"Very perceptive of you," Lynn said. "They *do* need a lot of help in that regard."

"She's the best analyst I've ever had on the squad," Doroz said. "It helps that she's had street experience like you, Randi. She's our resident expert on deciphering telephone traffic."

"The cell phone is today's criminal's biggest tool, and his Achilles' heel," Lynn said. "I just look at lots of numbers and identify patterns. All from the safety of my cubicle. No more drawing down on guys who outweigh me by a hundred pounds and want to kick my little butt. I was never an actual patrol officer like you, Randi. I don't know how you gals do it. I admire your courage."

"Lots of training, weapons, and bluffing," Rhodes deflected the compliment. "It gets a little dicey at times, but I have my big brother Sam here to protect me. He has something in common with you, Lynn—a real thing for phone numbers. Scribbles down every one he finds."

"Like the lady said, a tool and a problem for the perps," McInnis said.

"He really likes those that end in sixty-nine," Rhodes quipped.

"Dammit, Randi—" McInnis protested, but was cut off almost immediately by Lynn.

"As in nineteen sixty-nine?" Lynn asked.

"It's when I was born—" McInnis started to explain.

"Have you come into contact with this number?" Lynn cut him off again, writing the phone number down on a paper napkin and sliding it between Rhodes and McInnis.

"I think so," Sam said. "Let me check to make sure." He pulled a small spiral notepad out of his pocket, and flipped page after page backward until he found the entry.

"Yeah. Same number. November twenty-fourth. Last year. Little guy driving a ton-and-a-half with Texas plates dropped his cell phone outside a convenience store. That's the number that was displayed on it. Like I said, that's the year—"

"Did you say a ton-and-a-half?" It was Trask's turn to cut McInnis off.

"Yeah. Texas plates. I ran 'em. No hit on the company it was registered to, but I remember it was located in Laredo."

"Light-colored cab?" Trask asked.

"Yep. We followed it to—"

"To The Dome Racquet Club?" Lynn interrupted.

"Are you guys all mind readers or something?" McInnis asked, exasperated. A waitress showed up at the head of the table. "You folks ready to order?"

"Not yet," Trask said. "Give us about five minutes, okay?"

"Sure," she said, walking toward another table.

"Wait a minute," Doroz said, looking at Trask. "I know how Lynn knows about the phone number, but how do you know about the cab color—"

"On the truck?" Trask finished the question for him.

"See?" Randi patted McKinnis' arm. "They do it to each other, too."

"I've had a pole cam on the racquet club for a few weeks. I have a nice still shot of that truck from south Texas—a known supply route for the Zetas drug cartel and their China White heroin—leaving the joint. That is, if you'd like to see it."

"How the hell did you—"

"Get a pole cam up when you wouldn't authorize one, Bear?" Trask shrugged. "I have other contacts in law enforcement, some that are—"

"Some that are retired, I bet, and named Willie Sivella." Doroz shook his head. "I should have known that you wouldn't take 'No' for an answer."

"This is why I keep my mouth shut around them most of the time," Wisniewski said, looking knowingly at Officer Randi Rhodes. "I like to finish my own sentences." She giggled.

Oh my God. It's on for those two, Trask thought. He turned back to Doroz, not saying a word, but just raising his eyebrows. *I'll hold onto the info from Luis Aguilar for a while; I don't have to play that card yet.*

"Alright dammit. It's back on." Doroz threw his hands up in mock futility.

"Great." Trask nodded. "One thing we need to do is look at the records for that 1969 number and see who it might connect to in the Laredo area. That okay with you?"

"Makes sense," Doroz said, turning toward Lynn.

"I heard him," she said.

Trask motioned the waitress back over. "We're ready to order now, Miss. And the check goes to the gentleman at the head of the table who's shaking his head and frowning a lot."

———

5:30 p.m.

"So what songs were running through that crazy brain of yours at lunch today?" Lynn asked.

Trask steered the Jeep onto the Indianhead Highway, their first leg of the drive back toward Waldorf. "Let's see. Tim looks at Randi. That would have been "Infatuation" by Rod Stewart. Sam McInnis looks at Tim looking at Randi. That was The Gin Blossom's "Hey Jealousy."

"What about when *you* first saw Officer Randi Rhodes?"

"Silence is Golden."

"What?"

"It's an old song by The Tremeloes. Lots of falsetto. One of their biggest hits from the 1960s. I think 'Here Comes My Baby' was their other one."

"You're gonna get it when we get home, you know."

"I certainly hope so."

Chapter Twenty-Four

Hart Senate Office Building
Washington, D.C.
March 23, 2011, 1:45 p.m.

"Thank you for seeing me, Senator," Trask said. "I know I didn't give you much notice, but we've had some developments that I wanted to tell you about, and you asked to be kept current." He glanced at the chair to the side of Heidelberg's desk, noting that Senator Graves' schedule had to coincide closely with that of Senator Heidelberg's. *These guys really must be joined at the hip. I wonder which one has the dirty pictures of the other one.*

"Not a problem, Mr. Trask. What kind of developments?" Heidelberg crossed his arms and leaned back in the monstrous leather chair behind the desk.

"We've been able to identify both the Mexican drug cartel which is probably responsible for the China White coming into the District, and have made some significant progress identifying the local businessman who seems to be the local funnel for the drugs."

"Who's the businessman?" Graves asked.

"I'm sorry, Senator, but it's our department's policy not to provide names until after the suspects are charged." Trask gave Graves a warning glance. *Don't think you can push me off of that square, Digger.*

"Even to the families of the victims?" Heidelberg uncrossed his arms and leaned forward, his hands on the edge of his desk.

"To anyone, sir, *including* surviving family members. I'm sure you understand that some people might not be as controlled as yourself, and might try and take matters into their own hands, or could prematurely confront the suspects, all to the detriment of the investigation." *My playing field, not yours.*

"Do you have anything linking this 'businessman' as you call him to Janie?" Graves asked.

"Not yet. I'll make another appointment to let *Senator Heidelberg* know when and if that happens. Even at that point, I won't be able to provide an identity until we've charged him—or her. As soon as the indictment is unsealed, Janie's father will be the first person I notify." *He's got the victim's notification rights here, Digger; you don't.* Trask saw a long glance pass between Heidelberg and Graves, the latter breaking it off with a slight shrug.

"Very well, then," the older man said. "I'm glad you're making some progress, and am grateful for the update. Please call my secretary when you need to see us again."

"I'll certainly do that, Senator." Trask stood and made his way out of the office. *"Us," not "me." If I need to speak to him without Digger in the room, how do I set that up?*

———

FBI Field Office
Washington, D.C.
March 31, 2011, 3:12 p.m.

"All the Laredo calls from our 1969 phone—to our friend Adipietro—are from a damned prepaid cell. I couldn't get subscriber info on that Laredo phone if you gave me a subpoena and an IRS badge. The caller isn't using a credit card to put minutes on it, so we can't trace it through that, either. He's being careful." Lynn threw her arms up. "Sorry."

"You did what you could," Trask said. *Maybe Luis will have a name for me soon.*

"We could squeeze the driver," Carter suggested. "Grab him on the next trip in, catch him holding a load for delivery. If it's a substantial amount of heroin, he's looking at quite a bit of time to serve."

"A good idea, Dix, assuming we can stop him before he makes the drop," Trask said. "Since Bear has provided us with a spiffy new, real-time pole cam for surveillance of the racquet club, it's only a matter of monitoring it twenty-four-seven to make sure we're alerted, and then responding instantly to put the *habeas grabbus* on the truck driver and Adipietro when they're making the exchange."

"You know that's not likely," Doroz said. "Be glad you got your pole cam, Jeff. I *have* asked the security team to try and watch their monitor when we're not here—we have one monitor on the squad and they have one in the video room—but it's a crapshoot whether they'll spot it in real time, and a bigger problem to roll on it when we get the call."

"Dix, what about putting the word out on the western side of town to have the patrol units on the PD watch for the truck and give us a heads-up?" Trask asked.

"Your Metropolitan Police Department is ready to serve," Carter said, "but that's *another* crap shoot. We'd have to have the right car—with alert officers—in the right place at the right time. Couldn't really count on it."

"What about a tracker? A GPS unit?" Wisniewski offered. "Put one on the truck after it leaves the racquet club."

"Not a bad idea if it stops long enough and if we can get close to it without being seen," Doroz said. "If we get enough notice to follow it—"

"Then we follow the damned thing, whether we get close enough for a GPS or not," Trask said.

"To where?" Doroz asked.

"Wherever." Trask leaned over the conference table. "Look. Odds are good, *really* good, that this isn't his only stop. He's probably got customers in other towns." *At least that's what Luis tells me.* "I know the new generation of federal agents wants to solve every crime from the comfort of their chair in front of a computer, but this is one time when we're probably going to have to do some old-fashioned police work."

"*We?*" Wisniewski asked. "*You* coming along on this joyride, Jeff?"

"Maybe I shouldn't," Trask said. "My credentials lose their authority at the District line. You guys, however, are all either federal agents or are federally deputized. You can follow this guy anywhere he goes in the country."

"We'll need several cars and drivers to avoid getting burned," Doroz mused. "The guys on our surveillance squad *would* like a road trip."

"So would I," Trask said. "I guess I *am* coming."

"*What?!* What about your credentials?" Lynn asked.

"Just an observer along for the ride, on his own time," Trask said.

"What about me?" she asked.

"Someone has to feed the pups."

"I've been to surveillance school," she protested. "You haven't."

"I'll just be a tourist," Trask said. "Not on duty, remember?"

"As if," she snorted.

"I like it," Doroz said. "Our own forward legal advisor. Mobile, hostile, agile, and lee-gile."

"Just have somebody watch the pole cam, and have the cars and drivers ready," Trask said. "Everybody keep a bag packed at the office, and pack Tim's GPS, too. When this guy stops for sleep, we might get our shot to put it on the truck. At any rate, Tim will get a change of diet."

"Huh?" Wisniewski looked confused.

"I just hear that you've been taking all of your meals—lunch and dinner anyway—at the FOP," Trask said. "Since you forgot to ask for Randi Rhodes' number, don't you think it would be easier to have Dix call her partner and get it for you? She might not eat there again for another month."

"Shit. Thanks, Dix," Wisniewski said.

"Just concerned about my young and foolish partner's nutritional habits," Carter said innocently.

———

Laredo, Texas
April 2, 2011, 6:15 p.m.

The broker waited on the porch as the truck made its way up the road to the ranch house. The little man pulled the ton-and-a-half to a stop in front of the house and jumped down from the cab.

"Any problems?" the broker asked him.

"Nahh. Everything routine. Piece of cake." The little man handed him the gym bag. "Money and receipts are inside."

"Gas still going up?"

"Still high. Especially in the northeast and upper Midwest."

"Come on in and we'll settle up."

The broker sat down behind his desk and began tallying the receipts on a calculator, turning over those he'd already processed and placing them into a new stack to his right. He paused for a moment, and retrieved one from the stack on the right. He held it up next to one he'd just picked from the unprocessed stack on the left.

"I have a question."

"Sure," the little man said. "What's up?"

"Come take a look at this."

The little man came around the desk to where the broker was seated, and started to look at the two receipts. The broker's right hand shot up and grabbed the driver by the collar, then jerked his head down violently, bouncing the man's head on the edge of the desk.

"*Dammit!*" the little man yelled. "What the h—"

The broker's fist slammed into the smaller man's left eye socket and sent him sprawling.

"You stupid, greedy little son-of-a-bitch," the broker growled. "You want to get us both killed? That rat-faced Zeta bastard I have to deal with has already been asking me about your gas charges, and I find out that you're double pumping receipts on me. Why the hell do you think I ask you to keep the damned things?"

"Shit," the driver said, rubbing his eye as he rose from the floor. "I take all the risks, and you just sit here—"

Another right cross sent the little man sprawling again.

"I *just sit here?*" the broker mocked him. "Those bastards woke me up with a damned gun in my face in my own bedroom. They know where I live, and it's only because of me that they don't know *your* name or where *you* live. Maybe I should tell 'em. Just show 'em the paper and let 'em take your sorry little ass with them. I'm sure they'd have a lot of fun with you."

"Alright, already. Sorry. You didn't have to beat the shit out of me. It was just a few bucks."

"More like seven hundred over the last few trips, you stupid little weasel. Hang around another hour and wait 'til Ramón gets here and you'll have more to bitch about than a couple of punches to the head."

"What do you want me to do?" The little man was shaking now. "I'm sorry."

The broker stared at him. "Just go. I'll pull the double receipts out so he doesn't come looking for your ass, and I'll deduct the seven hundred from your pay for this trip, and give it to the Zetas. Maybe they won't force me to give you up. If they do, you're a dead man, 'cause I'm not dying for you. Now get the hell out of here."

The little man scurried for the door. The broker followed and watched as the driver ran to his car and sped off up the half-mile road to the gate, leaving the ton-and-half parked by the ranch house. As the car neared the gate, it had to make room for a red Bronco that was entering the property.

The broker hurried back to his desk and finished totaling the receipts, checking to make sure that he pulled any that had the same dates and locations indicated on them. He was done before the knock on the door.

"I found our expense problem," he told Dominguez as he handed him the bag of cash. "My problem, actually. The driver I hired has been throwing extra gas receipts in with the real ones. I figure I owed you an extra seven hundred. It's in there with the rest of the money, and the expense receipts."

"How did you handle this problem, my friend?"

"I kicked his ass, Ramón. Hard. It won't happen again."

"He should be replaced."

"That's easier said than done. He knows all the routes and the customers, and they trust him. I don't think we'll have the problem again."

"I know we won't. I will trust your judgment for now. I'll see you in a couple of weeks. Continue to show me the receipts until I can be sure the problem has been taken care of."

"You'll get them, and the money will be right."

Chapter Twenty-Five

"The papers are already calling it the 'Second San Fernando Massacre.' For once, I have no disagreement with them." Torres led Aguilar from one excavated pit to another. "We located seventeen different burial sites, Major. A hundred and ninety-three bodies." Torres wiped his brow with a handkerchief. "It's good to have you back, sir. I just wish—"

"We had no advance warning this time," Aguilar said, waving aside Torres' concern. "My informant was in Colombia. The Zetas had sent him there to check on some opium crops, and he had no idea this was happening. He called me when he returned to Nuevo Laredo. What did the survivors tell you?"

"There were two survivors. One younger man, one woman. Their stories were consistent, both with each other and with the three Zetas who were willing to talk after we arrested them and applied some persuasion. The victims were on buses headed for Reynoso. The buses were diverted from the main road by Zetas who blocked the highway with SUVs. They were holding automatic weapons, probably assault rifles. They boarded the buses and forced the drivers to drive to the ranch here. The men were split into two groups. Those that appeared to be able-bodied were paired up and forced to fight to the death, gladiator style, using sledge hammers and machetes. The survivors were invited to join the Zetas. Those that agreed to do so were spared. Those that refused were shot."

"What about the others?"

"The older men and those who appeared to be sickly were bound and forced to lie on the roadway. A Zeta then held a gun to the bus driver's head and forced him to drive the bus over them. After he did so, *he* was shot as well. Some of the women suffered the same fate. The prettier ones were taken to some of the buildings where they were raped first. Then *they* were shot. One of our survivors was being kept by a Zeta for more abuse, but we found her before she was killed. The dead were pushed into these pits and covered up."

Aguilar shook his head. The smell of decomposing flesh still hung in the air even though the last of the bodies had been removed. "How many Zetas have you rounded up?"

"More than eighty." Torres looked at the ground before returning his gaze to Aguilar. "I have to confess something, Major. After first speaking to the witnesses, we were able to arrest about forty Zetas. They were spread throughout San Fernando, sleeping drunken thugs occupying deserted homes. I had our men form a circle, and I told the Zetas to pair up inside the circle. I had them strip naked, and told them that *they* were going to fight to the death with their bare hands, and that only the winners would be allowed to survive. I told them that the survivors would then have to rape each other, and that any who refused would be shot."

Aguilar stared at his subordinate. "Did that happen? Did you force them to kill and rape each other, *Capitán* Torres?"

Torres shook his head. "No sir. I fired one shot to command them to start fighting, but fired another and stopped it after a few seconds. I'm sorry, Major. I was blinded by anger, and just wanted those degenerates to experience some of the same terror they'd caused."

Aguilar nodded. "At least you stopped it before you completely lowered yourself to their level." He looked around at the pits, smelling the stench. "If I had been here a few days earlier, I might not have stopped it myself."

"It always seems to be San Fernando," Torres said.

"It's the roads, Torres. This is the transportation hub leading to Reynoso, and Reynoso is the gateway to Nuevo Laredo, the big prize. Control Nuevo Laredo and you control the drug routes in the east into the US. My man inside the Zetas told me he heard that Lazcano ordered the bus attacks because he found out that Chapo Guzmán was bussing people into the area for reinforcements—trying to take back Nuevo Laredo from the Zetas. He ordered his second-in-command, the one they call *El Ratón*, to purge any buses carrying passengers who had cell phones with numbers linking them to Sinaloa or Michoacan."

"What are your orders, sir?"

"Sweep the town again. Arrest any Zetas you may have missed before—some may have been hiding—and disarm and arrest any of the worthless bastards who called themselves members of the local law enforcement. They could not have been unaware that this was happening for days. They either took bribes or hid themselves like cowards and allowed this catastrophe to occur. I am recommending to headquarters that we establish a permanent base here with several hundred troops. It is the only way we can prevent this from happening a third time."

Washington, D.C.
April 29, 2011, 5:51 p.m.

Detective Timothy Wisniewski sat at the corner of the bar of the Fraternal Order of Police. He had chosen the corner stool because it gave him a view of the front door.

"Another beer?" The girl behind the bar asked him.

"One more."

"Waitin' on someone?" She put another cold mug under the tap.

"No. Just killin' time. Winding the week down."

"Right," she said skeptically. "Wanna order anything?"

"Sure. It'll help soak up the beer before I hit the road. What's good tonight?"

"Special's the chicken parm. Pretty good, actually."

"That'll work."

He picked up the beer and sucked off a little of the head. Someone tapped him on the shoulder. He turned and stared—far too long—into the very pretty face of Officer Randi Rhodes. She was in her patrol uniform, but he didn't notice.

"Don't I know you from somewhere?" she asked.

"Could be," he finally said. "Where's your partner?"

"Day off." She slipped onto the stool beside him. "I hear you've been wait-ing for me."

"Who told you that?"

"*Your* partner."

"Not after today," Wisniewski said. "He's got a lot of nerve pulling that stunt."

"Well, *have* you been waiting for me?"

"Would it be okay with you if I had?"

"Might be."

"That's pretty vague."

"So were you—'would it be okay with you if I had'—he said."

"Okay, you got me. Yes."

"That's better. I hate games. Yes, it would be okay if you had been waiting for me, but it would have been *better* if *you'd* called me instead of Detective Carter."

He nodded. "I completely agree."

"Then why didn't you?"

"Have *you* been waiting for *my call*?" He raised an eyebrow.

"Would it be okay with you if I had?" she giggled.

He smiled. "Let's get a table."

A second order of chicken parmesan and an additional mug of beer later, she leaned back in her chair.

"I have a confession to make," she said.

"Okay. I'll brace myself."

"Carter didn't call just to hook us up. He called for Sam, but like I said, it's his day off. Carter said that the FBI surveillance team had too many irons in the fire to fully staff some kind of road trip you guys were setting up. He said he was asking our brass to detail us to your FBI squad for a month or so, since we were the ones who first saw this truck you're so interested in. *I* actually asked *Carter* if you were seeing anyone, and he told me you were seeing a lot of this place."

Wisniewski felt himself frowning.

"Did I say something wrong?" she asked.

"Not at all. I've just always made it a personal policy not to date any co-workers. If you're going to be working with us—"

"Then that's something we'll have to discuss and get by, or we'll discuss it and just keep things professional. Agreed?"

"Agreed," he nodded.

"I really enjoyed dinner. You have wheels?"

"A block down—at the Bureau garage."

"I live up toward Bethesda. Took the Metro here. Want to give me a lift?"

"Sure."

She lived in a modest townhome just inside the District line with Maryland, complying with the residency requirements for new cops on the force. He pulled to the curb, and walked around the car to open the door for her.

"Oh, a gentleman to boot," she said.

"It's how my mama raised, me ma'am," he said putting on his best western drawl.

"That is appreciated. Shall we have our discussion now or later?"

"We can talk it over now if you like."

He followed her up the stairs to the door, totally absorbed in her shape and in the way that that shape moved. Inside, she had him sit on a sofa.

"Another beer?"

"Better not. I had one before you got there, and I'm driving."

"Coffee?"

"Sure. Thanks."

"I'm gonna lose the uniform and the hardware first. Be back in just a sec."

He picked up a catalogue lying on the coffee table and saw that it was for all varieties of police tactical gear and clothing. He thumbed through it until he became aware that she was standing in the door to the hallway, smiling at him. She wasn't wearing a stitch.

"Still want to discuss something?" she asked.

He stood and walked toward her. He didn't say a word.

———

Tampico Naval Air Station
Tamaulipas, Mexico
May 9, 2011, 7:41 a.m.

"The numbers are in, Major." Torres handed Aguilar the report.

"Casualty totals for April. Fourteen hundred dead. The worst month since our war began." Aguilar nodded. "I suspected we'd get news like this after the San Fernando thing. Anything else?"

"Headquarters called. They've agreed with your suggestion. We are to start disarming all police forces in Tamaulipas, beginning with Matamoros, Reynosa, and San Fernando, if any of the cops there have any weapons remaining, of course."

Aguilar nodded. "About time."

Chapter Twenty-Six

Washington, D.C.
May 12, 2011, 4:17 p.m.

"I'd like to first introduce everybody," Doroz said, standing at the head of the squad conference table. "Some of you have already met. All of us from the squad know each other." He waved toward the left of the table. "Detectives Dixon Carter and Tim Wisniewski; Lynn, our analyst; and Jeff Trask, her husband and our AUSA. We also have two teams from our surveillance squad." He motioned to four agents along the right side of the table. "George Hurst, Frank Woodley—he goes by "FB"—Margie Camp and Bobby Thames. We also have Officers Sam McInnis and his partner Randi Rhodes as on-demand TFOs from the Police Department. They've actually seen our target vehicle."

Doroz flashed a photo of the truck on the screen at the end of the room. It was the one Trask had frozen on his computer. The front of the racquet club was behind the truck.

"Ton-and-a-half, light-colored cab, probably driven by a short white male, late forties," Doroz continued. "The only time anyone's seen the guy—those folks being Sam and Randi—he was driving alone. He'll probably have some boxes in the bed, some sort of cover load, but we believe his main cargo will be several kilos of heroin. China White, to be more specific.

"Our plan is a simple one. Be ready to roll when we call you. Bags packed for a short-notice road rally. When and if we see the truck at that same racquet club, we scramble. Standard surveillance protocol for multiple vehicles and long distance. We should be able to put six or seven sets of wheels behind this guy, and we'll rotate cars behind him and eyes on him 'til we see where he goes after he makes the first drop."

"Why not just get a search warrant for the racquet club after he makes that first drop?" Hurst asked.

"I'll take that, Bear," Trask said. "It's a good question, George. The answer is that we're in a completely unique situation here. We're operating on our best information—tips from far outside sources—but we have no history of reliability for those sources, no confirmation from anyone we could call into a Grand Jury or before a judge. In short, we have no probable cause to ask for a warrant."

"That's weird," Hurst said. "Who the hell are your sources?"

"I don't know," Trask said. "They're in Mexico. I know that's weird, but I think they're accurate, and it's all we have to go on."

Hurst rolled his eyes. "Okaaay, then."

"I have a question." Randi Rhodes half-raised her hand.

Trask saw that all the three male surveillance agents appeared to be very interested in the coming question, but that Wisniewski was trying hard not to be. *I wonder how long Tim and Randi are going to try and hide this.*

"Sure." Doroz said. "What?"

"Since Sam and I will still be on patrol out west, where we first saw this guy, what do we do if we spot him again—you know—coming into town before he makes it to the racquet club?"

Doroz thought for a moment. "Since you and Sam are only going to be coming with us if this materializes, and since you'll be in uniform and in a marked unit, call me if you see him, and hang back. Don't get burned or make him hinky at all. We'll put somebody else on him as he approaches and then leaves the club, and you guys can scramble back to your district for a change of clothes. We'll pick you up and bring you back here for one of our unmarked vehicles, and then you can catch up and join the parade. We'll have a radio in the car tuned to our frequency. Your call—if you're able to make it—will actually give us a few more minutes of lead time."

"Got it," McInnis said. He nodded approvingly toward his partner.

"Where are we going with this guy, or did your unknown Mexican sources give you that?" Hurst asked, looking at Trask.

"Probably New York." Trask answered. "More specifically, Long Island. Let's give this a shot, George. We've got reason to believe it may be a break in several overdose cases."

"Okay," Hurst shrugged. "Beats a traffic jam on the beltway."

———

9:40 p.m.

"So what was that little act of yours at the meeting today?" she asked him, rising up in the bed on an elbow.

"Act?" Wisniewski frowned as he flicked the hair from her eyes, caressing her face.

"Don't play dumb, *now*." Randi smirked at him. "That could get you an evening alone, and neither one of us would like that after the past week. You acted like you didn't know me, and never wanted to."

"I was just trying not to alienate your partner. He's already marked me as a threat of some kind. It's one of the dynamics I worried about when we started seeing each other. If we're on the same squad for any length of time I don't want it to be a complication."

"*Sam?* He's got no reason to be jealous. He's just my partner, my big brother in blue. Plus, he's o-o-old."

"Listen to me, Randi. My mom used to tell me that she could tell when some girls in school or in the neighborhood were on the hunt for *me*. I thought she was full of it, until her predictions proved to be true more than once. I think females read other females better on things like this. They know who's on the prowl when we dumb guys don't have a clue. I also think it works the same for men sometimes. We can sure read other guys more easily than we can women. I think Sam would like to be more than your partner, whether you can see that or not. I was trying to keep the water smooth."

"Great. That doesn't complicate *a squad*, it complicates my *patrol car*, and my relationship with my training officer. If you're right, anyway. I'm still not convinced."

"I hope I'm wrong, but I don't think so."

She leaned over and kissed him. "Tell me about the rest of the crew so *I* don't step on any toes."

"Okay. Who first?"

"Let's start at the top of the squad."

"Supervisory Special Agent Barry Doroz. Veteran of several mega-cases. International drug trafficking and smuggling, the Oklahoma City bombing, white slave trade, you name it, he's seen and done it all. Good man. Doesn't look down on us poor little local cops just because he's a fed. He works really well with Jeff Trask. They're a hard team to beat. I wouldn't want to be on the other side."

"Your *other* partner." She kissed him again. "You know, the *work* one."

"Dix? You know about him from all the old-timers on the force. Best detective in the metro. Works off-policy when he has to and usually gets away with it. He's got instincts I'll never have. He's still getting over the death of his old partner a couple of years back. Juan Ramirez. Good guy. I was around them both for a little while. Helluva team. Juan got surprised and suffocated by a Jamaican named Reid. Dix blames himself to this day, even though he shouldn't."

"What happened to Reid?"

"He took himself out. Jeff Trask worked with some Mounties to catch him up in Canada, got him into trial and shredded the shrink who was trying to get Reid off on an insanity defense. Reid saw he was about to go down hard and rushed Jeff in the courtroom. Jeff ducked and Reid cracked his head on the judge's bench. He died in the courtroom."

"I remember hearing about that now. Is Jeff that good?"

"He's scary. Never forgets anything. He's probably a better detective than anybody on the squad besides Dix, and he can wear three hats in the courtroom at the same time."

"Three hats?"

"One, the cop who can question anybody on the stand like he was getting a confession out of 'em in an interrogation room. Two, the attorney who's checking all the squares on the elements of the offense he has to prove, and getting the jury to agree with him. Three, doing it all by the book so that it's bulletproof on appeal."

"How'd you hook up with those three, then?"

"I worked with Jeff for a while in the US Attorney's office—"

"As an investigator?"

"As a prosecutor."

"*You have a law degree?*"

"I have the degree; I *had* the license."

"What happened?"

"A little dispute with my friendly bar association back in New Mexico. They didn't like that I was trying to use my position as a prosecutor to follow Supreme Court precedent and put bad guys in jail. They said I violated the rule against contact with a represented party when that party—a defendant—contacted me and said he didn't *want* his attorney representing him anymore 'cause he didn't trust him. The kid was right not to trust him. The mouthpiece was a total scumbag who just wanted the kid to keep his mouth shut so he wouldn't implicate the bigger bad guy who was paying the lawyer."

"So you were a lawyer."

"I know. I'm not proud of it."

She poked him. "I think that's impressive. So what's your role on the squad now?"

"I'm the muscle." He flexed a bicep. "See?"

She laughed and squeezed it. "OOOh yes, I can tell."

"Dixon Carter needed another partner. He's the best there is, but needed somebody to watch his back. I lucked out and drew the job."

"Trask seems to be lugging a little baggage of his own."

Wisniewski looked at her and shook his head. "Beauty *and* brains. Incredible. Very perceptive, actually. Jeff's mentor and close friend in the office, Bob Lassiter, was gunned down by a hit man Reid hired in case the trial didn't go his way. Lassiter was on the courthouse steps, stepping to the podium for a post-trial presser after Reid went down in the courtroom. He took a sniper round to the heart. His name is right under Juan Ramirez' on the memorial wall in Judiciary Square."

"God. I didn't know I was joining a combat unit. What happened to the sniper?"

Wisniewski paused. "*He* took two rounds to the head. Lynn Trask fired one, I fired the other one."

"*Jesus!*" She sat up in amazement, the sheets falling off her breasts. "Sweet little Lynn? You're kidding?"

He pulled her back down, and pulled the covers up to her shoulders. "If you want me to talk, you've got to cover those things up. Men are visual creatures, don't ya know." He caught his breath. "Don't let her fool you. That lady is as lethal as they come. She retired as a Special Agent for Air Force OSI—it's their version of the FBI. She was an undercover narc and used to do long-term operations, going under for months at a time. When she came up for air, people went to military prisons. She's a helluva shot, too. Some paramilitary types from El Salvador broke into their house in Waldorf a few months back and tried to take Jeff out. She killed 'em both. Head shots. Now she analyzes stuff. Nice and peaceful work, if the bad guys are smart enough to leave her alone."

"And what am I supposed to do while I'm attached to this unit?"

He rolled toward her and looked into her eyes. "Watch a truck."

Chapter Twenty-Seven

Nuevo Laredo, Tamaulipas, Mexico
May 17, 2011, 5:38 p.m.

"Was your mission successful, Ramón?" Lazcano looked up when he saw Dominguez standing in the doorway.

"Of course. Just some stupid farmers who were objecting to our using their property as a staging facility. The site was optimal—good barns and right off the road—in Guatemala just south of the border. We needed it to protect our supply lines. I left a few men to garrison the place."

"How many of the farmers opposed us?"

"Only a few. A couple of dozen, perhaps. They had tried to band together. A few had even managed to find guns. Now they are missing their heads."

"Excellent," Lazcano laughed. "Any casualties?"

"None of our men had a scratch. The Guatemalans were amateurs."

"Good. We'll need as many men here as we can muster. Guzmán is trying to move in on Nuevo Laredo again. We've set some traps for him."

"Speaking of traps, I've been thinking about that problem you mentioned. You know, the Americans sending guns to our enemies and their agents to our capital. I think I may have a way to take care of two problems at once."

"What are you thinking, Ramón?"

"We hit *their* capital. We already have the explosives, *and* the delivery system."

Nuevo Laredo, Tamaulipas, Mexico
May 21, 2011, 3:26 p.m.

Major Luis Aguilar walked down the center of the street, surveying the damage. *More burned-out buildings, broken windows everywhere, chipped bricks and mortar from bullet impacts. I can't blame the police this time. We're the police now.*

"You shouldn't be this exposed, sir," Torres said as he approached.

"The whole country is exposed, Torres. I won't hide anymore. If we retreat to the shadows, the civilians will never find the courage to oppose these thugs. What is your report?"

"It looks like a firefight over the last twenty-four hours between *Los Zetas* and Guzmán's men. We've counted thirty-one dead, mostly cartel gunmen, but a couple of bystanders. About forty more in the hospitals with wounds. We've arrested a hundred and ninety-six."

"A good number," Aguilar nodded. "It would have been better if we'd arrived sooner, but I called for the helicopters as soon as my friend inside the Zetas alerted me. Let's hope that some of those we've arrested stay behind bars this time. Any sign of Lazcano?"

"No, Major."

"Keep looking. I feel his eyes on us. He is priority one."

"Some of the civilians have been taking the guns from the dead, Major. Do you want us to disarm them?"

"No. Just make sure they are actually civilians, not cartel men."

"They might join the cartels, or try to sell them the guns, sir."

"Quite correct. Or they might try to defend themselves, Torres. If they can't do that, who will? We've disarmed the police, and we don't have enough men to be everywhere at once."

"What if they form vigilante groups?"

"Even better, as long as they oppose the cartels. You can call them vigilantes if you want. If they start taking care of themselves again, I'll celebrate their courage."

South of Nuevo Laredo
Tamaulipas, Mexico
May 28, 2011, 11:42 a.m.

"A toast, my friends, to our returning hero!" Heriberto Lazcano stood at the head of the table in the dining room of his hacienda. Twenty of his lieutenants stood with him. "Tell us your story, Ramón!"

"*Gracias,* Lazca." Dominguez bowed slightly, remaining standing while the others took a cue from Lazcano and sat down to await the report. "As you all know, last week *El Lazca*—Z3—had the foresight to set some traps for the Federation swine who attempted to retake Nuevo Laredo. They failed miserably, but since they had the stupidity to attempt to attack us in our most important plaza, *El Lazca* brilliantly decided that it was time for us to strike these cowards on their own turf.

"I was sent to Nayarit—just one state south of Sinaloa itself—on the shores of the Pacific. With a number of our men, I struck the Sinaloa Federation where they never expected to be struck. We ambushed one of their convoys outside a town called Ruiz. They never knew what hit them. We killed thirty of those pigs, and returned home yesterday without a single wound!"

The applause and cheers took almost an entire minute to die down.

"Now tell them about our plan for the Americans," Lazcano commanded.

Dominguez nodded. "For years our politicians and the Americans have plotted against us. The Americans released guns which went to *El Chapo* and his men—at least until we killed them and took the guns for ourselves." He waited for the laughter to stop. "Our own government, like Guzmán and his pussies, fear us more than any other force, so they arrange backdoor deals with the Americans, and we suspect the Americans of striking deals with Guzmán. We killed one of the American agents recently when he tried to travel our roads. Unfortunately, some of our men have paid a price for that attack.

"The Americans demanded arrests after the death of their cop, and Calderón and his puppets gave them our man '*El Toto*' in return. *El Lazca* then directed me to respond, and to hit the Americans themselves. We have prepared a surprise for them, and I have asked my little brother to make sure we have some movies to watch when that surprise unfolds."

The table erupted again with cheers and applause.

"We should not have to wait very long for our entertainment."

———

Washington, D.C.
June 10, 2011, 12:50 p.m.

"Now that just beat *the hell* out of FOP food," Dixon Carter said. "Didn't it, Tim? Of course, the scenery might suffer by comparison."

Wisniewski shrugged and nodded, leaning back away from the table.

"Jeff and I found this place a couple of years back," Lynn said. "I know it's way across town, but it's a good change of pace, and it's Friday."

"That it is," Trask agreed. "Georgetown's nice this time of year, and you can't beat the French for food. This place smells so good, I could do another plate, but my belt and my wallet won't stretch that far."

"I'm just glad I had the Escalade today," Doroz said. "It's the only G-car we could all fit in."

"How'd you come by *that* ride?" Trask asked. "Not normal government issue."

"A doper's car, of course, seized and forfeited to the government for facilitation of drug trafficking. It may have been the last heroin case we had before this one. Instead of giving it to the marshals to auction, we put it in service. It's a good undercover ride when we have to pretend to be high-rollers."

"Maybe we'll get some more good forfeitures out of *this* case when it's all done," Lynn said. "We've got to be part of the only government department that actually pays its own way."

"By billions to the good," Trask agreed. "I think DOJ as a whole raked in about eleven billion from the bad guys last year—mostly dope money and property bought with dope money—and the department's operating allowance was only two billion. But when it comes time for the new budget—if Congress ever does its job and passes one—we'll probably get cut again."

"They ought to be looking at the border when they do the next budget," Doroz said. He was looking at a priority message on his smart phone.

"What's up, Bear?" Wisniewski asked.

"A big sweep down in Texas. Some of our Bureau folks just helped arrest a hundred and twenty-seven of our own customs and border patrol agents for cooperating with the Mexican cartels."

"No punishment's too heavy for that," Trask said. "They're lucky they got arrested on this side of the border. On the other side, they'd be looked at not just as crooked cops, but as traitors, and for good reason. There are lots of folks dying down there."

"For now, it's just our junkies biting the dust," Carter nodded. "Some bright side of things, huh?"

A ring tone signaled that Doroz' phone was going off again.

"This is Doroz." A pause. "You're kidding. Where are you now?" Pause. "I'll call Hurst and the surveillance squad. We *had* to pick today to all ride to lunch together." Pause. "Yeah, but we're in Georgetown. We can sit on him for a minute or two while you guys back off." Pause. "Right. We'll see you in five."

Doroz put the phone back in his shirt pocket. "That was Sam McInnis. Our truck's back in town, stopped at a convenience store about five blocks from here. Sam and Randi are on it now. We'll scramble over there and keep eyes on things while they go change duds and cars, and I'll have the surveillance guys get ready to pick our target up as he goes across town. He's probably heading for our favorite racquet club, so we should have some time to get back to the office and gear up once Hurst takes over." He pitched the keys to Wisniewski. "Tim, you drive. I'll be on the phone. Is our tab paid? No time for change."

They all threw bills to the center of the table, leaving their server what was probably her biggest tip of the day.

———

1:07 p.m.

Wisniewski pulled the Escalade into a space on the far right of the store, next to a marked Metropolitan Police patrol car. Trask, in the front passenger seat, saw that McInnis and Rhodes were standing on the side of the building. To any casual onlooker, they were two cops just taking a coffee break. Each was holding a cup of something. *Good cover. They sure don't look like they're on the job at the moment.*

He looked to his left. The ton-and-a-half was parked in a spot just to the left of the front door. *The driver must be inside. I don't see him in the cab.*

They all bailed out of the Escalade and joined McInnis and Rhodes on the side of the building, a glass front convenience store with concrete block walls on the rear and sides.

"How long's he been inside, Sam?" Carter asked.

"Too damned long. He's in the head and I need to take a leak myself somethin' fierce."

"When he comes out, we'll take him," Doroz said. "You can go to the john and then you and Randi head out and change. Hurst and the other surveillance unit will pick him up at the racquet club while we double back to your district to pick you two up, then we'll all head to our place and break up into road teams."

Wisniewski peaked around the corner of the building. "Short guy climbing back into the cab. You're clear, Sam."

"Yeah, thanks," McInnis said gruffly as he brushed by Wisniewski on his way to the sidewalk.

Trask saw Wisniewski look at Officer Rhodes, and noticed a slight shrug in the detective's shoulders as he walked toward her. *One of our campers isn't happy. I think I was right about that jealousy thing.*

A loud, deep, booming noise and a roaring rush of air caused them all to duck reflexively. Trask, standing closest to the corner, looked around the edge of the building. The cab of the truck was on fire. He saw a uniformed figure running out the front door. *I wonder if Sam had time to—oh, no! No!* He pulled back away from the corner, hugging the wall. He looked up and saw a figure rushing at him.

"*SAM?!?*" Randi Rhodes was sprinting toward the corner of the building, Wisniewski hot on her heels.

Trask threw his right arm around Rhodes, knocking her back into Wisniewski and sending them both to the ground just as a second blast, this one much louder than the first, shook the ground.

"Jeff, *what the hell?!*" Rhodes was screaming. Trask was barely aware of her protest, his ears still ringing from the noise of the blast.

He got to his feet and staggered to the corner of the building. The scene that greeted him was like one from an apocalyptic horror movie. There were several bodies lying inside what had been the front of the store. The gasoline pumps were burning, and anything and anyone that had been in the front of the store had been blown into the back wall, which was now only partially erect. What was left of the ton-and-a-half was twisted and lying on its side, resting atop the remains of some sort of sedan that had been parked next to it. Trask turned and saw that the Escalade was burning as well. *The blocks on the side wall protected us just enough. Without them for cover, we'd all have been blown to hell.*

"Get fire and ambulances rolling," he told Doroz, who was getting to his feet. "We need to back up some. Those pumps might blow at any second." He saw the look on Rhodes' face. "I'm sorry, Randi. Sam's gone."

———

Four blocks away, the driver of a black Mustang tossed one cellphone onto the passenger seat. He got out of the car, and smiling, set another smart phone to video mode, and pointed the lens toward the pillar of black smoke rising into the air.

———

Laredo, Texas
June 13, 2011, 1:36 p.m.

The broker saw the red Bronco kicking up the dust on the road to the ranch house. *What the hell is he doing here today? The truck isn't due back for days.* He stepped out onto the porch and waited.

"Hello, my friend," Dominguez leered from the passenger window as the Bronco stopped in front of the house. He didn't get out of the truck.

"What's going on, Ramón? You know he's not back yet."

The broker stepped back from the door of the Bronco, reading something strange in Dominguez' face. *Is this ugly bastard drunk? Something's different.*

"Come here, my friend," Dominguez waved him over. "I have something to show you."

The broker stepped closer to the Bronco as Dominguez brought a tablet computer up to the window.

"Remember your friend in the truck—your little driver who stole from us? Watch this!"

The broker looked at the video on the tablet screen. He could make out the silhouette of the ton-and-a-half parked in front of what looked like a convenience store. He thought he saw an orange flash in the cab of the vehicle, and then, seconds later, the entire truck rose into the air in a huge ball of flame before falling back to earth on its side. He jumped back from the Bronco in horror.

"*What the fuck, Ramón?!!*" He jumped back toward the window of the Bronco, not stopping to think about where his rage was taking him. "*Dammit!* I told you I had taken care of—"

Dominguez grabbed him by the collar of his shirt, pulling him close. "Do not forget your place, my friend," he snarled. He shoved the broker away from the Bronco.

The broker collected himself. "Where am I supposed to find another driver? Our customers are going to wonder what happened. They won't trust just anybody. I have to find somebody else to learn the routes and locations." He felt his blood rising again. "If we're still in business, Ramón, where the hell do I find that guy on short notice?"

"We're still in business, my friend." The narrow jawline contracted into a hideous grin. "A new load in a new vehicle will be coming soon. Your FBI arrested our friend with the border patrol. I guess he got careless. We'll get the merchandise across at another location, and use different load cars. You'll know your new driver when you see him." The grin widened. "You can find him by looking in your mirror."

Dominguez laughed, and made a motion with his hand to his driver.

The broker stood speechless, watching as the Bronco headed back up the road toward the gate.

———

Waldorf, Maryland
10:45 p.m.

"I've got seventeen dead here now, Luis." Trask tried to keep from screaming into the phone. "Not just junkies overdosing on heroin. Completely innocent people, doing nothing wrong. One of the police officers on my team, too. A good man. They're all gone now, and your source had no idea this was going to happen?"

"I assure you that he did not, Jeff. I am so very sorry."

"We're beyond sorry, Luis. I'm mad as hell."

There was a sizable pause before Aguilar answered him.

"I gave you my word that I would keep you informed to the extent possible, Jeff. I will keep that promise. You must keep this in perspective."

"Exactly what *perspective* are you referring to? We don't have bombs going off on our streets that often."

"We do." Aguilar's voice was deliberate and calm. "Listen to me, my friend. You lost seventeen souls. I mourn them. I truly do. I mourn them as much as I mourn the innocents in the more than 75,000 that *my* country has lost. You lost a good police officer. We have lost thousands. Your victims are getting decent burials. We dig ours out of mass graves. Shall I go on?"

Trask caught himself and took a deep breath. "Point taken. I'm sorry, Luis. I didn't mean to blame you for any of this."

"No offense taken. I know how you feel, Jeff. I take that frustration and those emotions to bed with me every night. I wake up to them every morning."

"How the hell do you deal with that?"

"I told you. I have a tool that is not available to you. When we find the enemy, we shoot them. I estimate that I save twenty lives every time my marines kill a Zeta. I will never say that publicly, because we are supposed to be both the police and the military. We do not summarily execute anyone. But I must confess that I sleep more soundly after a successful operation."

Trask took another deep breath. "Good night, Luis. Keep me informed as you can. And good hunting."

Chapter Twenty-Eight

FBI Field Office
Washington, D.C.
June 15, 2011, 2:25 p.m.

"That was as impressive as it was sad," Trask said as he pulled into the parking garage.

"Yes it was," Lynn nodded. "All the dress uniforms, the badges with the black stripes, the pipes at the grave site. Poor Sam's end of watch."

They walked to the elevator and took it up.

"I have to use the ladies' room," she said. "See you in a minute or two."

Trask walked into the squad conference room.

"It was a nice service." Dixon Carter was in his police dress uniform sitting at the table and staring at nothing.

"Yes it was, Dix. I know there are cops, and then there are really good cops. From the number of brothers in blue that showed up today, I'd say you trained another good one." *This is the first time I've ever seen Dix in anything other than a suit or sport coat.*

"He was a good man." Carter sat silent for a moment, then turned and stared at Trask. "We've all been shaken up for a few days, Jeff. Seventeen dead at our crime scene, statements to write, all the somber stuff. I haven't had a chance to ask you before now. Just *how the hell* did you know to expect the *second* blast?"

"I was reading background files on the Zetas before our lunch that morning, Dix. I remembered something my friend from the Mexican marines told me. The original Zetas—the ones who deserted from the Mexican Army—were all special ops types. They'd been trained by some of our special forces, by some Canadian units, and by some Israeli operators, too. I had heard one of the Israeli security guys give a talk at one of our Air Force Bases before I left active duty. They've learned over the years that when a terrorist detonates a bomb—in Tel Aviv, for example—their first responders have to hang back for a bit.

"As counter-intuitive as it is for them—since they want to rescue the injured—they've learned the hard way that the first bomb is there to attract the police and rescue personnel. It's the second one that's the major charge, and it's designed to kill them as well as any who were injured in the first blast. I saw the cab, and it looked like a smaller bomb had gone off in the front of the ton-and-a-half. Something just clicked and I remembered thinking about the Israeli lecture. If they trained the Zetas, the Zetas could have picked up the dirty tricks from their trainers' experience."

Carter nodded. "Anyone who cleared that corner would have died from the blast force. You saved some lives out there, Jeff."

"Not enough. We can never seem to do enough."

"We can only do what we can." Carter paused again. "I hear that Officer Rhodes still wants to join the squad for the remainder of the investigation, if there is one."

Barry Doroz entered the conference room, followed by Lynn Trask.

"I heard that, Dix," Doroz said. "I'm not sure it's a good idea. Anything she testifies to will be attacked because of her relationship with Sam."

"She won't have to testify to anything if there's a second set of eyes on anything she sees," Carter replied. "She can partner with me."

"What about Tim?" Doroz asked.

"She sure as hell can't partner with *him*," Carter said. "Or have you gone blind in your advancing age?"

"Oh yeah. There is *that*." Doroz nodded. "He's probably at her place now."

"He *needs* to be there now," Lynn said. "And since all you *men* won't say it, I will. Dix is the perfect partner at the moment for Randi. Who *else* in this room knows what it's like to go through losing a partner? Nobody. It's taken Dix this long to deal with the way Juan died." She looked across the table at Carter. "You can help her through this. That will help you, too, and *she'll* feel like she's doing something to get back at whoever who did this. Tim's not a rookie, he can go solo, or he can ride with you, Bear."

Trask looked at Carter who was nodding in agreement. He thought he saw tears in the big man's eyes.

Doroz saw it, too. "I thought you were just the squad analyst, Lynn," he said.

"You know better than that," she said. She looked at Trask. "Any problems with that, babe?"

Trask nodded. "Yeah, actually, but none that we can't handle."

"What's our next play, Jeff?" Carter asked.

Trask leaned over the table. "I talked to my man in Mexico. His source tells him the supply line is still open, and that blowing the truck was a double-shot from the cartel. The driver had been ripping them off some way, so they used him to drive a bomb into the District. The Zetas blame us—America and our ATF in particular—for arming their opposition in the Fast and Furious mess. It was their method of retaliation. They've hung some signs around Nuevo Laredo taking credit for the bombing.

"All that means is that their vehicle and driver will be replaced, and that at some point they'll resume deliveries. They can't let their customers wait too long or the junkies will hook up with other suppliers. We keep the camera on the racquet club, and look for a similar pattern with another truck—or a car. It doesn't have to be a ton-and-a-half to haul a few kilos of heroin. If our Mexican source can peg the new driver or vehicle he'll do so, and I'll get a call. Otherwise it's up to us."

"I'll start watching the video feed," Lynn said. She half-smiled at Doroz. "It'll be something for me to *analyze*."

Trask's cell phone vibrated on his belt. He checked it and read the text message. "Oh, hell."

"What's up?" Doroz asked.

"It's from Ross Eastman. I'm being summoned by Heidelberg."

———

Hart Senate Office Building
3:35 p.m.

One thing was different when Trask entered the room. The big side chair beside Heidelberg's desk—the one usually occupied by Senator Sherwin "Digger" Graves—was empty.

Heidelberg noticed that Trask noticed.

"I didn't tell Senator Graves we'd be meeting today," Heidelberg explained.

"Any particular reason?" Trask asked. He measured the old man carefully. *He looks exhausted.*

"I just wanted the two of us to talk freely for a while."

"Good," Trask said. "I think that's necessary. Since he's not here, though, I have to ask you something. Did Digger ever date your daughter?"

The senator frowned. "Not that I know of. Like I said before, she had her own life and I never had Janie followed or anything like that. I *do* know, however, that he *wanted* to see her socially. Janie told me she 'shot him down,' as you Air Force types say."

"We do say that, sir."

"You don't think he's a suspect, do you?"

"I can't rule him in or out at this point. I just wondered why he was here at every prior meeting, and wondered why he was so interested in our progress. He wasn't really entitled to be present, but since he appeared to be here at your invitation I didn't say anything."

"If you prefer that he not be here in the future, we'll do it that way. At least until you can rule him out."

"I would prefer that."

"I saw the news reports about that truck blowing up and killing all those people. One of the telecasts showed some others on the scene helping with the initial response. I thought I saw you in those shots."

"You did."

"It was related to the case you've been working on, tied to Janie's death, wasn't it?"

"We have plenty of reason to believe it was."

The senator nodded. "I thought so. What can you tell me?"

"Do we have an agreement that this goes no farther than this room, Senator?"

"We do."

Trask remained silent for a moment, still studying the old man's face.

"You're wondering if you can trust me," Heidelberg noted. "Let me tell you this. You mentioned the other deaths caused by this China White heroin. Four or five prostitutes, as I recall. I have to admit that that news didn't really concern me. My daughter wasn't a hooker, Mr. Trask. I had a great deal of difficulty linking her in any way to those other women."

"They were other human beings who died from the same kind of heroin, and that heroin very probably came from the same supplier, Senator."

"I know, I know." The old man put his hands up. "I realize that now. I think the deaths of all those others in the bombing may have jolted me into seeing the magnitude of this whole thing."

Well, Trask thought, *maybe the old bird has had an epiphany.*

"Who were those people at the store—the victims?" Heidelberg asked.

"Except for the driver of the truck carrying the charges, just folks going about their everyday lives and tasks. Each had a story. If we ever catch the ones responsible, their surviving family members will get a chance to tell those stories."

"What can *you* tell me about them?"

An odd request. Trask shrugged. "Okay, we'll start with the driver. A little man named Robert Carey. No criminal record to speak of, just a few tickets while out on the road driving trucks. Our intelligence, which I'll explain later, indicates that he'd crossed the wrong people south of the border. Those people are the Zetas Cartel, a crew which may be the closest thing to the Nazis we've seen in the last few decades. They blame the US and the ATF in particular for providing weapons to their competition, the Federation Cartel, through the Fast and Furious disaster. They appear to have substituted C4 for the heroin this trip. Carey and the other victims never knew what hit them. Ironically, ATF's bomb experts were the ones tasked with processing the scene. They found bits and pieces of this and that after the blast, and they've concluded that the charges were detonated by a cell phone wired to the bomb."

"Do you trust these bomb experts?"

"I've never found any fault with the ATF worker bees, Senator. Many are former cops, and there are some fine investigators in that organization. For some reason, however, the cream doesn't seem to rise to the top of that barrel. Ruby

Ridge, Waco, and Fast and Furious were all operations severely lacking in the use of common sense. *We*—the folks in my office—have to get approval from the Pope and every cardinal at main Justice to let a couple of pounds of marijuana out of our control in a reverse sting operation, where we sell drugs to the bad guys. To let hundreds of assault rifles and other firearms walk out the door to the enemy is the most moronic thing I've ever seen."

Heidelberg nodded, and looked down at his desk. "I've never been satisfied with the answers we've gotten in our hearings on that operation. Very troubling." He looked back up at Trask. "You were telling me about the victims at the store."

Trask met the old man's gaze. *Something else is going on here.* "Yes, I was. You asked me about the ATF bomb squad, so I got sidetracked. Sorry. The other sixteen victims, Senator, were Wanda Blackwell and Newton Boyles, the clerks working the counter in the store; Sally Jean Butler, a nurse who had stopped for gas on her way home after her shift at one of the trauma centers; Ricky Carter, a fifteen-year-old dropout who was there running an errand for his mother— picking up a pizza—I believe; Taneesha DeLancey and her two-year-old daugh- ter Theressa, who were there to buy ice cream for the little girl—"

Trask looked hard at the Senator as he took a breath. *I understand now.*

"Sandra Freeman, who was there to get a powerball ticket for her father, an invalid who couldn't leave his house; Isaac Grady, who just liked to hang around the store; Jackie Grantham, an attorney from a firm on K Street who had stopped for gas; Billy Halliwell, a dental student who had been jogging and wanted one of those frozen fountain drinks; Brian Hendrix, a congressional staffer to Representative Hill from Tennessee; and Dana Holland, an off-duty police officer on her way to start her shift. Three of the last four victims were Hal Mauldin, a stay-at-home dad, and his kids Randy, and Carolyn. Hal was standing by a gas pump when the explosion hit. The kids were still in his mini- van. When we interviewed their mother she said they were on their way to the National Zoo. That's what we've learned so far from the surviving family mem- bers and friends."

Trask stared at Heidelberg. The old man's mouth was hanging open in disbelief.

"The last victim I have to mention is—was—Sam McInnis. He was the police officer who originally put us onto what we believe was the load truck that was bringing the heroin into town. This time the truck wasn't carrying heroin. It was carrying C4."

Trask waited for Heidelberg to say something. He didn't.

"Did I pass, Senator?"

Heidelberg reached down and pulled a newspaper clipping out from under a stack of papers on the top of his desk. He held it up sheepishly. "Yes, you passed."

"Where do you think *The Post* got most of that information, Senator? I gave it to our PR guy and he passed it on."

Heidelberg sat in stunned silence for a moment. "Why and how did you *remember* all that?"

"I never, *NEVER* forget the victims, Senator. That includes your daughter. Are we clear on that?"

"Yes. We are now."

"Are we done here?" *I resent the hell out of this little game. I don't care who you are.*

The senator leaned back in his chair, but this time there was no arrogance, no attitude. When he spoke, he spoke softly. "No, Mr. Trask. We aren't done. I'm from Texas. I've had some briefings about the Zetas. We have a common enemy here, so let's try a fresh start. I lost my only daughter, and it's hard to wait for answers. I'm sorry if I've pushed too hard, tried to rush things."

The old man started to tremble. He looked at Trask though eyes swollen with tears.

"How can I *help* you, Mr. Trask?"

Chapter Twenty-Nine

Tampico Naval Air Station
Tamaulipas, Mexico
June 17, 2011, 4:45 a.m.

"Hello." Aguilar answered the special phone he carried.

"It's me."

"Your information was perfect, my friend. I passed it on to our men in Zacatecas. They captured Lazcano's man Huerta—the one they call *El Wache*—and twenty-one others yesterday. Huerta confessed to being involved in the massacre at San Fernando, and showed them some mass graves from other murders. Well done, my friend. Well done. Your other information has been passed on to my friend in the US. Whatever other intelligence you can get on the heroin could also be very fruitful."

"I will do what I can."

"You have always provided heroic service for us. More than I thought would be possible when we began."

"I have to go, Major," the man said.

"I understand, my friend. Stay safe."

"How long has this been going on, Jeff?" Dr. Ramsey Huddleston asked.

"A few months. I thought it was psychosomatic. The Air Force docs in San Antonio ran some tests and couldn't find anything. First the hand just shook a lot, but when I got to work this morning I had to use my right arm to reach across and open the car door. My left was just too weak."

"No pain to speak of, just weakness?"

"Right."

"What kind of tests did they do in Texas?"

"Mostly nerve stuff."

"It was just the hand then?"

"Yeah. Now it's the whole arm. Like I said, it doesn't really hurt—"

"That's what you said when we found you had double pneumonia last year, and it nearly took you out. No chest pains, even when you were down more than twenty-five per cent on lung capacity. We're going to have to wake you up one day to tell you that you died during the night."

"I thought it was just a cold. I really didn't have any pain with it."

"Any past history of similar incidents, other than the pneumonia?"

"I played the second half of an intramural football game at the academy on a broken ankle. I collapsed when the game was over."

The doctor nodded. "This isn't unheard of, but cases of this degree are pretty rare. You have a ridiculously high pain threshold, especially when you're focused and concentrating on something else. On top of that, you've got an area across the upper chest area—at least on the inside—where your nerves just aren't talking to your brain at all."

"What do you call that?"

"Abnormal. But I suspect I'm not the first to call you that. I read a recent study on this kind of thing. Some researchers tested the pain sensitivity of a bunch of healthy folks by touching them with a hot probe. Then they gave the test subjects an MRI, and determined that the ones least sensitive to pain were the ones with the most grey matter in certain parts of the brain. You're a very bright guy, Jeff. You're probably better able to distract yourself from the pain messages your nerves are trying to get through to that head of yours."

The exam room door opened and a nurse handed Huddleston a large envelope. "Let's see what these tell us," he said, putting the X-rays of Trask's left
shoulder on the light rack. The doctor paused, then turned back toward Trask.

"Just how long have you been walking around with a shattered collar bone?"

"*What!?*"

"The end of the thing is all sharded, Jeff. Look here. The bone splinters are
digging into the muscle tissue in your shoulder. That's why the arm's shutting
down. Your muscle strength is probably down to near nothing. When did this
happen?"

"I had to tackle a couple of people at that bombing site—"

"No, no, no. This is an *old* injury. You can tell from the patterns in the bones
that some have tried to heal and set. You don't remember hurting it?"

"Sorry, no."

"No falls, impacts?"

"A tumble skiing last year, and I had a tussle with a couple of bad guys in
our house before Lynn shot 'em, but that was several months back."

"And you haven't felt any pain?"

"Not really."

"You, my friend, are not wired right."

"You're not the first to say that, either. How do we fix it?"

"Surgery, cowboy. I know a good ortho guy. He'll have to file down the end
of the bone here, smooth it out, re-attach the labrum, basically rebuild the entire
AC joint. He can do it on an out-patient basis, meaning you can go home after
the surgery, but there'll be some rehab therapy. They'll give you some pain pills
for after the surgery . . . oh what the hell. You probably won't even take them,
will you?"

"We'll see. When can he do it?

"I'll call him. Are you at a spot in your schedule where you can take some
time off?"

"No."

"Of course not. Just don't overdo it or you'll have to have the whole thing
re-done. Here—" The doctor wrote down the phone number for the referral.
"Call them Monday morning. I'll tell them to work you in as soon as they can."

"Thanks. It's a relief, actually. I was beginning to think something was
wrong with my head."

The doc just looked at him. "If you're waiting for me to say something to cast some doubt on that conclusion . . ."

"Thanks again." Trask smiled and headed for the door.

———

South of Nuevo Laredo
Tamaulipas, Mexico
June 21, 2011, 8:41 a.m.

"Why isn't he dead yet?" Heriberto Lazcano pounded the head of the table. "I do not hear an answer!"

"He is like a snake, Lazca. He strikes and then crawls back in his hole." The Zeta sitting closest to Lazcano on the left side of the table seemed impressed with his analogy.

Lazcano glared at the man. "Do snakes fly, Emilio?"

"No, Lazca," the man said, a confused look on his face. "Snakes cannot fly."

"Then why say something that stupid? We know where Aguilar's *hole* is. It is that damned base in Tampico, where we cannot reach him. He and his marines hide *there*, climb into their helicopters whenever they feel brave, and they can be anywhere within hours. They are not *snakes*, you fool. Finish your breakfast in silence."

The admonished Zeta fixed his eyes on his plate.

"Anyone else have anything better to offer, or are we all just waiting for the marines to ambush us again?" Lazcano asked.

"Your question is an excellent one, Lazca," Dominguez said, sitting on Lazcano's right. "And it suggests our answer. *We* must ambush the *marines*. We step up our attacks on targets which will attract Aguilar and his men. When they come to respond, we ambush *them*."

Lazcano clapped his hands together. "Finally! Ramón demonstrates why he is my second in command. Do you have some targets in mind, my friend?"

"Let's try something in an area that they do not know as well. We've fought them everywhere in Tamaulipas. We will set something in motion elsewhere, and lure them onto ground that they do not know."

"Yes," Lazcano said. "We will do that. And this time, we will not be outnumbered."

———

FBI Field Office
Washington, D.C.
June 24, 2011, 9:17 a.m.

"Well! The cast is gone. How's the wing?" Carter asked as Trask entered the squad room.

"Just came from my first rehab appointment," Trask said, "And quite probably, my last."

"What the hell did you do, Jeff?" Lynn was standing with her hands on her hips, looking over the top of her cubicle wall.

"Just followed directions."

"Explain, please." She folded her arms across her chest.

"I go in, and this guy—the head therapist—takes my medical history. I told him the whole story. No pain before or after the surgery. Never took any pills, never needed any. He asked to see the range of motion, so I gave him a full windmill with the arm. Nothing fast, I just showed him I could do the full three-sixty. He takes me over to a greased track with a metal weight on it—probably ten pounds or so—and hands me one end of a bungee cord. The other end is tied to the weight. He tells me to move the weight as fast as I can so he could measure my pain tolerance, despite what I'd told him. I gave the thing a good yank, it jumped the track at the far end, flew across the room and put a hole in the wall. End of rehab."

"*Oh, God!* I give up." Lynn sank back in her chair, shaking her head.

"I can do the rehab at home, babe. Low weights and low reps at first, build the shoulder back up gradually," Trask said. "Piece of cake."

"The man who feels no pain," Wisniewski quipped.

"Not true. Paper cut my fingers and I'll cry like a girl," Trask replied.

"I heard that," Lynn said from down behind her wall.

"It's just the upper torso where I don't feel much," Trask said. "I'm sure it'll come in real handy in our next bar fight."

"Anyway, welcome back," Carter said. "Enjoy the break?"

"Actually, I did." Trask walked into Lynn's cubicle and rubbed her shoulders. "I got to see what Lynn's been looking forward to in her retirement. Lots of time with three lovin' puppies who think I'm a superhero, as long as I give 'em a treat at least once an hour."

"I think Boo gained five pounds this past week," Lynn said, shaking her head again.

Trask patted her shoulders, then headed for Doroz' office. The squad supervisor was just hanging up the phone on his desk.

"Anything happen in my absence?" Trask asked.

"Nothing until just now. And that's not a good thing. As I'm sure you know, Lynn and Randi have both been taking shots at the video feed from the racquet club, and we haven't seen any vehicles that fit the pattern we saw from the truck before it blew up."

"So I heard. I asked my guy in Mexico to see what he could find out, but his source within the Zetas isn't that highly placed yet. No news for now. They could just be using different load cars."

"Or they could have shut down for a while to let things cool off. I was prepared to have that argument with you again about tabling the case until I got that phone call—the one I hung up just now. It was Kathy Davis at the medical examiner's office. We have another dead hooker. Heroin overdose. China White. They're still rolling."

———

Waldorf, Maryland
6:15 p.m.

"From the looks of that, I guess my diagnosis was wrong." Willie Sivella nodded toward the sling on Trask's left arm. The bartender handed Trask the frosted mug of beer.

"Only about the hand, Willie. I think everything else you said was spot on."

Sivella nodded. "Glad to hear it, and glad you feel that way. So your pitchers are following your signals again?"

"I'm talking more with them about what signals to put down. The communication's good all around. I think my ace just needed a day off from the rotation."

Sivella laughed. "Bear *can* get cranky from time to time, can't he?"

"That he can."

"So who'd you find to take his start?"

"A new ace, if he's not careful. Nobody you know, for once. I found him in the Mexican league."

Chapter Thirty

San José de Lourdes community
Fresnillo, Zacatecas, Mexico
June 30, 2011, 9:19 p.m.

"The bait is out, Lazca." Ramón Dominguez put his boots up on the desk in what was supposed to be the police station for the community. He shifted the cell phone to his other ear. "No, believe it or not, *you* are the bait, and you aren't even here! We hung a *narcomanta* from a pole on the main street next to the body of one of the cops who tried to interfere. It said that you—*El Lazca*—were taking an interest in removing the Federation sympathizers from Zacatecas. Anyone reading it would think that you are personally supervising things in Fresnillo. I don't think Aguilar will be able to resist it. *Comandante Ardila* and I have arranged a nice welcoming party for them when they arrive. I expect that they'll be here first thing in the morning. They like to strike at dawn, when they think we are asleep. I'll keep you posted."

Dominguez clicked off the phone and grinned at the other man in the room. "Well, *Comandante*, let's see how well the men you command have been trained."

"You'll find them in position. I instructed them to get some sleep, but there is a sentry on watch on both sides of our choke point. They are all to be awake before daybreak. We will have something to celebrate tomorrow."

Tampico Naval Air Station
Tamaulipas, Mexico
June 30, 2011, 10:41 p.m.

The helicopters lifted off and headed west, bound for the central highlands.

"The reports place Lazcano here, Major." Torres pointed to the map spread across his lap, the light mounted on his helmet illuminating the grid. "It's a little settlement northwest of the crossroads at Fresnillo. A place called San José de Lourdes. A small town of about five thousand people."

Aguilar studied the map. "There's an army installation in Fresnillo. Radio ahead and tell them we'd like to borrow some armored personnel carriers. We'll land at the post and go in from there. Tell the commander I'd like to see him when we land."

"We're going to use APCs instead of our usual operations plan, sir?"

"This doesn't smell right, Torres. Lazcano has used *narcomantas* before, but only after a significant victory, with lots of his enemies' bodies strewn all over the place. You say there was a single policeman hanging by this sign?"

"That is what was reported."

"I don't like it." He flicked a radio button, activating a communication channel to all the marines on the choppers. "This is Aguilar, gentlemen. We will hit the enemy at dawn, as usual, while he is wiping the sleep from his eyes. We will be using armored transports, however. If we experience crossfire, if we are the targets of an ambush, remember your training. It may be natural to steer or run away from a gun firing at you. You will live longer if you attack the points of fire. You can return fire at an enemy if you face him. You are marines, and you will prevail. If you show your enemy your backs, he will be firing and you will not. Follow your officers. Follow me. We will split our forces and attack. I know you will all make Mexico proud. You always have. Aguilar out." *It is a major risk, but if Lazcano is there, it is worth it.*

San José de Lourdes community
Fresnillo, Zacatecas, Mexico
July 1, 2011, 6:03 a.m.

The marines walked in two rows, one on each side of the street. The APCs rolled alongside of them, rumbling slowly through the dark. Each time a door was forced open, the transport beside the column would stop and wait to see if the latest structure housed a Zeta barracks, the gunners on the outside of the vehicles at the ready to offer fire support to the exposed marines.

As the company neared the center of the block, muzzle bursts from automatic weapons in buildings on each side of the road lit the pre-dawn darkness. The marines closest to the buildings dropped down to prone firing positions for seconds, just long enough for the gunners in the transports to return fire with their heavier caliber machine guns. After the return fire had shredded the ambush points, the marines were back on their feet, charging *into* the Zeta positions. The initial firefight lasted only moments.

Aguilar's radio squawked inside one of the transports. "Yes, Torres?"

"We're under heavy fire on this end, Major. The Zetas have blocked the streets behind us. They pulled trucks into the streets on either side of us. We are holding our own for now, but—"

"We're on our way." Aguilar pushed one button, then another. "We could use your reserves on the west side of town now, sir," he told the army colonel.

Five hours later, the last of the firing stopped.

"How are your men, Torres?" Aguilar asked.

"I have five disabled, Major. Mostly light wounds. One man took a knife in the leg. He bled a lot, but none of the wounded are in danger. How did you do?"

"One wounded," Aguilar said. "Not serious." He looked toward the side of the street. Some marines, assisted by men of the Mexican army who had joined them in the fight, were lining up bodies along the road.

"Fifteen enemy dead, and seventeen captured, Major," Torres reported.

"Lazcano?"

"No, sir. The prisoners who talked told us he was never here. They did say that Lazcano's number two, the one they call *El Ratón*, was setting the ambush up last night. We have not found him. We did get one of the local big fish, however.

Not Heriberto *Lazcano*, but Heriberto Centeno Madrid. The Zetas called him *Comandante Ardila*."

"Has he been interrogated?"

"That would be difficult, sir. He has very little brain matter left. A round took off the back of his skull."

"I see. What have we seized from them?"

"The usual homemade assault vehicles. We have one Toyota FJ cruiser with some impressive welding work on it—lots of steel plates—and another truck with a turret on top. A couple of dozen AK 47s and several thousand rounds of ammo. The army is taking control of the prisoners."

"Good. Let's go home, Torres." Aguilar looked around the street. The haze of the gunpowder was disappearing, and his marines were ushering their prisoners toward waiting trucks. *I love these men*, he thought. *I love them.*

———

Tampico Naval Air Station
Tamaulipas, Mexico
11:48 p.m.

Aguilar answered the cell phone when it rang on his night stand.

"Thank you, my friend. You saved lots of good marines today."

"Glad I could help, for once, Major."

"So they trust you more now?" Aguilar asked.

"Much more. I am on *El Ratón's* staff now; not highly placed yet, but more trusted, and with a better vantage point."

"Excellent."

"How did you let the men know, Major?"

"Relax, my friend. I never mentioned you, or even the fact that I had warning. They all think I am a military genius."

"I think you *are*, sir."

"No, my friend. Just fortunate to have good men beside me, and men like you looking out for me. Stay safe."

"Good night, Major."

———

Washington, D.C.
11:58 p.m.

"It's almost midnight, Tim. Are you coming to bed?" Randi asked.

Wisniewski clicked the television off with the remote and put his arm across her shoulders as they walked back toward the bedroom.

"I can't stop thinking about poor Sam, and I need to be with you. I'm glad you can stay with me. I can't spend too much time at your place in Bethesda. I have the residency requirement, you know. Still a rookie, have to reside in DC."

"Yeah; been there, done that. You know your bed's too little for the both of us; I'm not getting any sleep in that bassinet."

"Is it that big a problem?"

"Not if we conserve space."

"What?"

"The surface area of the bed is only big enough for one of us," he said. "It might work, however, if—"

"If what?"

He pulled the tee shirt up over her head and kissed her.

"If you just stay on top tonight."

———

Chapter Thirty-One

FBI Field Office
Washington, D.C.
July 15, 2011, 9:00 a.m.

"Sorry, but I got nuthin'. I mean nada and zilch." Lynn shook her head as the squad staff meeting convened in the conference room. "I haven't seen the same vehicle twice in any pattern at the racquet club, and no Texas plates. I know we think the dope is still coming in, but I can't find anything that might tell us how."

"Ideas?" Doroz asked, looking around the table.

"Hmmph." Carter cleared his throat, but didn't say anything.

"Spill it, Dix," Doroz said. "I've known you long enough to know when those wheels of yours are turning."

"Ever since we struck out—or thought we did, since Jeff disagrees—with our janitor friend, we've been concentrating on the supply line *into* the club. We all agree that the truck that exploded was probably the load vehicle. That all fits, and dovetails with what Jeff's sources in Mexico are telling him. If we aren't getting anything on the supply *into* the place, it might be time to take another look at what's coming *out* of the racquet club."

"What do you have in mind, Dix?" Trask asked.

"Before we take that road trip we had set up for out of town, let's try it at home. If we think our man Roscoe is part of the dope flow down to the hookers and other junkies, let's watch him—*carefully*—and see what he's up to. We'll at least get a more complete picture than the occasional encounters that Hammer has with Briggs' truck on the track."

"In the absence of any objection, and hearing none, the motion is seconded and passes," Doroz said.

"I don't remember voting," Wisniewski quipped.

"You didn't," Doroz said.

Randi Rhodes managed a smile.

"You're with *me*, Officer Rhodes," Carter said.

———

Tampico Naval Air Station
Tamaulipas, Mexico
4:15 p.m.

"I'm sorry to ruin your day, Major," Captain Torres said as he dropped the report on Aguilar's desk.

"I knew it had been too calm," Aguilar replied. "What is it?"

"There's been another mass escape from the federal prison in Nuevo Laredo. Sixty-six inmates escaped, including some of those Zetas we just captured in Zacatecas."

"Saddle up," Aguilar said. "Maybe when we find them this time, they won't surrender." He paused. "If they do, we'll take them back." He patted Torres on the shoulder. "Our rules of engagement. Make sure the men understand that."

"Yes, Major. I'll see you at the choppers."

———

"Briggs is coming out, Dix," Randi said, lowering the binoculars she'd had leveled on the racquet club. "He's got his tool box and the same duffle bag he carried in."

"About time," Carter said. "I was beginning to think he was going to spend the night in there."

"What if he was actually doing some janitor stuff?"

"What if he was? That doesn't eliminate the possibility that he's doing both that *and* muling some dope for Adipietro. When you take the detective's exam—either the one on paper, or more importantly, the one out here in the real world—don't treat any scenario as an either-or, zero-sum game. That's what our targets want us to do." He paused. "If Jeff Trask is right, that's the mistake that Barry Doroz and I made after our interrogation session with Mr. Briggs. We bought the cover and didn't stop to think that it might have *been* a cover."

Rhodes pulled the unmarked car into traffic behind the Metro Maintenance van, staying about four cars behind him in traffic. She was careful to make the lights without gunning the car through yellows.

"Thanks," she said to Carter.

"You're welcome. For what?"

"For not telling me how to do what I already know how to do. Sam used to do that. 'Stay back, don't get burned. Careful, not too close.'"

Carter chuckled. "He probably did that because I used to do that with him."

"You did?"

"We mellow with age. I'm sure he was mostly thinking out loud, almost talking to himself. That's why I did it. Then my new partner—Juan Ramirez—kept bringing it to my attention. He made me stop."

"How'd he do that?"

"He'd pour coffee in my lap. I learned not to do it pretty quickly."

The maintenance van pulled to the curb in front of a brownstone. Rhodes turned right at a cross street before reaching the van.

"I got the address," Carter said.

"How'd you see it? I turned before we got to the house. I was going to make the block."

"I know. I've been to that house before."

———

9:27 p.m.

The broker pulled the car with the DC plates out of the parking lot of the restaurant and headed for New York. He'd pick up the load car with the Missouri plates in the storage unit in Arlington, Virginia, on the return trip, parking the DC car in the unit until he returned with the next load. A car with DC plates raised no suspicion on the eastern seaboard, and a car with Missouri plates raised no eyebrows between Texas and the capital city. Missouri, unlike Texas, was not a source state for dope. It was, like most other states away from the border, a destination for the drugs. In DC, a Missouri driver was not a mule; he was a tourist, and so sometimes he'd use the Missouri car to drop the stuff with Adipietro; on other trips, he'd use the DC vehicle.

The Texas vehicle—the one the Zetas had given him loaded with the heroin—was parked in another storage facility in Oklahoma. He would park the Missouri car there on the way home.

What he liked to think of as a new version of the Pony Express made him feel eminently more comfortable than he had felt during his first delivery trip. He shuttered remembering it. He'd been in a cold sweat that entire week, worried that some alert cop or highway patrolman would peg him as a mule in the clunky looking Chevy with plates from south Texas, and also worried that the pounds of heroin packed in the big cooler in the trunk were actually explosives, and that he'd meet the same fate as his former driver.

He'd considered throwing the cooler off a bridge somewhere, but had decided that he'd be better off making the money a while longer. A few more trips and he could replace the ranch in Laredo with a nice place in Europe, somewhere far out of reach of the Zetas. *Just keep that bastard Ramón happy at all costs.*

I'm not having to pay a driver anymore, so the money's better. Enough to buy the ponies and the storage sheds, plus some.

The dope worried him, of course. He'd been to every underground page on the web looking for something new to mask the odors, petrified that a drug detection dog might alert on the cooler. Some recommended peppers, but he didn't want to have to explain to some state trooper why he had a load of cayenne powder or even jalapeños. The cops were already training their dogs to ignore the old standards—coffee grounds, fabric softeners, bleach, motor oil and grease—so he'd come up with his own system. The heroin was triple-wrapped, in plastic at the bottom of the cooler, and covered with layers of steaks, with the whole container filled with as much as ice as possible. If stopped, he'd just claim that his brother in some berg back up the road had gotten a helluva deal on the meat, and he was taking some home to his folks in some berg ahead on the road.

On the return trips, he wrapped the money in the same fashion that he'd wrapped the heroin, and recovered it with fresh meat, as required. The basic plan was, of course, not to get stopped at all. He didn't drive too fast or too slow, opting for the tried and true 'five over' rule to avoid suspicion. So far it had worked. So far.

He passed a Maryland State Trooper hiding in a cut on the median and looked down at his speedometer. *Fifty-nine in a fifty-five. Perfect.* He checked anyway, just a peek at the side mirror. *He's still there. I'm good.*

Chapter Thirty-Two

FBI Field Office
Washington, D.C.
July 18, 2011, 9:10 a.m.

"His name is Tommy Harris," Carter said, leaning forward on the table. He pushed out copies of a stack of papers, a booking photo on top of a rap sheet. "Several priors, all related to being what he is—a pimp. Hammer's brought him in at least three times, usually for getting rough with one of his girls. I've had to interview him on a couple of homicides. He wasn't good for either one. One of the dead girls was a victim of our old friend Demetrius Reid, the Jamaican that Jeff took out in the courtroom."

"He took himself out. I just ducked," Trask said. "No drug convictions, Dix?"

"No. Just assaults and pandering."

Trask looked puzzled. "Dix, as Hammer said, it would be bad for business for a pimp to be giving this crud to his own girls, reducing his stable. I think his words were 'bad for cash flow.'"

"He did say that."

"What if Harris isn't giving the dope to his own girls, but to his competition? You know, girls working for the other pimps on the track?" Rhodes asked. She saw the faces turned and staring at her. "Just a thought."

"And a good one," Doroz said. "We need to consider all possibilities."

"Sure was," Trask nodded. "No priors for dope, though? Nuts. That's going to limit our leverage a little. We'll drop from mandatory life under the statute to a twenty-year mandatory and whatever additional time the judge wants to throw at him. Of course, if we can put more than one death on him, we can try stacking the sentences. Still, a good lead and my mistake. Since Hammer had seen Briggs' truck on the track, I'd assumed Briggs was muling the stuff straight from Adipietro's racquet club to the working girls. I didn't stop to think there might be another level in the delivery chain."

"None of us did," Doroz said. "Nice work, Dix."

"I just had a thought," Trask looked down at the table, then reached for his cell phone. He hit an icon and waited for the phone to ring at the other end. "Kathy? Jeff Trask. Do you have the tox results back yet on our latest hooker OD? You do? How do they compare to the other victims? Yeah, that's significant. Do you have a last address for the latest girl? Thanks very much." He ended the call.

"I'm afraid my hunch was right," Trask said. "The first OD cases were all months ago, and while there was a significant amount of dope in the victims' bloodstreams—certainly enough to kill them—those deaths all appear to have been accidental. Those girls were all living in Adipietro's building, too."

Trask looked at Randi. "Your idea is one we need to consider, and it's still a possibility we'll need to follow up on it; we never want to have tunnel vision. The other possibility is this. The new, strong heroin hits town, and lots of working girls like their heroin. The initial deaths are just the result of junkies shooting stronger dope than they were used to using. There's no reason for Tommy Harris to be killing his own hookers, or for Adipietro to be whacking his own tenants."

"The latest one is different?" Carter asked.

"Yeah. She didn't live in the same building, and the amount of dope in her bloodstream was massive. Ten times what Kathy saw in the other dead girls."

"That makes it either a suicide or a hot shot," Wisniewski offered.

"Hot shot?" Randi asked.

"An intentionally fatal dose administered by someone other than the user," Carter explained. "Murder by overdose. I'll call Hammer and put him on that."

"Good idea again, Dix," Doroz said. "Any other thoughts?"

"If the only time Briggs is holding the dope is on the short trip between the racquet club and Harris' place, that's when we have to hit him," Trask said. "If he's actually doing some real work for Adipietro at the club, we can't assume that every time he leaves the joint, he'll be carrying. If we stop him and he's not holding anything, we blow it."

"So wait until he pulls up in front of Harris' house and then call a dope dog?" Wisniewski asked.

"We *could* do that, Tim, but then we might lose the case on Harris," Doroz said.

"Even if we rolled in after seeing Harris walk outside and take a package from Briggs' hands, we wouldn't be able to link him directly to the overdose deaths," Trask observed. "It's just heroin possession at that point, and no witness is saying that any of the victims got the stuff from Harris. At least not yet."

"We could have Hammer start looking at Harris real hard," Carter said. "He wouldn't have to make it look like anything out of the ordinary, or even tied to the dope. It's what Hammer does every day—I mean *night*."

"That's worth a shot," Trask said. "Let's try to make that happen yesterday. See if Hamilton can work us up a new source, if necessary. Maybe one of Harris' girls."

"We'll wake him up this afternoon," Doroz said. "Hammer is back on the squad for a while."

———

Tampico Naval Air Station
Tamaulipas, Mexico
August 4, 2011, 10:00 a.m.

Aguilar and Torres watched the little television monitor in Aguilar's office as the Mexican Secretariat of National Defense in Mexico City announced the continuation of *Operación Lince Norté*, a national initiative targeting *Los Zetas*. The speaker at the podium was trumpeting the seizure in recent weeks of more than 500,000 pesos, and the fact that more than thirty Zeta gunmen had been killed.

"Half a million out of a billion, and thirty out of a thousand or more," Aguilar said. "Drops in the bucket. Still, the politicians need to claim our successes, and the people need to have hope."

———

South of Nuevo Laredo
Tamaulipas, Mexico

Lazcano and Dominguez sat watching the same broadcast on a sixty-inch plasma set in Lazcano's office.

"You would think we were on the ropes and about to surrender." Lazcano rose from his chair and paced around the room. "We need some victories, Ramón. Something significant enough to prevent any doubt in the population that we are invincible. These little setbacks like the one in Zacatecas cannot be allowed to become propaganda tools for Calderón and his marines."

"I understand," Dominguez said. "We are stepping up our training. More rigorous, more structured drills. We have fewer and fewer real Zetas, Lazca. Those like you and me who were trained before we *became* Zetas are slowly disappearing—dead or captured. The new men are not as disciplined, not as brave. We had that bastard Aguilar surrounded in Fresnillo, but our men ran at the first sign of trouble. I had to shoot a couple myself when they would not stand and fight as we ordered."

"It was a good plan, and you are not to blame for its failure, my friend. We need another operation. Hand pick your men this time. Choose those you can trust to behave well in combat." Lazcano nodded toward the television screen. "We will make these stupid politicians eat their words."

———

Tampico Naval Air Station
Tamaulipas, Mexico
August 8, 2011, 3:49 p.m.

"I have three missing, Major. They were not at roll call this morning and there is still no sign of them."

"Who are they, Torres?" Aguilar looked up from his reports.

"Lozano, Gonzalez and Machado, sir."

Aguilar frowned. "Two of the men are new. I don't know them well enough yet to say that they would have never deserted. Corporal Machado has been with us for three years now. The Zetas killed his brother. He would never join them. Something is wrong, Torres."

A sergeant stood in the doorway, waiting for Aguilar to finish speaking. Aguilar noticed him and raised an eyebrow.

"Sorry to disturb you, sir. I think you should turn on your television. There is a disturbing report from Veracruz."

Aguilar grabbed the remote, and the little screen came to life. A pretty little news anchor was introducing a video transmission she claimed had been sent to her station by *Los Zetas*. There were the usual warnings that what was to be shown on the video that followed could be disturbing. For once, they were accurate.

The video showed the faces of four bound captives sitting on the floor of what appeared to be a warehouse somewhere. Aguilar recognized the faces of his three missing marines. The new men appeared to be terrified; Machado's face was one of defiant rage, and shows signs that he'd been beaten.

There was no sound on the video. After focusing on the captured men's faces for several seconds, the camera panned up to a *narcomanta* hanging on the wall behind and above them. The sign listed the captives by name and rank. Aguilar's men were all named, and the fourth prisoner was identified as a naval cadet. The sign indicated that the men would be executed unless all property seized from the Zetas during the past thirty days was returned, and all Zetas held in federal prisons were released. The camera left the sign and returned to the captives, panning slowly across their faces from left to right. As the camera left the face of the last man, there was a flash of light from the right of the screen.

"Did you see that, Torres?" Aguilar asked. "The open door to the right at the end? I saw water and a dock. I know that spot in Veracruz. We can be there in hours. Assemble the men and notify the helicopter crews. I will not desert our men as long as they are drawing breath."

Torres ran from the office. Aguilar began changing to his battle uniform. He was interrupted by the chirp of the cell phone he had just unclipped from his belt.

"Yes, my friend? Do you know the place where they are being held? Have they been moved?"

"I am very sorry, Major. You cannot save them."

"Why not? I know that place. We can—"

"You cannot save them, sir. They are already dead. I have seen their bodies. It is a trap. The open door to the water was shown *hoping* your company would fly down and try to rescue them. The Zetas have hand-held surface-to-air missiles, sir. They are waiting on your helicopters. More marines would die. I have to go, Major."

The phone went dead. Aguilar threw it onto the desk and sank back into his chair, staring at the ceiling.

Torres appeared in the doorway, a confused look on his face. "We can be airborne in twenty minutes, sir."

"Cancel the mission. They are beyond rescue now."

Torres nodded and closed the door.

Aguilar closed his eyes and began mentally drafting the first letter. "*Dear Señora Machado, It is with the heaviest of hearts that I must inform you of the death of your husband . . .*"

Chapter Thirty-Three

Washington, D.C.
August 11, 2011, 11:20 p.m.

Detective Gordon Hamilton pulled to the curb. She was waiting at her usual spot on the track. There was no game this time, as she knew the car by now. She opened the passenger door and got in without hesitation, eager to make more than her usual fee for far less than the usual effort.

"Hey, baby," Bootsy said. "You're getting to be my new favorite regular, you know."

"Happy to help," Hamilton said, passing her the money. He pulled away from the curb. "What can you tell me about Tommy Harris, Boots?"

"He's a pimp, Hammer, you know that."

"I know what I know, Boots, and I'm not stupid enough to think that I know more than I know. What I *need* to know *now* is what *you* know about any connection between Tommy and any of the dead girls."

"Okay. Easy enough. At least three of the first four girls that OD'd were workin' for him. I don't know about that Misty girl, but she was livin' in the same apartments as the other three."

"Did you ever find out who that double date john was that Misty saw the night she died? Ever talk to your friend about that? The one who did the double with Misty?"

"No."

"Think she'd be willing to talk about it now if you asked her?"

"No."

Hamilton looked at her and shook his head. "You ain't really earning your money tonight, Boots."

"I can't talk to her anymore, Hammer. She's dead."

Hamilton pulled into a fast food restaurant parking lot and turned the car's engine off. He turned to face her. "What happened to her?"

"I'm not sure, Hammer. I just know they came and carried her body out of her apartment, and she was all sealed up in one of them body bags. I tried to ask some of your cops on the scene what happened to her, but they wouldn't tell me nuthin'."

"When did that happen, Boots?"

"My birthday. June 23rd. Wasn't a very good birthday. She was as good a friend as I got out here."

"What was her name, Boots? Nobody can hurt her anymore."

"You knew her, Hammer. Her street name was Tiffany. She liked to wear her hair red, with extensions. Pretty thing, or at least she used to be before she hit the track. Her real name was Carol Freeman."

"Yeah, I remember her." Hamilton pulled out a notebook from his pocket and flipped the pages. "Was she into any particular kind of dope?"

"She was just into weed, Hammer, like me. That's one of the reasons we was close. A lot of the other girls didn't really trust you if you didn't smoke their shit with 'em, know what I'm sayin'?"

"Yeah, I know." Hamilton found the entry in the notebook. It was the one he thought it would be—the hot shot victim. "Only she died from a heroin overdose, Boots. That's what the blood work said. A helluva shot, too. A lot more than a normal hit."

"That don't make no sense, Hammer. She was like me. She was scared to death of smack. Specially with all them other girls dyin' from it. It just don't make no sense."

————

South of Nueva Laredo
Tamaulipas, Mexico
August 17, 2011, 10:25 a.m.

"We have another problem, Ramón," Lazcano said. He tossed another steak into the tiger's cage. "I know, Felix, I haven't brought you anything really fresh lately. I was hoping for a certain marine major to entertain you, but he was a coward, and did not want to play with us."

"Some other problem with Aguilar, Lazca?" Dominguez asked as he watched the tiger devour the beef.

"No. Aguilar remains a constant problem. It's the casinos. *Grupo Royale.* They seem to be reneging on our agreement. We have not been paid for the last three months."

"I was told personally that the money would be paid. The casino manager in Monterrey told me that to my face," Dominguez said.

"He lied. The corporation has apparently also failed to get some government permits for remodeling, and their city closed them down for a while. I got a call from a *Grupo* accountant who told me their receipts were down, and they'd try to make it up to us later."

"How did you respond, Lazca?"

"How do you think I responded? I told the pig that his problems were not my concern, but that my problems were certainly *his.* I gave him until midnight on the 25th to make all the payments. 130,000 pesos per week, his license fee for us to allow him to operate. If he does not, we will make an example of his casino."

"Do you wish me to travel to Monterrey?"

"Not this time, Ramón. I need you here. Our old Gulf bosses are hiring soldiers now, trying to reclaim what we took from them. There will be battles to fight here. Send *La Rana.* I just promoted him to be our third in command, behind you and myself. Let's see if I was correct in promoting him."

———

FBI Field Office
Washington, D.C.
August 22, 2011, 9:17 a.m.

"Bootsy told me she wasn't aware of any connection between the Freeman girl—our last OD—and Tommy Harris, but the first three overdose cases *were* all Tommy's girls." Hamilton said. "She also told me that her friend wasn't into using heroin at all."

"That makes the 'hot shot' scenario even more likely," Carter said. "It's not a distribution case, it's a homicide."

"A true 'smack-down'," Wisniewski quipped.

"Jesus, Tim," Lynn said, frowning.

"Sorry, bad joke," he apologized.

"What do we know about Harris, Dix?" Trask asked. "Aside from the fact that he's a pimp?"

"He lives alone in that brownstone. No family that I know of. He'll give his new girls what he calls 'tryouts' before he signs 'em up to his stable, likes to sample the merchandise himself. Gets 'em hooked on the money at first, then gets 'em hooked on the dope of their choice, and makes his own money off his pimp fees *and* the dope. Pretty soon, the girls can't afford to leave him because they're on the hook for the drugs. He's a real sweetheart."

"Where do you figure he's making the drops to his girls?" Doroz asked.

"Probably has 'em come to his car on the street," Carter said. "A quick hand-to-hand in the middle of the night. If we just see an exchange in the dark, he's all too ready to admit that he was making contact with them; he'll admit to being a pimp, but deny any knowledge of the dope. If we bust him for pandering, he's out on bond in an hour or two, and the jail at Lorton is so crowded with more serious cases, no judge is going to try and shoehorn him in there for much of a sentence."

"That means he'll have the dope in the car," Trask said. "How about this, Bear? We tail him and see if we can make a productive stop. Have Hammer make the initial arrest so it looks like just another vice stop, then run a drug dog on the car before we tow it in. We can do an inventory search of the vehicle if nothing else."

"That's the plan, then," Doroz said. "Dix, Randi, Tim, why don't you all head home now and rest up. We'll get with Hammer tonight when he gets in for his regular shift."

———

3:26 p.m.

Clarisse "Bootsy" Yelverton pulled the "rental" next to the curb in front of the brownstone. She had not rented the vehicle in the conventional, commercial sense of the word, but had bought time with the car by passing some of her stash of marijuana to a party driving the car. That party had "rented" it from another party for a quantity of cocaine. The danger of anyone running the plates was slim, given the fact that she wasn't going to be there long, but even if that happened, it would be very difficult to trace the car to her.

She took a moment before leaving the vehicle to gather her courage, and her motivation. She raised her head and spoke to the sky. "Little sister, I promised you I wouldn't tell anyone who you and Misty were with that night. I know you were scared to death of him, and it looks now like you had reason to be. I mean to make that right for you; for you and those other poor girls. Life's hard enough on the track to have to worry about your protection sending you to the grave."

She opened her purse and checked the gun, a compact .38. It was loaded, with a round chambered. She got out of the car and headed for the door. He opened it before she had a chance to ring the bell.

"Well, well, well," Tommy Harris said smiling. "If it isn't the queen of the track. Finally gettin' tired of the dangerous independent life, Bootsy?"

"I thought we'd talk about that, Tommy."

"C'mon in." He led her into the living room. You know my policy, baby. I gotta be *real familiar* with the merchandise I'm offering to my customers."

"I know. I'm gonna make you forget every other girl you ever had, baby."

She reached into her purse.

———

The Casino Royale
Monterrey, Nuevo León, Mexico
August 26, 2011, 3:50 p.m.

Four vehicles—a Mini Cooper, a Chevrolet Equinox, a blue GMC truck, and a gray Volkswagon Beetle—arrived at the entrance to the casino. Nine armed men piled out of the vehicles and stormed inside. One of the Zetas struck the receptionist in the face with the butt of his assault rifle.

"Everybody out! Now!" The one known as *La Rana* waved as a few patrons followed his direction and ran for the door. Many more ran in the opposite direction, seeking refuge in rear bathrooms and stairways. "We are *Los Zetas,* and the management here has proven that they do not recognize our authority."

The Zetas began dousing the walls with gasoline, and *La Rana* tossed a match into the pool on the floor, igniting the inferno. The patrons who had fled toward the rear of the casino tried the emergency exits, but found them locked.

———

Tampico Naval Air Station
Tamaulipas, Mexico
August 27, 2011, 9:12 a.m.

"Fifty-three dead in the casino fire, Major," Torres handed Aguilar the report. "Witnesses on the scene said it was *Los Zetas."*

"Any idea who was in charge of this little massacre?" Aguilar asked.

"Initial intelligence has identified the leader as someone calling himself '*La Rana.*'"

Aguilar nodded. "Carlos Oliva Castillo. My source told me he had been promoted. No sign of Lazcano?"

"None reported, sir. Are we going to Nueva León, Major?"

"Not this time, Torres. The president has ordered three thousand troops and federal police to the city. The rest of the state is being patrolled by Black Hawks—the helicopters we bought from the Americans. I imagine it's quite a dragnet. What have you learned about the victims?"

"Ten men, forty-two women. Two were pregnant. Most died from inhaling poisonous fumes. Only seven were actually burned. I don't have any word on their identities yet."

"Thank you, Torres. Keep me informed if there were any relatives of our men among the dead. They may need some leave to take care of their loved ones."

FBI Field Office
Washington, D.C.
August 29, 2011, 10:15 a.m.

Trask knocked on the frame of the open door to Barry Doroz' office.

"Morning, Bear. You said we had a major setback?"

Doroz didn't say a word, but handed Trask a police report. Trask sat down in one of the black plastic chairs facing the desk and scanned the paper. *Officers responded after neighbors complained of a foul odor emanating from the residence. After ringing the doorbell and receiving no response, entry was forced into the residence. The body of the sole occupant of the home, Tommy R. Harris, black male, DOB 07/15/1980, was found on the floor of the living room in an advanced state of decomposition. The deceased was transported to the office of the medical examiner. Autopsy revealed the cause of death to be a single gunshot wound to the head.*

Trask looked up at Doroz. "Guess that explains why we haven't been able to find him to follow him. Any leads on the shooter?"

"Nope. If I find him, I think we'll bill that citizen for our overtime last week, and then maybe give him a medal. Where does that leave us for now?"

"I'm thinking of a song: 'The Bug,'" Trask said. "You heard of Mark Knopfler? Dire Straits?"

"I know the band."

"'Sometimes you're the windshield. Sometimes you're the bug.' I feel a lot like a bug right now."

Chapter Thirty-Four

FBI Field Office
Washington, D.C.
August 31, 2011, 11:14 a.m.

"They can't stop making their deliveries," Carter said. "Tommy or no Tommy. They'll either have to find another distributor, or our friend Roscoe will have to pick up the slack. Heroin's too addictive for them to just cease operations. Every junky customer they have will be going into withdrawal—not a pretty sight if you've never seen it—and starting to act crazy out of desperation. They'll have to keep things calm, and keep their money flowing."

"Briggs is the most likely target at the moment," Doroz agreed. "We need to decide where and when to pick him off. It'll have to be the right time and place or we still risk blowing the case up completely. If he's not holding when we hit him, he'll run straight to his boss."

"Just a couple of questions, and maybe some ridiculous thoughts first," Trask said. "Dix, you've seen the homicide file. First, did the guys on the scene get Harris' phone, and second, did he keep any records of which girls worked for him?"

"The answers, respectively, are yes and yes."

"My third question, then, is this: Does anyone—Metro PD, FBI, whoever— have an undercover asset who could fill the void left by the untimely death of Mr. Harris?"

"What on earth are you thinking, Jeff?" Doroz asked. "Plug a UC in cold?"

"If done correctly, with the right, street-wise undercover cop, it wouldn't look cold even to Roscoe Briggs. Our UC moves into Harris' house. We pay the rent. He starts contacting the hookers first. We have a roster and probably contacts for them from the phone and other notes. UC tells the working girls that he's Tommy's cousin, and is taking over his business, same terms. That word gets back to Roscoe from one or more of the girls. If Roscoe is as nervous as I think he is about making the dope deliveries himself, he'll be glad to offer our new pimp an opportunity to make some more money on the side."

"Why do you think Roscoe's nervous about handling the dope himself?" Rhodes asked. "Just trying to learn the ropes here."

"Because he hasn't been doing it all along," Trask replied. "In the dope game, every level in the distribution chain costs money. It's why customers try to cut out their plugs and deal directly with that plug's supplier. They get the same amount for less because they're not paying another middleman. If Roscoe wasn't hinky about carrying the stuff, he could make more cash just doing it himself. Tommy Harris was either cutting the dope or raising the price—or both—before it went to the hookers. He wasn't working for free. Roscoe wasn't willing to do that himself for some reason."

"You think Briggs will buy that?" Wisniewski asked. "What about the club owner, Adipietro?"

"Odds are that Joe the tennis pro doesn't even know about Harris," Doroz said. "He's interested in insulation. We can't trace something directly to him if he didn't know about it. We have to go through Briggs to get to Adipietro, then through Adipietro to get to his suppliers."

"I know a guy in homicide," Carter said. "He just got there from Georgetown. He hasn't worked vice, so the girls on the track won't know him. If he's willing, he'd fit the bill."

"There's one big rub, maybe two," Doroz said. "I'm sorry to have to be the bureaucrat in the room, but first, what do we do when we get the dope, and two, is the Metropolitan Police Department going to be okay with us using one of their assets as a pimp?"

"If we get the dope, let's check the weight," Trask said. "A hundred grams of heroin gets the distributer—in this case, Briggs handing it to the UC—a mandatory minimum of five years. If we get lucky and he hands off a kilo, it's ten years. If we get some recorded conversation to establish the history of this thing, you know, the past deliveries to Tommy, the weight in the past deals drives the sentence a lot higher, even without proof that it was their dope that killed the victims. That's some leverage to throw at a first timer like Briggs with no prison record, especially at his age. He might well roll over on Adipietro.

"We don't even have to pay for the dope—or let it hit the street—if Briggs trusts the UC; it's probably getting handed off on consignment. Briggs gets paid after the hookers pay their pimp. If we have to pick up some cash from the working girls for the tricks they're doing, we can pay them back later if the police department gets queasy."

"A pimp rebate?" Wisniewski asked. "That's new."

"We're in uncharted waters, gang," Trask said. "This isn't 'out of the box,' it's off the map. I know that. We all know that if we have to make any payments to Briggs for the dope, we can record the bills and maybe find some of 'em back in Adipietro's mitts. That wouldn't hurt the case. We hold the dope for evidence."

"I might find enough money—with approval from up the chain—to go one or two rounds on that," Doroz said. "No more. Once we get enough for a sizeable charge on Roscoe, we'll have to move. Nobody in my chain of command is going to like paying thousands to Adipietro or the Zetas."

"If you have any trouble with that, let me know," Trask said. "I know a certain senator who's willing to intervene on our behalf."

"What about the girls going through withdrawal?" Lynn asked. "Are we giving them anything to prevent that?"

"We can't be in that business," Doroz said. "She's got you there, Jeff."

"Yes, she does," Trask said, smiling at his wife. "We can't be responsible for any overdoses ourselves, so we can't push the dope to the customers. We hold it for evidence, and hope we get enough dope and conversation from our initial contact with Briggs to charge him. The addicts will have to deal with their addictions on their own terms. Briggs is probably keeping them from their withdrawal pains at the moment."

"We'll need to move on this yesterday," Carter said. "I'll run over to homicide. We'll sign our man up and plug him in. I kind of like the idea."

"Speaking of homicide, any leads on the Harris murder, Dix?" Wisniewski asked.

"Nothing, from what I hear," Carter replied. "That file is on a fast track to the cold case shelves."

———

Washington, D.C.
September 12, 2011, 1:18 a.m.

"Hit your lights and siren and stay behind him long enough to make him think we're on him," Carter said. "We just want to heat him up."

"Yeah, I got it," Rhodes replied, shooting a look at Carter. "You're lucky I don't have a cup of coffee."

She was back in her patrol uniform, and they had borrowed a marked patrol cruiser for the night. She activated the equipment and waited for the van—about forty yards ahead—to pull over. She kept a constant speed, and veered just enough into the parking lane behind the van to give the driver reason to sweat before she steered back into the center right traffic lane and shot by him, pretending to be on the way to another call.

Inside the van, Roscoe Briggs was sweating profusely. He waited until he was sure that the police cruiser had gone by before he felt his heart rate start to slow. He sat for a moment, and finally reached for the small duffle bag that he'd kicked under his seat. His hands were shaking.

Three blocks ahead, Officer Rhodes made a right turn, then cut the lights and siren.

"Perfect," Carter said. "Let's do this again sometime. Like a couple of nights from now."

———

Tampico Naval Air Station
Tamaulipas, Mexico
September 15, 2011, 2:15 p.m.

"We have a report from a little town in Zacatecas, Major," Torres said. "It's called Juchipila. There are apparently eighty gunmen there who've seized the town and are claiming that they are there to wipe out any Zetas in the area."

"My source with the Zetas reported that they were expecting a fight with their old bosses from the Gulf Cartel," Aguilar said. "And so it begins. It would not be a problem if they'd just kill each other, but there are citizens to protect. Get the men ready. I'll see what assets might be available in the area. We'll be in the air to join them as soon as the choppers are fueled. We can form up outside the town and move in after dark."

———

Washington, D.C.
8:38 p.m.

Detective Jerry Winstead of the Metropolitan Police Department switched on the digital device hooked to his belt as he looked through the curtains of the brownstone. The device was designed to appear to be a smart phone, and could actually function as a cell phone if anyone checked, but its purpose for the next few minutes would be two-fold—to record any conversation that Detective Winstead might be having with the driver of the vehicle that had just pulled to the curb, and to transmit that conversation to another van waiting a block away. Winstead noted the lettering on the truck at the curb.

"Metro Maintenance Services. Here we go, Dix."

Winstead waited for the doorbell to ring. He shuffled to the door as if he'd just been awakened from a not-long-enough night's sleep. *Gotta look like I'm keeping pimp hours.* He opened the door to face a man wearing a shirt with a name embroidered in an oval over the right breast pocket. *Roscoe. Bingo.*

"Yeah? Help you with something?" Winstead asked.

"I'm lookin' for Tommy," Briggs said.

"Bullshit. I know who you are, and I know you know Tommy's dead. He told me 'bout you, Briggs, so get the hell off my porch."

"Easy, okay?" Briggs said, flashing his most apologetic smile. "I was just bein' careful, my man. Now who are *you*? What are you doin' livin' in Tommy's house, and what exactly did he tell you about me?"

"I'm his cousin, I'm takin' over his business, and he told me that it was your smack that was the reason he was havin' to recruit a bunch of new ho's to pay his bills. So why don't you get the hell off my porch?" *Like you said, Dix, best way to put 'em off guard is to make 'em think you don't want nuthin' to do with 'em.*

"Easy now, easy," Briggs said. "I may have a business proposition that might interest you."

"Business is goin' just fine, and it's goin' to get better. I don't need you or any bad dope complicatin' my life or my girls' lives right now, so—"

"How much of a complication would an extra five grand a week be?"

Winstead stepped back from the door, looking as if someone had just shown him a unicorn. *"What the hell did you just say?"*

"Five grand a week."

Winstead looked up and down the street as if he was checking for police surveillance. He looked back at Briggs. "Come on in."

They sat on opposite sides of the living room, Winstead still appearing skeptical.

"What's the deal?" he asked Briggs.

"Same deal I had with Tommy before he died. I supply the white, you piece it out to the girls, collect the money, keep your cut, and I'll be around to collect. Speaking of cut, you can step on the stuff before you hand it out. Cut it to fifty percent pure if you want and double your money. Makes no difference to me long as I get paid."

"I ain't into putting' nobody in the ground, even if it's just ho's. That ain't good for business, or stayin' outta the joint."

"That never has to happen, know what I'm sayin'? Tommy's girls that OD'd just didn't know how to use the product correctly. Once we got the word to 'em on the right amounts to shoot, everything was cool. We didn't have no problems at all after that."

"You sure?"

"Hell, yes, we went through a half a key a week to his bitches and other customers, and never had an issue or a complaint. When it's done right it's safe, and the money's real good, brutha."

"I'm still not too sure 'bout this. How much would I need to put together to start?"

"Not a dime. I'll front it to you. You pay me when *you* get paid. Just turn the stuff around quick. We've got other customers askin' for it, if you can't handle the job."

"I can handle it. Tommy told me about it. I used to stay with him some, but he didn't want you seein' me. He said that woulda made you nervous."

"He was right."

"When do we start?"

"Now if you want. The shit's in the van."

"Fine."

Briggs walked out the door and bounced down the steps from the porch to his van. He walked around to the driver's door, and was about to open it when he saw a police cruiser, its lights flashing and siren wailing, skid around the corner and head in his direction. He stepped close to the van, expecting it to pass him. Instead, the unit pulled in behind his truck just as two unmarked cars and another van pulled in front and beside his truck, boxing him in.

A female cop in uniform was out of the squad car in seconds, pointing a gun in his face and ordering him to the ground.

———

Juchipila, Zacatecas, Mexico
9:48 p.m.

"They all appear to have left yesterday, Torres," Aguilar said, walking out of the little town's administrative building. "The mayor says that the Gulf troops took over his city hall for about five hours, made all their proclamations, and then drove off."

"Kind of a wild goose chase for us, sir."

"It appears that way. If this is the worst the new Gulf bad asses can do, Lazcano will feed them to his damned cats. Let's go back to base."

———

FBI Field Office
Washington, D.C.
11:34 p.m.

Trask turned off the recorder. Roscoe Briggs sat across the table in the same interrogation room where he had answered questions from Carter and Wisniewski months before. This time he was in handcuffs, he had been read his Miranda warnings, waived them, and he had listened to his entire conversation with a man he now knew to be an undercover cop, not Tommy Harris' cousin.

"I just have one question for you, Mr. Briggs," Trask said, "and I'm not here to dance with you. This is the way it is, and there's no doubt about any of it. I wouldn't even be having this conversation with you if I didn't know that there are others out there who are at least equally guilty of killing five women with this poison—" Trask picked up the package of white powder and slammed it down on the table, "and probably more guilty of blowing up seventeen others. Your choices are cooperation, and by that I mean total, truthful, and *right now* cooperation, or life in a federal pen. What'll it be?"

"How much time do I serve if I help you?"

"You're forty-one now. Even if you do cooperate fully, you've got so much blood on your hands that no judge in our courthouse is going to sign off on a deal for less than thirty years. Keep your nose clean on the inside and you'll serve about eighty-five percent of that. You'll at least be out by your full social security age, if there's anything left in the fund. Otherwise, you've seen your last free sunrise."

"What do you want to know?"

Chapter Thirty-Five

"I hear you had a late night, Jeff. I wasn't expecting to see you in this early."

Ross Eastman offered Trask a cup of coffee from the machine behind his desk. Trask took it.

"Thanks. I'll probably have several of these today."

"What's next?"

"We have a criminal complaint filed charging Adipietro with the heroin conspiracy and also a search warrant for the racquet club. According to Briggs, there are at least two more pounds of heroin in one of the lockers."

"Are we going to offer Adipietro any slack for help with the truck bomb at the convenience store?"

"That's your call. You're the boss. I'd wait and see whether he's even interested in that. He may not be. He's supposed to be old school mob."

"He'll do life if he doesn't cooperate."

"Some of them don't. If he runs something up the flagpole, we'll get the details before we sign up for anything. No promises in advance."

"Good. When do you plan on briefing Senator Heidelberg?"

"After Adipietro's in cuffs. We'll indict him in the next grand jury, we'll forfeit the club property for facilitation of drug trafficking since he used the place to stash the heroin, and I'll hit him with a substitute asset count so that we can recoup any money he made from selling that junk. Whatever amount he made, he'll owe that back to the government."

"That wraps up everything downstream to the prostitutes. What about Heidelberg's daughter and the bombing victims? Let's not forget about them."

A rueful smile crossed Trask's face. "No, let's not."

———

1:15 p.m.

Trask stood outside The Dome Racquet Club next to Barry Doroz.

"They're bringing him out now, Jeff." Doroz clicked a button on the radio. "I let Dix and Randi handle this one. The heroin was in the locker, right where Briggs said it would be. A full kilo."

Trask saw the side door open. Wisniewski came out first, carrying a small gym bag that Trask figured contained the heroin. Carter and Rhodes followed, flanking a small man dressed entirely in white. White tennis shoes, socks, shorts, and a tennis sweater with red trim. Joe Adipietro hardly looked the part of a heroin dealing mobster. Trask walked over to the transport van that was waiting to take the new defendant to the marshals' lockup. Adipietro looked him over and stopped a few feet away.

"You the DA? Trask?" Adipietro's strong Brooklyn accent and deep baritone sounded like it should have come from a much larger man.

"I'm an Assistant United States Attorney. This is a federal case. Have you been read your rights?"

"Yeah. I heard all that stuff. I just got one question for ya. Who ratted me out? Was it that white bread pussy from the Hill?"

Trask couldn't help but look puzzled for an instant. "You'll get your answer when your attorney gets the discovery in the case."

"I saw your face. It wasn't him. That's funny. I always figured he was the one who'd do it. Whaddaya know."

_____

Hart Senate Office Building
4:45 p.m.

"Anything pointing to Janie's killer in all this mess?" Heidelberg asked.

"No, Senator, not yet." *He said Janie's 'killer.' That's the first time I've heard him call her dealer her killer.*

"That's disappointing, but you're still to be congratulated for today's events. As you've always reminded me, there have been other victims of this ring. What kind of sentence do you expect this guy to get?"

"I will ask for life imprisonment, and in this case, I expect to get it. We have at least five dead from the heroin alone, and reason to believe that it was his ties to the Zetas that resulted in the truck bomb at the store."

"And none of that includes Janie."

"Not yet, Senator."

"I know, Mr. Trask. You won't forget her. I appreciate that."

Trask nodded. "One question, sir. When we arrested Adipietro at the club, he mentioned someone on 'the Hill.' Are you aware of anyone in the Capitol who's had a heroin problem recently?"

"No," Heidelberg said. "I'll keep on the alert for that, if it might help."

"Thank you, Senator. It might."

_____

Boca del Rio, Veracruz, Mexico
September 20, 2011, 5:00 p.m.

Hundreds of drivers and passengers following two flatbed trucks were forced to stop and watch in horror as the trucks stopped on the Manuel Avila Camacho Boulevard in the middle of rush hour traffic. Gunmen from pickup trucks accompanying the flatbeds jumped out and began pulling bodies from the trucks and spreading them across the road. The gunmen then hung a *narcomanta* from an overpass. The sign read, "This will happen to all the Zeta shit that stay in Veracruz. The Plaza has a new owner. G.N."

———

Tampico Naval Air Station
Tamaulipas, Mexico
6:20 p.m.

"What do you make of this, Major?" Torres asked as the two men looked at the television in Aguilar's office.

"Apparently, the Gulf braggarts from Zacatecas may have some bite to go with their bark," Aguilar replied. "The 'G.N.' on the sign refers to the *Gente Nueva*, a group of thugs who work for Guzmán and the Sinaloa/Federation Cartel."

"That would confirm that some of the old Gulf bosses are now with Chapo."

"Correct." Aguilar nodded. "I just hung up with one of the Army commanders on the scene. They have thirty-five dead. Twenty-three men and twelve women, all linked to *Los Zetas*. Unfortunately, Lazcano was not among them. The victims had been bound and gagged, most of them tortured, and shot in the head. As my American wife likes to say, sometimes what goes around comes around. We will not mourn these dead, but we should be prepared if the cartel wars are escalating in our sector."

"Any particular instructions, Major?"

"Of course." Aguilar said, shaking his head. "Be prepared for the announcement of another grand government *operación* in response. The war has come to Veracruz, Torres. That will mean that *we* will go to Veracruz."

———

555 4th Street, N.W.
Washington, D.C.
September 23, 2011, 9:57 a.m.

"Trask." The desk phone's caller ID light was out, so Trask was cautious.

"Harold Lewis, Mr. Trask. I've been retained to represent Joseph Adipietro."

"My condolences."

"I'm sorry to hear you feel that way. I've always found Joe to be a rather refreshing change of pace from some of my other clients. He's always been very direct with me."

"I'd appreciate it if you'd do the same, Mr. Lewis. What can I do for you?"

"Of course. Direct it is. Any offers I can convey to my client?"

"I've got five dead from his dope, Mr. Lewis. What kind of offer do you think would be appropriate under those circumstances?"

"There's always a bigger fish to fry."

"Then talk to your client and let me know what—or whom—he wants to put in the frying pan."

"Thanks. I'll do that. Not for attribution?"

"Of course not. He tells you, you tell me, and I can't use it against him. But one thing . . ."

"Yes?"

"He'd better be talking Hitler's meaner brother or I won't be interested."

"I understand."

———

Waldorf, Maryland
11:00 p.m.

The phone was answered on the fourth ring.

"Hello, Jeff?"

"Yes, Luis. Glad I caught you. I was about to hang up."

"I just got out of the shower. A cold one. My water heater picked tonight to stop working."

"That always sucks."

"It certainly does. What's up?"

"I just wanted to let you know that we've been able to cut off your Zetas' cash flow—from Washington, anyway. We weren't able to follow the trail up the coast. Your information helped a great deal. Without it, I might still have a closed investigation and nothing to show for it."

"That's wonderful news, my friend. Wonderful. I'm happy we could be of service to each other. Let's stay in touch."

"Let's do that. Good night, Luis. Please give my best to Linda."

"I will. Good night."

Chapter Thirty-Six

555 4ᵗʰ Street, N.W.
Washington, D.C.
September 26, 2011, 10:21 a.m.

The desk phone's ring pulled Trask's eyes off of his paperwork. "Jeff Trask."

"Mr. Trask, Harold Lewis again. I had an opportunity to speak to Mr. Adipietro over the weekend. He is not willing to cooperate against anyone else."

"Can't say I'm surprised, given his history."

"Yes, it's the mob connection thing. He said that he's the one who has to look in the mirror every day, and he can't be staring back at a rat."

"How noble. Then he can stare at whatever he calls himself for the rest of his life."

"You're still not willing to tender any plea offers?"

"None."

"As I told you before, he's direct with me. I do know that he has some significant information on at least one fatality. Would it do me any good to press him on that?"

"Is the person he's not willing to talk about *upstream* or *downstream*, Mr. Lewis?"

"I don't follow you."

"Assuming this is a drug-related fatality that we're talking about, did he give the dope to somebody who then caused the death, or does this information concern someone who was supplying your client with drugs?"

"The former; I guess what you called 'downstream.'"

"Then I'm not interested. I'm not putting a bass on the hook to try and catch a minnow, Mr. Lewis. No deals, even if he decides he's willing to give up this downstream guy."

"I see. That may mean a trial, then. It'll cost a lot of money to try this case. He's got nothing to lose."

"Don't bluff me, Lewis." Trask felt his blood rising. "And don't hand me that hooey about it costing a lot to try this case. I won't get paid any extra for it and neither will the judge or most of my witnesses—the cops and agents. We're all on salary and make the same money whether we're in trial or not. The press always blows up these costs, but it's funny money, already spent. The cops get a little overtime and we'll have to pay some juror fees, and that's about it. It'll cost the same to warehouse your client for the rest of his life whether he goes down on a plea or a verdict."

"You're that confident of your case?"

"Absolutely. And one more thing. I know it's another myth around the mob that the mafia isn't in the dope business. They always *have* been, whether the dope *du jour* was booze or heroin, but I also know that some of the crime families take their mythology seriously, and they won't be happy to have your client's antics blasted all over the front pages of the papers for weeks in a row. Anyway, it doesn't matter to me. Your call. Just let me know how Little Joe wants to proceed."

"Little Joe?"

"That's what we call him now."

"That's a bit insulting."

"I hope so. Goodbye, Mr. Lewis."

Trask hung up the phone. *Sorry, Senator, I'm not getting there that way.*

———

Boca del Rio, Veracruz, Mexico
October 7, 2011, 8:18 a.m.

"We've caught eight of Guzman's men, Major." Captain Torres stood by the passenger door of the car carrying his commander. "They have confessed to being involved in the murders of *Los Zetas*."

"Good work, Torres. Any more bodies from the feud?"

"Thirty-six in three houses last night, sir. Another ten this morning scattered across the state, according to the reporting units."

"That's more than a hundred the past two weeks. Who's winning, Torres, Guzmán's Federation, or *Los Zetas*?"

"I'd call it a draw, based upon the tattoos we've seen on the corpses."

"Good. If they fight a war of attrition, and no innocents are caught in the middle, it's good for us all."

E. Barrett Prettyman Federal Courthouse
Washington, D.C.
10:00 a.m.

Just another arraignment, and the news vultures haven't caught on yet that nothing will actually happen. Trask scanned the spectators' section of the courtroom, noting that virtually every seat was filled with the ample backside of some variety of reporter. *Rafferty from one paper, Kirby from the other one. I count two radio stations, four TV outlets from D.C., more from Baltimore. Amazing coverage for a non-event.*

"Do you understand the charges against you, Mr. Adipietro?" Chief Magistrate Judge Thomas Noble asked.

"Yes." Adipietro spoke softly. Only the microphone in front of him made it possible for his mumbles to be heard.

"And how does your client plead, Mr. Lewis?" Noble asked.

"We're pleading not guilty today, Your Honor, but my client has directed me to schedule a change of that plea before Judge King as soon as possible." Lewis glanced at Trask from the defense table, and gave a slight shrug.

I'll be damned, Trask thought. *That's the closest to a guilty plea at an arraignment I'll ever see. I guess the mob bosses got the word to the little jerk that they didn't want the bad press.*

"Pleas of not guilty will be entered today, then," Noble said, "and I'll leave it to counsel to schedule the disposition with Judge King's chambers. We're in recess."

Trask left the courthouse through a rear entrance, avoiding the press, and walked back toward his office. *No point in telling the reporters that I can't tell 'em anything yet. They can call our public affairs guys.*

He made his way through Judiciary Square and stopped at the National Law Enforcement Officers' Memorial to gaze briefly at the names of Juan Ramirez and Robert Lassiter etched in the stone wall. *Looks like we won another one today, guys. As always, thanks for the help. Anytime I need a buck-up or some motivation, you're always here.*

The light on his phone was flashing again when he entered his office. The recorded message indicated Eastman wanted to see him.

Trask winked at Julia Forrest as he walked by her desk. She gave him a warning nod toward Eastman's office as he passed. When he cleared the doorway, he saw why. Eastman was not alone.

"Hello, Digger."

"Hello, Jeff," Senator Graves was flashing his biggest campaign grin. "I stopped by to congratulate you on the Adipietro arrest. I knew if anyone could clean this up, you could."

"Thanks. We're not done yet."

"Yes, I know, those poor people at the store."

"And Janie Heidelberg."

"Oh, you haven't been able to tie Adipietro to Janie's death?"

"Not yet."

"I see." Graves looked puzzled. "I just assumed you'd cleared that, too. I haven't been to any of your meetings with Senator Heidelberg recently."

"I know, Digger," Trask said. "That was at my request." Trask looked past Graves at Eastman, whose face looked like he was searching for a bomb shelter.

"Why the hell would you do that?" Graves asked angrily.

"Because I haven't been able to clear you as a suspect yet."

"*A suspect?* Are you accusing me of giving the heroin to that girl, Jeff?"

"Of course not," Trask said calmly. *Just like I'm back at the Academy in a hazing session. Always keep calm, and make the upperclassman do the work.* "You know how this works, Digger. Everyone who knew the victim remains a suspect until they get cleared. You've seen the drill dozens of times. You never accuse anyone until you're sure, until you're ready to convict. Up until that point, you could be dead wrong, and you never want to *falsely* accuse anyone. That could have disastrous consequences for everyone concerned. If and when I'm ready to accuse *anyone* of involvement in Janie's death, I'll bring the cops and some handcuffs."

Graves said nothing, but glared at Trask as he stormed out of the office.

"That was fun," Eastman said when the senator was gone.

"It really *was*, for me," Trask said. "I don't think he'll be interfering for a while."

"And what exactly was the purpose of that little exchange? *With a United State Senator?*"

"An old military ploy," Trask said. "When in doubt, fire for effect. Sometimes it flushes the enemy out."

———

FBI Field Office
Washington, D.C.
4:39 p.m.

"Anything of note in that safe deposit box at the bank?" Doroz asked. "That *was* what the key in his desk was for, right?"

"Yep." Wisniewski picked up a cardboard box from the end of the table. "The warrant was good enough for the bank to hand over everything. I'm sorting through and tagging all the evidence now. There are some ledgers. Looks like Little Joe was pretty meticulous about his accounts, whether it was for rent or dope debts. He tried to use some code, but it's not an enigma machine. Easy to crack. Once you know the going price for a gram on the street, everything lines up—numbers and weights—even if he does refer to them as 'tennis lessons.'"

"What about that?" Doroz pointed to a computer disc lying on the table beside the box.

"I just looked at a minute of it, then I turned it off," Wisniewski said. "It looks like a surveillance video of Joe's office at the club. Nobody was in the room for the part I saw. Since our warrant was for cash and financial records I was nervous about watching any more of it."

"Good call," Doroz said. "Just mark it and seal it. You agree, Dix?"

"Sounds good," Carter said as he fed bills into a machine. "Looks like we have something north of $100,000 here, if the counter's accurate. We've paid *my* salary for the year anyway."

Chapter Thirty-Seven

"Your man on the inside has proven his value once again, Major. His tip was dead on. *La Rana*, the Zeta who led the attack on the casino in Monterrey, was captured yesterday in Saltillo."

"If anything ever happens to me, Torres, you must take this second phone on my belt," Aguilar said, patting the cell holster. "He is the bravest man I know. We'll have to be careful not to over-utilize his information, or Lazcano may figure out that he has a spy in his camp."

"It's Saturday, Major. You haven't taken a day off in weeks. If you'd like to go home, I can cover the office alert duty today."

"No, you go home, *Capitán*. You are the one with a family to go home to. I'll stay."

"I'll check back in the morning then, sir."

South of Nuevo Laredo
Tamaulipas, Mexico
10:46 a.m.

"I am sick of losing men to these Gulf bastards, Ramón," Lazcano said, throwing the newspaper to the floor. "I want you to organize another mission. Take as many good men as you need, make sure they are ready, and hit Guzmán hard. Keep him off balance. The last raid into Federation territory kept their heads down for weeks. It is time to remind them that they are not safe anywhere."

"It will be a pleasure, Lazca. This time, I suggest that we hit them in Sinaloa itself, not in a neighboring state."

"A good suggestion. Just make sure your raid is a success. If it is not, it will only embolden the enemy, and we will have to fight harder just to defend our own plazas."

"There will be no failure, Lazca. Within a month, we will drive the Federation mice back into their burrows."

————

Waldorf, Maryland
11:30 a.m.

Trask rolled over and put his arm over Lynn, who was still sleeping soundly. He kissed her cheek and then climbed out of the bed and headed for the den, where three elevated dog bowls of varied sizes awaited, each with a hungry animal sitting patiently beside it.

"Sorry guys, I didn't mean to keep you waiting this long on breakfast."

It looks like the three bears live here, a big bowl for Boo, a medium-sized bowl for Nikki, and a baby bowl for Tasha the perma-puppy. He mixed some of the expensive canned stuff with the expensive dry stuff, and the dogs were soon cleaning their bowls while he sat on an arm of the couch and watched.

"I can't believe you let me sleep this late. It's almost noon." Lynn was standing behind him, an oversized tee shirt serving as her pajamas.

"We both needed it. We haven't been able to relax in weeks with all the pressure from this case."

"Will you be able to take a break now?"

"For a while. We have the sentencing hearings coming up for Briggs and Adipietro. After that we're back to looking for leads on the Heidelberg girl and the truck bomb."

"Anything promising? It seems like we've exhausted everything we have for now."

"That's because we have. I don't have any ideas at the moment. I'm kind of at the mercy of Luis Aguilar. I promised him I wouldn't move on anyone in the cartel until he had his shot at them first."

"How long will you give him?"

He stood and walked over to her, holding her and kissing her neck. "As long as he wants," he said. He grabbed her hand and headed back toward the bedroom.

"Are you still sleepy?" she asked.

"Nope, not a bit."

Tampico Naval Air Station
Tamaulipas, Mexico
November 25, 2011, 11:34 a.m.

"How are you, Jorge? It has been a while since we talked," Aguilar said, pressing the speakerphone button so that Torres could hear the call.

"Not bad, Luis, but I'd be better if you'd keep your Zetas on your side of Mexico. They're stirring up all kinds of trouble for me at the moment."

"Really? Zetas in Sinaloa? That's news to me, Jorge."

"Either that, or someone is doing their dirty work for them and hanging *narcomantas* to give them credit for it. We found twenty-three bodies in abandoned cars and trucks two days ago. They were all Guzmán's men. Sixteen of them had been burned to death."

"That sounds like Lazcano's number two. Ramón Dominguez. They call him '*El Ratón.*' I've heard that he favors fire as a method of execution."

"Our men in Jalisco found twenty-six more bodies yesterday in Guadalahara. All Sinaloa guys again. It seems as if your Zetas are working their way down the west coast."

"Probably in response to Guzmán's raids over here," Aguilar said. "Lazcano couldn't just stand by and defend Nuevo Laredo without pushing back hard. Maybe these raids will actually calm things down a bit for a little while."

"A Christmas lull, Luis?"

"Wishful thinking on my part, I'm sure. We should be so lucky."

"Stay alert and safe, Major."

"You too, Jorge."

———

E. Barrett Prettyman Federal Courthouse
Washington, D.C.
December 22, 2011, 10:00 a.m.

"Your objections to the Presentence Investigation Report are overruled, Mr. Lewis," Judge Edie King said, looking down from her bench. "I have heard the testimony of Mr. Briggs, and while I understand that he is trying to earn the relatively light sentence of thirty years granted to him by the government, I find that he is credible, and substantially corroborated by the government's other evidence, including—but not limited to—the drug ledgers which were found in your client's safe deposit box. The defendant and counsel will rise and come to the lectern."

Here you go, Little Joe, Trask said to himself. *Merry Christmas.* He made eye contact across the table with Barry Doroz, who was sitting with him as the lead case agent. Doroz nodded. *Bear knows it's a done deal. Edie King won't give an inch on this one.*

"You and others who distributed this poison on our streets are responsible for a minimum—*and I do mean a minimum*—of five deaths, Mr. Adipietro.

And while Mr. Trask didn't say it, because he can only assert in this court what he can back up with proof, I strongly suspect that other members of your conspiracy are responsible for that hell that erupted near Georgetown and killed so many others. I am not sentencing you for those deaths, however. I am sentencing you for what the proof here has established, and that is this:

"You may not have intended to kill these women who died using your heroin, but you killed them just as if you had put a gun to their heads and pulled the trigger. Even worse, you continued to sell this garbage long after you became aware of the first overdose death, showing me that you have no regard at all for anything other than your own pocketbook.

"The maximum sentence that I am allowed to impose is life imprisonment without the possibility of release, and that is the sentence that you have earned. I am also ordering the forfeiture of the racquet club that you used to facilitate these crimes, as well as the sum of three million dollars, which is a plausible estimate of the street value of the heroin that you sold in this city. You have ten days to file a notice of appeal, should you desire to do so."

The judge rapped her gavel a little louder than Trask was used to hearing.
"We are adjourned."

———

Zapata, Texas
December 24, 2011, 6:07 a.m.

Aguilar bent over the bed and kissed her. She awoke and threw her arms around his neck, holding him as tightly as she could.

"You made it, Luis." She kissed him hard, then pulled back a little, holding his face in her hands. "Which way did you come this time?"

"Through my home town, as usual."

She sat up in bed, angry at him. "Nuevo Laredo is also the home plaza for *Los Zetas*. It is the most dangerous city in Mexico, Luis."

"Only for those who do not know it well. If the Zetas were looking for me, they would have a road block on the highway into town from Reynosa. I got off the highway before I got into town and went through the back streets. No problem."

"At least you are here. That's all I need for now."

He kissed her again. "Merry Christmas, my love."

———

South of Nuevo Laredo
Tamaulipas, Mexico
January 3, 2012, 3:45 p.m.

"How much money are we losing because of the arrests in our D.C. market?" Lazcano asked.

"It is minor, Lazca. Our friend in Laredo was still able to make his deliveries to New York, but we are down about a third in terms of weight and profits on his run. We still have our other couriers making deliveries into Chicago and elsewhere."

"Instruct him to increase the deliveries to New York or some other place to make up the difference. Tell him if he does not do so, he can be replaced. Leave no doubt in his mind as to what that will mean."

"I understand."

Chapter Thirty-Eight

Brooklyn, New York
April 30, 2012, 1:27 a.m.

"Sorry, bud, but I just can't handle this much weight right now. Here's what I owe ya for the seven, and here's the three pounds I couldn't move. You'll just have to take them back with you. You're lucky I'm still dealin' with ya at all, after Joe and his guy got grabbed in D.C. My capo here was hell-bent on tellin' me to pull the plug completely. If it wasn't for the money we're makin' he would have told ya to stay home."

"Thanks. See you next trip."

"Yeah, if there is a next trip. I'll keep ya posted."

The broker nodded, and carried the bag back to his car. The alley was dark, so he had time to pull back the ice and meat and bury the bag at the bottom of the cooler. Once the ice was smoothed back over on top, he shut the lid.

How the hell am I gonna unload the other three pounds?

———

Nuevo Laredo
Tamaulipas, Mexico
May 4, 2012, 12:45 a.m.

The broker pulled his car to the shoulder of Mexican Federal Highway 85D and gazed up in horror and disgust. The bodies of nine people—seven men and two women—were hanging from nooses tied to the overpass above him, next to a large sheet of plastic. The plastic was weighted at the bottom by three ropes tied to stones so that all who passed below could read the message printed on it without interference from any passing breeze. His Spanish was good enough to let him read the hanging banner, the *narcomanta.*

"Fucking Federation Cartel whores, this is how I'm going to finish off every fucker you send to heat up the turf . . . here are your guys. The rest went away but I'll get them. Sooner or later. See you around, fuckers."

The broker shuddered. He knew the author of the message. He was on his way to meet *"El Raton"* now. He reached for the briefcase under his seat in the Toyota Highlander almost involuntarily. The case was still there. He felt himself sweating, even though the night air was cool and the sun that seared every daylight sky along the border would not rise for hours.

He had been unable to unload the last three pounds of heroin, and had had to make up the difference by pulling cash out of his own stash of money. The total was good for now, but he knew it was a routine he could not sustain. *I'll have to ask Ramón for permission to scale it back a little.* He drove ahead, his mind racing. *What am I gonna do if the guys in Brooklyn cut me off?*

The broker exited the highway and navigated the city streets from memory. He approached the entrance to the hacienda, and was waved through by the armed guards at the gate. He parked the SUV and pulled the case from under the seat. When he closed the car door, he turned to see *El Raton* smiling at him.

"Welcome, back, my friend!" Ramón Dominguez said, slapping him on the shoulders.

Dominguez took the case and handed it to one of the men standing beside him. The man nodded and carried the case toward the main house.

"Did you see our little exhibit on your way in?" Dominguez asked.

"I don't think I could have missed it," the broker replied.

Dominguez laughed. "Exactly! The whole point! *No one* could miss it. Especially not those fools from Sinaloa who think they can come into our plazas without consequences."

The broker nodded, and studied Dominguez' face. *Is part of this message for me? Have I given him any more reason not to trust me? If I have, I'm a dead man.*

"I have something else to show you," Dominguez said. "Another demonstration." He threw his left arm across the broker's shoulders and led him around a corner of the main house into a small courtyard.

The broker stopped involuntarily. Fifty feet in front of him stood a fifty-five gallon drum. His nostrils picked up a strong odor of diesel fuel. Inside the drum a man stood crying pathetically, his arms bloody and bruised. Men with assault rifles stood guard, laughing at him and taunting him.

"He would love to climb out and run, but he cannot, because his arms are both broken," Dominguez explained. "He can't run, and he doesn't splash too much, so the fuel he's standing in won't spill out too fast. He knows what is coming, but can do nothing. He can only stand, and cry and whine like a dog. Excuse me; I have a little speech to make."

El Raton patted the broker on the shoulder and walked to the center of the courtyard. He nodded to one of the men closer to the stack of tires. The recipient of the order wrapped a gag around the mouth of the man inside the drum. *El Raton* was not to be interrupted.

"Compadres! You all know our history here, our mission. We are *Los Zetas.* The Gulf Cartel hired us to protect their business here against the other cartels, but when we asked for fair payment for our services, they tried to sell us out! They actually tried to kill us!"

The men gathered around *El Raton* roared with laughter, as if the very idea that they could die was an outrageous farce.

"We discovered their treachery, and killed most of them instead!"

More laughter.

"We now own the business, the trade routes, the profits of what used to be the Gulf Cartel!"

The men cheered and pumped their fists and weapons in the air in agreement with *El Raton.*

"Those who remain loyal to those Gulf Cartel whores have run to join forces with the Sinaloa bastards," Dominguez continued. "And unfortunately, hollow promises and money can sometimes persuade the weak to stab their friends in the back, something a true Zeta would never think of doing."

There were more cheers, and a few of the men fired their guns into the air.

"Someone who would sell out his friends is not a soldier. He is not a Zeta!" Dominguez shouted. "He is scum. We found *this* scum's telephone number in one of the phones taken from one of the *putas* whose body now dangles from the end of a rope on the highway." Dominguez pointed at the man in the barrel who was now frantically shaking his head back and forth. "And in his pockets, we found this!"

Dominguez reached into his vest and pulled out a roll of American cash, then held it high, turning so that all in the courtyard could see it. The men shouted angrily, and several more shots were fired skyward. Dominguez nodded again toward one of the men closest to the wretch in the drum, and the man removed the gag. He then grabbed a five gallon can, and poured more diesel fuel into the barrel. The man inside cried pitifully.

"As you can see, we have topped off his drink!" Dominguez shouted.

The men circled around the drum again roared in laughter.

"Let's cook our little stew!" Dominguez ordered.

The man who had poured the diesel fuel pulled a cigarette lighter from his pocket and tossed it into the barrel. The flames jumped quickly around the helpless victim inside the tires. He screamed in agony for a few minutes, and then slumped silently across the upper edge of the fuel drum as the blaze consumed him.

The broker stood frozen in shock. He was jolted by another pat on the shoulder from Dominguez. The man who had taken the case had returned, and had returned the case—now empty—to Dominguez.

"Gracias, Miguel." Dominguez nodded. "The count was good," he said, turning to the broker. "You can go now. We will see you again soon."

Driving in a daze, the broker retraced his route, crossing the border back into Laredo, Texas. *I couldn't ask for lighter loads with that going on. I've gotta find another market, now and fast. I don't have the cash to keep buying three pounds of every load myself.*

"Anything to declare, sir?" the agent at the customs station asked him.

The broker stared blankly at him before snapping back to the moment. He handed his driver's license and passport to the agent. "Sorry. No, nothing to declare. Just visiting some business contacts."

"Have a nice day, sir."

"Thanks. You, too."

He drove through the empty streets as the sun came up over Laredo, involuntarily staring at every overpass he approached to make sure there were no bodies dangling from them.

———

Nuevo Laredo
Tamaulipas, Mexico
7:48 a.m.

Mexican police officers found fourteen decapitated bodies inside a vehicle parked in front of the Customs Agency in Nuevo Laredo. The heads were found in ice coolers left in front of the city's Municipal Palace. Along with the bodies, the police found a message from the head of the Federation Cartel, demanding that the mayor of Nuevo Laredo publicly acknowledge the presence of the Federation Cartel in their city, and claiming that the Federation would deliver and soon display the heads of all of *Los Zetas.*

———

South of Nuevo Laredo
Tamaulipas, Mexico
May 5, 2012, 9:30 a.m.

Ramón Dominguez looked up from his newspaper with a sneer of contempt that contorted his already repulsive face. "Miguel!" he barked.

After a knock seeking permission to enter, the summoned subordinate appeared in the office doorway.

"Yes, Ramón?"

"Tell The Rider I want to see him—immediately!"

Miguel nodded deferentially and scurried off.

So the Federation wants to play in our backyard, to flex their muscles in our plaza, Dominguez thought. *They attack us in our homes, assassinate our men. We will see who can play the roughest now.*

A voice from the doorway interrupted his thoughts. There had been no knock this time.

"You wanted to see me?"

"Have you seen the morning paper?" Dominguez asked, tossing the folded daily across his desk toward the other man.

"Of course," his visitor responded, not bothering to pick up the paper. "What should we do to respond?"

"*El Verdugo, El Lazca,* wants us to respond quickly and dramatically. We will leave these *putas* a message they cannot ignore and will not forget."

"It's done," the visitor said, a satisfied smile crossing his face. "What if the cowards are not to be found? They tend to run to ground after showing their faces for a moment or two."

"We will find the ones we can, and then use suitable substitutes, as we find them. You know, like we did at San Fernando."

"Understood," the visitor said, smiling again. He turned and walked briskly from the office.

Chapter Thirty-Nine

Cardereyta Jiménez
Nuevo Leon, Mexico
May 13, 2012

The one they called "The Rider" stepped up to the door of the crowded bus. He waved his pistol back and forth, covering the packed seats and aisle as he spoke.

"Everyone gets off here. Now."

"But we paid to go to the border," a woman in the left front seat protested.

The Rider smiled at her, then quickly raised a pistol and fired. Blood began pouring from the small hole in the center of the woman's head and she slumped forward. Screams erupted from the other passengers, and The Rider fired twice more, ventilating the roof of the bus.

"As I said before, everyone gets off here, now."

The terrified passengers poured past him, forming a single file line on the side of the road as directed by several men who were waiting beside the bus with automatic weapons.

A young man in his early twenties stood holding the girl next to him. "Please, sir," he addressed The Rider, "we are all just trying to find work in the north. We will cooperate with you completely. We are not your enemies. We have no weapons. We pose no threat to you."

The girl next to him dropped to her knees in front of The Rider.

"I am pregnant," she said, tears running down her face. "We want to make a home for our child where there is work."

"*Lo siento mucho*, little sister," The Rider said, shaking his head, "but today you are all part of a much bigger, more important plan."

He stepped back, pointed the pistol at the young man's head, and fired. The next shot killed the girl. Taking their cues, the men on either side of him opened fire. The echoes of gunfire did not stop until all those from the bus stopped moving.

The Rider pulled a machete from a sheath on his belt. "Let's get to it," he shouted. "Quickly. No survivors this time. Make sure of your work."

———

Tampico Naval Air Station
Tamaulipas, Mexico
May 14, 2012

Aguilar felt the vibrations of the phone on his belt. It could be only one caller, using the walkie-talkie function that was pre-programmed to dial only Aguilar's phone.

"How are you, my friend?" Aguilar asked.

"Well, enough, Major. As well as I can be after helping these vermin dismember about fifty people with machetes." Even though his contact spoke in a whisper, Aguilar could recognize the rage in his voice.

"You have to maintain your cover. You do what you do to remain safe. Any problems?"

"No sir."

"Who ordered the killings this time?"

"Lazcano again. At least that's what Dominguez told everyone. *El Ratón* and his little brother—the one they call The Rider—were right in the middle of it. At least I didn't have to kill any of those poor devils myself. I fired some shots into some bodies, pretending to finish them off, but they were already dead."

"Any idea where you're heading next?"

"Back toward Nuevo Laredo."

"Keep me informed when you can."

"Yes sir."

Aguilar returned the phone to his belt. He walked out of his office and into a conference room, where he stood in front of his company. On a screen behind him, the first screen of an electronic slideshow displayed two carbines crossed in front of an anchor, the symbol of Mexico's Infanteria de Marina — the Naval Infantry Force, or Marines. Each one of his men was dressed in camouflaged battled dress uniforms, or "bdu's," with the word "Marina" displayed in large white letters across the chest. A black mask designed to be pulled up like a bank robber's bandana rested around each man's neck. Aguilar's uniform included one as well.

"Have the new men sit up front," Aguilar instructed a sergeant. Six young troops obeyed the NCO's commands and took the center seats in the front row of the room. "For some of you men, this is new information; for others, a refresher course." The major walked to the side of the screen.

"August 24, 2010." Aguilar pressed a button on the remote in his hand, and the screen behind him changed to a photograph of blood stained corpses piled on top of each other against a wall. "What the press now calls the 'Tamaulipas massacre.' Some of you men were there with me. We recovered 72 bodies from a ranch. The victims had been executed with bullets through their brains. Fifty-eight men and fourteen women, mostly migrants trying to cross the border into the United States. One young man named Freddy survived and was able to tell us his story."

Aguilar pressed the remote button again. The screen changed to another grisly scene, the bullet-riddled body of an elderly man.

"November 22, 2010. Ciudad Victoria. This is the body of Don Alfredo Guerrero Torrejon. He refused to give away his ranch when the cartel demanded it, and shot it out with them when they came for him. He actually killed four and wounded two before they killed him." Aguilar turned away from the screen and looked at his men. "Don Alfredo was seventy-seven years old. We defend our heroes as well as the sheep in our herds. I expect each of you to demonstrate the same courage as that shown by Don Alfredo."

The screen changed again, showing a large prison compound.

"December 18, 2010. Nuevo Laredo. One-hundred and fifty-one inmates, many of them the very cartel scum we worked very hard to apprehend, walked out the front door of this prison. Let me say that again. *They walked out the front door.* We fight not only against the gunmen who fire at us, but against their money and the corruption that their illegal wealth spreads, and against those who accept it."

The screen changed again, showing seven bodies covered with sheets in a prison yard.

"July 15, 2011," Aguilar said. "The same federal prison in Nuevo Laredo. A new facility director could not be counted on to prevent sixty-six more inmates from escaping. The escapees killed seven of their cartel rivals before they left."

The screen now showed several corpses hanging from a highway overpass.

"May 4. Ten days ago. Nuevo Laredo. These nine were hanged for opposing *Los Zetas.* The Federation Cartel responded by decapitating fourteen others. The Zetas apparently believe in massive retaliation."

Aguilar pressed the remote button. A gruesome scene of dismembered body parts filled the screen.

"Yesterday. The reporters still brave enough to write about such things are calling this the Cadereyta Jiménez massacre. We found the beheaded and dismembered bodies of forty-nine people left along Highway 40 in Nuevo Leon, between Monterrey and Reynosa. A *narcomanta* written on a wall nearby claimed these murders were committed by *Los Zetas.*"

The screen changed to a photograph of a dark-haired, clean-shaven young man in a coat and tie.

"At least one common denominator in all of the prior events is this gentleman," Aguilar said, heavily lacing the word "gentleman" with sarcasm. "This is Heriberto Lazcano Lazcano, otherwise known as Z-3, or '*El Verdugo*.' He was born on December 25, 1974, Satan's own Christmas present to the Republic.

"He was once one of us. Like each of us in this room, Lazcano took an oath to defend Mexico, and was even chosen by the Army as one of our *Grupo Aeromovil de Fuerzas Especiales*, the GAFEs. He and thirty others then deserted from the special forces because the Gulf Cartel needed enforcers to combat their rivals in Sinaloa. They became '*Los Zetas.*' They call Lazcano 'Z-3' because he was the third Zeta to desert and join the Gulf Cartel. They call him '*El Verdugo*' because he executes some of his victims by feeding them to some lions and tigers that he stole from a zoo and keeps on his ranch. He runs *Los Zetas* in

Tamaulipas, and President Calderon has designated him as our Public Enemy Number One.

"*Los Zetas* grew dissatisfied with the financial benefits afforded to them by the Gulf Cartel, so they took over that Cartel from their employers, and now run their own criminal enterprise. I remind you that they are former GAFE operators, trained by the American and Israeli special forces. They have joined with some other former special forces operators—deserters from Guatemala—and now use beheading and dismemberment as part of their techniques of terror.

"These are, gentlemen, the most dangerous men in Mexico. They are a serious threat to our nation and to our families. They are a threat to each of you. Those masks around your necks are not useless rags. They are to be used any time you are in public and in uniform. Your lives and those of your families— your parents, wives, siblings and children—depend on your using them. We have lost police chiefs, mayors, members of the press, and marines to *Los Zetas*. That is why some of you new men are sitting in the front row where other marines once sat before you."

Aguilar thought of Linda's concerns for them, their paltry salaries, the temptations that they always faced.

"You men can never appreciate the respect I have for all of you. It is you who remain to loyally serve instead of chasing the dirty money dangled before you by the traitors who seek to turn our nation into a cesspool."

He turned to the screen for another look at the photograph of Lazcano. He turned back to face his marines.

"I want this traitor dead or alive, and without losing any more of you in the process. He is trying to turn Nuevo Laredo into his own personal fort. We are going to catch him, and if he resists, as I frankly hope he will, we will return him to hell." He started to leave, then paused and returned to the podium. "One more thing, gentlemen. If any of you finds the cartels' money more attractive than your uniform, and chooses to join *Los Zetas*, rest assured that the rest of us will hunt you down and kill you."

———

Brooklyn, New York
May 18, 2012, 10:37 p.m.

"Sorry, bud, you'll have to keep those. Got my orders. We're outta the smack business. The guys at the top think you might be hot, anyway."

The broker stood at the bottom of the loading dock steps, his mouth hanging open. "C'mon, Pete, you can't mean that. What am I supposed to do with ten pounds of this shit? You were the only market I had left!"

"Sell it, use it yourself. I don't care. We're done, buddy. See ya."

The big man on the dock closed the door behind him.

The broker went back to his car and repacked the heroin. He got back into the driver's seat and sat there, staring at the darkness. *I can't go home without the money.* He buried his face in his hands for a moment, took a deep breath, and exhaled. *I've got about fifty g's with me, all the cash I had left. That'll stake me someplace for a while.*

———

South of Nuevo Laredo
Tamaulipas, Mexico
May 22, 2012, 9:29 a.m.

"Our friend never returned with the money from the last shipment," Dominguez said.

Lazcano raised an eyebrow and shrugged. "When you find him, kill him. We can always find another mule. On the bright side, Ramón, your raid on the west coast and our little show on the highway seem to be having the desired effect. I think Chapo's boys are going to be keeping their heads down for a while."

Dominguez nodded. "We will remain alert, anyway."

———

Washington, D.C.
June 3, 2012, 2:51 a.m.

Officer Randi Rhodes suddenly sat up in bed, shaking, her breathing rapid and shallow.

Wisniewski shook himself out of his sleep and sat up himself, wrapping his arms around her shoulders. "The nightmare again?"

"Yes," she said quietly. "I don't—can't—cry any more. I just keep hearing those explosions, feeling the heat from the fires, seeing those poor people, or what was left of them, and Sam."

"We'll get their killers. It'll just take some time."

She looked at him and shook her head. "How can you so sure, Tim? It's already been months. Sure, Adipietro and Briggs are locked up, but they weren't the ones who blew up that truck. I haven't even seen Jeff Trask around the squad room in weeks. It's like he's forgotten all about the other victims."

Wisniewski pulled her head to his shoulder. "You can be sure of one thing in this world, even if you doubt everything else. There are four other people on that squad—Bear, Dix, Lynn, and me—who will never forget about that day, and even if we did, Jeffrey Trask wouldn't. I was up in his office on Friday. He wasn't in, but his door was open. There were stacks of papers on a table behind his desk, some a foot high. I looked at 'em. Every page had something to do with the Zetas. He still has his contacts in Mexico. He's working on something, believe me. He'll never forget Sam or the others, or even that stupid little daughter of Heidelberg's. He won't let go of it. That's just who he is."

He felt her relax a little.

"Okay. Thanks." There were tears welling up in her eyes.

"I won't tell anybody if you cry about it, you know."

She just nodded, and managed a smile.

"One other thing you should never forget."

"What's that?"

"I love you."

Chapter Forty

Tampico Naval Air Station
Tamaulipas, Mexico
July 1, 2012, 7:39 p.m.

"How are the election returns, Luis?" Linda Aguilar asked.

"Not good," he said, dropping his eyes from the television in his office to check the cell phone's battery indicator. He had a couple of bars left. "Peña Nieto will be the new president of Mexico. His PRI will sweep back into power in December. President Calderón did all he could, but the country has lost its stomach for the killing."

There was a pause on the other end of the line. "What does that mean *for us* now, Luis?"

"I will keep my promise to you, my love, as soon as I am sure that I have kept my promises to Mexico. I have to give the new administration a chance. If the campaign promises are kept, there will be no quarter for any of the cartels, just some sort of change in strategy. I have to wait and see what that means. Do you understand?"

"I'm not sure anymore, Luis." She didn't say anything for a moment. "Daddy has offered me a job with his company in San Antonio. I'm going to take it. It's just office work, but I can't just sit around and wait and worry and do nothing anymore."

"I understand."

"I hope so. I can be at the lake house in Zapata anytime you can get leave."

"I know. I'll try to take some time off very soon."

"I'd like that. Please be careful."

The dial tone told him the call was over.

—————

555 4ᵗʰ Street N.W.
Washington, D.C.
July 2, 2012, 9:29 a.m.

"Hello, Luis. How are you?" Trask leaned back and threw one foot up on his desk.

"I have been better, my friend. I think I know how your military felt when they saw the helicopters leaving Saigon."

"I saw your election returns. What does that mean for you?"

"I'm not sure yet. There will almost certainly be a reduction in our enforcement efforts against the cartels, or at least some of them."

"Some of them?"

"There have always been rumors about links between the new president elect and Chapo Guzmán, Jeff. The PRI—the party returning to power—may concentrate on Guzmán's enemies and leave the control of the entire drug trade to Chapo."

"Yeah, I know. I've been doing a lot of reading."

"I thought you might. You have probably seen, then, that the Federation Cartel brings in billions of your dollars each year."

"Yep, and politicians love their money, wherever they are."

"That they do, my friend, and the PRI has always been rumored to love cartel money. I hope I am mistaken in my assessment, but I don't know what to think at this point.At any rate, I do not know how long I can continue to make an effective contribution, or more accurately, I do not know how long I will be allowed to make such a contribution. As long as I can, I will, but I think we should talk about a contingency plan."

"I'm listening, Luis."

"If you were to indict those responsible for the bomb in your city, would that be a matter of public knowledge?"

"Not if I don't want it to be. We can get either a criminal complaint or an indictment, and hold it under seal—that means a court secret which can't be released to anyone without a judge's order—until an arrest is made. We don't even have to enter the indictment in any national system until we're ready to do so."

"Would anyone have to be there to testify?"

"Not necessarily. If we file a complaint, the information just has to establish probable cause for the charge and arrests; we can use what we call hearsay—what someone told someone else. A federal agent just has to satisfy the judge that the source of his information is reliable."

"I see." Aguilar paused. "I think it is time that Linda and I invited you back to Zapata, and I think you should bring one of your agent friends. If you know one who speaks Spanish, that would be even better. It would eliminate the need for a translator, and time might be crucial."

"I know just the guy."

———

Zapata, Texas
July 9, 2012, 1:48 a.m.

"He should be calling any minute now," Aguilar said. "I am sorry about the hour, but I'm sure you understand that he has to be extremely careful about the times he chooses to use the phone."

"We understand," Trask said. He pushed his mug forward as Linda Aguilar brought the coffee pot out from the kitchen. Next to him, Wisniewski did the same.

"How many is that?" Trask asked, yawning.

"Apparently, not enough," Linda said. "I'll put some more on."

Trask was stirring the sugar into his coffee when the phone rang on the table in front of Aguilar.

"Hello, my friend," Aguilar said. "Yes, I'm going to hand the phone to another friend of ours, as we discussed. Tell him everything you know about the truck explosion in Washington first. Then, if you have time and it is safe, tell him about the other matters we discussed." Aguilar handed the phone to Wisniewski, who immediately began speaking in Spanish and taking notes on a legal pad that Trask shoved in front of him.

"I can vouch for some of what he is saying," Aguilar said.

"And I've collected news reports and photographs from some of the incidents you've described," Trask replied. "There should be plenty to corroborate what he's saying and establish his reliability for our judge once we're back in D.C."

Wisniewski's conversation in Spanish continued for another minute or two. He paused, holding his hand over the phone, and looked up at Trask. "I've got enough for all three of them on the bombing—Lazcano and both of the Dominguez brothers—Lazcano ordered it, Ramón planned it and his little brother Vicente, the one they call 'The Rider,' detonated it. The source says he's heard them all joking about and admitting their roles in it. They were all involved in the heroin conspiracy as well, from harvesting through manufacture to delivery."

Trask smiled. "Great, spend what time he has left with the other incidents."

Wisniewski went back to his conversation.

"You can charge them even though only one pushed the button on the bomb, Jeff?" Aguilar asked.

"Anyone who directed it, procured it, agreed to it, or otherwise aided or abetted it," Trask said, nodding. "Our federal conspiracy laws are a lot broader than those in your country."

"I see."

Wisniewski was wrapping up his questions. The call had lasted five minutes and forty seconds. He handed the phone back to Aguilar.

"We are once more in your debt," the major said in Spanish. "Be safe my friend."

"Interesting stuff?" Trask asked.

Wisniewski nodded solemnly. "Enough to make your skin crawl."

"Give me the rest of the year, if you can, Jeff," Aguilar said. "The PRI doesn't take over until December. We will step up our efforts and try to resolve these problems in Mexico first."

"Done," Trask said. "We'll be ready to roll when you need us to."

Chapter Forty-One

Progreso, Coahuila, Mexico
October 7, 2012, 4:20 p.m.

"We are in place, Major."

"Excellent, Torres. Hold your position until I give the word. There are hundreds of civilians around the field. We don't want unnecessary casualties." Aguilar surveyed the situation from the window of his vehicle. He and his men had taken helicopters to a field located miles from the little town and had transferred to unmarked cars and trucks so as not to spook their target. They were about 130 miles south of the U.S. border, so the flights had not required any coordination with the Americans. *Good,* thought Aguilar. *One less possible weak link. One less opportunity for a leak. Even our friends to the north have security problems. Tonight they will not be our problems. If my friend's information was correct just one last time, then all our efforts have been worthwhile.*

"I have eyes on the target, Major," Torres reported. "Lazcano is here, just as our friend reported he would be."

"Good. Hold until I give the order." Aguilar's blood raced in excitement, but his command instincts, honed by years of fighting the cartels, cautioned him not to give in to any impulse. Acting too rashly might mean throwing his men into the wrong side of an ambush. In addition, the small baseball park was too crowded to storm, and he had too few men to undertake a frontal assault.

"Torres, how many Zetas do you think he has with him?" Aguilar asked, releasing the transmit button on his radio and waiting for the answer.

"There are just a handful in his party, Major. Just five that I can count. They are sitting with him."

It is just as our friend said it would be. El Verdugo has gotten sloppy, too confident. Our friend is elsewhere with El Ratón, so there are some details he could not be sure of, but what he did report was on the mark. "Torres, set up a roadblock on your side. We will do the same here. Search each vehicle leaving the field, and post sentries on each side to watch and stop those on foot. Lazcano is known to drive a gold Dodge Charger, but may have used a different vehicle today."

"*Sí,* Major."

Aguilar motioned the men on his team into position. The baseball game ended, and the slow procession of cars and small pickups began to filter through the checkpoints.

Nothing unusual yet, Aguilar thought. *Maybe—Yes! That one.*

A dark colored Ford Ranger stood out from the rest of the traffic. It was newer than most of the vehicles in the line approaching the roadblock, and Aguilar saw that the wheels of the Ranger had twice turned as if the truck's driver was contemplating breaking out of line. His eyes locked on the passenger in the front seat. *It could be him. Baseball hat and sunglasses, so I can't be sure, but it certainly looks like him.*

"The Ranger. Watch it," Aguilar ordered.

His squad of marines split in two, with men advancing down each side of the line toward the crew-cab pickup. Aguilar noticed that the windows on the passenger side of the truck were rolling down. There was a silence for what seemed like several minutes. Suddenly he saw flashes of muzzle fire from inside the vehicle, and three dark objects came flying out of the truck's windows.

"Grenades!" Aguilar heard himself screaming the warning at the same time as some of his men. His marines were instantly diving to the ground, taking cover behind barrels, other vehicles, whatever they could find. Before the smoke from the explosions could clear, Aguilar rushed forward through the confusion and screams of the crowd, firing his .45. The reports from his pistol joined those of his marines' rifles, and he could see through the haze that the Ranger was being riddled in the crossfire. He was about to order his men to cease fire when he felt a smashing blow to his right thigh. He looked down to see the bloodstain forming on the leg of his battle fatigues. *Oh hell, not again!* His marines, seeing him fall, emptied their weapons in anger at the pickup.

"Cease fire!" Aguilar shouted. A medic was already at his side, ripping the pants leg open and applying pressure to the wound. "How is it?" he asked the corpsman.

"No arteries, Major. We'll need to get the bullet out, and—"

"Then help me up. I'm going over there!" Aguilar ordered.

The medic tied a bandage around the wound and pulled the Major's right arm over his shoulder. They approached the pickup, and one of the marines pulled open the front passenger door. A body, oozing blood from more than a dozen bullet wounds, spilled out onto the ground at Aguilar's feet. The dead man's head was a mass of blood and torn tissue.

It's him, I'm almost certain, but we must make sure. "Fingerprint the bodies before you take them to a mortuary," Aguilar ordered.

"Yes, Major." Captain Torres was taking over now, barking orders to the men, moving the onlookers away from the area.

Aguilar nodded in satisfaction. *Good man. He is doing as he was trained, assuming command.* Aguilar nodded to the corpsman. "You can find me a hospital now."

―――

FBI Field Office
Washington, D.C.
October 8, 2012, 9:17 a.m.

"Luis?" Trask nodded to those standing around him in the squad conference room. "I'm going to put you on speakerphone, if that's okay with you. You have some fans in the room." He pushed the button and placed his cell phone on the table.

"Hello, Jeff. Can you hear me?"

"Loud and clear, *amigo*. We've seen the news about your fight with Lazcano, Luis. It's not every day that someone brings down their nation's public enemy number one. Congratulations, Major." Trask led a round of applause which was joined in by the others in the room.

"Thank you, Jeff, and all my other friends there. I have had the pleasure of meeting Detective Wisniewski, and I have heard many good things about all the rest of you. I hope we can all meet someday."

"How are you, Luis?" Trask asked. "Linda said you'd managed to get yourself shot again."

"A leg wound this time," Aguilar said. "At first we didn't think it was anything too serious, but the doctors who took the bullet out last night tell me there was some nerve damage. They're medically retiring me next week, Jeff."

"I'm sorry and happy to hear that at the same time, Luis," Trask said. "You've fought the good fight. Time for someone else to carry the flag for a while. Your Captain Torres sounds very able, from what you've told me."

"Very able," Aguilar agreed. "You've just paid him a compliment, which I will translate for him. You're on speakerphone on this end, and Captain Torres is here with me. So is Linda. She flew into Tampico last night."

"Then you're in good hands. I know Linda will be glad to have you home for good."

"You're damned straight," Linda Aguilar said, leaning toward the phone in the hospital room. "And he's flying back with me this time, not driving through Nuevo Laredo like some suicidal maniac. We'll be in Zapata very soon."

"Excellent," Trask replied. "We'll knock the top name off our criminal complaint here, Luis. Any word on the other two?"

"Only that my friend tells me that he thinks *El Ratón* will be smarter and even more dangerous than Lazcano. Unfortunately, he was not at the baseball game, and neither was his brother."

"We'll only move if we get them on this side of the river, Luis. Tell Torres he still has first shot."

"I understand. You are a man of your word, Jeff. You must bring your wife and come visit us in Zapata. I think I'll be doing a lot of fishing."

Lynn leaned across the table. "It's a date Luis. I think Linda and I might have a lot in common, since she's married to a maniac and my husband is a lunatic."

Aguilar's laughter could be heard through the chuckles in the conference room. "Excellent. As you *Norté Americanos* say, 'Come on down.' We'd love to have you."

"Rest and heal, Luis. Congratulations again." Trask switched off the speakerphone.

"Thank you, Jeff. I was serious about our invitation. You can't leave me alone with this woman for too long, you know."

"I heard that!" Linda said. Trask could tell that the speaker function on the other end was still engaged.

"It's a good day for both our countries," Trask said. "I know that several families here, and hundreds in Mexico, cheered your victory yesterday. I'll talk to you again soon, Luis."

"Thank you, Jeff."

———

Hospital Naval de Tampico
Tamaulipas, Mexico

"That was nice of Jeff to call," Linda Aguilar said, taking the phone from her husband. "You need to rest, now, Luis."

Before he could say anything, Aguilar was distracted by another phone ringing, this one in the hands of Captain Torres. He waited until Torres finished the call.

"Bad news, Major. Some Zetas broke into the funeral parlor in Sabinas where we took Lazcano's body. They've stolen it."

"It never ends," Aguilar said. "I'm glad we fingerprinted the bodies before we took them there. Compare the fingerprints with Lazcano's enlistment records. We'll still be able to confirm the kill."

Torres saluted. "It has been an honor serving in your command, Major."

Aguilar returned the salute. "It has been a privilege commanding officers like you Torres. Take care of our men." He pointed at the phone in Torres' hand. "Our friend will be calling *you* now. Keep it charged, and don't let that out of your sight. Let me know if I can help with anything."

———

Brooklyn, New York
October 12, 2012, 11:46 p.m.

The broker rolled off the bed in the motel room when he heard the knock on the door. He had not been asleep. In fact, he was fully dressed and well rested. These were, after all, his new business hours. He'd had nowhere else to go but back to the old neighborhood. The money he left the ranch with was running out, and he had turned to the only commercial asset he had left.

He'd cut the heroin, mixing it with a blend of milk sugar and quinine to double the volume of the ten pounds to twenty. The milk sugar was a fairly safe adulterant, and the quinine kept the taste bitter in case any of the junkie customers wanted to taste it first. Too much sugar, they got suspicious.

He'd run the numbers before taking the plunge. Twenty pounds equaled 9,080 grams. At fifty bucks a gram—a competitive street rate—he could turn the white powder into almost half a million dollars, and that was an amount he could live on. He'd already gone through a couple of pounds without any problems. The money was stacking up.

He took the pistol from underneath the pillow and walked to the corner of the window to see who was at the door. He recognized the man as a regular customer, a gram buyer who was good for about three grams per week. It had been two days since the junkie had been by, so everything was on schedule.

"Be right there."

He pulled his shirttail up and stuck the pistol inside his belt. Walking to the dresser, he opened a shaving kit that contained nothing related to shaving. The gram baggies filled the kit, each gram weighed on the digital scales he kept with the main stash of dope in the trunk of the car parked outside. He pulled one of the little baggies from the kit and walked over to the door.

The moment the knob turned, the door flew open and the broker felt himself being lifted off the ground as two large men bull-rushed him, spinning him around and throwing him onto the bed.

"*Federal Agents! You're under arrest!*" One of the men was yelling in his ear. The other already had a cuff on one of his arms, and was pulling the other arm behind his back. The man's hand brushed against the pistol as he pulled the broker's hand backward.

"*GUN!*" The second man yelled in his other ear.

He felt himself being thrown to the floor. One of the men had a knee digging into his back while he was patted down. He could hardly breathe.

"He's secure."

The broker felt himself being lifted by his arms. The men put him in the rolling desk chair that came with the room. One was reading him his rights. The other was telling him something about a search warrant for his car. It was over.

Chapter Forty-Two

Zapata, Texas
November 24, 2012, 11:45 a.m.

"How wide is the lake here, Luis?" Lynn asked as they looked southwestward from the deck of the lake house.

"Almost exactly a mile," Aguilar said. He pointed out across the lake. "There's a point right out there on the other side where I used to fish a lot as a boy. A good spot. A stream feeds the lake on the north side, and we could catch a lot of bass feeding on the smaller fish entering the main lake." He smiled. "We could still catch them today, if it were not for the Zetas. They control Nuevo Laredo to the northwest, and their boats often come out trying to retrieve the drugs that their planes drop into the lake."

"How's the fishing been for you?" Trask asked.

"Fair. It slows a bit this time of year. We take the boat out a couple of times a week. I find myself wishing we could go back to that little point on the other side. Perhaps someday we will be able to."

"How's the leg?" Trask asked him.

"Not bad. I honestly think I could have continued to serve. It's a little numb, and slower than the other one when it comes to accepting instructions from my brain. I have to be careful not to move too quickly or I find myself stumbling."

"You're a lucky guy, Luis," Lynn said. "Surviving all those wounds at the hands of those bastards. Jeff's shown me a lot of the research he's done into all their mass killings. Incredible brutality. Now you're here with Linda. It's all good."

"Thank you, Lynn," Linda said. "I think he needs to be reminded of that sometimes."

"I just feel like I left some things unfinished, my love," Aguilar said, patting his wife's knee.

"Captain Torres can handle that for you now," she said. "You did much more than your share."

A timer went off in the kitchen, the bell ringing through the screen doors to the deck.

"Finally," Trask said. "I was gaining weight smelling that, Linda."

"Stay here too long and you will," Aguilar said, pointing to his waist. "I'm up ten pounds since I got here. With this leg slowing me down, it's hard to get much exercise."

———

South of Nuevo Laredo
Tamaulipas, Mexico
November 25, 2012, 12:27 a.m.

Once he was sure that the others were asleep, he rolled out of the bed in the bunkhouse of the hacienda. He headed down the hallway on what would seem to any of the others to be a trip to the latrine. Instead of entering the bathroom, however, he kept going, walking outside into the courtyard. He found his car, a run-down looking Subaru, in the row of vehicles parked outside the bunkhouse. For all the dents and missing paint, the car's engine and drivetrain still functioned well.

He stopped at the gate and smiled at the man with an AK-47 strapped to his shoulder.

"Ah, Miguel," the guard said, smiling back at him. "Off to see that little *chiquita* of yours again?"

"What can I say? Duty calls."

The guard laughed and waved him on.

A soon as he was out of sight of the hacienda, he turned right. He did not take the road into Nuevo Laredo, but drove eastward toward the lakefront. He checked the mirrors as he drove. *No lights. I am not being followed.* He found the little park with its picnic tables, and pulled into the parking lot. It was a good spot. He had used it before.

He turned the engine off and pulled out the cell phone.

"Hello?"

"It's me, *Capitán.*"

"How are you, my friend?"

"Well enough. I have something to—"

A movement in his rearview mirror caught his attention. Another car was entering the parking lot, it's headlights off. *It's probably nothing. Maybe some amorous teenagers looking for a place to make out.* Instead of turning toward another area of the parking lot, however, the other vehicle pulled in directly behind him and stopped. A brief ray of moonlight shining through the clouds provided just enough definition for him to make out the model of the other car. *A black Mustang!*

The driver of the Mustang climbed out and walked to the driver's side of the Subaru. He had a pistol in his hand.

"I told Ramón it had to be you," Vicente Dominguez said, sneering. "The meeting tonight was to flush out our spy—the one who kept alerting Aguilar about our traps for him, the one who tipped him off about Lazcano being at that baseball game. I told Ramón it had to be you, but he would not believe me. He believes me now. He's bringing one of his little stewpots. We're going to be cooking tonight. Get out."

Miguel raised his left hand by his face, indicating his surrender. His right hand, rising more slowly, was not empty. The .45 fired twice, and Vicente Dominguez fell lifeless to the pavement.

Miguel cranked the Subaru's engine, turned the car across the Zeta's body, and sped out of the park, his own headlights turned off this time. He heard Torres' voice on the phone lying on the seat next to him.

"Are you alright? I heard gunfire! Are you alright?"

Miguel picked up the phone. "I am alright for now, *Capitán,* but I may not be for long. My cover is blown. I just had to kill The Rider. *El Ratón* and the others are already looking for me. I cannot go back to the hacienda, and they will have roadblocks set up in Nuevo Laredo. Where should I go? I do not have much fuel."

He waited for an answer, Torres was strangely silent.

"*Capitán?* Are you there?"

"Yes, my friend. I'm afraid I have no answer for you at the moment. We are too far away from you to arrange a pickup on such short notice. Which direction are you heading?"

"South and east, away from Nuevo Laredo."

"Keep going that way. I'll call you back as soon as I can."

———

Zapata, Texas
1:06 a.m.

The phone rang beside Aguilar's bed. He shook off the sleep and answered the call. "Yes?"

"Major, I'm sorry to disturb you."

"Torres? What's wrong?"

"It's our friend, sir." Torres relayed the details of the call from Miguel. "I have nothing to offer him, sir. I didn't know anyone else to call."

Aguilar was already pulling on some clothes. "Tell him to head for the point, Torres, do you understand? Hide his car and just make it to the point."

"The point? Yes, Major, I'll tell him."

"What is it, Luis?" Linda was awake now, sitting up in bed. "Where are you going?"

"I have to take the boat out. Our man with the Zetas is in trouble."

"Where are you going?" she demanded.

He leaned over and kissed her. He spoke calmly, slowly. "I have to do this. If you want to help, call your brother and tell him I'm heading for the point."

"I'm going with you."

He held a hand up. "No. *You* must call your brother; *I* must leave now."

Aguilar slipped on a pair of deck shoes and opened the bedroom door. Trask was standing there shirtless, barefoot and in a pair of jeans.

"Too many beers. I had to pee. Trouble?"

"My source with the Zetas is about to be killed unless I can rescue him. Can you shoot?"

"Yeah. Some."

"You don't have to do this. It could go badly."

"I'm in."

"Let's go then."

Trask ran toward the boat house, following Aguilar down the dark boardwalk from the house. He turned when he heard Lynn calling after him.

"Jeff?"

"Talk to Linda, Lynn. Help her. I'm going with Luis."

"Where?"

"Talk to Linda."

They reached the boathouse. Aguilar reached above the doorway and brought down a long object before tossing it to Trask. *A rifle. Remington 700, I think, night vision scope.* Trask jumped in the front after Aguilar took the seat in the rear by the outboard. The motor roared to life, and Aguilar pointed the little boat out toward the middle of the lake.

"Where exactly are we heading, Luis?" Trask yelled over the noise of the engine.

"Mexico, *amigo.*" Aguilar yelled back. "Can you use that, or should we switch places?"

Trask checked the bolt and the safety on the rifle, and peered through the scope.

"I've used one of these—or at least one like it—a lot more than I have one of those," he said, pointing to the outboard.

"Stay there, then. Hopefully, you won't have to use either one tonight."

Amen to that, Trask said to himself. He looked at the night sky. *Good. Lots of cloud cover. At least we've got that going for us.*

The trip across the mile of water seemed like an eternity, the little outboard driving the old boat as hard as it could at full throttle. Trask watched the approaching coastline through the scope.

"Do you see anything, Jeff?"

Trask looked back at Aguilar, stunned to have heard the whisper so clearly.

I got it now. He's killed the engine. We're coasting toward the bank. "Nothing yet, Luis," he said quietly.

"Keep looking. Sweep the bank with the scope."

Trask did as he was instructed, moving the rifle from side to side along the spit of scrub-lined sand that jutted out into the water. Suddenly, a figure crouched by the water's edge was waving at them.

"I've got him. There."

"We can't risk the motor yet. He may have been followed." Aguilar barked a command softly in Spanish. "I told him to swim to us," he explained.

Trask looked through the scope again. The man was already in the water, breast-stroking quietly toward the boat. Trask swept the coastline with the scope again. "All clear for now, Luis."

"Excellent."

The swimmer reached the boat, and Trask and Aguilar pulled him in. The man hugged Aguilar, and babbled something very rapidly in Spanish.

Whatever language that was in, it sure sounded like thank you forever and I owe you my life and let's get the hell out of here, Trask thought.

Aguilar cranked the outboard back to life.

"Jeff, Let's switch now. Just keep it pointed that way." Aguilar pointed back toward the center of the lake. Trask crawled back to the rear of the boat and took the outboard's control bar, handing the rifle back to Aguilar.

"It's on full throttle," Aguilar said. "Hold it steady and straight." He took the rifle and lay prone, facing the rear of the boat and the Mexican shore.

Trask was starting to breathe easier. *I think we just pulled this off.* Suddenly he heard something whiz by his head, and saw a splash in the water ahead of the boat. A microsecond later, the sounds caught up with them. *Shit, was that gunfire? Is somebody shooting at us?* Trask ducked low instinctively. Any doubt he may have had was erased a fraction of a second later by the sound of the rifle in Aguilar's hands as he returned fire. Two lights started sweeping the water around them. He heard automatic weapons firing.

"Searchlights. *Zigzag!*" Aguilar yelled.

It was a command that Trask was following before it was issued. He kept the throttle wide open, driving the boat left and right at irregular angles and intervals. He heard the sounds of other engines approaching them. For the first time since picking up their passenger, Trask took a look behind the boat. He wished he hadn't.

Two high speed boats, long and sleek with lights mounted forward, were rapidly gaining on them. Riflemen in each of the boats were firing, the muzzle flashes of their weapons piercing the darkness. Trask heard Aguilar's rifle fire a shot, and the light on one of the chase boats went out. A round from one of the Mexican snipers struck the back edge of the bass boat, and Trask felt an impact on the back of his left shoulder. *Damn. Probably a big splinter. Lynn's going to give me hell about this. I just had that one fixed.*

He took another glance behind them. One of the Zetas' boats was a mere thirty yards behind them now. Trask thought he saw one of the men on the boat zero in with his rifle. *He's aiming at my head!*

Then the Zetas' boat exploded.

Trask whipped his head toward the front of the boat. Racing by them, toward the remaining Zeta vessel, was a big gunboat with the words, "Texas Highway Patrol" painted proudly on her side. Each of the three machine gun batteries was blazing away.

The gunboat made straight for the Zeta vessel, and the Zetas' craft seemed to disintegrate before his eyes. He saw one figure leap into the water just before the Highway Patrol boat sliced through the debris field which seconds before had been a real threat to end his time on the planet.

Trask felt the outboard begin to shake; then the motor died. He looked at Aguilar with a question on his face.

"You did nothing wrong, Jeff. It is out of fuel. I had no time to fill it before we left."

Before Trask could respond with the very sharp words that were forming on his tongue, the Highway Patrol boat was pulling alongside them. A light from the larger craft illuminated the bass boat.

"You seem to be taking on water there, skipper," Sergeant Jimmy Avila called down.

Trask looked around the little boat. She had taken many more hits than he'd realized. A six inch gash had been cut toward the bow where some of the wood had been shot away. He looked down and saw that his bare feet were already ankle deep in water.

"You'd all better come on up," Avila said, tossing down a chain ladder. "We'll try and tow her back, but odds are that sis here is gonna owe our daddy a new bass boat."

Trask saw both Linda Aguilar and Lynn looking down at him. He followed Aguilar and their passenger up onto the gunboat. Avila was there with another trooper.

"I saw all three batteries firing," Trask said.

Linda smiled. "I was a gunnery officer in the Navy. Your wife can pull a trigger herself. The boat was short-handed, and we got drafted."

"Everyone okay?" Avila asked.

"I think we're fine, thanks to you," Trask said.

"You're not, Jeff." Lynn slapped a towel onto the back of Trask's left shoulder. "You're bleeding like a stuck pig."

"I think it's a wood splinter from the boat. I heard a round hit the back rail—"

"That's no splinter," Avila said, shining a flashlight onto the wound. "It's a ricochet. Not deep. That hard old teak took a lot of the steam out of it. You're lucky." He looked at Lynn. "Keep some pressure on it."

"We've got a prisoner over here, Sarge." Trask saw the trooper on the other side of the boat reach down and pull an exhausted figure over the rail. The man collapsed on the deck of the gunboat, muttering in Spanish. The patrolman was on him immediately, cuffing him.

"What's he saying?" Trask asked Aguilar.

Aguilar smiled. "*El Ratón* is very upset at our friend here for killing his brother. He also says that he cannot swim."

Chapter Forty-Three

Zapata, Texas
November 26, 2012, 11:51 a.m.

"There's some guy at the front door who's asking for you, Jeff," Lynn said. "Stuffed shirt type. He looks pissed."

Trask got up from the recliner, wincing as he did so.

"That actually hurts?" Lynn asked.

"Yeah. I've never been shot before, you know."

"Pull a stunt like that and it could happen again. Friendly fire."

"Thank you for your support," he said.

He steadied himself, took a deep breath, and headed for the front of the lake house. There were actually two stuffed shirts waiting for him at the doorway.

"Are you Trask?" one of the men in a suit asked him.

"Yes, and you are?"

"Gordon Lovitt, Mr. Trask. I'm the chief of the criminal division in the US Attorney's Office for the Western District of Texas. Our offices are in San Antonio. This is AUSA Ward Walton."

"Nice to meet you." Trask held out his hand, but none was offered in return. He shrugged and pulled it back. "Okay. What's up?"

"What's up is we don't take too kindly to someone from Washington flying down here without any notice or coordination and getting involved in an international incident, kidnapping an international priority target defendant, and then thinking he's just going to whisk that defendant back to D.C. after we genuflect and hold a removal hearing for him. That's what's up, Trask."

"I see." Trask turned back and called toward the rear of the house. "Jimmy?"

Sgt. Avila walked up the hallway to join them. "Yeah, Jeff?"

"Sergeant, please tell these fine gentlemen what actually occurred last night while I make a quick phone call."

Trask stepped back and listened to the conversation at the door while he punched the icon on the telephone.

"We were in Texas waters, and came to the assistance of an American vessel which was under fire by pirates on Falcon Lake. Zeta pirates," Avila explained. "We pulled one out of the drink after we sank his boat."

Trask waited for the secretary to patch him through.

"Yes sir, I am a sergeant in the Highway Patrol, and I was the gunboat commander."

"Thank you, sir," Trask spoke into the phone. "It will be just a minute." He turned back toward the front door.

"No sir," Avila was saying. "It was my understanding that Mr. Trask was here for no other purpose than a well-deserved vacation. He's a family friend."

"Let's cut to the chase, guys," Trask interrupted them. He handed the cell phone to Lovitt.

"Who the hell is this?" Lovitt asked.

"Some other Texan," Trask said. "The one who got your boss—the United States Attorney for the Western District of Texas—appointed to his current position."

After an extended conversation in which Lovitt set what Trask figured was the world record for the number of times someone could say, "Yes, Senator Heidelberg," in a five-minute span, Lovitt handed the phone back.

"I guess I didn't understand what happened here. Sorry, Mr. Trask. What can we do to help?"

"You can take the copy of the now unsealed criminal complaint charging Ramón Dominguez with murder and drug conspiracy which you found on your fax machine this morning, give him his removal hearing, prove who he is with the help of the two witnesses who are in this very house and who are more than willing to testify, and get him on a con-air flight to Washington as soon as the United States Marshals Service can accommodate him. If you would be so kind?"

"Certainly. Happy to help."

"I thought you might be."

"Anything else?"

"Yeah. You can expect a motion to oppose removal and transfer to D.C. based upon the same silly allegations that you've apparently already heard from some cartel mouthpiece defense attorney—you know, that Dominguez was kidnapped and all that rot?"

"Yes."

"You might want to re-acquaint yourself with the Ker-Frisbie doctrine before the hearing, Gordon. I'm sure you've heard of it. That's the line of Supreme Court cases holding that it doesn't even matter if we *did* kidnap that murdering slug, even though we didn't. All that matters is that he was found in a territory within the jurisdiction of the United States. The courts don't give a damn how he got here. I'm sure you remember those cases from your Constitutional Law course."

"Yes, of course. Glad to help."

"Thanks very much."

Trask watched as Lovitt and Walton drove away.

Lynn was standing behind him. "The Ker-Frisbie doctrine? Did you just make that up?"

"Actually, no. The cases are *Ker v. Illinois* and *Frisbie v. Collins*. Decided in 1886 and 1952, respectively. Once in a while the Supremes get something right."

Chapter Forty-Four

FBI Field Office
Washington, D.C.
November 30, 2012, 8:45 a.m.

"Did we get the indictment returned?" Carter asked.

"Yep," Trask replied. "About four o'clock yesterday. The grand jury certainly had no trouble with it. Once our Mexican spy friend told them his story, I think they were ready to convict Dominguez on the spot. Unfortunately, we have to wait for a *trial* jury to do that."

"If it's the same story he told me, that's certainly understandable," Wisniewski said.

"We're still weak on the dope conspiracy in one area," Trask said. "Miguel the spy said he has seen Dominguez handle everything related to the China White from the harvesting of the poppies in Colombia to processing the paste in Mexico. He's helped pack the stuff in vehicles to get it through the border checkpoints. He only came across with it once, however.

"Our linkage gets pretty thin between the border and the District. The photos of the truck at the racquet club provide some connection, since we found some dope there, and since Dominguez loaded the same truck with the bomb. It's still thin, though. It was good for the grand jury but the standards of proof are a lot higher at trial. We may have to offer that skunk Adipietro a sweetened deal to get him to testify."

"Maybe not." Lynn walked in with a small stack of papers in her hand. "I had your man Miguel—or whatever his real name is—point out the ranch he said he went to in Laredo, you know, the staging point where they handed off the heroin. I brought it up on a satellite map and Miguel was certain it was the right place. I ran the property records. The ranch is owned by a Frank Aurrichio. He was originally a stockbroker from New York. He moved to Laredo a few years back."

"So now all we have to do is find your Mr. Aurrichio—" Doroz said.

"Already found him," Lynn said. "He's pending trial in the Eastern District of New York. They have him in custody."

"What are the charges?" Doroz asked.

"Distribution of heroin, possession of heroin with intent to distribute, and possession of a firearm in furtherance of drug trafficking. I called Brooklyn. DEA did a few undercover buys and then hit him with a search warrant. He was holding eight pounds."

"I could kiss you," Trask said to Lynn.

"We have a license that says you can do that," she replied.

"Road trip," Wisniewski said. "I called it first."

"Approved," Doroz said. "You too, Dix."

"What's the offer?" Carter asked Trask.

"How old is our Mr. Aurrichio, babe?" Trask asked Lynn.

"Forty-nine."

"Not a day less than twenty-five years. He's looking at that on the New York charges alone. I'll call my counterparts up there and grease this with them and his defense counsel. We'll do a two-for-one sale. He pleads there and we don't charge him here. It's basically the same thing we offered Briggs—a chance to die outside of prison if he lives that long."

Doroz saw that Randi Rhodes was looking a bit lost. "Dix, take your other partner with you, too," he said, nodding in her direction. "Ever been to New York, Randi?"

"Not until now," she said smiling.

"I think we can save the taxpayers some money by just renting two hotel rooms," Carter said. "Tim and I can stay in one, and Randi can have the other one."

"*As if!*" Lynn Trask laughed. "How could you even say that with a straight face, Dix?"

"Two rooms are approved," Doroz said. "Occupancy to be determined by the travel party. Everybody get moving. We have work to do."

"Bear, I need to speak with you and Jeff privately," Carter said.

"My office then," Doroz replied.

Once the door was closed, Carter pulled the DVD from his jacket pocket. "You both need to see this. It's the surveillance video from the racquet club office. Once Adipietro entered his guilty plea, I didn't see any harm looking at it. Bear, advance the timer to just before the seven minute mark."

Doroz took the disc and inserted it into his desk computer. The image flickered to life on the screen, showing an empty office at first. Doroz fast-forwarded the video, resuming normal speed when the timer indicated six minutes and fifty seconds.

The video was from an elevated corner angle looking across the room toward Adipietro's desk. The club owner was sitting at his desk at first, then looking up as two people entered the room. A man and a young woman, both with their backs to the camera, stood talking with Adipietro, who remained seated at his desk. After about twenty seconds, Adipietro reached into a desk drawer and pulled out a small, clear envelope.

"Freeze it there and zoom in," Carter said.

Doroz followed the directions. A close-up view of Adipietro's hand showed that the little baggie contained a white powder.

"Now back out and push play," Carter said.

The video resumed. The man with his back to the camera handed the heroin to the woman. He shook hands with Adipietro, then the couple turned to leave and faced the camera for the first time.

"That's Janie Heidelberg!" Trask exclaimed.

"Yes. And look at her escort," Carter said. "Zoom in on his face, Bear."

Doroz enlarged the frozen image of the man's face. "Holy shit," he said.

Hart Senate Office Building
Washington, D.C.
December 3, 2012, 9:00 a.m.

Trask sat with Ross Eastman in the waiting room outside the senator's office. Trask was holding a laptop computer.

"Are you sure about this?" Eastman asked.

"I made the man a promise, Ross. He *is* the girl's father."

"I suppose there's no other way."

Heidelberg opened the door and waved them in. He waited for them, and shook their hands as they entered the office.

"Amazing work, you've done, Mr. Trask. Working around our extradition problem as well. I fully expected the new government in Mexico to be raising hell about your capital case against Dominguez, but they haven't made a sound."

"I don't think they care to protect any members of the Zetas, Senator," Trask said.

"I see. I understand you have some more *personal* updates for me?"

Trask put the copy of the disc in the laptop.

"Before I show you this, Senator, understand that without the cooperation of Joe Adipietro, we could not introduce this into evidence at any court proceeding. We think it was taken by a surveillance camera in his office. When we executed the search warrant on that office, the holes in the wall from the camera mounts were visible, but even the camera had been removed, We found the original of this disc in Adipietro's safe deposit box at his bank.

"Our rules of evidence require the authentication of a photograph or film by someone with personal knowledge of the scene. That witness would have to testify that the scene shown was accurately depicted by the photograph or film. Without such a witness, this has no evidentiary value."

"You're saying you'd have to cut a deal with Adipietro."

"That's correct, sir, and he's told us he's not willing to testify, even if we offered him one."

"I see."

Trask looked at Eastman, who nodded. Trask walked to the side of Heidelberg's desk and played the video. The old man leaned forward, concentrating hard on the computer screen, and shaking his head. Trask stopped the video.

The senator sat back in his chair, stunned, his hands over his face.

"Has anyone outside your investigative team seen this?" he finally asked.

"No sir. I promised that you'd be the first to know."

Heidelberg nodded. "Thank you both. I'm very grateful for all your efforts. If you'll please excuse me now?"

"Of course," Eastman said as he and Trask stood.

———

Waldorf, Maryland
December 5, 2012, 7:05 p.m.

"It's the committee's last hearing session before the Christmas break," Trask said.

The television was again tuned to C-Span. The Senate Foreign Relations Committee was still trying to hash out some last minute funding for the troops in Afghanistan.

"I can't believe he's sitting there so composed, knowing what he knows now," Lynn said.

Heidelberg, the chair of the committee, sat at his usual center spot, flanked by Senator Graves, the ranking member of the majority party, and Senator Anderson, the minority's ranking member. Heidelberg gaveled the session to order.

"I'd like to thank all the members of the committee for coming to what I honestly believe to be an equitable and bipartisan solution which will guarantee that our brave men and women in the field in the Afghan theater of operations will receive everything they need to complete this vital mission," Heidelberg said. "And I'd like to also take this opportunity to personally thank some individual members of the committee for their critical contributions to the crafting of this compromise."

"Do you think he'll just spring it as a political torpedo?" Lynn asked. "The guy is up for re-election this year isn't he?"

"He is, and that's certainly one strong possibility," Trask agreed.

"And now for the true architects of this agreement," Heidelberg said. "Senators Graves and Anderson, the ranking members of this committee, who set aside all political concerns in order to reach the goals of this committee. Gentlemen, I'd like to shake each of your hands."

"Incredible," Lynn said, shaking her head.

Heidelberg stood and first turned to Graves, giving him a hearty handshake, smiling for the camera, and then slapping Graves on the shoulder. He turned to Anderson, again mugging for the camera during the handshake, and reaching for what appeared to be a playful hug with his left hand around Anderson's shoulder. Once that hug was made, however, Heidelberg never let go, and his right hand was suddenly holding a gun to Anderson's throat.

"*Oh my God!*" Lynn gasped.

"Everyone stay back," Heidelberg warned, backing away from the table with his hostage. "No one else needs to get hurt today. No one but the rattlesnake I'm holding who ate dinners in my home, called himself my friend, and then poisoned my little girl."

Trask heard screams from the television, and saw staffers running for the wings of the table as Heidelberg backed up toward the wall.

"I'm *sorry*, Hugh. I never meant that to happen, you've got to believe that," Anderson whimpered. "I *loved* Janie. I really did."

"*Shut up,*" Heidelberg growled. "She was less than half your age, Bob. You used her, and you fed her the heroin that killed her, you son of a bitch. I've sent a video to the media. It shows *you* giving her the dope."

The first shot that Heidelberg fired traveled upward through Anderson's lower jaw, entered his skull through the soft palate, and exited the top of his head. The second shot traveled a similar route through Heidelberg's own brain. The C-Span feed suddenly went black.

Trask stared at the blank screen and shook his head. "It just never stops."

Chapter Forty-Five

555 4ᵗʰ Street, N.W.
Washington, D.C.
January 30, 2013

Trask looked up from his desk when he sensed someone standing in the doorway. "Hello, Digger." He remained seated.

"I would have thought that by now you'd have called, Jeff. I think you owe me an apology. I also think you got a good man killed, and I'm not happy about that."

Trask leaned back and stared at Graves for a moment.

"I'm a United States Senator, dammit!" Graves shouted. "The least you could do is stand up when I come into your office!"

"I'm comfortable where I am, Senator," Trask said. "You're welcome to have a seat if you like."

Graves stood a moment longer before snorting and then dropping into one of the modest chairs facing Trask's desk.

"Can I get you some coffee or something?" Trask asked.

"You are insufferable, Jeff. Still no apology?"

"I don't owe you one, Digger. I was doing my job, that's all. If it's any consolation to you, I was very happy that you weren't the one on that video."

"That's comforting." The sarcasm was heavy in Graves' voice. "I am not at all happy about the way you've handled this whole thing."

Trask had had enough. He leaned forward in his chair. "Get this straight, *Senator*. I am not at all happy with *your* conduct in this whole thing."

"What the hell are you talking about?"

"The fact that you still don't have a clue makes my point. You guys are sent up here to represent the people, then all of a sudden the rules that we poor mortals have to obey just don't apply to you anymore. You stick your nose in an investigation when you don't have any dog in the fight, expect to be briefed every morning like you were a Wing Commander monitoring aircraft availability, and lean on a good man like Ross Eastman, threatening his job if the speed of the process doesn't tickle your fancy. I don't think it's any coincidence that all that pressure stopped once I carved you out of the updates with Heidelberg."

Graves eyes hit the floor for a moment.

"You've forgotten some of the trial tactics I taught you, Digger. Never let the other side see you flinch."

"I just cared about the girl, Jeff."

"I don't doubt that. But you tried to use your position to manipulate me, and to manipulate the process. Hell, even Hugh Heidelberg couldn't let the system work in the end. I can't say that I wouldn't have done the same thing in his shoes, but it just frosts me to watch you guys hamper the hell out of us with every restriction or rules change that you think might help your next election effort, and then toss every rule in the book aside when it suits you. Where do you stand on mandatory minimum sentencing, the one good tool we've got left in our toolboxes? I see that all you experts in the senate are talking about discarding them."

"I think there are problems with them. We've got too many folks in jail—"

"*Folks*? You think we walk around looking for '*folks*' to throw in the can? *Hells bells!* We generally have to wait for the little darlings to graduate from the state systems first where nothing happens to them until they've committed four or five felonies. When they finally get to *this* system they hardly resemble '*folks*,' Digger. They're as hard as they come, and we don't have the luxury or time or assets or—thanks to you clowns on the Hill—the *money* to waste processing poor little '*folks*.' You need to take a reality pill, my friend, or at least talk to somebody who doesn't share your little ivory tower. You know where I work, what I do, but you've never called me or anyone else in the trenches to discuss the issue because all the answers reside up there on Olympus."

"I'm sorry you feel that way. There are important matters that you can't understand unless you're exposed to them on a much broader scale."

Trask looked at Graves for a moment, shaking his head. "You can do me a favor, Senator."

"What?"

"Get the hell out of my office."

Chapter Forty-Six

555 4ᵗʰ Street, N.W.
Washington, D.C.
November 15, 2013, 5:20 p.m.

"Are you ready to go?" Ross Eastman stood in the doorway to Trask's office. "As ready as we can be. Trial starts Monday."

"J.T. Burns represents him?"

"Who else? He's the default appointee of the defense bar whenever we try and go for the death penalty."

"He's good at it. I don't think any of his defendants have been sentenced to death, have they?"

"Nobody has been sentenced to death in this town for decades. It's a little different this time, though."

"All the aggravation evidence?"

"There's certainly that. It's not every day that you have literally hundreds of murders to throw at the defendant at sentencing. I think that's had an effect on Burns as well."

"What kind of effect?"

"I don't think J.T. likes his client very much."

Eastman nodded. "Good luck."

"Thanks, Ross."

Trask took the elevator down to the parking garage and hopped into the Jeep. As he nosed out into traffic, a rare Washington snow storm began dropping flakes onto his windshield.

He headed southeast on the Indianhead Highway, and opted for a rural road to connect with Maryland 5 into Waldorf. He rarely took this road, but was all too familiar with it. He paraphrased Frost's poem as he made the turns. *Driving through the woods on a snowy evening.* When he pulled over at the spot, the snow had already covered the ground. He turned the engine off, but didn't get out of the Jeep; he just fixed his eyes on the spot about fifty yards into the pasture. *That's where we found poor Juan Ramirez buried.*

The sterile, quiet flakes began to thicken the blanket of white on the ground. Trask started the engine again. *For I have promises to keep.* He pulled back onto the road. *And a murderer to put to sleep.*

Chapter Forty-Seven

E. Barrett Prettyman Federal Courthouse
Washington, D.C.
November 27, 2013, 9:00 a.m.

" Call your next witness, Mr. Trask," Judge King said after the jury had filed in.

"Frederico Alcantar, Your Honor," Trask said. Randi Rhodes nodded in the back of the room, and walked out to relay the signal. The witness would appear shortly.

While he waited, Trask mentally reviewed the trial so far. He had presented a lot of things in reverse order, setting the stage for this witness, his smoking gun for the case. Kathy Davis had testified about her findings regarding the deaths of the prostitutes. Roscoe Briggs had testified about getting the dope from Adipietro. Aurrichio, the broker, had testified about his arrangements with Dominguez, the rodent-faced defendant who wasn't helping his own cause by sneering at every witness who took the stand.

Aurrichio had concluded his testimony by relating how Dominguez had proudly shown him the video of the truck exploding at the convenience store. That testimony was followed by all the crime scene technicians, and by Kathy Davis, making a second appearance to discuss the causes of deaths of the seventeen who died at the scene.

The witness appeared at the doors in the rear of the courtroom, and walked down the center aisle, past the spectators, through the gate, and stopped in front of the courtroom clerk. He raised his hand.

Good. Just like we practiced. He's ready.

"Do you promise that the testimony you are about to give will be the truth, the whole truth, and nothing but the truth, so help you God?" the clerk asked.

The witness waited for the interpreter to translate the English into Spanish, then nodded and spoke. "*Sí.*"

Trask stepped to the lectern in the center of the room while the witness stepped into the witness stand and took his seat.

Trask spoke a little more slowly than usual, giving the interpreter time to make notes as required. He waited for the Spanish spoken by his witness to be converted to English by the translator before moving to the next question.

"State your name, please."

"Frederico Alcantar."

"Where were you born, sir?"

"In Hidalgo state, Mexico."

"If I could direct your attention first to the date of August 22nd, 2010, do you recall where you were and what you were doing on that date?"

"I was taking a bus, trying to get to the United States."

"Why were you coming to America?"

"Trying to find work."

"Did you have permission to enter the United States?"

"No. I was going to try and come across the border illegally, without permission."

Very good. No hesitation. Admit the bad stuff, be candid about it. Dilute any potential cross examination. Very credible.

"Did you make it to the United States?"

"No."

"Tell us why you didn't make it to the border."

"The bus I was traveling on was ambushed. Everyone was ordered off the bus and taken to an old building on a farm."

"What happened there?" *He's doing fine. He's the star, now. The prep work is paying off. Here comes the devastation. Keep it matter of fact. Help him stay in control.*

The young man dropped his head. He looked straight at Dominguez, who was sneering again. The witness pointed at him. "That man and the other Zetas who were with him shot us."

"Do you know that man? His name?"

"Yes. He is Ramón Dominguez. All the Zetas called him *El Ratón*, The Rat."

Trask glanced at Dominguez. The mention of the nickname angered him, and his sneer grew meaner. *Good. He looks even more like a rat now. A very mean rat.*

"How many were in your party that day, traveling on the bus with you?"

"More than seventy."

"How many survived?"

"Only me."

"After that experience and your recovery, what did you decide to do with your life?"

"I decided to do whatever I could to fight the Zetas."

"Was there someone who helped you to do that?"

"Yes. Captain—I mean Major—he was promoted—Luis Aguilar. He was a marine."

"How did he help you?"

"He personally trained me. He put me through the same kind of training that the rest of his marines went through."

"Why did he do that?"

"Our plan was to make it appear that I was a marine deserter, to make it credible for the Zetas to accept me as a deserter."

"How long did you train with the Major?"

"For five months."

"And did he provide you with a new identity?"

"Yes. Identification papers, enlistment papers, all that."

"And what was your assumed name on these papers?"

"Miguel Espinoza."

Trask directed the witness through all of his knowledge of the heroin conspiracy, through the poppy fields in the mountains of Colombia, the processing station on the stolen hacienda, and the packing of the drugs into the load vehicles. He asked Freddy about the one trip he had made to the broker's ranch in Laredo, about the laughter shared between Lazcano and Dominguez when they planned and then celebrated the truck bomb, and about the role Vicente Dominguez had played in the conspiracy.

Freddy described his undercover role, how he worked his way up into the Zetas' inner circle, and how he provided information to Aguilar by phone when he could.

Trask was satisfied. *We'll save the rest for sentencing Freddy. You've done well.* He concluded the direct examination.

"And what role did the defendant Ramón Dominguez play in all of that?" Trask asked.

"While *El Verdugo*—the executioner—Lazcano was alive, Ramón was the Zetas' second in command. After Lazcano was killed, he led them."

"No further questions, Your Honor."

J.T. Burns approached the lectern to begin his cross-examination. "That's quite a story, young man."

The gavel almost exploded in Judge King's hand as she brought it down. "You know better than that, counsel. Ask a question. You can present your argument later."

Good, Trask thought. *She's not going to have any nonsense today.*

"Sorry, Judge," Burns said.

He's off balance. Maybe he'll go fishing. He's really got nothing to work with here.

"You say that you are the only survivor of this incident in which you were shot. Is that correct?"

The interpreter translated the question.

"As far as I know."

"So we have only your word for that, given the fact that no other witnesses lived to tell the tale?"

More argument, but I don't need to object to that. Freddy's doing fine.

"There are photographs of the massacre at San Fernando, sir. Major Aguilar will testify about that."

Nice work, Freddy. You asked for that, Burns.

"You don't like Mr. Dominguez very much, do you?"

"I despise him."

Maybe a bit strong, but okay. If bias is all he's got to work with, Burns is dead.

"That's about as biased as you can be, isn't it? You despise him? Do you hate him?"

"Of course."

Good. No hesitation, no apologies here.

"Yet you ask us to believe everything you said, even though it comes from a mind filled with hate?"

The gavel came down hard again. "Do you have something substantive to ask this witness, Mr. Burns, or do you intend to try and argue your case now?" Judge King asked, the anger evident in her voice.

"Just one more question," Burns said. "Did you hate my client's brother, Vicente, like you hate my client?"

"I did."

"In fact, you hated him so much that you murdered him. Isn't that true?"

Trask noticed that the judge was looking at him, almost inviting an objection. *Not this time, Judge. He's asked for it, and we'll give him his answer. Let it stand.*

"I killed his brother. That much is true."

Burns nodded, folded his papers, and returned to the defense table. He sat down next to Dominguez.

"Redirect, Mr. Trask?" the judge asked.

"Just a few questions," Trask said, returning to the lectern.

"Freddy, where were you shot?"

"In the head, sir."

"Please show the jury your scar."

The young man stood and pulled back the collar-length dark hair from the left side of his head. A wide, ugly scar ran from the back of his head past his ear, almost to the temple, mapping the track where the bullet had followed the shape of his skull under the skin.

"Thank you. You admitted to having killed Vicente Dominguez, the Zeta they called The Rider?"

"Yes."

"Why did you do that?"

"Ramón had a favorite way of killing his enemies. I saw him do it several times. He would prepare what he called a *guiso*—a "stew"—and would burn the victim alive in diesel fuel—"

Burns was on his feet screaming objections.

"Overruled, Mr. Burns," Judge King said. "You opened the door to this."

"You were describing the defendant's stews, I believe," Trask said, returning to the redirect.

"Yes," Freddy continued. "Vicente—The Rider—caught me trying to telephone the marines and warn them about a raid the Zetas were planning. He told me they were going to cook me in one of Ramón's stews. I had to kill him in self-defense and run for my life."

"And how did you escape?"

"Major Aguilar had told me about a fishing spot on Falcon Lake that he liked to go to when he was a boy. He told me to go there. He picked me up in a boat and brought me to America. The Zetas tried to stop us, but the Texas Navy sank their boats."

Beautiful job, Freddy. We'll have to have Luis explain the "Texas Navy," but that's fine. Now Luis will take the stand with the credibility of a hero. He is one, after all. And thank you for not mentioning that I was in the boat.

"No further questions."

Chapter Forty-Eight

December 2, 2013, 9:00 a.m.

"The jury having returned guilty verdicts on all counts, including those of premeditated murder, we will now proceed to sentencing," Judge King said. "Mr. Burns, your objections regarding the scope of the government's aggravation evidence are overruled. The evidence is graphic, horrific, appalling. I concede all of that, but it is relevant, convincing and credible, and I am not going to allow your client to use the horror of his own conduct as a shield."

Trask recalled Freddy and Luis to the stand, and the testimony about the other massacres at San Fernando and Cardereyta Jiménez went in as smoothly as had the initial testimony. Trask watched the jury, evaluating, reading their faces. *I could put on more, but they've had enough. I don't want them to become numb to all this carnage. They're ready.*

"The United States rests, Your Honor."

Burns had little to offer. Dominguez refused to testify, or Burns wouldn't let him. The usual mitigation specialists were absent, as Burns couldn't very well send amateur death-penalty abolitionist investigators crawling all over Mexico in the middle of a cartel war. There was a shrink who testified that the defendant suffered from a narcissistic personality disorder. Trask got him to admit that Dominguez shared that trait with about eighty percent of the world's criminals.

"You may present argument, Mr. Trask."

Trask summarized the evidence before the jury, beginning with the seventeen victims at the convenience store. He mentioned each by name, not pausing once to look at a note of any kind.

"Ladies and Gentlemen, I would like to give you a similar list of each of the victims who fell to this man's brutality in Mexico, but the list is too long, and I could not begin to remember each of their names, or begin to know each of their tragic stories.

"The death penalty should always be used sparingly, only when truly necessary, but the evidence in this case asks its own questions. If seventeen deaths are not enough, are two hundred? Three hundred? At what point do we say that the murder of this victim or that one does not justify the imposition of the ultimate punishment, but when we throw a few *more* bodies on the pile of this murderer's record, now we've had enough?"

He left the lectern and walked back to his counsel table before he turned and faced the jury again.

"If not now, ladies and gentlemen, when?" He let the question sink in. "When?"

He knew what Burns would say before he said it. Having no facts from the case to work with, the defense counsel was left to make a philosophical attack on the death penalty itself. Trask pulled a transcript of Burns' last penalty summation from the box beside his table. *I'll bet he gives this again, almost verbatim.*

"Ladies and gentlemen, search your memories to try and recall the last execution in this city. Odds are that you can't remember one. We don't undertake such things lightly. There have been terrible crimes, *horrific* crimes, *senseless* crimes committed without the smallest fragment of justification, and we have not inflicted death just because someone else did so. Is *this* really the case in which we should change course?"

He's reading his own argument from the Moreno case! Unbelievable. Well, it worked that time, so why not?

Burns rattled on, attacking again the bias and hatred that he claimed were held against his client by Freddy and Aguilar, a hatred he claimed was "born in the hot sands of Mexico and in the heat of warfare, where his client was not a bloodthirsty murderer, but a soldier in combat."

"All we've heard about in this case is killing," Burns shouted. "Killing after killing. Do you want to add your names to the list of those responsible for the killing of another human being? To lower yourselves and this government and this city to the levels of a murderer out of revenge? Each of you is better than that, yes, better than my client, but better than what the government is asking you to be. I ask you to activate that one thing in your sense of humanity that will prevent us from following down this inhumane path. When the government asks you to vote for death, they in effect ask you to personally throw the kill switch that will end the life of this man. And, ladies and gentlemen, for all his faults, he *is* a man, a human being."

'*Kill switch.' I can run with that.*

"Rebuttal, Mr. Trask?" the judge asked.

Trask walked slowly to the lectern. He looked into the jurors' eyes. *Good. Lots of eye contact. None of them are turning away. They actually want me to give them a reason.*

"Kill switch. Mr. Burns mentioned a 'kill switch.' He says we are better than this. He mentions the 'kill switch' because he knows that each of you shudders at the idea of throwing one. He's right—very right—to mention that switch.

"It's important to mention that 'kill switch' because, ladies and gentlemen, each of you with an ounce of humanity *has* a 'kill switch.' It is *your* 'kill switch,' however, that actually kills the temptation to do violence against another human being. You learned it as a young child when your parents taught you how cruel it was to do violence against another living thing, how evil it was to cause pain to your brother or sister, or even to the family puppy or kitten.

"It is your 'kill switch,' then, which gives you the respect for human life and makes you a member of civilized society. Unfortunately, there are those who *do not have* that restriction on their personalities. There are evil men in the world like Ramón Dominguez. So when you find yourselves brushing up against that civilized reluctance to kill, the repulsion that naturally *should* boil up in you at the very idea of taking another life, please remember *at that very instance* that all the evidence in this case has shown that *this* man does not feel that same reluctance. *That* is the difference between him, and you. Remember that he has shown, time after time after time after time—I could repeat that phrase once for every victim, but we'd be here for days—that his 'kill switch' has no off position, but instead is always set on 'kill.'

"He is, genetically, a human being, but he is missing that essential piece of humanity that Mr. Burns is speaking to when he asks *you* to spare him."

Trask walked back to his table before turning and facing the jury one last time. "I can speak no more for the victims of this murderer. That task now falls to you."

———

The jury would be out for a while deliberating. Trask elbowed his way through the crowded hallway, trying to reach the sanctuary of the office space reserved for trial preparation by the United States Attorney. The courthouse was packed with interested spectators, attorneys, and security personnel, and there was the usual crush of reporters clamoring for a statement.

"You folks know that you're supposed to contact our public affairs officer," he said, shoving at least three microphones out of his face with a single sweep of his hand.

"C'mon, Jeff, you know that if the jury comes back with the death penalty, it will be the first capital sentence in this town in decades. Give me a quote."

Trask stopped and looked at the reporter from *The Post*. He thought about saying something, but thought better of it. *I should just shove on past, get to the prep tank.* He looked at the man, half-smiled, and shook his head.

"You just asked those people to kill a man, Trask. You can't actually believe that's something civilized people should do. You can't believe that's justice."

Trask froze in his tracks, and turned to face the reporter.

"Now you're questioning my ethics and my own motives and beliefs, Rafferty, so I'll answer you. That defendant in there got his due process of law, more than he was ever actually entitled to. Don't you *dare* imply that I asked for the death penalty just to put some kind of notch on my gun. I don't need one. Capital punishment should always be the last resort, used only when we are certain as a society that it's appropriate. I'd *never* ask for it if I didn't think it was justified."

"So you're *that* sure? You're willing to let your own judgment play judge, jury and executioner?"

Trask stared hard, burning fires into the reporter's eyes with his own. "Rafferty, I couldn't say this to the jury. It would have been *the truth*, but *not allowed* under the law. There are times when the law *is* an ass, and some of those times the rules still have to be followed. But you're not a juror, and we're not in that room anymore, so make no mistake about it. If the jury comes back with a death verdict, and after all the appeals run out," he lowered his voice to a mea-sured growl, "once they strap that monster to the gurney in a death chamber, if they ask me to push the plungers, I'll jump at the chance, and never think twice about it afterward. He actually deserves a lot worse. I'm only sorry that we're too civilized to give it to him."

One of the television reporters stuck a microphone back in his face. "Just one question, Mr. Trask. I know that you're a student of legal history. If you had to compare this trial to any in the past, which one do you think of?"

Trask thought for a moment. "Nuremberg."

Chapter Forty-Nine

"Congratulations, Jeff. This has been a long road for you, hasn't it?" Sivella asked, switching the empty beer mug with a full one.

"Too long, Will. As usual, I had a helluva lot of help."

"I think they were all happy to give it."

Trask just nodded. Lynn smiled at him from the next bar stool and tapped his mug with one of her own, winking at him.

Dixon Carter patted him on the back from stool on the other side. "That's truly one for the history books. I never thought I'd hear that verdict in this town," Carter said.

"Dominguez wouldn't have gotten it if he didn't deserve it," Barry Doroz said, leaning around Carter from the other side. "And he still wouldn't have gotten it without our favorite prosecutor." He held his glass up in a salute.

"Thanks, Bear," Trask said. He heard a commotion near the front door of the bar.

Luis Aguilar and Freddy were being ushered in by Wisniewski and Randi Rhodes. The bar erupted in applause.

"I'm the designated driver tonight," Randi said. "Besides, they didn't know how to find the place."

Trask pulled a disc from his jacket pocket.

"Uh, oh," Doroz said. "Here we go again."

"Not this time," Trask said. "Willie, I need your help a second with the jukebox."

Sivella followed him over to the machine and opened it. "Put it in this slot here, Jeff."

Trask stepped back while Sivella closed the Wurlitzer. The bartender nodded, and Trask pushed the button.

The sound of thundering tympani filled the bar, quietening the crowd. The drum strikes were repeated, followed by chords from trumpets and French horns.

"What kind of song is that?" Sivella asked. "Sounds like the theme from the Olympic games or something."

Trask walked over and faced Luis Aguilar. He came to attention and saluted the major. "He knows," Trask said.

Aguilar came to attention, returning the salute.

"Aaron Copeland," the major said. "Fanfare for the Common Man."

Epilogue

Nuevo Italia
Michoacan, Mexico
January 13, 2014

Captain Jorge Lopez of the Mexican marines halted his convoy on a side road and watched as more than a hundred pickup trucks rolled out of the town. Each of the trucks carried several armed men, standing in the truck beds and shouting in celebration. They had just pushed the Knights Templar Cartel out of one of their strongholds in their war-torn state on the Pacific coast.

"Should we stop them and disarm them, *Capitán?*" a lieutenant asked over the radio.

"No. Let them pass, Felipé. They are on their way to Apatzingan. If they are able to repeat their success here and kick the cartel out of *that* town, then the most corrupt state in Mexico may actually be the first to see peace again."

"But these are nothing more than unorganized vigilantes, sir."

"No, they are much more than that, Felipé. They are *men*, and they've come to take their country back. We will wait in reserve. If they need help, we will be their cavalry. Have your men stand down for now. They can use the rest. They will need to be fresh. We have new orders. There are reports that we've located Chapo Guzmán, and we're heading to Mazatlán."

Other Books
By Marc Rainer

Capital Kill (Book One in the Jeff Trask Series)

A few short blocks from the safety of the museums and monuments on the National Mall, a ruthless killer prowls the streets of Washington DC. Federal prosecutor Jeff Trask joins a team of FBI agents and police detectives as they try and solve the series of brutal murders. As the body count rises, the investigation leads to a chilling confrontation with the leader of an international drug smuggling ring, and no one is safe, not even the police.

Reviews of Capital Kill:

"Jeff Trask is an Assistant U.S. Attorney who becomes embroiled in a high-stakes international case . . . Characters are well developed. The streets of Washington, D.C. come alive; those who have lived or worked in the nation's capital will recognize Rainer's cunning use of seedy locales to give the action in the book a realistic tone. Trask, an engaging main character, works to find out who is behind the heinous murders plaguing D.C. Despite being extremely intelligent, he comes across as an everyman. The book's intense action, realistic tone and memorable characters will keep readers engrossed in this thriller with a superb payoff." *Kirkus Reviews*

"Marc Rainer has joined the ranks of trial attorneys turned fiction writers with Capital Kill, a legal thriller. Rainer introduces us to what may be the most diabolically inventive method of homicide since the south end of King Edward II met the north end of a red-hot poker. The climax is a blockbuster - it's as good as anything I've read in courtroom fiction." *The Reporter*

"The best crime drama I have read in a long time." *Editor, EBookObsessed*

"Mr. Rainer is capable of writing a hell of a good sentence. The writing is crisp, hard, nearly flawless. The love story woven in has a way of arriving with perfect pitch; it is warm and right. I can safely recommend Capital Kill to anyone who wants a thrill, scented with a world of truth." *Palmetto Reviews*

Horns of the Devil (Book Two in the Jeff Trask Series)

The beheaded body of an ambassador's son is dumped on the curb in front of his father's embassy just blocks from the White House. Federal prosecutor Jeff Trask and an FBI task force are called upon to solve the murder. Their search for the killers leads to the MS-13, a hyper-violent gang from El Salvador, but Trask and his team soon learn that someone else is also tracking their suspects, and with deadly efficiency. When Trask himself becomes a target, he realizes that he is caught in a cross-fire between two of the most ruthless organizations in the western hemisphere.

Reviews of Horns of the Devil:

Federal prosecutor Jeff Trask returns to work on a case involving Salvadoran gang members. The author's second legal thriller keeps the questions coming. Trask is an engaging lead character: His extraordinary intelligence and eidetic memory are the same reasons he sometimes has trouble concentrating. Rainer also turns the spotlight on other, equally gripping characters. A well-paced mystery featuring an entertainingly complicated protagonist, supported by a robust cast. *Kirkus Reviews.*

Another great thriller by Marc Rainer. With an author who doesn't hesitate to harm a character, either major or minor, it keeps you on your toes wondering if the killers might just win this time. An intriguing story with great characters in real danger. Like any good thriller, it kept you guessing until the very end. *Editor, EBookObsessed.*

With *Horns of the Devil,* author Marc Rainer has given us another brilliant ride, a genuinely suspenseful book full of intrigue and action, the twists often leaving the reader in fear for the characters they've come to love. The command Mr. Rainer has over his material, the pure writing skill, not only keeps things flowing, but never lets it seem that any of what is going on is less than real. The story goes along in a thrilling way, right until the end, where there is one more twist waiting. The whole tale is unnerving and great fun. Highly recommend it. *Palmetto Reviews.*

Acknowledgements

As always, I am deeply indebted to my wife Lea, for her keen eye and loving support, to my editors Jamie, Jennifer, and Tania, and to the thousands of readers who have purchased and found pleasure in reading the books in this series. I also owe a great debt to an astounding collection of good folks with whom I grew up and shared so many great times in a previous and much simpler life. Their support got these books off the ground. Here's to you, HHS 1969.

About the Author

Marc Rainer is a graduate of the United States Air Force Academy, and is a former Air Force JAG Circuit Prosecutor and former federal prosecutor in Washington, D.C. In his more than thirty years of experience, he has tried hundreds of both military and federal (civilian) major cases, including prosecutions of homicide cases, federal conspiracy trials, and mafia and other organized crime cases. He weaves scenes from his investigative and trial experiences into the plot lines of his novels, which have been hailed by those in the criminal justice fields for their realism. He has co-authored a manual on how to try murder cases, which was published by the American Bar Association's Criminal Law Section. He lives in a suburb of a major Midwestern city with his wife, a retired Special Agent of the Air Force's Office of Special Investigations (OSI), and their three rescue mutts. His web page may be found at www.marcrainer.com

CPSIA information can be obtained
at www.ICGtesting.com
Printed in the USA
BVHW051901161218
535740BV00013B/247/P